Mary Higgins Clark is the author of twenty-two bestselling novels of suspense, a memoir, three collections of short stories, and with her daughter, Carol Higgins Clark, is co-author of two Christmas novellas. She lives with her husband in Saddle River, New Jersey.

First published in Great Britain by Simon & Schuster UK Ltd, 1997
This edition published by Pocket Books, 2004
An imprint of Simon & Schuster UK Ltd
A CBS COMPANY

7 9 10 8 6

Simon & Schuster UK Ltd
Africa House
64–78 Kingsway
London WC2B 6AH

Simon & Schuster Australia
Sydney

www.simonsays.co.uk

A CIP catalogue record for this book is available from
the British Library

'Pretend You Don't See Her', words and music by Steve Allen.
Copyright © 1957. Revised 1966, 1985.
Meadowlane Music, Inc. ASCAP.

ISBN-10: 0-7434-8433-9
ISBN-13: 978-0-7434-8433-6

Printed and bound in Great Britain by
Cox & Wyman Ltd, Reading, Berkshire

MARY HIGGINS CLARK

PRETEND YOU DON'T SEE HER

**POCKET
BOOKS**

LONDON • SYDNEY • NEW YORK • TORONTO

ACKNOWLEDGMENTS

People often ask, "Where do you get your idea for a book?"

The answer in this instance is very specific. I was considering several plot possibilities with not one of them as yet triggering my imagination. Then one night I was having dinner in Rao's Bar and Grill, a legendary New York restaurant.

Toward the end of the evening, Frank Pellegrino, one of the owners and a professional singer, picked up a mike and began to sing a song Jerry Vale made popular many years ago, "Pretend You Don't See Her." As I listened to the lyrics, an idea I'd been considering crystallized: A young woman witnesses a murder and to save her life has to go into the Witness Protection Program.

Grazie, Frank!

Kudos and heartfelt thanks to my editors, Michael Korda and Chuck Adams. In my school days, I was always the one who worked best under looming deadlines. Nothing's changed. Michael and Chuck, copy supervisor Gypsy da Silva, assistants Rebecca Head and Carol Bowie, you're the best and the greatest. May your names be inscribed in the Book of Saints.

Bouquets to Lisl Cade, my publicist, and Gene Winick, my literary agent, dear and valued friends.

An author's research is immeasurably strengthened by talking to the experts. I am grateful to author and retired FBI manager Robert Ressler, who discussed the Witness Protection Program with me; attorney Alan Lippel, who clarified legal ramifications of plot points; retired detective Jack Rafferty, who answered my queries about police procedure; and Jeffrey Snyder, who actually lived as a protected witness. Thanks to all of you for sharing your knowledge and experiences with me.

A tip of the hat to computer expert Nelson Kina of the Four Seasons Hotel in Maui, who reclaimed crucial chapters I thought I had lost.

Continuing thanks to Carol Higgins Clark, my daughter and fellow author, who is always my splendidly on-target sounding board.

Warm wishes to good friend Jim Smith of Minneapolis, who sent me the information I needed about the city of lakes.

Deep gratitude to my cheering section, my children and grandchildren. Even the little ones were asking, "Have you finished the book yet, Mimi?"

And finally, a special award to my husband, John Conheeney, who married a writer with a deadline and, with infinite patience and good humor, survived the experience.

Bless you all. And now to quote again a fifteenth-century monk, "The book is finished. Let the writer play."

For my husband, John Conheeney,
and our children

Marilyn Clark
Warren and Sharon Meier Clark
David Clark
Carol Higgins Clark
Patricia Clark Derenzo and Jerry Derenzo

John and Debbie Armbruster Conheeney
Barbara Conheeney
Patricia Conheeney
Nancy Conheeney Tarleton and David Tarleton

With love.

PRETEND YOU DON'T SEE HER

Later Lacey tried to find comfort in the thought that even if she had arrived seconds earlier, rather than being in time to help she would have died with Isabelle.

But it didn't happen that way. Using the key she had been given as realtor, she had entered the duplex apartment on East Seventieth Street and called Isabelle's name in the exact instant that Isabelle screamed "Don't . . . !" and a gunshot rang out.

Faced with a split-second decision to run or to hide, Lacey slammed the apartment door shut and slipped quickly into the hall closet. She had not even had time to fully close that door before a sandy-haired, well-dressed man came running down the stairs. Through the narrow opening she could see his face clearly, and it became imprinted on her mind. In fact, she had seen it before, only hours ago. The expression was now viciously cold, but clearly this was the same man to whom she had shown the apartment earlier in the day: affable Curtis Caldwell from Texas.

1

From her vantage point she watched as he ran past her, holding a pistol in his right hand and a leather binder under his left arm. He flung open the front door and ran out of the apartment.

The elevators and fire stairs were at the far end of the corridor. Lacey knew that Caldwell would realize immediately that whoever had come into the apartment was still there. A primal instinct made her rush out of the closet to shove the door closed behind him. He wheeled around, and for a terrible moment their eyes locked, his pale blue irises like steely ice, staring at her. He threw himself against the door but not fast enough. It slammed shut, and she snapped the dead bolt just as a key clicked in the lock.

Her pulse racing, she leaned against the door, trembling as the knob twisted, hoping there was no way Caldwell could get back in now.

She had to dial 911.

She had to get help.

Isabelle! she thought. That had to have been her cry that Lacey heard. Was she still alive?

Her hand on the banister, Lacey raced up the thickly carpeted stairs through the ivory-and-peach sitting room where in these past weeks she had sat so frequently with Isabelle and listened as the grieving mother told her over and over that she still could not believe that the death of her daughter, Heather, had been an accident.

Fearing what she would find, Lacey rushed into the bedroom. Isabelle lay crumpled across the bed, her eyes open, her bloodied hand frantically pulling at a sheaf of papers that had been under a pillow beside her. One of the pages fluttered across the room, carried by the breeze from the open window.

Lacey dropped to her knees. "Isabelle," she said. There were many other things she wanted to say—that she would call an ambulance; that it would be all right—but the words

2

refused to pass her lips. It was too late. Lacey could see that. Isabelle was dying.

Later *that scene was played out in the nightmare that came more and more frequently. The dream was always the same: She was kneeling beside Isabelle's body, listening to the dying woman's last words, as Isabelle told her about the journal, entreating her to take the pages. Then a hand would touch her shoulder, and when she looked up, there stood the killer, his cold eyes unsmiling, aiming the pistol at her forehead as he squeezed the trigger.*

1

IT WAS THE WEEK AFTER LABOR DAY, AND FROM THE steady ringing of the phones in the offices of Parker and Parker, it was clear to Lacey that the summer doldrums finally were over. The Manhattan co-op market had been uncommonly slow this past month; now, finally, things would start to move again.

"It's about time," she told Rick Parker as he delivered a mug of black coffee to her desk. "I haven't had a decent sale since June. Everybody I had on the hook took off for the Hamptons or the Cape, but thank God they're all drifting back into town now. I enjoyed my month off, too, but now it's time to get back to work."

She reached for the coffee. "Thanks. It's nice to have the son and heir wait on me."

"No problem. You look great, Lacey."

Lacey tried to ignore the expression on Rick's face. She always felt as though he were undressing her with his eyes. Spoiled, handsome, and the possessor of a phony charm that he turned on at will, he made her distinctly uncomfortable. Lacey heartily wished his father hadn't moved him from the West Side office. She didn't want her job jeopardized, but lately keeping him at arm's length was becoming a balancing act.

Her phone rang, and she grabbed for it with relief. Saved by the bell, she thought. "Lacey Farrell," she said.

"Miss Farrell, this is Isabelle Waring. I met you when you sold a co-op in my building last spring."

A live one, Lacey thought. Instinctively she guessed that Mrs. Waring was putting her apartment on the market.

Lacey's mind went into its search-and-retrieve mode. She'd sold two apartments in May on East Seventieth, one an estate sale where she hadn't spoken to anyone except the building manager, the second a co-op just off Fifth Avenue. That would be the Norstrum apartment, and she vaguely remembered chatting with an attractive fiftyish redhead in the elevator, who had asked for her business card.

Crossing her fingers, she said, "The Norstrum duplex? We met on the elevator?"

Mrs. Waring sounded pleased. *"Exactly!* I'm putting my daughter's apartment on the market, and if it's convenient I'd like you to handle it for me."

"It would be very convenient, Mrs. Waring."

Lacey made an appointment with her for the following morning, hung up, and turned to Rick. "What luck! Three East Seventieth. That's a great building," she said.

"Three East Seventieth. What apartment?" he asked quickly.

"Ten B. Do you know that one by any chance?"

"Why would I know it?" he snapped. "Especially since my father, in his wisdom, kept me working the West Side for five years."

It seemed to Lacey that Rick was making a visible effort to be pleasant when he added, "From what little I heard on this end, someone met you, liked you, and wants to dump an exclusive in your lap. I always told you what my grandfather preached about this business, Lacey: You're blessed if people remember you."

"Maybe, although I'm not sure it's necessarily a blessing," Lacey said, hoping her slightly negative reaction would end their conversation. She hoped also that Rick would soon come to think of her as just another employee in the family empire.

He shrugged, then made his way to his own office, which overlooked East Sixty-second Street. Lacey's windows faced Madison Avenue. She reveled in the sight of the constant traffic, the hordes of tourists, the well-heeled Madison Avenue types drifting in and out of the designer boutiques.

"Some of us are born New Yorkers," she would explain to the sometimes apprehensive wives of executives being transferred to Manhattan. "Others come here reluctantly, and before they know it, they discover that for all its problems, it's still the best place in the world to live."

Then if questioned, she would explain: "I was raised in Manhattan, and except for being away at college, I've always lived here. It's my home, my town."

Her father, Jack Farrell, had felt that way about the city. From the time she was little, they had explored New York City together. "We're pals, Lace," he would say. "You're like me, a city slicker. Now your mother, God love her, yearns to join the flight to the suburbs. It's to her credit that she sticks it out here, knowing I'd wither on the vine there."

Lacey had inherited not only Jack's love of this city, but his Irish coloring as well—fair skin, blue-green eyes, and dark brown hair. Her sister Kit shared their mother's English heritage—china-blue eyes, and hair the shade of winter wheat.

A musician, Jack Farrell had worked in the theater, usually in the pit orchestra, although sometimes playing in clubs and the occasional concert. Growing up, there wasn't a Broadway musical whose songs Lacey couldn't sing along with her dad. His sudden death just as she had finished college was still a shock. In fact, she wondered if she ever would get over it. Sometimes, when she was in the theater district, she still found herself expecting to run into him.

After the funeral, her mother had said with wry sadness, "Just as your dad predicted, I'm not staying in the city." A pediatric nurse, she bought a condo in New Jersey. She wanted to be near Lacey's sister Kit and her family. Once there, she'd taken a job with a local hospital.

Fresh out of college, Lacey had found a small apartment on East End Avenue and a job at Parker and Parker Realtors. Now, eight years later, she was one of their top agents.

Humming, she pulled out the file on 3 East Seventieth and began to study it. I sold the second-floor duplex, she thought. Nice-sized rooms. High ceilings. Kitchen needed modernizing. Now to find out something about Mrs. Waring's place.

Whenever possible, Lacey liked to do her homework on a prospective listing. To that end, she'd learned that it could help tremendously to become familiar with the people who worked in the various buildings Parker and Parker handled. It was fortunate now that she was good friends with Tim Powers, the superintendent of 3 East Seventieth. She called him, listened for a good twenty minutes to the rundown of his summer, ruefully reminding herself that Tim had always been blessed with the gift of gab, and finally worked the conversation around to the Waring apartment.

According to Tim, Isabelle Waring was the mother of Heather Landi, a young singer and actress who had just begun to make her name in the theater. The daughter as well of famed restaurateur Jimmy Landi, Heather had died early last winter, killed when her car plunged down an embankment as she was driving home from a weekend of skiing in

Vermont. The apartment had belonged to Heather, and now her mother was apparently selling it.

"Mrs. Waring can't believe Heather's death was an accident," Tim said.

When she finally got off the phone, Lacey sat for a long moment, remembering that she had seen Heather Landi last year in a very successful off-Broadway musical. In fact, she remembered her in particular.

She had it all, Lacey thought—beauty, stage presence, and that marvelous soprano voice. A "Ten," as Dad would have said. No *wonder* her mother is in denial.

Lacey shivered, then rose to turn down the air conditioner.

On Tuesday morning, Isabelle Waring walked through her daughter's apartment, studying it as if with the critical eye of a realtor. She was glad that she had kept Lacey Farrell's business card. Jimmy, her ex-husband, Heather's father, had demanded she put the apartment on the market, and in fairness to him, he had given her plenty of time.

The day she met Lacey Farrell in the elevator, she had taken an instant liking to the young woman, who had reminded her of Heather.

Admittedly, Lacey didn't *look* like Heather. Heather had had short, curly, light brown hair with golden highlights, and hazel eyes. She had been small, barely five feet four, with a soft, curving body. She called herself the house midget. Lacey, on the other hand, was taller, slimmer, had blue-green eyes, and darker, longer, straighter hair, swinging down to her shoulders, but there was something in her smile and manner that brought back a very positive memory of Heather.

Isabelle looked around her. She realized that not everyone would care for the birch paneling and splashy marble foyer tiles Heather had loved, but those could easily be changed; the renovated kitchen and baths, however, were strong selling points.

After months of brief trips to New York from Cleveland, and making stabs at going through the apartment's five huge closets and the many drawers, and after repeatedly meeting with Heather's friends, Isabelle knew it had to be over. She had to put an end to this searching for reasons and get on with her life.

The fact remained, however, that she just didn't believe Heather's death had been an accident. She knew her daughter; she simply would not have been foolish enough to start driving home from Stowe in a snowstorm, especially so late at night. The medical examiner had been satisfied, however. And Jimmy was satisfied, because Isabelle knew that if he *hadn't* been, he'd have torn up all of Manhattan looking for answers.

At the last of their infrequent lunches, he had again tried to persuade Isabelle to let it rest, and to get on with her own life. He reasoned that Heather probably couldn't sleep that night, had been worried because there was a heavy snow warning, and knew she had to be back in time for a rehearsal the next day. He simply refused to see anything suspicious or sinister in her death.

Isabelle, though, just couldn't accept it. She had told him about a troubling phone conversation she had had with their daughter just before her death. "Jimmy, Heather wasn't herself when I spoke to her on the phone. She was worried about something. Terribly worried. I could hear it in her voice."

The lunch had ended when Jimmy, in complete exasperation, had burst out, "Isabelle, get *off* it! Stop, please! This whole thing is tough enough without you going on like this, constantly rehashing everything, putting all her friends through the third degree. Please, let our daughter rest in peace."

Remembering his words, Isabelle shook her head. Jimmy Landi had loved Heather more than anything in the world. And next to her, he loved power, she thought bitterly—it's what had ended their marriage. His famous restaurant, his investments, now his Atlantic City hotel and casino. No room for me ever, Isabelle thought. Maybe if he had taken on a partner years ago, the way he has Steve Abbott now, our marriage wouldn't have failed. She realized she had been walking through rooms she wasn't really seeing, so she stopped at a window overlooking Fifth Avenue.

New York is especially beautiful in September, she mused, observing the joggers on the paths that threaded through Central Park, the nannies pushing strollers, the elderly sunning themselves on park benches. I used to take Heather's baby carriage over to the park on days like this, she remembered. It took ten years and three miscarriages before I had her, but she was worth all the heartbreak. She was such a special baby. People were always stopping to look at her and admire her. And she knew it, of course. She loved to sit up and take everything in. She was so smart, so observant, so talented. So trusting . . .

Why did you throw it away, Heather? Isabelle asked herself once more the questions that she had agonized over since her daughter's death. *After that accident when you were a child—when you saw that car skid off the road and crash—you were always terrified of icy roads. You even talked of moving to California just to avoid winter weather. Why then would you have driven over a snowy mountain at two in the morning? You were only twenty-four years old; you had so much to live for. What happened that night? What made you take that drive? Or who made you?*

The buzzing of the intercom jolted Isabelle back from the smothering pangs of hopeless regret. It was the doorman announcing that Miss Farrell was here for her ten o'clock appointment.

* * *

Lacey was not prepared for Isabelle Waring's effusive, if nervous, greeting. "Good heavens, you look younger than I remembered," she said. "How old *are* you? Thirty? My daughter would have been twenty-five next week, you know. She lived in this apartment. It was hers. Her father bought it for her. Terrible reversal, don't you think? The natural order of life is that I'd go first and someday she'd sort through *my* things."

"I have two nephews and a niece," Lacey told her. "I can't imagine anything happening to any of them, so I think I understand something of what you are going through."

Isabelle followed her, as with a practiced eye Lacey made notes on the dimensions of the rooms. The first floor consisted of a foyer, large living and dining rooms, a small library, a kitchen, and a powder room. The second floor, reached by a winding staircase, had a master suite—a sitting room, dressing room, bedroom and bath.

"It was a lot of space for a young woman," Isabelle explained. "Heather's father bought it for her, you see. He couldn't do enough for her. But it never spoiled her. In fact, when she came to New York to live after college, she wanted to rent a little apartment on the West Side. Jimmy hit the ceiling. He wanted her in a building with a doorman. He wanted her to be safe. Now he wants me to sell the apartment and keep the money. He says Heather would have wanted me to have it. He says I have to stop grieving and go on. It's just that it's still so hard to let it go, though . . . I'm trying, but I'm not sure I can . . ." Her eyes filled with tears.

Lacey asked the question she needed to have answered: "Are you sure you want to sell?"

She watched helplessly as the stoic expression on Isabelle Waring's face crumbled and her eyes filled with tears. "I wanted to find out why my daughter died. Why she rushed out of the ski lodge that night. Why she didn't wait and come back with friends the next morning, as she had planned. What changed her mind? I'm sure that somebody knows. I need a reason. I know she was terribly worried about something but wouldn't tell me what it was. I thought I might find an answer here, either in the apartment or from one of her friends. But her father wants me to stop pestering people, and I suppose he's right, that we have to go on, so yes, Lacey, I guess I want to sell."

Lacey covered the woman's hand with her own. "I think Heather would want you to," she said quietly.

That night Lacey made the twenty-five-mile drive to Wyckoff, New Jersey, where her sister Kit and her mother both lived. She hadn't seen them since early August when she had left the city for her month away in the Hamptons. Kit and her husband, Jay, had a summer home on Nantucket, and always urged Lacey to spend her vacation with them instead.

As she crossed the George Washington Bridge, Lacey braced herself for the reproaches she knew would be part of their greeting. "You only spent three days with us," her brother-in-law would be sure to remind her. "What's East Hampton got that Nantucket doesn't?"

For one thing it doesn't have *you,* Lacey thought, with a slight grin. Her brother-in-law, Jay Taylor, the highly successful owner of a large restaurant supply business, had never been one of Lacey's favorite people, but, as she reminded herself, Kit clearly is crazy about him, and between them they've produced three great kids, so who am I to criticize? If only he wasn't so damn pompous, she thought. Some of his pronouncements sounded like papal bulls.

As she turned onto Route 4, she realized how anxious she was to see the others in her family: her mother, Kit and the kids—Todd, twelve, Andy, ten, and her special pet, shy four-year-old Bonnie. Thinking about her niece, she realized that all day she hadn't been able to shake thoughts about poor Isabelle Waring, and the things she had said. The woman's pain was so palpable. She had insisted that Lacey stay for coffee and over it had continued to talk about her daughter. "I moved to Cleveland after the divorce. That's where I was raised. Heather was five at that time. Growing up, she was always back and forth between me and her dad. It worked out fine. I remarried. Bill Waring was much older but a very nice man. He's been gone three years now. I was so in hopes Heather would meet the right man, have children, but she was determined to have a career first. Although just before she died I had gotten the sense that maybe she had met someone. I could be wrong, but I thought I could hear it in her voice." Then she had asked, her tone one of motherly concern, "What about you, Lacey? Is there someone special in your life?"

Thinking about that question, Lacey smiled wryly. Not so you'd notice it, she thought. And ever since I hit the magic number thirty, I'm very aware that my biological clock is ticking. Oh well. I love my job, I love my apartment, I love my family and friends. I have a lot of fun. So I have no right to complain. It will happen when it happens.

Her mother answered the door. "Kit's in the kitchen. Jay went to pick up the children," she explained after a warm hug. "And there's someone inside I want you to meet."

Lacey was surprised and somewhat shocked to see that a man she didn't recognize was standing near the massive fireplace in the family room, sipping a drink. Her mother blushingly introduced him as Alex Carbine, explaining that they had known each other years ago and had just met again, through Jay, who had sold him much of the equipment for a new restaurant he'd just opened in the city on West Forty-sixth Street.

Shaking his hand, Lacey assessed the man. About sixty, she thought—Mom's age. Good, solid-looking guy. And Mom looks all atwitter. What's up? As soon as she could excuse herself she went into the state-of-the-art kitchen where Kit was tossing the salad. "How long has this been going on?" she asked her sister.

Kit, her blond hair pulled back at the nape of her neck, looking, Lacey thought, for all the world like a Martha Stewart ad, grinned. "About a month. He's nice. Jay brought him by for dinner, and Mom was here. Alex is a widower. He's always been in the restaurant business, but this is the first place he's had on his own, I gather. We've been there. He's got a nice setup."

They both jumped at the sound of a door slamming at the front of the house. "Brace yourself," Kit warned. "Jay and the kids are home."

From the time Todd was five, Lacey had started taking him, and later the other children, into Manhattan to teach the city to them the way her father had taught it to her. They called the outings their Jack Farrell days—days which included anything from Broadway matinees (she had now seen *Cats* five times) to museums (the Museum of Natural History and its dinosaur bones being easily their favorite). They explored Greenwich Village, took the tram to Roosevelt Island, the ferry to Ellis Island, had lunch at the top of the World Trade Center, and skated at Rockefeller Plaza.

The boys greeted Lacey with their usual exuberance. Bonnie, shy as always, snuggled up to her. "I missed you very much," she confided. Jay told Lacey she was looking very well indeed, adding that the month in East Hampton obviously had been beneficial.

"In fact, I had a ball," Lacey said, delighted to see him wince. Jay had an aversion to slang that bordered on pretension.

At dinner, Todd, who was showing an interest in real estate and his aunt's job, asked Lacey about the market in New York.

"Picking up," she answered. "In fact I took on a promising new listing today." She told them about Isabelle Waring, then noticed that Alex Carbine showed sudden interest. "Do you know her?" Lacey asked.

"No," he said, "but I know Jimmy Landi, and I'd met their daughter, Heather. Beautiful young woman. That was a terrible tragedy. Jay, you've done business with Landi. You must have met Heather too. She was around the restaurant a lot."

Lacey watched in astonishment as her brother-in-law's face turned a dark red.

"No. Never met her," he said, his tone clipped and carrying an edge of anger. "I used to do business with Jimmy Landi. Who's ready for another slice of lamb?"

It was seven o'clock. The bar was crowded, and the dinner crowd was starting to arrive. Jimmy Landi knew he should go downstairs and greet people but he just didn't feel like it. This had been one of the bad days, a depression brought on by a call from Isabelle, evoking the image of Heather trapped and burning to death in the overturned car that haunted him still, long after he had gotten off the phone.

The slanting light from the setting sun flickered through the tall windows of his paneled office in the brownstone on West Fifty-sixth Street, the home of Venezia, the restaurant Jimmy had opened thirty years ago.

He had taken over the space where three successive restaurants had failed. He and Isabelle, newly married, lived in what was then a rental apartment on the second floor. Now he owned the building, and Venezia was one of the most popular places to dine in Manhattan.

Jimmy sat at his massive antique Wells Fargo desk, thinking about the reasons he found it so difficult to go downstairs. It wasn't just the phone call from his ex-wife. The restaurant was decorated with murals, an idea he had copied from his competition, La Côte Basque. They were paintings of Venice, and from the beginning had included scenes in which Heather appeared. When she was two, he had the artist paint her in as a toddler whose face appeared in a window of the Doge's Palace. As a young girl she was seen being serenaded by a gondolier; when she was twenty, she'd been painted in as a young woman strolling across the Bridge of Sighs, a song sheet in her hand.

Jimmy knew that for his own peace of mind he would have to have her painted out of the murals, but just as Isabelle had not been able to let go of the idea that Heather's death must be someone else's fault, he could not let go of the constant need for his daughter's presence, the sense of her eyes watching him as he moved through the dining room, of her being with him there, every day.

He was a swarthy man of sixty-seven, whose hair was still naturally dark, and whose brooding eyes under thick unruly brows gave his face a permanently cynical expression. Of medium height, his solid, muscular body gave the impression of animal strength. He was aware that his detractors joked that the custom-tailored suits he wore were wasted on him, that try as he might, he still looked like a day laborer. He almost smiled, remembering how indignant Heather had been the first time she had heard that remark.

I told her not to worry, Jimmy thought, smiling to himself. I told her that I could buy and sell the lot of them, and that's all that counts.

He shook his head, remembering. Now more than ever, he knew it wasn't really all that counted, but it still gave him a reason to get up in the morning. He had gotten through the last months by concentrating on the casino and hotel he was building in Atlantic City. "Donald Trump, move over," Heather had said when he'd showed her the model. "How about calling it Heather's Place, and I'll perform there, yours exclusively, Baba?"

She had picked up the affectionate nickname for father on a trip to Italy when she was ten. After that she never called him Daddy again.

Jimmy remembered his answer. "I'd give you star billing in a minute—you know that. But you better check with Steve. He's got big bucks in Atlantic City too, and I'm leaving a lot of the decisions to him. But anyway, how about forgetting this career stuff and getting married and giving me some grandchildren?"

Heather had laughed. "Oh, Baba, give me a couple of years. I'm having too much fun."

He sighed, remembering her laugh. Now there wouldn't be any grandchildren, ever, he thought—not a girl with golden-brown hair and hazel eyes, nor a boy who might someday grow up to take over this place.

A tap at the door yanked Jimmy back to the present.

"Come in, Steve," he said.

Thank God I have Steve Abbott, he thought. Twenty-five years ago the handsome, blond Cornell dropout had knocked on the door of the restaurant before it was open. "I want to work for you, Mr. Landi," he had announced. "I can learn more from you than in any college course."

Jimmy had been both amused and annoyed. He mentally sized up the young man. Fresh, know-it-all kid, he had decided. "You want to work for me?" he had asked, then pointed to the kitchen. "Well, that's where I started."

That was a good day for me, Jimmy thought. He might

have looked like a spoiled preppie, but he was an Irish kid whose mother worked as a waitress to raise him, and he had proved that he had much of the same drive. I thought then that he was a dope to give up his scholarship but I was wrong. He was born for this business.

Steve Abbott pushed open the door and turned on the nearest light as he entered the room. "Why so dark? Having a seance, Jimmy?"

Landi looked up with a wry smile, noting the compassion in the younger man's eyes. "Woolgathering, I guess."

"The mayor just came in with a party of four."

Jimmy shoved back his chair and stood up. "No one told me he had a reservation."

"He didn't. Hizzonor couldn't resist our hot dogs, I suppose . . ." In long strides, Abbott crossed the room and put his hand on Landi's shoulder. "A rough day, I can tell."

"Yeah," Jimmy said. "Isabelle called this morning to say the realtor was in about Heather's apartment and thinks it will sell fast. Of course, every time she gets me on the phone, she has to go through it all again, how she can't believe Heather would ever get in a car to drive home on icy roads. That she doesn't believe her death was an accident. She can't let go of it. Drives me crazy."

His unfocused eyes stared past Abbott. "When I met Isabelle, she was a knockout, believe it or not. A beauty queen from Cleveland. Engaged to be married. I pulled the rock that guy had given her off her finger and tossed it out the car window." He chuckled. "I had to take out a loan to pay the other guy for his ring, but I got the girl. Isabelle married me."

Abbott knew the story and understood why Jimmy had been thinking about it. "Maybe the marriage didn't last, but you got Heather out of the deal."

"Forgive me, Steve. Sometimes I feel like a very old

man, repeating myself. You've heard it all before. Isabelle never liked New York, or this life. She should never have left Cleveland."

"But she *did,* and you met her. Come on, Jimmy, the mayor's waiting."

2

IN THE NEXT FEW WEEKS, LACEY BROUGHT EIGHT POTEN-
tial buyers to see the apartment. Two were clearly window-
shoppers, the kind whose hobby was wasting realtors' time.

"But on the other hand, you never know," she said to
Rick Parker when he stopped by her desk early one evening
as she was getting ready to go home. "You take someone
around for a year, you want to kill yourself before you go
out with her again, then what happens? The person you're
ready to give up on writes a check for a million-dollar
co-op."

"You have more patience than I do," Rick told her. His
features, chiseled in the likeness of his aristocratic ancestors,
showed disdain. "I really can't tolerate people who waste
my time. RJP wants to know if you've had any real nibbles
on the Waring apartment." RJP was the way Rick referred
to his father.

"I don't think so. But, hey, it's still a new listing and
tomorrow is another day."

"Thank you, Scarlett O'Hara. I'll pass that on to him. See you."

Lacey made a face at his retreating back. It had been one of Rick's edgy-tempered, sarcastic days. What's bugging him now, she wondered. And why, when his father is negotiating the sale of the Plaza Hotel, would he give a thought to the Waring apartment? Give me a break.

She locked her desk drawer and rubbed her forehead where a headache was threatening to start. She suddenly realized that she was very tired. She had been living in a whirl since coming back from her vacation—following up on old projects, getting new listings, catching up with friends, having Kit's kids in for a weekend . . . and devoting an awful lot of time to Isabelle Waring.

The woman had taken to calling her daily, frequently urging her to come by the apartment. "Lacey, you must join me for lunch. You do have to eat, don't you?" she would say. Or just, "Lacey, on your way home, stop in and have a glass of wine with me, won't you? The New England settlers used to call twilight 'sober light.' It's a lonesome time of day."

Lacey stared out into the street. Long shadows were slanting across Madison Avenue, a clear indication that the days were becoming shorter. It *is* a lonesome time of day, she thought. Isabelle is such a very *sad* person. Now she's forcing herself to go through everything in the apartment and dispose of Heather's clothes and personal effects. It's quite a job. Heather apparently was a bit of a pack rat.

It's little enough to ask that I spend some time with Isabelle and listen to her, Lacey thought. I really don't mind. Actually, I like Isabelle very much. She's become a friend. But, Lacey admitted to herself, sharing Isabelle's pain brings back everything I felt when Dad died.

She stood up. I am going home and collapse, she thought. I need to.

Two hours later, at nine o'clock, Lacey, fresh from twenty minutes in the swirling Jacuzzi, was happily preparing a BLT. It had been her dad's favorite. He used to call bacon, lettuce, and tomato New York's definitive lunch-counter sandwich.

The telephone rang. She let the answering machine take it, then heard the familiar voice of Isabelle Waring. I'm not going to pick up, Lacey decided. I simply don't feel like talking to her for twenty minutes right now.

Isabelle Waring's hesitant voice began to speak in soft but intense tones. "Lacey, guess you're not home. I had to share this. I found Heather's journal in the big storage closet. There's something in it that makes me think I'm not crazy for believing her death wasn't an accident. I think I may be able to prove that someone wanted her out of the way. I won't say any more now. I'll talk to you tomorrow."

Listening, Lacey shook her head, then impulsively turned off the answering machine and the ringer on the phone. She didn't even want to know if more people tried to reach her. She wanted what was left of the night all to herself.

A quiet evening—a sandwich, a glass of wine, and a book. I've earned it, she told herself!

As soon as she got to the office in the morning, Lacey paid the price for having turned off the answering machine the night before. Her mother called, and an instant later Kit phoned; both were checking up on her, concerned that they had gotten no answer when they had called her apartment the night before. While she was trying to reassure her sister, Rick appeared in her office, looking decidedly annoyed. "Isabelle Waring has to talk to you. They put her through to me."

23

"Kit, I've got to go and earn a living." Lacey hung up and ran into Rick's office. "I'm sorry I couldn't get back to you last night, Isabelle," she began.

"That's all right. I shouldn't talk about all this over the phone anyhow. Are you bringing anyone in today?"

"No one is lined up so far."

As she said that, Rick slid a note across his desk to her: "Curtis Caldwell, a lawyer with Keller, Roland, and Smythe, is being transferred here next month from Texas. Wants a one-bedroom apartment between 65th and 72nd on Fifth. Can look at it today."

Lacey mouthed a thank-you to Rick and said to Isabelle, "Maybe I *will* be bringing someone by. Keep your fingers crossed. I don't know why, but I've got a hunch this could be our sale."

"A Mr. Caldwell's waiting for you, Miss Farrell," Patrick the doorman, told her as she alighted from a cab.

Through the ornate glass door, Lacey spotted a slender man in his mid-forties drumming his fingers on the lobby table. Thank God I'm ten minutes early, she thought.

Patrick reached past her for the door handle. "A problem you need to know about," he said with a sigh. "The air-conditioning broke down. They're here now fixing it, but it's pretty hot inside. I tell you, I'm retiring the first of the year, and it won't be a day too soon. Forty years on this job is enough."

Oh, swell, Lacey thought. No air-conditioning on one of the hottest days of the year. No wonder this guy's impatient. This does not bode well for the sale.

In the moment it took to walk across the lobby to Cald-well, her impression of the man, with his tawny skin, light sandy hair, and pale blue eyes, was uncertain. She realized that she was bracing herself to be told that he didn't like to be kept waiting.

But when she introduced herself to Curtis Caldwell, a smile brightened his face. He even joked. "Tell the truth now, Miss Farrell," he said, "how temperamental *is* the air-conditioning in this building?"

When Lacey had phoned Isabelle Waring to confirm the time of the appointment, the older woman, sounding distracted, had told her she would be busy in the library, so Lacey should just let herself in with her realtor's key.

Lacey had the key in hand when she and Caldwell stepped off the elevator. She opened the door, called out, "It's me, Isabelle," and went to the library, Caldwell behind her.

Isabelle was at the desk in the small room, her back to the door. An open leather loose-leaf binder lay to one side; some of its pages were spread across the desk. Isabelle did not look up or turn her head at Lacey's greeting. Instead, in a muffled voice, she said, "Just forget I'm here, please."

As Lacey showed Caldwell around, she briefly explained that the apartment was being sold because it had belonged to Isabelle Waring's daughter, who had died last winter in an accident.

Caldwell did not seem interested in the history of the apartment. He clearly liked it, and he did not show any resistance to the six-hundred-thousand-dollar asking price. When he had inspected the second floor thoroughly, he looked out the window of the sitting room and turned to Lacey. "You say it will be available next month?"

"Absolutely," Lacey told him. This is it, she thought. He's going to make a bid.

"I don't haggle, Miss Farrell. I'm willing to pay the asking price, provided I absolutely can move in the first of the month."

"Suppose we talk to Mrs. Waring," Lacey said, trying not to show her astonishment at the offer. But, she reminded herself, just as I told Rick yesterday, this is the way it happens.

Isabelle Waring did not answer Lacey's knocks at the library door. Lacey turned to the prospective buyer. "Mr. Caldwell, if you don't mind waiting for me just a moment in the living room, I'll have a little talk with Mrs. Waring and be right out."

"Of course."

Lacey opened the door and looked in. Isabelle Waring was still sitting at the desk, but her head was bowed now, her forehead actually touching the pages she had been reading. Her shoulders were shaking. "Go away," she murmured. "I can't deal with this now."

She was grasping an ornate green pen in her right hand. She slapped it against the desk. "Go away."

"Isabelle," Lacey said gently, "this is very important. We have an offer on the apartment, but there's a proviso I have to go over with you first."

"Forget it! I'm not going to sell. I need more time here." Isabelle Waring's voice rose to a high-pitched wail. "I'm sorry, Lacey, but I just don't want to talk now. Come back later."

Lacey checked her watch. It was nearly four o'clock. "I'll come back at seven," she said, anxious to avoid a scene and concerned that the older woman was on the verge of hysterical tears.

She closed the door and turned. Curtis Caldwell was standing in the foyer between the library and the living room.

"She doesn't want to sell the apartment?" His tone was shocked. "I was given to understand that—"

Lacey interrupted him. "Why don't we go downstairs?" she said, her voice low.

They sat in the lobby for a few minutes. "I'm sure it will be all right," she told him. "I'll come back and talk to her this evening. This has been a painful experience for her, but she'll be fine. Give me a number where I can call you later."

"I'm staying at the Waldorf Towers, in the Keller, Roland, and Smythe company apartment."

They stood to go. "Don't worry. This will work out fine," she promised. "You'll see."

His smile was affable, confident. "I'm sure it will," he said. "I leave it in your hands, Miss Farrell."

He left the apartment building and walked from Seventieth Street to the Essex House on Central Park South, and went immediately to the public phones. "You were right," he said when he had reached his party. "She's found the journal. It's in the leather binder the way you described it. She's also apparently changed her mind about selling the apartment, although the real estate woman is going back there tonight to try to talk some sense into her."

He listened.

"I'll take care of it," he said, and hung up. Then Sandy Savarano, the man who called himself Curtis Caldwell, went into the bar and ordered a scotch.

3

HER FINGERS CROSSED, LACEY PHONED ISABELLE WARING at six o'clock. She was relieved to find that the woman now was calm.

"Come over, Lacey," she said, "and we'll talk about it. But even if it means sacrificing the sale, I can't leave the apartment yet. There's something in Heather's journal that I think could prove to be very significant."

"I'll be there at seven," Lacey told her.

"Please. I want to show what I've found to you too. You'll see what I mean. Just let yourself in. I'll be upstairs in the sitting room."

Rick Parker, who was passing by Lacey's office, saw the troubled expression on her face and came in and sat down. "Problem?"

"A big one." She told him of Isabelle Waring's erratic behavior and about the possibility of losing the potential sale.

"Can you talk her out of changing her mind?" Rick asked quickly.

Lacey saw the concern on his face, concern that she was fairly certain wasn't for her or for Isabelle Waring. Parker and Parker would lose a hefty commission if Caldwell's offer was refused, she thought. That's what's bothering him.

She got up and reached for her jacket. The afternoon had been warm, but the forecast was for a sharp drop in temperature that evening. "We'll see what happens," she said.

"You're leaving already? I thought you said you were meeting her at seven."

"I'll walk over there, I think. Probably stop for a cup of coffee along the way. Marshal my arguments. See you, Rick."

She was still twenty minutes early but decided to go up anyway. Patrick, the doorman, was busy with a delivery, but smiled when he saw her. He waved her to the self-service elevator.

As she opened the door and called Isabelle's name, she heard the scream and the shot. For a split second she froze, then sheer instinct made her slam the door and step into the closet before Caldwell came rushing down the stairs and out into the corridor, a pistol in one hand, a leather binder under his arm.

Afterwards she wondered if she imagined that somewhere in her brain she heard her father's voice saying, "Close the door, Lacey! Lock him out!" Was it his protective spirit that gave her the strength to force the door closed as Caldwell pushed against it, and then to bolt it?

She leaned against the door, hearing the lock click as he tried to get back into the apartment, remembering the look of the stalking predator in his pale blue eyes in that instant in which they had stared at each other.

Isabelle!

Dial 911 . . . Get help!

She had stumbled up the winding staircase, then through the ivory-and-peach sitting room and into the bedroom, where Isabelle was lying across the bed. There was so much blood, spreading now to the floor.

Isabelle was moving, pulling at a sheaf of papers that were under a pillow. The blood was on them too.

Lacey wanted to tell Isabelle that she would get help . . . that it would be all right, but Isabelle began to try to speak: "Lacey . . . give Heather's . . . journal . . . to her father." She seemed to be gasping for air. "Only to him. . . . Swear that . . . only . . . to him. You . . . read it . . . Show . . . him . . . where . . ." Her voice trailed off. She drew in a shuddering breath, as though trying to stave off death. Her eyes were becoming unfocused. Lacey knelt next to her. With the last of her strength, Isabelle squeezed Lacey's hand. "Swear . . . please . . . man . . . !"

"I do, Isabelle, I do," Lacey said, her voice breaking with a sob.

Suddenly the pressure on her hand was gone. She knew that Isabelle was dead.

"Y ou all right, Lacey?"

"I guess so." She was in the library of Isabelle's apartment, seated in a leather chair facing the desk where Isabelle had been seated just a few hours ago, reading the contents of the leather loose-leaf binder.

Curtis Caldwell had been carrying that binder. When he heard me he must have grabbed it, not realizing that Isabelle had taken pages out of it. Lacey hadn't seen it that closely, but it looked heavy, she thought, and fairly cumbersome.

The pages she had picked up in Isabelle's room were in

Lacey's briefcase now. Isabelle had made her swear to give them only to Heather's father. She had wanted her to show him something that was in them. But show him what? she wondered. And shouldn't she tell the police about them?

"Lacey, drink some coffee. You need it."

Rick was crouching beside her, holding a steaming cup out to her. He had already explained to the detectives that he had no reason to question a phone call from a man claiming to be an attorney with Keller, Roland, and Smythe, an attorney transferring to New York from Texas. "We do a lot of business with the firm," Rick had explained. "I saw no reason to call and confirm."

"And you're sure this Caldwell guy is the one you saw running out of here, Ms. Farrell?"

The older of the two detectives was about fifty and heavy-set. But he's light on his feet, Lacey thought, her mind wandering. He's like that actor who was Dad's friend, the one who played the father in the revival of *My Fair Lady*. He sang "Get Me to the Church on Time." What *was* his name?

"Ms. Farrell?" An edge of impatience had crept into the detective's voice.

Lacey looked back up at him. Detective Ed Sloane, that was this man's name, she thought. But she still couldn't remember the name of the actor. What had Sloane asked her? Oh, yes. Was Curtis Caldwell the man she'd seen running down the stairs from Isabelle's bedroom?

"I'm absolutely sure it was the same man," she said. "He was carrying a pistol and the leather binder."

Mentally she gave herself a hard slap. She hadn't meant to talk about the journal. She had to think all this through before talking about it.

"The leather binder?" Detective Sloane's tone became sharp. "What leather binder? That's the first you've mentioned it."

Lacey sighed. "I really don't know. It was open on Isabelle's desk this afternoon. It's one of those leather binders that zips closed. Isabelle was reading the pages in it when we were in here earlier." She should tell them about the pages that *weren't* inside the leather binder when Caldwell took it. Why wasn't she telling them? she thought. Because she'd sworn to Isabelle that she would give them to Heather's father. Isabelle had struggled to stay alive until she had heard Lacey's promise. She couldn't go back on her word . . .

Suddenly Lacey felt her legs begin to shake. She tried to hold them still by pressing her hands on her knees, but they still wouldn't stop trembling.

"I think we'd better get a doctor for you, Ms. Farrell," Sloane said.

"I just want to go home," Lacey whispered. "Please let me go home."

She knew Rick was saying something to the detective in a low voice, something she couldn't hear, didn't really *want* to hear. She rubbed her hands together. Her fingers were sticky. She looked down, then gasped. She hadn't realized that her hands were sticky with Isabelle's blood.

"Mr. Parker is going to take you home, Ms. Farrell," Detective Sloane was saying. "We'll talk to you more tomorrow. When you've rested." His voice was very loud, Lacey thought. Or was it? No. It was just that she was hearing Isabelle scream *Don't . . . !*

Was Isabelle's body still crumpled on the bed? she wondered.

Lacey felt hands under her arms, urging her to stand. "Come on, Lacey," Rick was saying.

Obediently she got up, allowed herself to be guided through the door, then down the foyer. Curtis Caldwell had stood in the foyer that afternoon. He had heard what Isabelle said to her about not selling the apartment.

"He didn't wait in the living room," she said.

"Who didn't?" Rick asked.

Lacey didn't answer. Suddenly she remembered her brief-case. That's where the pages from the journal were.

She remembered the feel of the pages in her hand, crumpled, blood soaked. That's where the blood came from. Detective Sloane had asked her if she had touched Isabelle.

She had told him that she had held Isabelle's hand as she died.

He must have noticed the blood on her fingers. There must be blood on her briefcase too. Lacey had a sudden moment of total clarity. If she asked Rick to get it for her from the closet, he would notice the blood on the handle. She had to get it herself. And keep them from seeing it until she could wipe it clean.

There were so many people milling around. Flashes of light. They were taking pictures. Looking for fingerprints, dusting powder on tables. Isabelle wouldn't have liked that, Lacey thought. She was so neat.

Lacey paused at the staircase and looked up toward the second floor. Was Isabelle still lying there? she wondered. Had they covered her body?

Rick's arm was firmly around her. "Come on, Lacey," he said, urging her toward the door.

They were passing the closet where she had put her brief-case.

I can't ask him to get it for me, Lacey reminded herself. Breaking away, she opened the closet door and grabbed her briefcase in her left hand.

"I'll carry it," Rick told her.

Deliberately she sagged against him, weighing down his arm with her right hand, making him support her, tightening her grip on the handle of her briefcase.

"Lacey, I'll get you home," Rick promised.

She felt as though everyone's eyes were staring at her, staring at the bloody briefcase. Was this the way a thief felt?

she wondered. *Go back. Give them the journal; it's not yours to take,* a voice inside her insisted.

Isabelle's blood was on those pages. *It's not mine to give, either,* she thought hopelessly.

When they reached the lobby, a young police officer came up to them. "I'll drive you, Miss Farrell. Detective Sloane wants to make sure you get home okay."

Lacey's apartment was on East End Avenue at Seventy-ninth Street. When they arrived there, Rick wanted to come upstairs with her, but she demurred. "I just want to go to bed," she said, and kept shaking her head at his protests that she shouldn't be alone.

"Then I'll call you first thing in the morning," he promised.

She lived on the eighth floor and was alone in the elevator as it made what seemed to be an interminably long ascent before stopping. The corridor reminded her of the one outside Isabelle's front door, and Lacey looked around fearfully as she ran down it.

Once inside her apartment, the first thing she did was to shove the briefcase under the couch. The living room windows overlooked the East River. For long minutes Lacey stood at one of the windows, watching the lights as they flickered across the water. Finally, even though she was shivering, she opened the window and gulped in the fresh, cool night air. The sense of unreality that had overwhelmed her for the past several hours was beginning to dissipate, but in its place was an aching awareness of being as tired as she had ever felt in her life. Turning, she looked at the clock.

Ten-thirty. Only a little over twenty-four hours ago, she had refused to pick up the phone and talk to Isabelle. Now Isabelle would never call her again . . .

Lacey froze. The door! Had she double-locked the door? She ran to check it.

Yes, she had, but now she threw the dead bolt and wedged a chair under the handle. She realized suddenly that she was shaking again. I'm afraid, she thought, and my hands are sticky—sticky with Isabelle Waring's blood.

Her bathroom was large for a New York apartment. Two years ago, when she had modernized the whole space, she had added the wide, deep Jacuzzi. She had never been as happy she had gone to the expense as she was tonight, she thought, as steaming water clouded the mirror.

She stripped, dropping her clothes on the floor. Stepping into the tub, she sighed with relief as she sank into the warmth, then held her hands under the faucet, scrubbing them deliberately. Finally she pushed the button that sent the water swirling around her body.

It was only later, when she was snugly wrapped in a terry-cloth robe, that Lacey allowed herself to think about the bloodied pages in her briefcase.

Not now, she thought, not now.

Still unable to shake the chilling sensation that had haunted her all evening, she remembered there was a bottle of scotch in the liquor cabinet. She got it out, poured a little into a cup, filled the cup with water, and microwaved it. Dad used to say there was nothing like a hot toddy to help shake off a chill, she thought. Only his version was elaborate, with cloves and sugar and a cinnamon stick.

Even without the trimmings, however, it did the trick. As she sipped the drink in bed, she felt a calmness begin to settle over her and fell asleep as soon as she turned off the light.

And almost immediately awakened with a shriek. *She was opening the door to Isabelle Waring's apartment; she was bending over the dead woman's body; Curtis Caldwell was aiming the pistol at her head.* The image was vivid and immediate.

It took her several moments to realize that the shrill sound was the ringing of the telephone. Still shaking, she picked up the receiver. It was Jay, her brother-in-law. "We just got back from dinner and heard on the news that Isabelle Waring was shot," he said. "They reported that there was a witness, a young woman who could identify the killer. Lacey, it wasn't you, I hope."

The concern in Jay's voice was comforting. "Yes, it was me," she told him.

For a moment there was silence. Then he said quietly, "It's never good to be a witness."

"Well, I certainly never wanted to be one!" she said angrily.

"Kit wants to talk to you," Jay said.

"I *can't* talk now," Lacey said, knowing full well that Kit, loving and concerned, would ask questions that would force her to tell it all again—all about going to the apartment, hearing the scream, seeing Isabelle's killer.

"Jay, I just can't talk now!" she pleaded. "Kit will understand."

She hung up the phone and lay in the darkness, calming herself, willing herself to go back to sleep, realizing that her ears were straining to hear another scream, followed by the sound of footsteps racing toward her.

Caldwell's footsteps.

Her last thought as she drifted off to sleep was of something Jay had said in his call. He said it was never good to be a witness. Why did he say that? she wondered.

W hen he had left Lacey in the lobby of her apartment building, Rick Parker had taken a taxi directly to his place on Central Park West and Sixty-seventh Street. He knew what would be awaiting him there, and he dreaded it. By now, Isabelle Waring's death would be all over the news. There had been reporters outside her building when they had come out, and chances were that he had been caught on-camera getting into the police car with Lacey. And if so, then his father would have seen it, since he always watched the ten-o'clock news. Rick checked his watch: it was now quarter of eleven.

As he had expected, when he entered his dark apartment he could see that the light on his telephone answering machine was flashing. He pressed the PLAY button. There was one message; it was from his father: "No matter what time it is, call me when you get in!"

Rick's palms were so wet that he had to dry them on his handkerchief before picking up the phone to return the call. His father answered on the first ring.

"Before you ask," Rick said, his voice ragged and unnaturally high pitched, "I had no choice. I had to go over there because Lacey had told the police that I'd been the one who'd given her Caldwell's number, so they sent for me."

Rick listened for a minute to his father's angry voice, then he finally managed to break in to respond: "Dad, I've told you not to worry. It's all fine. Nobody knows that I was involved with Heather Landi."

4

SANDY SAVARANO, THE MAN KNOWN TO LACEY AS CURTIS Caldwell, had raced from Isabelle Waring's apartment and down the fire stairs to the basement and out through the delivery entrance. It was risky, but sometimes you had to take risks.

Quick strides took him to Madison Avenue, the leather binder tucked under his arm. He took a taxi to the small hotel on Twenty-ninth Street where he was staying. Once in his room, he tossed the binder on the bed and promptly poured a generous amount of scotch into a water glass. Half of it he bolted down; the rest he would sip. It was a ritual he followed after a job like this.

Carrying the scotch, he picked up the binder and settled in the hotel room's one upholstered chair. Up until the last-minute glitch the job had been easy enough. He had gotten back into the building undetected when the doorman was at the curb, helping an old woman into a cab. He had let himself into the apartment with the key he had taken off the table in the foyer when Lacey Farrell was in the library with the Waring woman.

He had found Isabelle in the master bedroom, propped up on the bed, her eyes closed. The leather binder had been on the night table beside the bed. When she realized he was there, she had jumped up and tried to run, but he had blocked the door.

She hadn't started screaming. No, she'd been too scared. That was what he liked most: the naked fear in her eyes, the knowledge that there would be no escape, the awareness that she was going to die. He savored that moment. He always liked to take his pistol out slowly, keeping eye contact with his victim while he pointed it, taking careful aim. The chemistry between him and his target in that split second before his finger squeezed the trigger thrilled him.

He pictured Isabelle as she started shrinking away from him, returning to the bed, her back to the headboard, her lips struggling to form words. Then finally the single scream: *"Don't!"*—mingling suddenly with the sound of someone calling her from downstairs—just as he shot her.

Savarano drummed his fingers angrily on the leather binder. The Farrell woman had come in at that precise second. Except for her, everything would have been perfect. He had been a fool, he told himself, letting her lock him out, forcing him to run away. But he *did* get the journal, and he did kill the Waring woman, and that was the job he was hired to do. And if Farrell became a problem he would kill her too, somehow . . . He would do what he had to; it was all part of the job.

Carefully Savarano unzipped the leather binder and looked inside. The pages were all neatly clamped in place, but when he thumbed through them he found they were all blank.

Unbelieving, he stared down at the pages. He started turning them rapidly, looking for handwriting. They were blank, all of them—none had been used. The actual journal pages must still be in the apartment, he realized. What should he do? He had to think this through.

It was too late to get the pages now. The cops would be swarming all over the apartment. He'd have to find another way to get them.

But it wasn't too late to make sure that Lacey Farrell never got the chance to ID him in court. That was a chore he might actually enjoy.

5

SOMETIME NEAR DAWN LACEY FELL INTO A HEAVY, DREAM-filled sleep in which shadows moved slowly down long corridors and terrified screams came relentlessly from behind locked doors.

It was a relief to wake up at quarter of seven even though she dreaded what she knew the day would bring. Detective Sloane had said he would want her to go to headquarters and work with an artist to come up with a composite sketch of Curtis Caldwell.

But as she sat wrapped in her robe, sipping coffee and looking down at the barges slowly making their way up the East River, she knew there was something she had to decide about first: the journal.

What am I going to do about it? Lacey asked herself. Isabelle thought there was something in it that proved Heather's death was not an accident. Curtis Caldwell stole the leather binder after he killed Isabelle.

Did he kill her because he was afraid of what Isabelle had

found in that journal? Did he steal what he thought was the journal to make sure no one else could read it?

She turned and looked. Her briefcase was still there, under the couch; the briefcase in which she had hidden the bloodstained pages.

I have to turn them over to the police, she thought. But I believe I know a way I can do it and still keep my promise to Isabelle.

At two o'clock, Lacey was in a small office in the police station, sitting across a conference table from Detective Ed Sloane and his assistant, Detective Nick Mars. Detective Sloane seemed to be a little short of breath, as though he had been hurrying. Or maybe he's just been smoking too much, Lacey decided. There was an open pack of cigarettes poking out of his breast pocket.

Nick Mars was another story. He reminded her of a college freshman football player she had had a crush on when she was eighteen. Mars was still in his twenties, baby faced with full cheeks, innocent blue eyes, and an easy smile, and he was nice. In fact, she was sure that he was being set up as the good guy in the good guy/bad guy scenario interrogators play. Sloane would bluster and occasionally rage; Nick Mars would soothe, his manner always calm, solicitous.

Lacey had been at the station for almost three hours, plenty of time to figure out the scenario they had worked up for her benefit. As she was trying to describe Curtis Caldwell's face to the police artist, Sloane was clearly annoyed that she wasn't being more specific.

"He didn't have any scars or birthmarks or tattoos," she had explained to the artist. "At least none that I could see. All I can tell you is that he had a thin face, pale blue eyes, tanned skin, and sandy hair. There was nothing distinguishing about his features. They were in proportion—except for his lips, maybe. They were a little thin."

But when she saw the artist's sketch, she had said, hesitantly, "It isn't really the way he looked."

"Then how *did* he look?" Sloane had snapped.

"Take it easy, Ed. Lacey's had a pretty rough time." Nick Mars had given her a reassuring smile.

After the artist had failed to come up with a sketch she felt resembled the man she had seen, Lacey had been shown endless mug shots. However, none of them resembled the man she knew as Curtis Caldwell, another fact that clearly upset Sloane.

Now Sloane finally pulled out a cigarette and lit up, a clear sign of exasperation. "Okay, Ms. Farrell," he said brusquely, "we need to go over your story."

"Lacey, how about a cup of coffee?" Mars asked.

"Yes, thank you." She smiled gratefully at him, then warned herself again: Watch out. Remember—good guy/ bad guy. It was clear Detective Sloane had something new on his agenda.

"Ms. Farrell, I'd just like to review a few things about this crime. You were pretty upset when you dialed 911 last night."

Lacey raised her eyebrows. "With good reason," she said, nodding.

"Absolutely. And I'd say you were virtually in shock when we talked with you after we got there."

"I guess I was." In truth, most of what had happened last evening was a haze to her.

"I didn't escort you to the door when you left, but I understand you had the presence of mind to remember that you'd left your briefcase in the hall closet next to the door of the Waring apartment."

"I remembered it as I passed the closet, yes."

"Do you remember that the photographers were taking pictures at that time?"

She thought back. The film of powder on the furniture. The flashes of light.

"Yes, I do," she replied.

"Would you look at this picture then, please?" Sloane slid an eight-by-ten photograph across the desk. "Actually," he explained, "what you see is an enlargement of a section of a routine shot taken in the foyer." He nodded to the younger man. "Detective Mars picked up this little detail."

Lacey stared at the picture. It showed her in profile, gripping her briefcase, holding it away from Rick Parker as he reached for it.

"So you not only remembered to get your briefcase, but you insisted on carrying it yourself."

"Well, in good part that's my nature. And with my co-workers I feel it's especially important to be self-reliant," Lacey explained, her voice low and calm. "In truth, though, I probably was acting on automatic pilot. I really don't remember what was in my head."

"No, I think you do," Detective Sloane said. "In fact, I think you were acting very deliberately. You see, Ms. Farrell, there were traces of blood in that closet—Isabelle Waring's blood. Now how would it have gotten there, do you suppose?"

Heather's journal, Lacey thought. The bloodstained loose-leaf pages. A couple of them had fallen on the carpet in the closet as she was jamming them into the briefcase. And of course her hands had been bloody. But she couldn't tell this to the detective—not yet, anyway. She still needed time to study the pages. She looked at her hands, resting in her lap. I should say something, she thought. But what?

Sloane leaned across the desk, his manner more aggressive, even accusatory. "Ms. Farrell, I don't know what your game is, or what you're not telling us, but clearly this was no ordinary murder. The man who called himself Curtis Caldwell didn't rob that apartment or kill Isabelle Waring at random. The whole crime was carefully planned and executed. Your appearance on the scene was the only thing that probably did not go according to plan." He paused, then continued, his voice filled with irritation. "You told us he was carrying Mrs. Waring's leather binder. Describe it to me again."

"The description won't change," Lacey said. "It was the size of a standard loose-leaf binder and had a zipper around it so that when it was closed nothing would fall out."

"Ms. Farrell, have you ever seen this before?" Sloane shoved a sheet of paper across the table.

Lacey looked at it. It was a loose-leaf page covered with writing. "I can't be sure," she said.

"Read it, please."

She skimmed it. It was dated three years earlier. It began, *Baba came to see the show again. Took all of us back to the restaurant for dinner . . .*

Heather's journal, she thought. I must have missed this page. How many more did I miss? she wondered suddenly.

"Have you ever seen this before?" Sloane asked her again.

"Yesterday afternoon when I brought the man I know as Curtis Caldwell to see the apartment, Isabelle was in the library, seated at the desk. The leather binder was open, and she was reading loose-leaf pages that she'd taken out of it. I can't be positive that this is one of them, but it probably is."

At least that much is true, she thought. Suddenly she regretted not taking time this morning to make copies of the journal before going to the station.

That was what she had decided to do—give the original to the police, a copy to Jimmy Landi, and keep a copy for herself. Isabelle's intention was that Jimmy read the journal; she clearly had felt that he might see something significant in it. He should be able to read a copy as well as the original, as could she, since, for whatever reason, Isabelle had made her promise to read the pages too.

"We found that page in the bedroom, under the chaise," Sloane told her. "Maybe there were other loose pages. Do you think that's possible?" He didn't wait for her to answer. "Let's get back to the smear of Isabelle Waring's blood we found in the downstairs closet. Do you have any idea how that got there?"

"I had Isabelle's blood on my hands," Lacey said. "You know that."

"Oh, yes, I know that, but your hands weren't dripping with blood when you grabbed that briefcase of yours as you were leaving last night. So what happened? Did you put something in that briefcase before we got there, something you took from Isabelle Waring's bedroom? I think so. Why don't you tell us what it was? Were there perhaps more pages like the one you just read scattered around her room? Is that a good guess?"

"Take it easy, Eddie. Give Lacey a chance to answer," Mars urged him.

"Lacey can have all the time she wants, Nick," Sloane snapped. "But the truth is going to be the same. She took something from that room; I'm sure of it. And don't you wonder why an innocent bystander would take something like that from the victim's home? Can you guess why?" he asked Lacey.

She wanted desperately to tell them she had the journal, and why she had it. But if I do, she thought, they'll demand I turn it over immediately. They won't let me make a copy for Heather's father. And I certainly can't tell them I'm making a copy for myself; they're reacting as though I had something to do with Isabelle's death, she thought. I'll give the original to them tomorrow.

She stood up. "No, I can't. Are you finished with me, Detective Sloane?"

"For today I am, Ms. Farrell, yes. But please keep in mind that being an accessory after the fact in a murder investigation carries serious penalties. *Criminal* penalties," he added, putting a touch of menace into the words. "And one other thing: if you did take any of those pages, I have to wonder just how 'innocent' a bystander you were. After all, you did happen to be responsible for bringing the killer into Isabelle Waring's home."

Lacey left without responding. She had to get to the office, but first she was going to go home to get Heather Landi's journal. She would stay at her desk this evening until everyone else had left and make the copies she needed. Tomorrow she would turn over the original to Sloane. I'll try to make him understand why I took it, she thought nervously.

She started to hail a cab, then decided to walk home. The midafternoon sun felt good. She still had the sensation of being chilled to the bone. As she crossed Second Avenue, she sensed someone close behind her and spun around quickly to meet the puzzled eyes of an elderly man.

"Sorry," she mumbled as she darted to the curb.

I expected to see Curtis Caldwell, Lacey thought, upset to realize she was trembling. If the journal was what he was after, then he didn't get it. Would he come back for it? He knows I saw him and can identify him as a murderer. Until the police caught Caldwell—if they caught him—she was in danger, she was certain of that. She tried to force the thought out of her mind.

The lobby of her building felt like a sanctuary, but when Lacey got off at her floor, the long corridor seemed frightening and, key in hand, she hurried to the apartment and quickly dashed inside.

I'll never carry this briefcase again, she vowed as she retrieved it from under the couch and carried it into the bedroom and set it on her desk, carefully avoiding touching the bloody handle.

Gingerly she removed the journal pages from the brief-case, wincing at the sight of the ones stained with blood. Finally she put them all in a manila envelope and fished around in her closet for a tote bag.

Ten minutes later, that bag firmly under her arm, she stepped out onto the street. As she nervously hailed a cab she tried to convince herself that whoever Caldwell was, and for whatever reason he had killed Isabelle, he must surely be miles away by now, on the run.

6

Sandy Savarano, alias Curtis Caldwell, was taking no chances of being recognized as he used a pay phone down the block from Lacey Farrell's apartment building. He wore a gray wig over his sandy hair, there was a graying stubble covering his cheeks and chin, and his lawyer's suit had been replaced by a shapeless sweater worn over faded jeans. "When Farrell left the police station she walked home and went inside," he said as he glanced down the street. "I'm not going to hang around. There's a squad car parked across from her building. It may be there to keep an eye on her."

He had started walking west, then changed his mind and turned back. He decided to watch the police car for a while as a test of his theory that the policemen had been assigned to guard Lacey Farrell. He didn't have to wait long. He watched from half a block away as the familiar figure of a young woman in a black suit, carrying a tote bag, emerged from the building and hailed a cab. As it sped away, he looked to see what the cops in the squad car would do. A moment later a car ran the red light at the corner, and the flashing lights on the roof of the squad car went on as it leaped from the curb.

Good, he thought. That's one less thing to get in my way.

7

AFTER THEY RETURNED TO THE RESTAURANT FROM MAKING arrangements for Isabelle's cremation, Jimmy Landi and Steve Abbott went directly to Jimmy's office. Steve poured liberal amounts of scotch into tumblers and placed one of them on Landi's desk, commenting, "I think we both need this."

Landi reached for the glass. "I know I do. This has been an awful day."

Isabelle would be cremated when her body was released and her ashes taken to Gate of Heaven Cemetery in Westchester to be placed in the family mausoleum.

"My parents, my child, my ex-wife will be together up there," he said, looking up at Abbott. "It doesn't make sense, does it, Steve? Some guy claims he's looking to buy an apartment, then comes back and kills Isabelle, a defenseless woman. It's not like she was flashing expensive jewelry. She didn't have any. She never even cared for that stuff."

His face contorted in a mixture of anger and anguish. "I

told her she had to get rid of the apartment! Her going on and on about Heather's death, worrying that it wasn't an accident! She was driving herself crazy over it—and me too —and being in that apartment just made it worse. Besides, she needed the money. That Waring guy she married didn't leave her a dime. I just wanted her to get on with her life. And then she gets killed!" His eyes glistened with tears. "Well, she's with Heather now. Maybe that's where she wanted to be. I don't know."

Abbott, in an obvious effort to change the subject, cleared his throat and said, "Jimmy, Cynthia is coming over around ten for dinner. How about joining us?"

Landi shook his head. "No, but thanks, I appreciate it. You've been wet-nursing me for almost a year, Steve, ever since Heather died, but it can't go on. I'll be okay. Stop worrying about me and pay attention to your girlfriend. Are you going to marry her?"

"I'm not rushing into anything," Abbott said, smiling. "Two divorces are enough."

"You're right. That's why I stayed single all these years. And you're young still. You've got a long way to go."

"Not so long. Don't forget I turned forty-five last spring."

"Yeah? Well, I turn sixty-eight next month," Jimmy said with a grunt. "But don't go counting me out yet. *I've* still got a long way to go before I cash in my chips. *And don't you forget it!*"

Then he winked at Abbott. Both men smiled. Abbott swallowed the last of his scotch and stood. "You bet you have. And I'm counting on it. When we open our place in Atlantic City, the rest of them might as well close their doors. Right?"

Abbott noticed Jimmy Landi glancing at his watch and said, "Well, I'd better get downstairs and do some glad-handing."

Shortly after Abbott had left, the receptionist buzzed

Jimmy. "Mr. Landi, a Miss Farrell wants to talk to you. She says to tell you she's the realtor who was working with Mrs. Waring."

"Put her on," he snapped.

Back in the office, Lacey had responded to Rick Parker's questions about her interview with Detective Sloane with noncommittal answers. "He showed me pictures. Nobody looked anything like Caldwell."

Once again she declined Rick's offer of dinner. "I want to catch up on some paperwork," she said with a wan smile.

And it's true, she thought.

She waited until everyone in the domestic real estate division left before carrying the tote bag to the copier, where she made two copies of Heather's journal, one for Heather's father, one for herself. Then she placed a call to Landi's restaurant.

The conversation was brief: Jimmy Landi would be waiting for her.

Pretheater was a busy taxi time, but she was in luck: a cab was just discharging a passenger right in front of her office building. Lacey raced across the sidewalk and jumped in the taxi just before someone else tried to claim it. She gave the address of Venezia on West Fifty-sixth Street, leaned back and closed her eyes. Only then did she relax her grip on the tote bag, though she still held it securely under her arm. Why was she so uneasy? she wondered. And why did she have the sensation of being watched?

At the restaurant she could see that the dining room was full and the bar jammed. As soon as she gave her name, the receptionist signaled the maitre d'.

"Mr. Landi is waiting for you upstairs, Ms. Farrell," he told her.

On the phone she had said simply that Isabelle had found Heather's journal and wanted him to have it.

But when she was in his office, sitting opposite the brooding, solid-looking man, Lacey felt as though she were firing at a wounded target. Even so, she felt she had to be straight-forward in telling him Isabelle Waring's dying words.

"I promised to give the journal to you," she said. "And I promised to read it myself. I don't know why Isabelle wanted me to read it. Her exact words were 'Show . . . him . . . where.' She wanted me to show you something in it. I suspect that for some reason she thought I'd find what it was that apparently confirmed her suspicion that your daughter's death was not a simple accident. I'm trying to obey her wishes." She opened her tote bag and took out the set of pages she had brought with her.

Landi glanced at them, then turned away.

Lacey was sure that the sight of his daughter's handwrit-ing was starkly painful to the man, but his only comment was a testy, "These aren't the originals."

"I don't have the original pages with me. I'm giving them to the police in the morning."

His face flushed with sudden anger. "That's not what Isabelle asked you to do."

Lacey stood up. "Mr. Landi, I don't have a choice. Surely you understand that it's going to take a lot of explaining to the police to make them understand why I removed evidence from a murder scene. I'm certain that eventually the original pages will be returned to you, but for now, I'm afraid you'll have to make do with a copy." As will I, she said to herself as she left.

He did not even look up as she walked out.

When Lacey arrived at her apartment, she turned on the entrance light and had taken several steps inside before the chaos in front of her registered. Drawers had been spilled, closets ransacked, furniture cushions had been tossed on the floor. Even the refrigerator had been emptied and left open. Appalled and terrified, she stared at the mess, then stumbled through the debris to call the superintendent; while he dialed 911, she put in a call to Detective Sloane.

He arrived shortly after the local precinct cops. "You know what they were looking for, don't you," Sloane said matter-of-factly.

"Yes, I do," Lacey told him. "Heather Landi's journal. But it's not here. It's in my office. I hope whoever did this hasn't gone there."

I n the squad car on the way to her office, Detective Sloane read Lacey her rights. "I was keeping the promise I made to a dying woman," she protested. "She asked me to read the journal and then give it to Heather Landi's father, and that's what I've done. I took him a copy this evening."

When they got to her office, Sloane did not leave her side as she unlocked the cabinet and reached for the manila envelope in which she had placed the original pages of the journal.

He opened the clasp, pulled out a few of the sheets, studied them, then looked at her. "You're sure you're giving me everything?"

"This is everything that was with Isabelle Waring when she died," Lacey said, hoping he wouldn't press her. While it was the truth, it wasn't the whole truth: The copy of the journal pages that she had made for herself was locked in her desk.

"We'd better go down to headquarters, Ms. Farrell. We need to talk about this whole thing a bit more, I believe."

"My apartment," she protested. "Please. I have to clean it up." *I sound ridiculous,* she thought. *Someone may have killed Isabelle because of Heather's journal, and I might* have been killed if I'd been home tonight, and all I can think of is the mess there. She realized that her head was aching. It was after ten o'clock and she hadn't had anything to eat for hours.

"Your apartment can wait to be cleaned," Sloane told her brusquely. "We need to go over all this now."

But when they reached the precinct station, he did have Detective Nick Mars send out for a sandwich and coffee for her. Then he began. "All right, let's take this from the top again, Ms. Farrell," he said.

The same questions over and over, Lacey thought, shaking her head. Had she ever met Heather Landi? Wasn't it odd that on the basis of a chance meeting in an elevator months earlier, Isabelle Waring had called her to offer an exclusive on the apartment? How often had she seen Waring in the last weeks? For lunches? dinners? end-of-the-day visits?

"She called early evening 'sober light,' " Lacey heard herself saying, searching her mind to try to find anything she could tell them that they might not have heard before. "She said that was what the Pilgrims called it; she said she found it a very lonely time."

"And she had no old friends to call?"

"I only know that she called me. Maybe she thought that because I was a single woman in Manhattan, I might be able to help her get some insight into her daughter's life," Lacey said. "And death," she added as an afterthought. She could visualize Isabelle's sad face, the high cheekbones and wide-set eyes hinting at the beauty she must have been as a young woman. "I think it was almost the way one might talk to a cabdriver or a bartender. You find a sympathetic ear, knowing that you don't have to worry about that person reminding you of what you said when you get over the difficult time."

Do I make sense? she wondered.

Sloane's demeanor didn't give any indication of his reaction. Instead he said, "Let's talk about how Curtis Caldwell got back into the Waring apartment. There was no sign of forced entry. Isabelle Waring clearly didn't let him in, then go back and prop herself up on the bed with him there. Did you give him a key?"

"No, of course not," Lacey protested. "But wait a minute! Isabelle always left a key in a bowl on the table in the foyer. She told me she did it so that if she ran downstairs for her mail she didn't have to bother with her key ring. Caldwell could have seen it there and taken it. But what about my apartment?" she protested. "How did someone get in there? I have a doorman."

"And an active garage in the building and a delivery entrance. These so-called secured buildings are a joke, Ms. Farrell. You're in the realty business. You know that."

Lacey thought of Curtis Caldwell, pistol in hand, rushing to find her, wanting to kill her. "Not a very good joke." She realized she was fighting tears. "Please, I want to go home," she said.

For a moment she thought that they might keep her there longer, but then Sloane got up. "Okay. You can go now, Ms. Farrell, but I must warn you that formal charges may be pending against you for removing and concealing evidence from a crime scene."

I should have talked to a lawyer, Lacey thought. How could I have been such a fool?

Ramon Garcia, the building superintendent, and his wife, Sonya, were in the process of straightening up Lacey's apartment when she arrived. "We couldn't let you come back to this mess," Sonya told her, running a dust cloth over the top of the bureau in the bedroom. "We put things back in the drawers for you, not your way, I'm sure, but at least things are not still on the floor."

"I don't know how to thank you," Lacey said. The apartment had been full of police when she left, and she was dreading what she would find when she returned.

Ramon had just completed replacing the lock. "This was taken apart by an expert," he said. "And he had the right tools. How come he didn't pick up your jewelry box?"

That was the first thing the police had told her to check. Her several gold bracelets, her diamond stud earrings, and her grandmother's pearls were there, undisturbed.

"I guess that wasn't what he was after," Lacey said. To her own ears her voice sounded low and tired.

Sonya looked at her sharply. "I'll come back tomorrow morning. Don't worry. When you get home from work everything will be shipshape."

Lacey walked with them to the door. "Does the dead bolt still work?" she asked Ramon.

He tried it. "No one's gonna get in while that's on, at least without a battering ram. You're safe."

She closed and locked the door behind them. Then she looked around her apartment and shuddered. What have I gotten myself into? she wondered.

8

Mascara and a light lip liner were usually all the cosmetics Lacey wore, but in the morning light, when she saw the shadows under her eyes and noted the pallor of her skin, she added blush and eye shadow and fished in the drawer for lipstick. They did little, however, to brighten her outlook. Even wearing a favorite brown-and-gold jacket didn't help dispel a sense of gloom. A final check in the mirror told her she still looked limp and weary.

At the door of the office she paused, took a deep breath, and straightened her shoulders. An incongruous memory hit her. When she was twelve and suddenly taller than the boys in her class, she had started to slump when she walked.

But Dad told me height was delight, she thought, and he made a game of the two of us walking around with books on our heads. He said walking tall made you look confident to other people.

And I *do* need that confidence, she said to herself a few

59

minutes later, when she was summoned to Richard Parker Sr.'s office.

Rick was in with his father. The elder Parker was obviously angry. Lacey glanced at Rick. No sympathy there, she thought. It really *is* Parker and Parker today.

Richard Parker Sr. did not mince words. "Lacey, according to security, you came in here last night with a detective. What was that all about?"

She told him as simply as she could, explaining that she had decided she had to turn the journal over to the police, but first she needed to make a copy for Heather's father.

"You kept concealed evidence in this office?" the older Parker asked, raising an eyebrow.

"I intended to give it to Detective Sloane today," she said. She told them about her apartment having been burglarized. "I was only trying to do what Isabelle Waring asked me to do," she said. "Now it seems I may have committed an indictable offense."

"You don't have to know much law to know that," Rick interjected. "Lacey, that was really a dumb thing to do."

"I wasn't thinking straight," she said. "Look, I'm sorry about this, but—"

"I'm sorry about it too," Parker Sr. told her. "Have you any appointments today?"

"Two this afternoon."

"Liz or Andrew can handle them for you. Rick, see to it. Lacey, you plan on working the phones for the immediate future."

Lacey's sense of lethargy disappeared. "That's not fair," she said, suddenly angry.

"Nor is it fair to drag this firm into a murder investigation, Ms. Farrell."

"I'm sorry, Lacey," Rick told her.

But you're Daddy's boy on this one, she thought, fighting down the urge to say more.

As soon as she got to her desk, one of the new secretaries, Grace MacMahon, came over with a cup of coffee and handed it to her. "Enjoy."

Lacey looked up to thank her, then strained to hear as Grace tried to tell her something without being over-heard. "I got in early today. There was a detective here talking with Mr. Parker. I couldn't tell what he was saying, but I did hear that it had something to do with you."

Sloane was fond of saying that good detective work began with a hunch. After twenty-five years on the force, he had ample proof, for many of his hunches had turned out to be correct. That was why he expounded his theories to Nick Mars as they studied the loose-leaf pages that comprised Heather Landi's journal.

"I say that Lacey Farrell still isn't coming clean with us," he said angrily. "She's more involved in this thing than she's letting on. We know she took the journal out of the apartment; we know she made a copy of it to give to Jimmy Landi."

He pointed to the bloodstained pages. "And I'll tell you something else, Nick. I doubt we'd have seen these if I hadn't scared her yesterday by telling her that we'd found traces of Isabelle Waring's blood on the floor of the closet, right where she'd left her briefcase."

"And have you thought of this, Eddie?" Mars asked. "Those pages aren't numbered. So how do we know that Farrell hasn't destroyed the ones she didn't want us to see? It's called editing. I agree with you. Farrell's fingerprints aren't just all over these pages. They're all over the whole case."

* * *

An hour later, Detective Sloane received a call from Matt Reilly, a specialist in the Latent Print Unit housed in room 506. Matt had run a fingerprint that had been lifted from the outer door of Lacey's apartment through SAFIS, the Statewide Automated Fingerprint Identification System. He reported it was a match with the fingerprint of Sandy Savarano, a low-level mobster who had been a suspect in a dozen drug-related murders.

"Sandy Savarano!" Sloane exclaimed. "That's crazy, Matt. Savarano's boat blew up with him in it two years ago. We covered his funeral in Woodlawn Cemetery."

"We covered someone's funeral," Reilly told him dryly. "Dead men don't break into apartments."

For the rest of the day, Lacey watched helplessly as clients she had developed were assigned to other agents. It galled her to pull out the tickler files, make follow-up calls regarding potential sales, and then have to turn the information over to others. It was the way she had started out when she was a rookie, but that was eight years ago.

She was also made uncomfortable by the feeling of being watched. Rick was constantly in and out of the sales area where her cubicle was located, and she sensed that he was keeping close tabs on her.

Several times when she went to get a new file, she caught him looking at her. He seemed to be watching her all the time. She had a hunch that by the end of the day, she would be told to stay away from the office until the investigation was concluded, so if she was going to take the copy of Heather's journal with her, she would have to get it out of her desk when Rick wasn't looking.

She finally got her chance to retrieve the pages at ten

minutes of five, when Rick was called into his father's office. She had barely managed to slip the manila envelope into her briefcase when Richard Parker Sr. summoned her to his office and told her she was being suspended.

9

"NOT TOO HUNGRY, I HOPE, ALEX?" JAY TAYLOR ASKED AS he checked his watch again. "Lacey isn't usually this late."

It was obvious that he was irritated.

Mona Farrell jumped to her daughter's defense. "The traffic is always terrible this time of day, and Lacey might have gotten delayed before she even left."

Kit shot her husband a warning glance. "I think with what Lacey has been through, nobody should be upset that she's a little late. My God, she came within a hair of being killed two days ago, then had her apartment burglarized last night. She certainly doesn't need to be hassled anymore, Jay."

"I agree," Alex Carbine said heartily. "She's had a rough couple of days."

Mona Farrell looked at Carbine with a grateful smile. She was never totally at ease with her frequently pompous son-in-law. It didn't take much to make him testy, and he usually had little patience with anyone, but she had noticed that he was deferential to Alex.

This evening they were having cocktails in the living room, while the boys were watching television in the den. Bonnie was with the grown-ups, however, having begged to stay up past her bedtime to see Lacey. She was standing at the window, watching for her.

It's eight-fifteen, Mona thought. Lacey was due here at seven-thirty. This really isn't like her. What can be keeping her?

The full impact of everything that was happening hit Lacey when she arrived home at five-thirty and realized that for practical purposes she was out of a job. Parker Sr. had promised that she would continue to receive her base salary —"For a short time to come, at least," he had said.

He's going to fire me, she realized. He's going to use the excuse that I jeopardized the firm by copying and concealing evidence there. I've worked for him for eight years. I'm one of his best agents. Why would he even *want* to get rid of me? His own son gave me Curtis Caldwell's name and told me to set up an appointment. And I bet he's not planning to give me any of the severance due after so many years of employment. He'll say the firing's for cause. Can he get away with that? It looks like I'm about to be in trouble on several fronts, she thought, shaking her head at the sudden bad fortune that had come her way. I need to talk to a lawyer, but who?

A name came to her mind. Jack Regan!

He and his wife, Margaret, a couple in their mid-fifties, lived on the fifteenth floor of her building. She had chatted with them at a cocktail party last Christmas and remembered hearing people ask him about a criminal case he had just won.

She decided to call right away, but then found that their phone number wasn't listed.

The worst thing that can happen is that they'll slam the door in my face, Lacey decided, as she took the elevator to the fifteenth floor. Ringing their bell, she realized that she was glancing nervously around in the corridor.

Their surprise at seeing her gave way to a genuinely warm welcome. They were having a predinner sherry and insisted she join them. They had heard about the burglary.

"That's part of the reason that I'm here," she began.

Lacey left an hour later, having retained Regan to represent her in the likely event that she was facing indictment for holding on to the journal pages.

"The least of the charges would be obstructing governmental administration," Regan had told her. "But if they believe you had an ulterior motive for taking the journal, it could get a lot more serious than that."

"My only motive was to keep a promise to a dying woman," Lacey protested.

Regan smiled, but his eyes were serious. "You don't have to convince *me,* Lacey, but it wasn't the smartest thing to do."

She kept her car in the garage in the basement of her building, a luxury that, if everything went as she feared, she probably could no longer afford. It was one of several unpleasant realizations she had had to face that day.

The rush hour was over, but even so there was a lot of traffic. I'll be an hour late, Lacey thought as she inched her car across the George Washington Bridge, where a blocked lane was creating havoc. Jay must be in a wonderful mood, she thought, smiling ruefully but genuinely worried about keeping her family waiting.

As she drove along Route 4 she debated how much she would tell them about what was going on. Everything, I guess, she finally decided. If Mom or Kit call me at the office and I'm not there, they'll have to know why.

Jack Regan is a good lawyer, she assured herself as she turned onto Route 17. He'll straighten this out.

She glanced in her rearview mirror. Was that car following her? she wondered, as she exited onto Sheridan Avenue. Stop it, she warned herself. You're getting paranoid.

K it and Jay lived on a quiet street in a section of pricey homes. Lacey pulled up to the curb in front of their house, got out of the car, and started up the walk.

"She's here," Bonnie called out joyously, "Lacey's here!" She ran for the door.

"About time," Jay grunted.

"Thank God," Mona Farrell murmured. She knew that despite Alex Carbine's presence, Jay was about to explode with irritation.

Bonnie tugged at the door and opened it. As she raised her arms for Lacey's hug, there was the sound of shots, and bullets whistled past them. A flash of pain coursed through her head, and Lacey threw herself forward, her body covering Bonnie's. It sounded as though the screams were coming from inside the house, but at that moment Lacey's whole mind seemed to be screaming.

In the sudden quiet that followed the shots, she quickly ran a mental check of the situation. The pain she felt was real, but she realized with a stab of anguish that the gush of blood against her neck was coming from the small body of her niece.

10

In the waiting room on the pediatrics floor of Hackensack Medical Center, a doctor smiled reassuringly at Lacey. "Bonnie had a close call, but she'll make it. And she's very insistent, Ms. Farrell, that she wants to see you."

Lacey was with Alex Carbine. After Bonnie was wheeled out of the operating room, Mona, Kit, and Jay had followed her crib to her room. Lacey had not gone with them.

My fault, my fault—it was all she could think. She was only vaguely aware of the headache caused by the bullet that had creased her skull. In fact, her whole mind and body seemed numb, floating in a kind of unreality, not yet fully comprehending the horror of all that was happening.

The doctor, understanding her concern and aware that she was blaming herself, said, "Ms. Farrell, trust me, it will take a while for that arm and shoulder to mend, but eventually she'll be as good as new. Children heal fast. And they forget fast too."

As good as new, Lacey thought bitterly, staring straight

ahead. She was rushing to open the door for me—that's all she was doing. Bonnie was just waiting for me. And it almost cost her her life. Can anything ever be "good as new" again?

"Lacey, go on in and see Bonnie," Alex Carbine urged.

Lacey turned to look at him, remembering with gratitude how Alex had dialed 911 while her mother tried to stem the blood that was spurting from Bonnie's shoulder.

In her niece's room, Lacey found Jay and Kit sitting on either side of the crib. Her mother was at the foot, now icy calm, her trained nurse's eyes observant.

Bonnie's shoulder and upper arm were heavily bandaged. In a sleepy voice she was protesting, "I'm not a baby. I don't want to be in a crib." Then she spotted Lacey and her face brightened. "Lacey!"

Lacey tried to smile. "Snazzy-looking bandage, girl-friend. Where do I sign it?"

Bonnie smiled back at her. "Did you get hurt too?"

Lacey bent over the crib. Bonnie's arm was resting on a pillow.

As she died, Isabelle Waring's arm had been reaching under a pillow, pulling out the bloodied pages. It's because I was there two days ago that Bonnie is here tonight, Lacey thought. *We could be planning her funeral right now.*

"She really is going to be all right, Lacey," Kit said softly.

"Didn't you have any sense that you were being fol-lowed?" Jay asked.

"For God's sake, Jay, are you crazy?" Kit snapped. "Of course she didn't."

Bonnie is hurt and they're at each other's throats because of me, Lacey thought. I can't let this happen.

Bonnie's eyelids were drooping. Lacey leaned down and kissed her cheek.

"Come back tomorrow, please," Bonnie begged.

"I have some stuff to do first, but I'll be back real soon," Lacey promised her.

Her lips lingered for a moment on Bonnie's cheek. I'll never expose you to danger again, she vowed.

Back in the waiting area, Lacey found detectives from the Bergen County prosecutor's office waiting for her. "We've been contacted by New York," they told her.

"Detective Sloane?" she asked.

"No. The U.S. Attorney's office, Miss Farrell. We've been asked to see that you get home safely."

11

GARY BALDWIN, UNITED STATES ATTORNEY FOR THE
Southern District of the state, generally wore a benign
expression that seemed incongruous to anyone who had ever
seen him in action at a trial. Rimless glasses enhanced the
scholarly look of his thin face. Of medium height and slender build, and soft-spoken in his demeanor, he nevertheless
could annihilate a witness during cross-examination and ac-
complish it without even raising his voice. Forty-three years
old, he was known to have national political ambitions and
clearly would like to crown his career in the U.S. Attorney's
office with a major, headline-grabbing case.

That case might have just landed in his lap. It certainly
had all the proper ingredients: A young woman happens on
a murder scene in an apartment on Manhattan's expensive
Upper East Side, the victim the ex-wife of a prominent
restaurateur. Most important, the woman has seen the assail-
ant and can identify him.

Baldwin knew that if Sandy Savarano had come out of

hiding to do this job, it *had* to be tied to drugs. Thought to be dead for the past two years, Savarano had made a career of being an enforcer who eliminated anyone who got in the way of the drug cartel he worked for. He was about as ruthless as they get.

But when the police had shown Lacey Farrell the mug shots they had of Savarano, she had not recognized him. Either her memory was faulty, or Savarano had had enough plastic surgery to successfully disguise his identity. Chances are it's the latter, Baldwin thought, and if so, then it means that Lacey Farrell is just about the only person who can actually identify him.

Gary Baldwin's dream was to arrest and prosecute Savarano, or better yet, get him to plea-bargain and give evidence against the real bosses.

But the call he had just received from Detective Eddie Sloane had infuriated him. The journal that seemed to be a key part of this case had been stolen from the precinct. "I was keeping it in my cubby in the squad room—locked, of course—while Nick Mars and I read it to see if there was anything useful in it," Sloane explained. "It disappeared sometime last night. We're turning the station house upside down to find out who lifted it."

Then Sloane had added, "Jimmy Landi has the copy Farrell gave him. I'm on my way to get it from him."

"Make sure you get it before that disappears too," Baldwin said.

He slammed the phone down. Lacey Farrell was due in his office, and he had a lot of questions for her.

Lacey knew that she was being naïve in hoping that turning over Heather Landi's journal to the police would end her involvement in the case. When she finally got home from New Jersey the night before, it was almost dawn, but still she was unable to sleep, alternating between self-recrimination that she had put Bonnie in mortal danger, and a sense of bewilderment at the way that her whole life seemed to be falling apart. She felt like a pariah, knowing that because she could identify the man she knew as Curtis Caldwell, not only was she in danger, but anyone close to her was as well.

I can't go to visit Mom or Kit or the kids, she thought. I can't have them visit me. I'm afraid to go out on the street. How long is this going to last? And what will make it end?

Jack Regan had joined her in the waiting room outside the U.S. Attorney's office. He gave her a reassuring smile when a secretary said, "You can go in now."

It was Baldwin's habit to keep people waiting once inside his office while he ostensibly completed making notes in a folder. Under lowered eyelids, he studied Lacey Farrell and her lawyer as they took seats. Farrell looked like a woman under severe stress, he decided. Not surprising given the fact that only last night, in a spray of gunfire, a bullet had grazed her skull and another had seriously injured a four-year-old child. It was a miracle that no one had been killed in the shooting, Baldwin added to himself as he finally acknowledged their presence.

He did not mince words. "Ms. Farrell," he said, "I am very sorry for the problems you've been having, but the fact is you seriously impaired a major criminal investigation by removing evidence from a crime scene. For all we know, you may have destroyed some of that evidence. What you did turn over is now missing, which is a stunning sign of its significance."

"I did *not* destroy—" Lacey began in heated protest, just

as Jack Regan snapped, "You have no right to accuse my client—"

They were interrupted by Baldwin, who held up his hand for silence. Ignoring Regan, his voice icy, he said, "Ms. Farrell, we have only your word for that. But you have my word for this: The man you know as Curtis Caldwell is a ruthless killer. We need your testimony to help convict him, and we intend to make sure that nothing happens to prevent that."

He paused and stared at her. "Ms. Farrell, it is within my power to hold you as a material witness. I promise you it won't be pleasant. It would mean that you'd be kept under twenty-four-hour guard in a special facility."

"How long a time are you talking about?" Lacey demanded.

"We don't know, Ms. Farrell. It would be however long it takes to apprehend and, with your help, convict the murderer. I do know that until Isabelle Waring's killer is arrested, your life isn't worth a plugged nickel, and until now we've never had a case against this man where we thought we'd be able to prosecute him successfully."

"Would I be safe after I testify against him?" Lacey asked. As she sat facing the U.S. Attorney, she had a sudden sense of being in a car that was hurtling down a steep hill, out of control, about to crash.

"No, you wouldn't be," Jack Regan said firmly.

"On the contrary," Baldwin told them. "He's claustrophobic. He will do anything to avoid going to prison. Now that we can link him to a murder, he may well be persuaded to turn state's evidence once we've got him, in which case we would not even bring him to trial. But until that happens we must keep you safe, Ms. Farrell."

He paused. "Have you ever heard of the witness protection program?"

12

IN THE QUIET OF HIS LOCKED OFFICE, HE STUDIED HEATHer's journal again. It was in there, all right. But he had taken care of the problem. The cops were following up all the names they had. Good luck to them. They were on a wildgoose chase.

Finally he turned the pages over. The blood on them had dried a long time ago, probably just minutes after it had been shed. Even so, his hands felt sticky. He wiped them with his handkerchief, dampened by water from the alwayspresent pitcher. Then he sat completely still, the only movement the opening and closing of his fingers, a sure sign of his agitation.

Lacey Farrell had not been seen for three months. They were either holding her as a material witness, or she had disappeared into the witness protection program. She supposedly had made one copy of the journal, for Jimmy Landi, but what would have stopped her from making another copy for herself?

Nothing.

Wherever she was, she would have figured out that if the journal was worth killing for, it had to have something of value in it. Isabelle had talked her head off to Farrell. God knows what she had said.

Sandy Savarano was back in hiding. He had seemed to be the perfect one to send to retrieve the journal and to take care of Isabelle Waring, but he had been careless. Stupidly careless. Twice. He had let Farrell see him at Waring's apartment at the time of the murder, and now she could identify him. (And if the Feds catch him, he told himself, she will.) Then he had left a fingerprint at Farrell's apartment that tied him to the burglary. Sandy would give everything up in a minute rather than go to prison, he reflected.

Farrell had to be tracked down, and Savarano sent to eliminate her.

Then, just maybe, he would be safe at last . . .

13

THE NAME ON THE BELL AT THE SMALL APARTMENT BUILD-
ing on Hennepin Avenue in Minneapolis was "Alice Carroll." To the neighbors, she was an attractive young woman
in her late twenties who didn't have a job and kept pretty
much to herself.

Lacey knew that was the way they described her. And
they're right about keeping to myself, she thought. After
three months, the sensation of sleepwalking was ending and
an intense sense of isolation setting in.

I didn't have a choice, she reminded herself, when at
night she lay awake remembering how she had been told to
pack suitcases with heavy clothing but bring neither family
pictures, nor items with her name or initials.

Kit and her mother had come to help her pack and to say
good-bye. We all thought of it as temporary, a kind of forced
vacation.

At the last minute her mother had tried to come with her.
"You can't go off alone, Lacey," she had argued. "Kit and
Jay have each other and the children."

"You'd be lost without the kids," Lacey had reminded her, "so don't even think that way, Mom."

"Lacey, Jay is going to keep paying the maintenance on your apartment," Kit had promised.

Her knee-jerk response—"I can handle it for a while"— had been an empty boast. She had realized immediately that once she moved and took on her new identity, she could have no involvement with anyone or any part of her life in New York. Even a maintenance check signed with an assumed name could be traced.

It had happened quickly and efficiently. Two uniformed cops had taken her out in a squad car as though she were going to the precinct for questioning. Her bags were brought down to the garage, where an unmarked van was parked. Then she was transferred to an armored van that took her to what they called "a safe site" and orientation center in the Washington, D.C., area.

Alice in Wonderland, Lacey would think as she passed the time in that enclosure, watching her identity disappear. In those weeks she worked with an instructor to create a new background for herself. All the things she had been were gone. They existed in her memory, of course, but after a time she began to question even that reality. Now there were only weekly phone calls from safe hookups, letters mailed through safe channels—otherwise there was no contact. None. Nothing. Only the overwhelming loneliness.

Her only reality became her new identity. Her instructor had walked her to a mirror. "Look in there, Lacey. You see that young woman? Everything you think you know about her isn't so. Just forget her. Forget all about her. It'll be rough for a while—you'll feel like you are playing some kind of game, pretending. There's an old Jerry Vale song that says it all. I can't sing, but I do know the lyrics; they go like this:

Pretend you don't see her at all . . . it's too late for running . . . look somewhere above her . . . pretend you don't see her at all . . .

That was when Lacey had chosen her new name, Alice Carroll, after Alice in *Alice's Adventures in Wonderland* and *Through the Looking Glass,* by Lewis Carroll.

It fit her situation perfectly.

14

THE RACKET FROM THE RENOVATION GOING ON IN THE apartment next to the one that had belonged to Heather Landi assaulted the ears of Rick Parker as soon as he stepped off the elevator in the building at Fifth Avenue and Seventieth Street. Who the hell was the contractor, he wondered, fuming with irritation. A demolition expert?

Outside, the sky was heavy with snow clouds. Flurries were predicted by evening. But even the vague, gray light coming through the windows revealed the general look of neglect that permeated the foyer and living room of Heather Landi's apartment.

Rick sniffed. The air was stale, dry, and dusty. He turned on the light and saw that a thick layer of powdery dust covered the tabletops, bookshelves, and cabinets.

He swore silently. Damn superintendent, he thought. It was his job to see to it that a contractor thoroughly sealed off the premises he was renovating.

He yanked the intercom off the hook and shouted to the

doorman, "Tell the good-for-nothing super to get up here. Now."

Tim Powers, large and by nature amiable, had been superintendent of 3 East Seventieth for fifteen years. He knew full well that in the landlord-tenant world, it was the super who was always caught in the middle, but as he would tell his wife philosophically at the end of a bad day, "If you can't stand the heat, then get the hell out of the kitchen." He had learned to sympathize with irate co-op dwellers when they complained that the elevator was too slow, the sink was dripping, the toilet running, or the heat uneven.

But standing in the doorway as he listened to Rick Parker's tirade, Tim decided that in all these years of putting up with angry complaints, he had never experienced the near manic fury that was being hurled at him now.

He knew better than to tell Rick where to get off. He might be a young jerk riding on his papa's coattails, but that didn't make him any the less a Parker, and the Parkers owned one of the biggest real estate/building management companies in Manhattan.

Rick's voice grew louder and his anger more pronounced. Finally, when he stopped for breath, Tim seized the opportunity to say, "Let's get the right person in here to hear this." He went back into the hall and pounded on the door of the next apartment, shouting, "Charley, get out here."

The door was yanked open, and the sounds of hammering and banging grew louder. Charley Quinn, a grizzled-faced man dressed in jeans and a sweatshirt, and carrying a roll of blueprints, came out into the corridor. "I'm busy, Tim," he said.

"Not busy enough," Powers said. "I've talked to you before about sealing up that job when you start ripping the walls out. Mr. Parker, maybe you'll explain why you're so upset."

"Now that the police have finally released this apartment," Rick shouted, "we are responsible for selling it for the owner. But will you tell me how the hell we can bring anyone in here with all the mess you're causing? The answer is, we can't."

He shoved Tim aside, stalked out into the hall, and rang for the elevator. When the door closed behind him, the superintendent and the contractor looked at each other.

"He's on something," Powers said flatly. "What a jerk."

"He may be a jerk," Quinn said quietly, "but he looks to me like the kind of guy who could go off the deep end." He sighed. "Offer to get a cleaning service in here, Tim. We'll pay for it."

Rick Parker knew better than to go directly to the office. He didn't want to run into his father. I shouldn't have blown my stack like that, he told himself. He was still shaking with anger.

January was a lousy month in New York, he thought. As he turned in to Central Park and walked rapidly along a jogging path, a runner brushed into him. "Watch out!" Rick snapped.

The jogger didn't break pace. "Cool it, man," he yelled back over his shoulder.

Cool it! Sure, Rick thought. The old man's finally letting me handle some sales again, and that nosy detective has to show up this morning of all times.

Detective Sloane had come by, asking the same questions, going over the same territory. "When you got that call from the man who identified himself as Curtis Caldwell, did it ever occur to you to check with the law firm he claimed was his employer?" he had asked for the umpteenth time.

Rick jammed his hands in his pockets, remembering how lame his response had sounded. "We do a lot of business with Keller, Roland, and Smythe," he had said. "Our firm manages their building. There was no reason not to take the call on faith."

"Have you any idea how the caller would have *known* his background wouldn't be checked? I understand that Parker and Parker has a standing policy of screening all applicants, of being sure that the people you take to look at upscale apartments are on the level."

Rick remembered the dread he had experienced when, without knocking, his father had joined them.

"I have told you before and I'll tell you again, I have no idea how that caller knew enough to use the law firm's name," Rick had said.

Now he kicked at a ball of crusted, dirty snow that was lying in his path. Were the police getting suspicious of the fact that he had been the one to set up the meeting? Were they starting to suspect that there never had been a phone call?

I should have figured out a better story, he thought, kicking savagely at the frozen earth. But it was too late now. He was stuck with it, so he *had* to make it stick.

15

THE KEY WORD IN THIS PROGRAM IS "SECURITY," LACEY thought as she started a letter to her mother. What do you write about? she asked herself. Not about the weather. If I were to mention that it's ten degrees below zero and there's been a record twenty-six-inch snowfall in one day, it would be a dead giveaway that I'm in Minnesota. That's the sort of information they warn you about.

I can't write about a job because I don't have one yet. I *can* say that my fake birth certificate and my fake social security card just came through, so now I can *look* for a job. I suppose I can tell them that now I have a driver's license, at least, and my advisor, a deputy U.S. marshal, took me to buy a secondhand car.

The program pays for it. Isn't that great? But of course I can't say that the marshal's name is George Svenson, and I certainly won't let Mom and Kit know that I bought a three-year-old maroon Bronco.

Instead she wrote:

My advisor is a good guy. He's got three teenaged daughters.

No, take that last part out, she thought. Too specific.

My advisor is a good guy. Very patient. He went with me to buy furniture for the studio.

Too specific. Make that *apartment*.

But you know me. I didn't want a lot of matched stuff, so he humored me and we went to some garage sales and house sales and I found some really nice secondhand furniture that at least has character. But I sure miss my own digs, and do tell Jay that I'm really grateful to him for keeping up the maintenance on the place for me.

That was safe enough, Lacey thought, and I really am grateful to Jay. But I *will* pay him back every nickel, she vowed to herself.

She was allowed to call home once a week on a secure telephone hookup. The last call she had made, she could hear Jay in the background, hurrying Kit. Well, it *was* a pain in the neck to have to sit and wait for a call at a specific time; she couldn't deny that. And no one could call her back.

It sounds as though the holidays were fun for the kids, and I'm so happy that Bonnie's arm is getting stronger. Sounds like the boys' skiing trip was a blast. Tell them I'm nutty enough to try snowboarding with them when I get back.

Take care of yourself, Mom. Sounds as though you and Alex are having fun. So what if he talks your ear off once in a while? I think he's a nice guy, and I'll never forget how helpful he was that awful night while Bonnie was in surgery.

Love you all. Keep praying that they find and arrest Isabelle Waring's murderer and he plea-bargains and I get off the hook.

Lacey signed her name, folded the letter and put it in an envelope. Deputy Marshal Svenson would mail it for her through the secure mail-forwarding channel. Writing to her mother and Kit or speaking to them on the phone took away something of the sense of isolation. But when the letter was finished or the phone call completed, the letdown that followed was rough.

Come on, she warned herself, knock off the self-pity. It won't do any good and, thank God, the holidays are over. "Now *they* were a genuine problem," she said aloud, realizing suddenly that she was getting in the habit of talking to herself.

To try to break up Christmas Day she had gone to the last Mass at St. Olaf's, the church named for the warrior king of Norway, then ate at the Northstar Hotel.

At Mass when the choir sang *"Adeste Fidelis"* tears had sprung to her eyes as she thought of the last Christmas her father was alive. They had gone to midnight Mass together at St. Malachy's in Manhattan's theater district. Her mother had always said that Jack Farrell could have made it big if he had chosen to try for a career as a singer rather than as a musician. He really did have a good voice. Lacey remembered how that night she had stopped singing herself, just to listen to the clarity of tone and warmth of feeling he put into the carol.

When it was over, he had whispered, "Ah, Lace, there's something grand about the Latin, isn't there?"

At her solitary meal, her tears had welled up again as she thought about her mother and Kit and Jay and the children. She and her mother always went to Kit's house on Christmas, arriving with the presents for the kids that "Santa had dropped off" at their houses.

At ten, Andy, like Todd at that age, was still a believer. At four, Bonnie was already savvy. Lacey had sent gifts to everyone through secure channels this year, but that didn't hold a candle to *being* there, of course.

As she had tried to pretend she was enjoying the food she

had ordered at the Northstar, she found herself thinking of Kit's festive holiday table with the Waterford chandelier sparkling, its lights reflected off the Venetian glassware.

Knock it off! Lacey warned herself as she dropped the envelope into a drawer, where it would await Deputy Marshal Svenson's pickup.

For lack of something else to do, she reached into the bottom drawer of her desk and pulled out the copy she had made of Heather Landi's journal.

What could Isabelle possibly have wanted me to see in it? she asked herself for the hundredth time. She had read it so often she felt as though she could quote it word for word.

Some of the entries were in a close sequence, daily and sometimes several times a day. Others were spaced a week, a month, or as much as six weeks apart. In all, the journal spanned the four years Heather had spent in New York. She wrote in detail about looking for an apartment, about her father insisting she live in a safe building on the East Side. Heather clearly had preferred Manhattan's West Side; as she put it, "It isn't stuffy and has life."

She wrote about singing lessons, about auditioning and getting her first part in a New York production—an Equity showcase revival of *The Boy Friend*. That entry had made Lacey smile. Heather had ended it by writing "Julie Andrews, move over. Heather Landi is on her way."

She wrote in detail about the plays she had attended, and her analysis of them and of the actors' performances was thoughtful and mature. She wrote interestingly as well about some of the more glamorous parties she attended, many of them apparently through her father's connections. But some of the gushing about her boyfriends was surprisingly *imma*-ture. Lacey got the clear impression that Heather had been pretty much held down by both her mother and father until, after two years of college, she opted to come to New York and try for a career in the theater.

It was obvious that she had been close to both parents. All the references to them were warm and loving, even though several times she had complained about the need to please her father.

There *was* one entry that had intrigued Lacey from the first time she read it:

Dad exploded at one of the waiters today. I have never seen him that angry before. The poor waiter was almost crying. I see what Mom meant when she warned me about his temper and said that I should rethink my decision to tell him that I wouldn't live on the East Side when I moved to New York. He'd kill me if he ever found out how right he was about that. God, I was stupid!

What had happened to make Heather write that? Lacey wondered. It can't be too important. Whatever it was, it took place four years before she died and that's the only reference to it.

It was clear from the last few entries that Heather was deeply troubled about something. She wrote several times about being caught "between a rock and a hard place. I don't know what to do." Unlike the others, those last entries were on unlined paper.

There was nothing specific in those entries, but obviously they had triggered Isabelle Waring's suspicions.

But it could have had to do with a job decision, or a boyfriend, or anything, Lacey thought hopelessly, as she put the pages back in the drawer. God knows *I'm* between a rock and a hard place right now.

That's because someone wants to kill you, a voice inside her head whispered.

Lacey slammed the drawer shut. Stop it! she told herself fiercely.

A cup of tea might help, she decided. She made it, then sipped it slowly, hoping to dispel the heavy sense of fear-filled isolation that was again threatening to overwhelm her.

Feeling restless, she turned on the radio. Usually she flipped the dial to a music station, but it was set on the AM band, and a voice was saying, "Hi, I'm Tom Lynch, your host for the next four hours on WCIV."

Tom Lynch!

Lacey was shocked out of her homesickness. She had made a list of all the names mentioned in Heather Landi's journal, and one of them was Tom Lynch, an out-of-town broadcaster on whom it seemed Heather had once had a mild crush.

Was it the same person? And, if so, was it possible Lacey could learn something about Heather from him?

It was worth pursuing, she decided.

16

Tom Lynch was a hearty Midwesterner. Raised in North Dakota, he was one of the breed of stalwarts who thought twenty degrees was a bracing temperature, and believed that only sissies complained about the cold.

"But today they've got a point," he said with a smile to Marge Peterson, the receptionist at Minneapolis radio station WCIV.

Marge looked at him with maternal affection. He certainly brightened her day, and since he had taken over the station's afternoon talk show, he apparently had been having the same effect on many other people in the Minneapolis–St. Paul area. She could tell from the steadily increasing volume of fan mail that crossed her desk that the popular thirty-year-old anchorman was headed for big-time broadcasting. His mixture of news, interviews, commentary, and irreverent humor attracted a wide age range of listeners. And wait until they get a look at him, she thought as she looked up at his bright hazel eyes, his slightly rumpled medium brown hair, his warm smile, and his attractively uneven features. He's a natural for television.

Marge was happy at his success—and therefore the station's—but realized that it was a double-edged sword. She knew that several other stations had tried to hire him away, but he had announced his strategy was to build WCIV into the number-one station in the listening area before considering moving on. And now it's happening, she thought with a sigh, and soon we'll be losing him.

"Marge, anything wrong?" Tom asked, his expression solicitous. "You look worried."

She laughed and shook her head. "Nothing wrong at all. You're off to the gym?"

As Lynch was signing off that afternoon, he had told his listeners that since even a penguin couldn't jog outside in this weather, he would be heading off to the Twin Cities Gym later on, and he hoped to see some of them there. Twin Cities was one of his sponsors.

"You bet. See you later."

"How did you hear about us, Miss Carroll?" Ruth Wilcox asked as Lacey filled out the membership form for the Twin Cities Gym.

"On the Tom Lynch program," Lacey said. The woman was studying her, and she felt the need to elaborate. "I've been thinking of joining a gym for some time, and since I can try this one out a few times before deciding . . ." She let her voice trail off. "It's also convenient to my apartment," she finished lamely.

At least this will give me some practice in trying to get a job, she told herself fiercely. The prospect of filling out the form had frightened her, since it was the first time she had actually used her new identity. It was all very well to practice it with her advisor, Deputy Marshal George Svenson, but quite another to actually try to live it.

On the drive to the gym she had mentally reviewed the details: She was Alice Carroll, from Hartford, Connecticut, a graduate of Caldwell College, a safe alma mater because the school was now closed. She had worked as a secretary in a doctor's office in Hartford. The doctor retired at the same time that she broke up with her boyfriend, so it just seemed like the right time to make a move. She had chosen Minneapolis because she visited there once as a teenager and loved it. She was an only child. Her father was dead, and her mother had remarried and was living in London.

None of which matters at the moment, she thought as she reached into her purse for her new social security card. She would have to be careful; she had automatically started to write her real number but caught herself. Her address: One East End Avenue, New York, NY 10021 flashed into her mind. *No,* 520 Hennepin Avenue, Minneapolis, MN 55403. Her bank: Chase; *no,* First State. Her job? She put a dash through that space. Relative or friend to notify in case of accident: Svenson had provided her with a phony name, address, and telephone number to use in that situation. Any call that was made to the number would go to him.

She got to the questions on medical history. Any problems? Well, yes, she thought. A slight scar where a bullet creased my skull. Shoulders that always feel tense because I always have the feeling that someone is looking for me, and that someday when I'm out walking, I'll hear footsteps behind me, and I'll turn and . . .

"Stuck on a question?" Wilcox asked brightly. "Maybe I can help."

Instantly struck with paranoia, Lacey was sure she detected a skeptical look appear in the other woman's eyes. She can *sense* that there's something phony about me, she thought. Lacey managed a smile. "No, not stuck at all."

She signed "Alice Carroll" to the form and pushed it across the desk.

Wilcox studied it. "Purr-fect." The pattern on her sweater was kittens playing with a spool of yarn. "Now let me show you around."

The place was attractive and well equipped with a good supply of exercise paraphernalia, a long jogging track, airy rooms for aerobics classes, a large pool, steam and sauna facilities, and an attractive juice bar.

"It gets fairly crowded early in the morning and right after work," Wilcox told her. "Oh, look, there he is," she said, interrupting herself. She called out to a broad-shouldered man who was headed away from them and toward the men's locker room: "Tom, come here a minute."

He stopped and turned, and Ms. Wilcox vigorously waved her arm, gesturing for him to come over.

A moment later she was introducing them. "Tom Lynch, this is Alice Carroll. Alice is joining us because she heard you talk about us on your radio program," Ms. Wilcox told him.

He smiled easily. "I'm glad I'm so persuasive. Nice to meet you, Alice." With a quick nod, and another bright smile, he left them.

"Isn't he a doll?" Wilcox asked. "If I didn't have a boyfriend I really like . . . well, never mind that. The trouble is, the single women sometimes come on too strong to him, keep trying to talk to him. But when he's here, he's here to exercise."

Helpful hints, Lacey thought. "So am I," she said crisply, hoping she sounded convincing.

17

MONA FARRELL SAT ALONE AT A TABLE IN THE POPULAR
new restaurant, Alex's Place. It was eleven o'clock, and the
dining room and bar were still crowded with after-theater
patrons. The pianist was playing "Unchained Melody," and
Mona felt a sharp sense of loss. That song had been one of
Jack's favorites.

The lyrics drifted through her mind. *And time can do so
much . . .*

Mona realized that lately she seemed always to be on the
verge of tears. Oh, Lacey, she thought, where *are* you?

"Well, I guess I can take some time to sit with a pretty
woman."

Mona looked up, startled back into reality, and watched
as Alex Carbine's smile faded.

"You crying, Mona?" he asked anxiously.

"No. I'm fine."

He sat across from her. "You're not fine. Anything special, or just the way things are?"

She attempted a smile. "This morning I was watching CNN, and they showed that minor earthquake in Los Angeles. It wasn't *that* minor. A young woman lost control of her car, and it flipped over. She was slim and had dark hair. They showed her being placed on a stretcher." Mona's voice quivered. "And for an awful moment I thought it was Lacey. She could be there, you know. She could be anywhere."

"But it wasn't Lacey," Alex said reassuringly.

"No, of course not, but I'm at the point that whenever I hear about a fire or flood or an earthquake, I worry that Lacey might be there and be caught in it."

She tried to smile. "Even Kit is getting sick of listening to me. The other day there was an avalanche on Snowbird Mountain, and some skiers were caught in it. Fortunately they were all rescued, but I kept listening for the names. Lacey loves to ski, and it would be just like her to go out in a heavy storm."

She reached for her wineglass. "Alex, I shouldn't be dumping all of this on you."

Carbine reached for her hand. "Yes, you should, Mona. When you talk to Lacey, maybe you should tell her what this whole thing is doing to you. I mean, maybe if you just had some idea of where she is, it would be easier to cope."

"No, I can't do that. I have to try *not* to let her know. It would be that much harder for her. I'm lucky. I've got Kit and her family. And you. Lacey's all alone."

"Tell her," Alex Carbine said firmly. "And then keep what she tells you to yourself."

He patted her hand.

18

"WHEN YOU CREATE SOMEONE LIKE THE MYTHICAL BOY-friend, have a real person in mind," Deputy Marshal George Svenson had warned Lacey. "Be able to visualize that guy and the way he talks so that if you have to answer questions about him, it will be easier to be consistent. And remember, develop the trick of answering questions by asking questions of your own."

Lacey had decided that Rick Parker was the mythical boyfriend she had broken up with. She could imagine breaking up with him more easily than having him as a boy-friend, but thinking of him at least did make consistency easier.

She began going to the gym daily, always in the late afternoon. The exercise felt good, and it gave her a chance to focus her thoughts as well. Now that she had the social security card she was anxious to get a job, but Deputy Marshal Svenson told her the protection program would not provide false references.

"How am I supposed to get a job without a reference?" she had asked.

"We suggest you volunteer to work without pay for a couple of weeks, then see if you're hired."

"*I* wouldn't hire someone without references," she had protested.

It was obvious, though, that she would just have to try. Except for the gym, she was without any human contact. Being alone so much, the time was passing too slowly, and Lacey could feel depression settling over her like a heavy blanket. She had even come to dread the weekly talk with her mother. It always ended the same way, with her mother in tears, and Lacey ready to scream with frustration.

In the first few days after she started going to the gym, she had managed to make something of a friend of Ruth Wilcox. It was to her that she first tried out the story of what had happened to bring her to Minneapolis: her mother had remarried and moved to London; the doctor she worked for retired; and she had ditched her boyfriend. "He had a quick temper and could be very sarcastic," she explained, thinking of Rick.

"I know the type," Wilcox assured her. "But let me tell you something. Tom Lynch has been asking me about you. I think he likes you."

Lacey had been careful not to seem too interested in Lynch, but she had been laying the groundwork for a planned encounter. She timed her jogging to be finished just as he was starting. She signed up for an aerobics class that looked out on the jogging track and chose a spot where he would see her as he ran by. Sometimes on his way out he stopped in the juice bar for a vitamin shake or a coffee. She began to go into the shop a few minutes before he finished his run and to sit at a table for two.

The second week, her plan worked. When he entered the bar, she was alone at the small table and all the other tables were taken. As he looked around, their eyes met. Keeping her fingers crossed, she pointed casually to the empty chair.

Lynch hesitated, then came over.

She had combed Heather's journal and copied down any mention of him. The first time he appeared had been about a year and a half ago, when Heather had met him after one of the performances of her show.

The nicest guy came out with us to Barrymore's for a hamburger. Tom Lynch, tall, really attractive, about thirty, I'd guess. He has his own radio program in St. Louis but says he is moving to Minneapolis soon. Kate is his cousin, that's why he came to the show tonight. He said that the hardest thing about being out of New York was not being able to go to the theater regularly. I talked to him a lot. He said he was going to be in town for a few days. I hoped he'd ask me out, but no such luck.

An entry four months later read:

Tom Lynch was in town over the weekend. A bunch of us went skiing at Stowe. He's really good. And nice. He's the kind of guy Baba would love to see me with. But he isn't giving me or any of the girls a second look, and anyhow it wouldn't make any difference now.

Three weeks later Heather had died in the accident—if it *was* an accident. When she copied the references to him,

Lacey had wondered if either Isabelle or the police had ever spoken to Lynch about Heather. And what had Heather meant by writing "anyhow it wouldn't make any difference now"?

Did she mean that Tom Lynch had a serious girlfriend? Or did it mean that Heather was involved with someone herself?

All these thoughts raced through Lacey's head as Lynch settled down across the table from her.

"It's Alice Carroll, isn't it," he asked in a tone that was more affirmation than question.

"Yes, and you're Tom Lynch."

"So they tell me. I understand you've just moved to Minneapolis."

"That's right." She hoped her smile did not look forced.

He's going to ask questions, she thought nervously. This could be my first real test. She picked up the spoon and stirred her coffee, then realized that very few people felt the need to stir black coffee.

Svenson had told her to answer questions with questions. "Are you a native, Tom?"

She knew he wasn't, but it seemed like a natural thing to ask.

"No. I was born in Fargo, North Dakota. Not that far from here. Did you see the movie, *Fargo*?"

"I loved it," she said, smiling.

"And after seeing it, you still moved here? It was practically banned in these parts. Folks thought it made us look like a bunch of hicks."

Even to her own ears it sounded lame when she tried to explain the move to Minneapolis: "My mother and I visited friends here when I was sixteen. I loved everything about the city."

"It wasn't in weather like this, I trust."

"No, it was in August."

"During the black fly season?"

He was teasing. She knew it. But when you're lying, everything takes on a different slant. Next he asked her where she worked.

"I'm just settling in," she replied, thinking that at least that was an honest statement. "Now it's time to look for a job."

"What kind?"

"Oh, I worked in billing in a doctor's office," she replied, then added hastily, "but I'm going to try something different this time around."

"I don't blame you. My brother's a doctor, and those insurance forms keep three secretaries busy. What kind of doctor did you work for?"

"A pediatrician." Thank God, after listening to Mom all these years, I can sound as though I know what I'm talking about there, Lacey thought. But why on earth did I mention the billing department? I don't know one insurance form from another.

Anxious to change the drift of the conversation, she said, "I was listening to you today. I liked your interview with the director of last week's revival of *Chicago*. I saw the show in New York before I moved here and loved it."

"My cousin Kate is in the chorus of the road company of *The King and I* that's in town now," Lynch said.

Lacey saw the speculative look in his eyes. He's trying to decide whether to ask me to go with him to see it. Let him, she prayed. His cousin Kate had worked with Heather; she was the one who introduced them.

"It's opening tomorrow night," he said. "I have two tickets. Would you like to go?"

19

In the three months that followed Isabelle's death, Jimmy Landi felt detached. It was as if whatever part of his brain controlled his emotions had been anesthetized. All his energy, all his thinking were channeled into the new casino-hotel he was building in Atlantic City. Situated between Trump Castle and Harrah's Marina, it was carefully designed to outshine them both, a magnificent gleaming white showcase with rounded turrets and a golden roof.

And as he stood in the lobby of this new building and watched the final preparations being made for the opening a week away, he thought to himself, I've done it! I've actually done it! Carpets were being laid, paintings and draperies were being hung, cases and cases of liquor disappeared into the bar.

It was important to outshine everyone else on the strip, to show them up, to be different in a special way. The street kid who had grown up on Manhattan's West Side, who had dropped out of school at thirteen and gone to work as a dishwasher at The Stork Club, was on top now, and he was going to rub another success in everyone's face.

Jimmy remembered those old days, how when the kitchen door swung open, he would try to sneak a glance at the celebrities in the club's dining room. In those days they all had glamour, not just the stars but everyone who came there. They'd never dream of showing up looking as if they had slept in their clothes.

The columnists were there every night, and they had their own tables. Walter Winchell. Jimmy Van Horne. Dorothy Kilgallen. Kilgallen! Boy, did they all kowtow to her. Her column in the *Journal-American* was a must-read; everybody wanted her on his side.

I studied them, Jimmy thought, as he stood in the lobby, workmen milling around him. And I learned everything I needed to know about this business in the kitchen. If a chef didn't show up, I could take over. He had worked his way up, becoming first a busboy, then a waiter, then maitre d'. By the time Jimmy Landi was in his thirties, he was ready to have his own place.

He learned how to deal with celebrities, how to flatter them without surrendering his own dignity, how to glad-hand them, but make them glad to get his nod of recognition and approval. I also learned how to treat my help, he thought —tough, but fair. Nobody who deliberately pulled anything on me got a second chance. Ever.

He watched with approval as a foreman sharply reprimanded a carpet layer who had placed a tool on the mahogany reservations desk.

Looking through wide, clear-glass doors, he could see gaming tables being set up in the casino. He walked into the massive space. Off to the right, glittering rows of slot machines seemed to be begging to be tried. Soon, he thought. Another week and they'll be lined up to use them, God willing.

He felt a hand on his shoulder. "Place looks okay, doesn't it, Jimmy?"

"You've done a good job, Steve. We'll open on time, and we'll be ready."

Steve Abbott laughed. *"Good* job? I've done a *great* job. But you're the one with vision. I'm just the enforcer, the one who rides herd on everyone. But I wanted it done on time too. I wasn't going to have painters slopping around on opening night. It'll be ready." He turned back to Landi. "Cynthia and I are on our way back to New York. What about you?"

"No. I want to hang around here for a while. But when you get back to the city, would you make a call for me?"

"Sure."

"You know the guy who touches up the murals?"

"Gus Sebastiani?"

"That's right. The artist. Get him in as fast as possible and tell him to paint Heather out of all the pictures."

"Jimmy, are you sure?" Steve Abbott searched his partner's face. "You may regret doing that, you know."

"I won't regret it. It's time." Abruptly he turned away. "You better get going."

Landi waited a few minutes, then walked over to the elevator and pushed the top button.

Before he left he wanted to stop in again at the piano bar.

It was an intimate corner room with rounded windows overlooking the ocean. The walls were painted a deep, warm blue, with silver bars of music from popular songs randomly scattered against drifting clouds. Jimmy had personally selected the songs. They all had been among Heather's favorites.

She wanted me to call this whole operation Heather's

Place, he thought. She was kidding. With a glimmer of a smile, Jimmy corrected himself. She was half kidding.

This *is* Heather's place, he thought as he looked around. Her name will be on the doors, her music is on these walls. She'll be part of it all, just the way she wanted, but not like in the restaurant where I have to look at her picture all the time.

He had to put it all behind him.

Restlessly he walked to a window. Far below, just above the horizon, the half-moon was glistening on churning waves.

Heather.

Isabelle.

Both gone. For some reason, Landi had found himself thinking more and more about Isabelle. As she was dying, she'd made that young real estate woman promise to give him Heather's journal. What was her name? Tracey? No. Lacey. Lacey Farrell. He was glad to have it, but what was so important in it? Right after he got it, the cops had asked to take his copy to compare it with the original.

He had given it to them, although reluctantly. He had read it the night Lacey Farrell gave it to him. Still he was mystified. What did Isabelle think he would find in it? He had gotten drunk before he tried to read it. It hurt too much to see her handwriting, to read her descriptions of things they did together. Of course, she also wrote about how worried she was about *him*.

"Baba," Jimmy thought.

The only time she ever called me "Dad" was when she thought I was sore at her.

Isabelle had seen a conspiracy in everything, then ironically ended up a random victim of a con man who cased the apartment by pretending to be a potential buyer, then came back to burglarize it.

It was one of the oldest games in the world, and Isabelle

had been an unsuspecting victim. She simply had been in the wrong place at the wrong time.

Or *had* she? Jimmy Landi wondered, unable to shake the worrisome residue of doubt. Was there even the faintest chance that she had been right, that Heather's death *hadn't* been an accident? Three days before Isabelle died, a columnist in the *Post* had written that Heather Landi's mother, Isabelle Waring, a former beauty queen, "may be on the right track in suspecting the young singer's death wasn't accidental."

The columnist had been questioned by police and admitted she had met Isabelle casually and had gotten an earful of her theories about her daughter's death. As for the mention in the column, she had completely fabricated the suggestion that Isabelle Waring had proof.

Was Isabelle's death related to that item? Jimmy Landi wondered. Did someone panic?

These were questions that Jimmy had avoided. If Isabelle had been murdered to silence her, it meant that someone had deliberately caused Heather to burn to death in her car at the bottom of that ravine.

Last week the cops had released the apartment, and he had phoned the real estate people, instructing them to put it back on the market. He needed closure. He would hire a private detective to see if there was anything the cops had missed. And he would talk to Lacey Farrell.

The sound of hammering finally penetrated his consciousness. He looked around him. It was time to go. With heavy steps he walked across the room and entered the corridor. He pulled the heavy mahogany doors closed, then stood back to look at them. An artist had designed the gold letters that were to be fastened on the doors. They should be ready in a day or two.

"Heather's Place," they would read, for Baba's girl, Jimmy thought. If I find that someone deliberately hurt you, baby, I'll kill him myself. I promise you *that*.

20

IT WAS TIME TO CALL HOME, AN EVENT THAT LACEY BOTH longed for and dreaded. This time the location for the secure phone call was a room in a motel. "Never the same place," she said when George Svenson opened the door in response to her knock.

"No," he agreed. Then he added, "The line's ready. I'll put the call through for you. Now, remember everything I told you, Alice."

He always called her Alice.

"I remember every word." Chanting, she recited the list: "Even to name a supermarket could give away my location. If I talk about the gym, don't dare refer to it as the Twin Cities Gym. Stay away from the weather. Since I don't have a job, that's a safe subject. Stretch it out."

She bit her lower lip. "I'm sorry, George," she said contritely. "It's just that I get an attack of nerves before these calls."

She saw a flicker of sympathy and understanding in his craggy face.

"I'll make the connection, then take a walk," he told her. "About half an hour."

"That's fine."

He nodded and picked up the receiver. Lacey felt her palms get moist. A moment later she heard the door click behind him as she said, "Hi, Mom. How's everyone?"

Today had been more difficult than usual. Kit and Jay were not home. "They had to go to some cocktail reception," her mother explained. "Kit sends her love. The boys are fine. They're both on the hockey team at school. You should see how they can skate, Lacey. My heart's in my mouth when I watch them."

I taught them, Lacey thought. I bought ice skates for them when they barely had started to walk.

"Bonnie's a worry, though," her mother added. "Still so pale. Kit takes her to the therapist three times a week, and I work out with her weekends. But she misses you. So much. She has an idea that you're hiding because someone may try to kill you."

Where did she get that idea? Lacey wondered. Dear God, who put that notion in her head?

Her mother answered the unasked question: "I think she overheard Jay talking to Kit. I know he irritates you sometimes, but in fairness, Lace, he's been very good, paying for your apartment and keeping up your insurance. I also learned from Alex that Jay has a big order to sell restaurant supplies to the casino-hotel that Jimmy Landi is opening in Atlantic City, and apparently he has been worried that if Landi knew he was related to you, the order might get canceled. Alex said that Jimmy felt terrible about what happened to his ex-wife, and Jay was afraid that he'd start to blame you somehow for her death. You know, for bringing that man in to see the apartment without checking on him first."

Maybe it's too bad I wasn't killed along with Isabelle, Lacey thought bitterly.

Trying to sound cheerful, she told her mother that she was going to a gym regularly and really enjoying it. "I'm okay, really I am," she said. "And this won't go on too long, I promise. From what they tell me, when the man I can identify is arrested, he'll be persuaded to turn state's evidence rather than go to prison. As soon as they make a deal with him, I'll be off the hook. Whoever he fingers will be after him, not me. We just have to keep praying that it happens soon. Right, Mom?"

She was horrified to hear deep sobs coming from the other end of the connection. "Lacey, I can't live like this," Mona Farrell wailed. "Every time I hear about a young woman anywhere who's been in an accident, I'm sure it's you. You've got to tell me where you are. You've got to."

"Mom!"

"Lacey, please!"

"If I tell you, it's strictly between us. You can't repeat it. You can't even tell Kit."

"Yes, darling."

"Mom, they'd withdraw the protection, they'd throw me out of the program if they knew I told you."

"I have to know."

Lacey was looking out the window. She saw the ample frame of George Svenson approaching the steps. "Mom," she whispered. "I'm in Minneapolis."

The door was opening. "Mom, have to go. Talk to you next week. Kiss everybody for me. Love you. Bye."

"Everything okay at home?" Svenson asked.

"I guess so," Lacey said, as a sickening feeling came over her that she had just made a terrible mistake.

21

Landi's restaurant on West Fifty-sixth Street was filled with a sparkling after-theater crowd, and Steve Abbott was acting as host, going from table to table, greeting and welcoming the diners. Former New York Mayor Ed Koch was there. "That new TV show you're on is fabulous, Ed," Steve said, touching Koch's shoulder.

Koch beamed. "How many people get paid that kind of money for being a judge in small-claims court?"

"You're worth every penny."

He stopped at a table presided over by Calla Robbins, the legendary musical-comedy performer who had been coaxed out of retirement to star in a new Broadway show. "Calla, the word is that you're marvelous."

"Actually, the word is that not since Rex Harrison in *My Fair Lady* has anyone faked a song with such flair. But the public seems to like it, so what's wrong with that?"

Abbott's eyes crinkled as he bent down and kissed her cheek. "Absolutely nothing." He signaled to the captain hovering nearby. "You know the brandy Ms. Robbins enjoys."

"There go the profits," Calla Robbins said, laughing. "Thanks, Steve. You know how to treat a lady."

"I try." He smiled.

"I hear the new casino will knock everyone dead," chimed in Robbins's escort, a prominent businessman.

"You heard right," Steve agreed. "It's an amazing place."

"The word is that Jimmy is planning to get you to run it," the man added.

"The word is this," Steve said decisively. "Jimmy's principal owner. Jimmy's the boss. That's the way it is, and that's the way it's going to be. And don't you forget it. He sure doesn't let *me* forget it."

From the corner of his eye he saw Jimmy enter the restaurant. He waved him over.

Jimmy joined them, his face wreathed in a big smile for Calla.

"Who is boss in Atlantic City, Jimmy?" she asked. "Steve says you are."

"Steve has it right," Jimmy said, smiling. "That's why we get along so good."

As Jimmy and Steve moved away from Robbins's table, Landi asked, "Did you set up a dinner with that Farrell woman for me?"

Abbott shrugged. "Can't reach her, Jimmy. She's left her job, and her home phone is disconnected. I guess she's off on some kind of vacation."

Jimmy's face darkened. "She can't have gone too far. She's a witness. She can identify Isabelle's killer when they find him. That detective who took my copy of Heather's journal has to know where she is."

"Want me to talk to him?"

"No, I'll do it. Well, look who's here."

The formidable figure of Richard J. Parker was coming through the restaurant doors.

"It's his wife's birthday," Steve explained. "They have a reservation for three. That's why R. J.'s wife is with him for a change."

And that punk son of his completes the happy family, Jimmy thought, as he hurried across to the foyer to welcome them with a warm smile.

The elder Parker regularly brought his real estate clients there for dinner, which was the only reason Jimmy hadn't banned his son, Rick Parker, from the restaurant ages ago. Last month he had gotten drunk and noisy at the bar and had had to be escorted to a cab. A few times when he had come in for dinner, it was obvious to Jimmy that Rick was high on drugs.

R. J. Parker returned Jimmy Landi's hearty handshake. "What more festive place to bring Priscilla than Landi's, right, Jimmy?"

Priscilla Parker gave Landi a timid smile, then looked anxiously at her husband for approval.

Jimmy knew that R. J. not only cheated on his wife, but that he bullied her unmercifully as well.

Rick Parker nodded nonchalantly. "Hi, Jimmy," he said with a slight smirk.

The aristocrat condescending to greet the peasant inn-keeper, Jimmy thought. Well, without his father's clout that jerk couldn't get a job cleaning toilets.

Smiling broadly, Jimmy personally escorted them to their table.

As Priscilla Parker sat down, she looked around. "This is such a pretty room, Jimmy," she said. "But there's something different. What is it? Oh, I see," she said, "the paintings of Heather are gone."

"I thought it was time to remove them," Jimmy said gruffly.

He turned abruptly and left, so he did not see R. J. Parker's angry glance at his son, nor the way Rick Parker stared at the mural of the Bridge of Sighs, from which the painting of Heather as a young woman was now missing.

It was just as well.

22

IT HAD BEEN NEARLY FOUR MONTHS SINCE LACEY HAD HAD a reason to get dressed up. And I didn't bring dress-up clothes, she thought, as she looked in the closet for something that would be appropriate for a festive evening out.

I didn't bring many of my things because I thought that by now Caldwell, or whatever his real name is, would have been caught and made a deal to turn state's evidence, and I'd be out of the loop and back to real life.

That's the kind of thinking that gets me in trouble, she reminded herself as she reached for the long black wool skirt and evening sweater she had bought at an end-of-season closeout sale at Saks Fifth Avenue last spring, neither of which she'd had a chance to wear in New York.

"You look okay, Alice," she said aloud when she studied herself in the mirror a few minutes later. Even on sale the skirt and sweater had been an extravagance. But it was worth it, she decided. The effect of understated elegance gave a lift to her spirits.

And I certainly *need* a lift, Lacey thought as she fished in her jewelry box for earrings and her grandmother's pearls.

Promptly at six-thirty, Tom Lynch called on the intercom from the lobby. She was waiting with the apartment door open when he stepped out of the elevator and walked down the hall.

The obvious admiration in his face as he approached was flattering. "Alice, you look lovely," he said.

"Thanks. You're pretty fancy yourself. Come—"

She never finished saying come in. The door to the elevator was opening again. Had someone followed Tom up? Grabbing his arm, she propelled him into the apartment and bolted the door.

"Alice, is anything wrong?"

She tried to laugh, but knew the effort sounded false and shrill. "I'm so foolish," she stammered. "There was a . . . a deliveryman who rang the bell a couple of hours ago. He honestly was on the wrong floor, but my apartment was burglarized last year . . . in Hartford," she added hastily. "Then the elevator door opened again behind you . . . and . . . and I guess I'm just still jumpy," she finished lamely.

There was no deliveryman, she thought. *And my apartment was burglarized, but it wasn't in Hartford. I'm not just jumpy. I'm terrified that whenever an elevator door opens I'll see Caldwell standing there.*

"I can understand why you'd be nervous," Tom said, his tone serious. "I went to Amherst and used to visit friends in Hartford occasionally. Where did you live, Alice?"

"On Lakewood Drive." Lacey conjured up the pictures of a large apartment complex she had studied as part of her preparation in the safe site, praying that Tom Lynch wouldn't say his friends lived there too.

"Don't know it," he said, slowly shaking his head. Then,

as he looked around the room, he added, "I like what you've done here."

The apartment *had* taken on a mellow, comfortable look, she had to admit. Lacey had painted the walls a soft ivory and then painstakingly ragged them to give them texture. The rug she had picked up at a garage sale was a machine-made copy of a Chelsea carpet, and it was old enough to have acquired a soft patina. The dark blue velvet couch and matching love seat were well worn, but still handsome and comfortable. The coffee table, which had cost her twenty dollars, had a scarred leather top and Regency legs. It was a duplicate of the one she had grown up with, and it gave her a sense of comfort. The shelves next to the television were filled with books and knickknacks, all things she had bought at garage sales.

Lacey started to comment on how much she enjoyed shopping at garage sales, but stopped herself. Most people wouldn't be completely furnishing an apartment with garage-sale items. No, she thought, most people who relocate move their furniture as well. She settled for thanking Tom for his compliment and was glad when he suggested they get started.

He's different tonight, she thought as an hour later they sat companionably sipping wine and eating pizza. In the gym he had been cordial but reserved whenever they passed each other, and she assumed it had been a last-minute impulse that made him invite her to go with him to the opening tonight.

But now, being with him had taken on the feeling of an enjoyable and interesting date. For the first time since the night Isabelle died, Lacey realized, she was actually *enjoying* herself. Tom Lynch responded freely to the questions she asked him. "I was raised in North Dakota," he said. "I told you that. But I never lived there again after I went to college. When I graduated, I moved to New York, fully expecting to set the broadcast industry on fire. It didn't happen, of course, and a very wise man told me that the best way to make it was to start out in a smaller broadcast area, make a name for yourself there, then gradually work your way up to larger markets. So in the last nine years I've been in Des Moines, Seattle, St. Louis, and now here."

"Always radio?" Lacey asked.

Lynch smiled. "The eternal question. Why not go for television? I wanted to do my own thing, develop a program format, have the chance to see what works and what doesn't work. I know I've learned a lot, and recently I've had some inquiries from a good cable station in New York, but I think it's too soon to make that kind of move."

"Larry King went from radio to television," Lacey said. "He certainly made the transition fine."

"Hey, that's me, the next Larry King." They had shared one small pizza. Lynch eyed the last piece then started to put it on her plate.

"You take it," Lacey protested.

"I don't really want—"

"You're salivating for it."

They laughed together and a few minutes later when they left the restaurant and crossed the street to the theater, he put his hand under her elbow.

"You have to be careful," he said. "There are patches of black ice everywhere around here."

If only you knew, Lacey thought. My life is a sheet of black ice.

It was the third time she had seen a production of *The King and I*. The last time had been when she was a freshman in college. That had been on Broadway, and her father had been in the orchestra pit. Wish you were playing in this one tonight, Jack Farrell, she thought. As the overture began, she felt tears welling in her eyes and forced them back.

"You okay, Alice?" Tom asked quietly.

"I'm fine." How did Tom sense that she was distressed? she wondered. Maybe he's psychic, she thought. I hope not.

Tom's cousin, Kate Knowles, was playing the role of Tuptim, the slave girl who tries to escape from the king's palace. She was a good actress with an exceptional voice. About my age, Lacey thought, maybe a little younger. She praised her enthusiastically to Tom during intermission, then asked, "Will she be riding with us to the party?"

"No. She's going over with the cast. She'll meet us there."

I'll be lucky to get any time with her, Lacey worried.

Kate and the other leads in the play were not the only "stars" at the party, Lacey realized. Tom Lynch was constantly surrounded by people. She slipped away from him to trade her wine for a Perrier, but then did not rejoin him when she saw he was with an attractive young woman from the cast. Obviously impressed by him, she was talking animatedly.

I don't blame her, Lacey thought. He's good-looking, he's smart, and he's nice. Heather Landi apparently had been attracted to him, although the second time she wrote about him in her journal there was the suggestion that one of them was involved with someone else.

Sipping the Perrier, she walked over to a window. The party was in a mansion in Wayzata, a decidedly upscale suburb twenty minutes from downtown Minneapolis. The well-lighted property bordered on Lake Minnetonka, and standing at the window, Lacey could see that beyond the snow-covered lawn the lake was frozen solid.

She realized that the real estate agent in her was absorbing the details of the place—the fabulous location, the fine appointments in the eighty-year-old house. There were details in the design and construction you just don't come by anymore—at any price—in new homes, she thought as she turned to study the living room, where nearly one hundred people were gathered without even making the room seem crowded.

For a moment she thought longingly of her office in New York, of getting new listings, matching buyer to property, the thrill of closing a sale. I want to go home, she thought.

Wendell Woods, the host of the party, came over to her. "It's Miss Carroll, isn't it?"

He was an imposing man of about sixty with steel gray hair.

He's going to ask me where I'm from, Lacey thought.

He did, and she hoped she sounded credible when she gave the well-rehearsed version of her background in Hartford. "And now I'm settled in and ready to start job hunting," she told him.

"What kind of job?" he asked.

"Well, I don't want to go back to work in a doctor's office," she said. "I've always had an idea I'd like to try my hand at real estate."

"That's mostly commission income, you know. Plus you'd have to learn the area," he said.

"I understand that, Mr. Woods," Lacey said. Then she smiled. "I'm a quick study."

He's going to put me in touch with someone, she thought. I *know* he is.

Woods took out a pen and his own business card. "Give me your phone number," he said. "I'm going to pass it on to one of my depositors. Millicent Royce has a small agency in Edina; her assistant just left to have a baby. Maybe you two can get together."

Lacey gladly gave the number to him. *I'm being recommended by the president of a bank and I'm supposedly new to the real estate field,* she thought. *If Millicent Royce is interested in meeting me, she may not bother to check references.*

When Woods turned to speak to another guest, Lacey glanced about the room. Seeing that Kate Knowles was momentarily alone, she quickly made her way to her. "You were wonderful," she said. "I've seen three different productions of *The King and I,* and your interpretation of Tuptim was great."

"I see you two have gotten together."

Tom Lynch had joined them. "Alice, I'm sorry," he apologized. "I got waylaid. I didn't mean to leave you on your own so long."

"Don't worry, it worked out fine," she told him. *You don't know how fine,* she thought.

"Tom, I wanted a chance to visit with you," his cousin said. "I've had enough of this party. Let's take off and have a cup of coffee somewhere." Kate Knowles smiled at Lacey. "Your friend was just telling me how good I was. I want to hear more."

Lacey glanced at her watch. It was one-thirty. Not wanting to stay up all night, she suggested having coffee at her place. On the drive back into Minneapolis, she insisted that Kate sit in the front seat with Tom. She was sure they wouldn't stay long in the apartment, and at least they were getting some of the family gossip out of the way.

How can I bring up Heather Landi's name without seeming too abrupt? she wondered, reminding herself that Kate was only in town for a week.

* * *

119

"I made these cookies this morning," Lacey said as she set a plate on the coffee table. "Try them at your own risk. I haven't baked since high school."

After she poured the coffee, she tried to steer the conversation around so that she could introduce Heather's name. In her journal, Heather had written about meeting Tom Lynch after a performance. *But if I say that I saw the show, chances are I would have remembered if I'd seen Kate in it,* Lacey thought. She said, "I went down to New York about a year and a half ago and saw a revival of *The Boy Friend.* I read in your bio in the program tonight that you were in it, but I'm sure I'd remember if I'd seen you."

"You must have gone the week I was out with the flu," Kate said. "Those were the only performances I missed."

Lacey tried to sound offhand. "I do remember that there was a young actress with a really fine voice in the lead. I'm trying to think of her name."

"Heather Landi," Kate Knowles said promptly, turning to her cousin. "Tom, you remember her. She had a crush on you. Heather was killed in a car accident," she said, shaking her head. "It was such a damn shame."

"What happened?" Lacey asked.

"Oh, she was driving home from a ski lodge in Stowe and went off the road. Her mother, poor thing, couldn't accept it. She came around to the theater, talking to all of us, searching for some reason behind the accident. She said that Heather had been upset about something shortly before that weekend and wanted to know if we had any idea what it was about."

"Did you?" Tom asked.

Kate Knowles shrugged. "I told her that I had noticed that Heather was terribly quiet the last week before she died, and I agreed that she *was* worried about something. I suggested that Heather may not have been concentrating on driving when she went into the skid."

It's a dead end, Lacey thought. Kate doesn't know anything I don't already know.

Kate Knowles put down her coffee cup. "That was great, Alice, but it's very late, and I've got to be on my way." She stood, then turned back to Lacey. "It's funny that Heather Landi's name should come up; I'd just been thinking about her. A letter her mother had written to me, asking that I try again to remember anything I could that might give her a reason for Heather's behavior that weekend, finally caught up with me. It had been forwarded to two other cities before reaching me here." She paused, then shook her head. "There is one thing I might write her about, although it's probably not significant. A guy I've dated some—Bill Merrill, you met him, Tom—knew Heather too. Her name came up, and he mentioned that he had seen her the afternoon before she died, in the après-ski bar at the lodge. Bill had gone there with a bunch of guys, including a jerk named Rick Parker who's in real estate in New York and apparently had pulled something on Heather when she first came to the city. Bill said that when Heather spotted Parker she practically ran out of the lodge. It's probably nothing, but Heather's mom is so anxious for any information about that weekend that she'd surely want to know. I think I'll write her first thing tomorrow."

The sound of Lacey's coffee cup shattering on the floor broke the trancelike state she had entered when she heard Kate's mention of Isabelle's letter and then of Rick Parker's name. Quickly covering her confusion, and refusing their help, she busied herself with cleaning up the mess while calling out her good nights to Kate and Tom as they headed for the door.

Alone in the kitchen, Lacey pressed her back against the wall, willing herself to be calm, resisting the urge to call out to Kate not to bother with the letter to Isabelle Waring, since it was too late for it to matter to her.

23

AFTER NEARLY FOUR MONTHS OF INVESTIGATION, U.S. Attorney Gary Baldwin was no nearer to locating Sandy Savarano than he had been when he had still believed Savarano was buried in Woodlawn Cemetery.

His staff had painstakingly studied Heather Landi's journal, and had tracked down the people named in it. It was a process that Isabelle Waring also had attempted, Baldwin thought, as he once again studied the police artist's rendering of Sandy Savarano's face as drawn from Lacey Farrell's description of him.

The artist had attached a note to the drawing: "Witness does not appear to have a good eye for noticing the kind of detail that would make the suspect identifiable."

They had tried talking to the doorman in the building where the murder took place, but he remembered virtually nothing of the killer. He said he saw too many people come and go there, and besides, he was about to retire.

So that leaves me with only Lacey Farrell to personally

finger Savarano, Baldwin thought bitterly. If anything happens to her, there's no case. Sure, we got his fingerprint off Farrell's door after her apartment was burglarized, but we can't even prove he went inside. Farrell's the only one who can tie him to Isabelle Waring's murder. Without her to ID him, forget it, he told himself.

The only useful information his undercover agents had been able to glean about the killer was that before his staged death, Savarano's claustrophobia apparently had become acute. One agent was told: "Sandy had nightmares about cell doors clanging closed behind him."

So what had brought him out of retirement? Baldwin wondered. Big bucks? A favor he had to repay? Maybe both. And throw in the thrill of the hunt, of course. Savarano was a vicious predator. Part of it could have been simple boredom. Retirement might have been too tame for him.

Baldwin knew Savarano's rap sheet by heart. Forty-two years old, a suspect in a dozen murders, but hasn't seen the inside of a prison since he was a kid in reform school! A smart guy, as well as a born killer.

If I were Savarano, Baldwin thought, my one purpose in life right now would be to find Lacey Farrell and make sure she never gets the chance to finger me.

He shook his head, and his forehead creased with concern. The witness protection program wasn't foolproof; he knew that. People got careless. When they called home, they usually said something on the phone that gave away their hiding place, or they started writing letters. One mobster who was put in the program after cooperating with the government was dumb enough to send a birthday card to an old girlfriend. He was shot to death a week later.

Gary Baldwin had an uneasy feeling about Lacey Farrell. Her profile made her sound like someone who could find it difficult to be alone for a long stretch of time. Plus she seemed to be exceptionally trusting, a trait that could get her in real trouble. He shook his head. Well, there was nothing he could do about it except to send word to her through channels not to let her guard down, even for a minute.

24

Mona Farrell drove into Manhattan for what had become her standing Saturday dinner date with Alex Carbine. She always looked forward to the evening with him, even though he left the table frequently to greet his regular customers and the occasional celebrities who came to his restaurant.

"It's fun," she assured him. "And I really don't mind. Don't forget I was married to a musician. You don't know how many Broadway shows I sat through alone because Jack was in the orchestra pit!"

Jack would have liked Alex, Mona thought as she exited the George Washington Bridge and turned south onto the West Side Highway. Jack had been quick-witted and great fun, and quite gregarious. Alex was a much quieter man, but in him it was an attractive quality.

Mona smiled as she thought of the flowers that Alex had sent her earlier. The card read simply, "May they brighten your day. Yours, Alex."

He knew that the weekly phone call from Lacey tore her heart out. He understood how painful the whole experience was for her, and the flowers were Alex's way of saying it.

She had confided to him that Lacey had told her where she was living. "But I haven't even told Kit," she explained. "Kit would be hurt if she thought I didn't trust her."

It's funny, Mona thought, as the traffic on the West Side Highway slowed to a crawl because of a blocked right lane, things have always gone smoothly for Kit, but not for Lacey. Kit met Jay when she was at Boston College and he was in graduate school at Tufts. They fell in love, married, and now had three wonderful kids and a lovely home. Jay might be pontifical and occasionally pompous, but he certainly was a good husband and father. Just the other day, he had surprised Kit with an expensive gold-leaf necklace she had admired in the window of Groom's Jewelry in Ridgewood.

Kit said that Jay had told her business suddenly had become very good again. I'm glad, Mona thought. She had been worried for a while that things were not going well. Certainly in the fall it was obvious that he had a lot on his mind.

Lacey *deserves* happiness, Mona told herself. Now's the time for her to meet the right person and get married and start a family, and I'm sure she's ready. Instead she's alone in a strange city and she has to stay there and pretend to be someone else because her life is in danger.

She reached the parking lot on West Forty-sixth Street at seven-thirty. Alex didn't expect her at the restaurant until eight, which meant she would have time to do something that had occurred to her earlier.

A newsstand in Times Square carried out-of-town newspapers—she would see if they had any from Minneapolis.

It would make her feel closer to Lacey if she became familiar with the city, and there would be some comfort in just knowing that Lacey could be reading the paper as well.

The night was cold but clear, and she enjoyed the five-block walk to Times Square. How often we were here when Jack was alive, she thought. We'd get together with friends after a show. Kit was never as interested in the theater as Lacey. She was like Jack—in love with Broadway. She must be missing it terribly.

At the newsstand she found a copy of the *Minneapolis Star Tribune*. Lacey may have read this same edition this morning, she thought. Even touching the paper made Lacey seem closer.

"Would you like a bag, lady?"

"Oh, yes, please." Mona fished in her purse for her wallet as the vendor folded the paper and put it in a plastic bag.

When Mona reached the restaurant, there was a line at the checkroom. Seeing that Alex was already at their table, she hurried over to him. "Sorry, I guess I'm late," she said.

He got up and kissed her cheek. "You're not late, but your face is cold. Did you walk from New Jersey?"

"No. I was early and decided to pick up a newspaper."

Carlos, their usual waiter, was hovering nearby. "Mrs. Farrell, let me take your coat. Do you want to check your package?"

"Why not keep that?" Alex suggested. He took the bag from her and put it on the empty chair at their table.

It was, as always, a pleasant evening. By the time they were sipping espresso, Alex Carbine's hand was covering hers.

"Not too busy a night for you," Mona said teasingly. "You've only been up and down about ten times."

"I thought that might be why you bought a newspaper."

"Not at all, although I did glance at the headlines." Mona reached for her purse. "My turn to get up. I'll be right back."

Alex saw her to her car at eleven-thirty. At one o'clock the restaurant closed and the staff went home.

At ten of twelve a phone call was made. The message was simple. "Tell Sandy it looks like she's in Minneapolis."

25

WHAT HAD HAPPENED BETWEEN HEATHER LANDI AND Rick Parker?

Lacey was stunned to learn they had known each other. After Tom Lynch and Kate Knowles had left Friday night, she had been unable to sleep and had sat up for hours, trying to make sense of it all. Over the weekend her mind had constantly replayed the night of Isabelle Waring's death. What had Rick been thinking as he sat there, listening to her being quizzed about how well she had known Isabelle, and if she had ever known Heather? Why hadn't he *said* something?

According to what Kate had been told, on the last day of her life, Heather had been visibly upset when she saw Rick at the skiing lodge in Stowe.

Kate had referred to Rick as a "jerk who's in real estate in New York" and had said that he "had pulled something on Heather when she came to the city."

Lacey remembered that, in her journal, Heather alluded

to an unpleasant incident that happened when she was looking for an apartment on the West Side. Could that have
involved Rick? Lacey wondered.

Before being transferred to Madison Avenue, Rick had
spent five years in the West Side office of Parker and Parker.
He changed offices about three years ago.

Which means, Lacey thought, that he was working the
West Side at precisely the time Heather Landi came to New
York and was apartment hunting. Did she go to Parker and
Parker and meet Rick? And if she did, what had happened
between them?

Lacey shook her head in anger. Could Rick be involved
in *all* of this mess? she wondered. Am I stuck here because
of him?

Rick was the one who gave me Curtis Caldwell's name
as a potential buyer for Isabelle's apartment, she reminded
herself. It was because of *him* that I brought Caldwell there.
If Rick had known Caldwell somehow, then maybe the police would be able to track Caldwell down through Rick.
And if they arrest Caldwell, then I'll be able to go home.

Lacey stood up and began to pace the room excitedly.
This could be part of what Isabelle had seen in the journal.
She had to get this information to Gary Baldwin at the U.S.
Attorney's office.

Lacey's fingers itched to pick up the phone and call him,
but direct contact was absolutely forbidden. She would have
to leave a message for George Svenson to call her, then
either write or talk to Baldwin through secure channels.

I have to talk to Kate again, Lacey thought. I have to
find out more about Bill Merrill, the boyfriend who had
mentioned Heather's reaction to Rick Parker, and I have to
find out where he lives. Baldwin will want to talk to him,
I'm sure. He can place Rick Parker in Stowe only hours
before Heather died.

Kate had mentioned that the cast was staying at the Radisson Plaza Hotel for the week. Lacey glanced at her watch. It was ten-thirty. Even if Kate was a late sleeper, like most show-business people, she probably would be awake by now.

A still slightly sleepy voice answered the phone, but when she realized who was calling, Kate livened up and seemed pleased enough at Lacey's suggestion that they get together for lunch the next day. "Maybe we should try to get Tom to join us, Kate," she suggested. "You know how nice he is. He'll take us to a good restaurant and pay the tab to boot." Then laughing, she added, "Forget it. I just realized, his program goes on at noon."

Just as well, Lacey thought. No doubt Tom would pick up on the fact that she was pumping Kate for informaton. But he *is* nice, she thought, remembering how concerned he had been that he wasn't paying her enough attention at the party.

She arranged to meet Kate at the Radisson at twelve-thirty the next day. As she replaced the receiver, she felt a sudden surge of hope. It's almost like seeing the first ray of sunshine after a long, terrible storm, she decided, as she walked to the window and pulled back the curtain to look out.

It was a perfect Midwestern winter's day. The outdoor temperature was only twenty-eight degrees, but the sun was shining warmly in a cloudless sky. There appeared to be no wind, and Lacey could see that the sidewalks were clear of snow.

Until today, she had been too nervous to go for a real run, afraid that she would look over her shoulder and see Caldwell behind her, his pale, icy eyes fixed on her. But suddenly, feeling as though there was the possibility of some sort of breakthrough in the case, she decided that she had to *try,* at least, to resume some kind of normal life.

When she had packed to move, Lacey had brought her cold-weather jogging clothes: a warm-up suit, jacket, mittens, hat, scarf. She quickly put them on and headed to the door. Just as she was turning the knob, the phone rang. Her first instinct was to let it go, but then she decided to pick it up.

"Ms. Carroll, you don't know me," a crisp voice told her. "I'm Millicent Royce. I hear you may be looking for a job in the real estate field. Wendell Woods talked to me about you this morning."

"I *am* looking, or rather, just about to start looking," Lacey said hopefully.

"Wendell was quite impressed with you and suggested we should meet. The office is in Edina."

Edina was fifteen minutes away. "I know where that is."

"Good. Take down the address. Are you free this afternoon by any chance?"

When Lacey left the apartment and jogged down the street, it was with the sense that her luck might be changing at last. If Millicent Royce *did* hire her, it would mean she would have something to do to fill her days until she could go home.

After all, she thought wryly, as Ms. Royce just told me, real estate can be a very *exciting* career. I bet she doesn't know the half of it!

Tom Lynch's four-hour program was a mixture of news, interviews, and offbeat humor. It was broadcast each weekday from noon till four o'clock, and his guests ran the spectrum from political figures, authors, and visiting celebrities to local VIPs.

He spent most mornings before the show in his office at

the station, roaming the Internet in search of items of interest, or poring over newspapers and periodicals from all over the country, looking for unusual subjects to discuss.

On the Monday morning following the opening of *The King and I*, he was not comfortable with the fact that he had been thinking about Alice Carroll all weekend. Several times he had been tempted to call her, but he always replaced the receiver before the connection was made.

He reminded himself that he would almost certainly see her at the gym during the week; he could just suggest casually that they go out for dinner or to a movie. Phoning and planning a date might potentially take on undue significance, and then it would be uncomfortable if he didn't ask her out again, or if she refused, and they still kept running into each other.

He knew his concern on that subject was a standing joke with his friends. As one of them had told him recently, "Tom, you're a nice guy, but if you don't call some girl again, trust me, she'll get through the day."

Remembering that conversation, Tom silently acknowledged that if he had a few dates with Alice Carroll and then didn't call her again, she clearly would get through the day very well without him.

There was something so quietly contained about her, he thought, as he watched the clock and realized he was an hour away from air time. She didn't talk much about herself, and something in her told him that she didn't invite questions. That first afternoon, when they had coffee together in the gym, she hadn't seemed happy when he teased her about moving to Minneapolis. Then Friday evening he had sensed that when the overture to *The King and I* began, she had been close to tears.

Some girls have a fit if their date doesn't give them full attention at a party. But it hadn't bothered Alice a bit that he had left her on her own when people came up to talk to him.

133

The clothes she had worn to the opening were expensive. A blind man could see that.

He had overheard her tell Kate that she had seen *The King and I* three times. And she had talked knowledgeably with Kate about the revival of *The Boy Friend.*

Expensive outfits. Trips in and out of New York from Hartford to go to the theater. These generally weren't the kinds of things one was able to do on the salary of a clerk in a doctor's office.

Tom shrugged and reached for the phone. It was no use. His questions were a sign of his interest in her, and the fact was, he couldn't stop thinking of her. He was going to call Alice and ask her if she wanted to have dinner tonight. He wanted to see her. He reached for the phone, dialed, and waited. After four rings the answering machine clicked on. Her voice, low and pleasing, said: "You've reached 555-1247. Please leave a message and I'll get back to you."

Tom hesitated, then hung up, deciding to call back later. He felt more uncomfortable than ever over the fact that he was so intensely disappointed at not having reached her.

26

On Monday morning Sandy Savarano took Northwest flight 1703 from La Guardia Airport in New York to Minneapolis–St. Paul International Airport in Minneapolis.

He rode first class, as he had on the flight from Costa Rica, where he now lived. He was known to his neighbors there as Charles Austin, a well-to-do U.S. businessman who had sold his company two years ago at age forty and retired to the tropical good life.

His twenty-four-year-old wife had driven him to the airport in Costa Rica and made him promise not to stay away too long. "You're supposed to be retired now," she had said, pouting lovingly as she kissed him good-bye.

"That doesn't mean that I turn down found money," he had said.

It was the same answer he had given her about the several other jobs he had undertaken since he staged his death two years ago.

"Lovely day to fly."

The voice was that of a young woman in her late twenties who was seated next to him. In a way, she reminded him very slightly of Lacey Farrell. But then, Farrell was on his mind, since she was the reason he was on his way to Minneapolis now. The only person in the world who can finger me for a murder, he thought. She doesn't deserve to live. And she won't for long.

"Yes, it is," he agreed shortly.

He saw the look of interest in the young woman's eyes and was amused. Women actually found him attractive. Dr. Ivan Yenkel, a Russian immigrant who had given him this new face two years ago, had been a genius, no doubt about it. His remolded nose was thinner; the bump caused by the break he had suffered in reform school was gone. The heavy chin was sculpted, his ears smaller and flat against his head. Formerly heavy eyebrows were thinned and spaced farther apart. Yenkel had fixed his drooping eyelids and removed the circles under his eyes.

His dark brown hair was now the color of sand, a whimsy he had chosen in honor of his nickname, Sandy. Pale blue contact lenses completed the transformation.

"You look fabulous, Sandy," Yenkel had boasted when the last bandage came off. "No one would ever recognize you."

"No one ever will."

Sandy always got a thrill, remembering the look of astonishment in Yenkel's eyes as he died.

I don't intend to go through it again, Sandy thought, as with a dismissive smile to his seatmate he pointedly picked up a magazine and opened it.

Pretending to read, he reviewed his game plan. He had a two-week reservation at the Radisson Plaza Hotel under the name James Burgess. If he hadn't found Farrell by then, he would move to another hotel. No use arousing curiosity by staying too long.

He had been supplied with some suggestions as to where he might find her. She regularly used a health club in New York. It made sense to assume she would do the same thing in Minneapolis, so he would make the rounds of health clubs there. People didn't change their habits.

She was a theater buff. Well, the Orpheum in Minneapolis had touring shows virtually every week, and the Tyrone Guthrie Theater would be another place to look.

Her only job had been in real estate. If she was working, the odds were she would be in a real estate agency.

Savarano had located and eliminated two other witnesses who had been in the witness protection program. He knew the government did not give false references—most of the people in the program began jobs in small outfits where they had gotten to know someone and had been hired on faith.

The flight attendant was making her announcement: "We are beginning our descent into the Twin Cities . . . place your seats in the upright position . . . fasten your seat belts . . ."

Sandy Savarano began to anticipate the look he would see in Lacey Farrell's eyes when he shot her.

27

ROYCE REALTY WAS LOCATED AT FIFTIETH STREET AND France Avenue South in Edina. Before leaving the apartment, Lacey studied the map, trying to determine the best way to drive there. Her mother had once remarked that it was a wonder how Lacey could have such good practical sense and such a lousy sense of direction. She surely was right about the last part, Lacey thought, shaking her head. New York had been a snap—she and the client would hail a cab, and it took them wherever they wanted. A sprawling city like Minneapolis, though, with so many scattered residential areas, was another matter. How will I ever take people around to see properties if I get lost every five minutes? she wondered.

Following the map carefully, however, she got to the office having made only one wrong turn. She parked her car, then stood for a moment in front of the entrance to Royce Realty, looking in through the wide glass door.

She could see that the agency office was small, but attractive. The reception room had oak-paneled walls that were covered with pictures of houses, a cheerful red-and-blue checked carpet, a standard desk, and comfortable-looking leather chairs. There was a short corridor leading off the reception area to an office. Through the open door she could see a woman working at a desk.

Here goes nothing, she thought, taking a deep breath. If I get through this scene successfully, I'll be ready to make my Broadway debut soon. That is, of course, if I ever get back to New York. As she opened the door to the agency, chimes signaled her arrival. The woman looked up, then came out to meet her.

"I'm Millicent Royce," she said as she extended her hand, "and you must be Alice Carroll."

Lacey liked her immediately. She was a handsome woman of about seventy whose ample girth was clothed in a well-tailored brown knit suit, and whose clear unlined complexion was devoid of makeup. Her shiny gray-white hair was swept back into a bun, a hairstyle that reminded Lacey of her grandmother.

Her smile was welcoming, but as Lacey sat down she could see that Millicent Royce's keen blue eyes were studying her intently. She was glad she had decided to wear the maroon jacket and gray slacks. They were conservative, but attractive—no-nonsense, but with style. Besides, she had always believed the outfit brought her luck on sales calls. Now maybe it would help her get a job.

Millicent Royce waved her to a chair and sat down opposite her. "It's turning out to be a terribly busy day," she said apologetically, "so I don't have much time. Tell me about yourself, Alice."

Lacey felt as though she were in an interrogation room with a spotlight shining on her. Millicent Royce's eyes did not leave Lacey's face as she answered. "Let's see. I just turned thirty. I'm healthy. My life has changed a lot in the last year."

God knows that's true, Lacey thought.

"I'm from Hartford, Connecticut, and after finishing college I worked for eight years for a doctor who retired."

"What kind of work?" Mrs. Royce asked.

"Receptionist, general office, some billing, submitting the medical forms."

"Then you're experienced with a computer?"

"Yes, I am." She watched as the older woman's eyes glanced at the computer on the reception room desk. There was a stack of papers beside it.

"This job entails answering the phones, keeping listings up to date, preparing flyers of new listings, calling potential buyers when a new listing comes in, helping with an open house. No actual selling. That's my job. But I've got to ask: What makes you think you'd like real estate?"

Because I love matching people to places, Lacey thought. *I love guessing right and seeing someone's eyes light up when I take that person into a house or apartment and know that it's exactly what he or she wants. I love the wheeling and dealing that goes into settling on a price.*

Dismissing these thoughts, she said instead, "I know I don't want to work in a doctor's office anymore, and I've always been intrigued by the idea of your business."

"I see. Well, let me call your retired doctor and talk to him, and if he vouches for you—as I'm sure he will—then I say, let's give it a try. Do you have his phone number?"

"No. He changed it and made it unlisted. He was adamant about not wanting to be contacted by his former patients."

Lacey could tell from the slight frown on Millicent Royce's face that this obviously sharp lady was finding her answers too evasive.

She remembered what George Svenson had told her: "Offer to work free for a couple of weeks, or even a month."

"I have a suggestion," Lacey said. "Don't pay me anything for a month. After that, if you're happy with me, you'll hire me. Or if you feel I have no aptitude for the work, you'll tell me to forget it."

She met Millicent Royce's steady gaze without flinching. "You won't regret it," she said quietly.

Mrs. Royce shrugged her shoulders. "In Minnesota, the Land of Lakes, that's known as an offer I can't refuse."

28

"WHY WASN'T MR. LANDI INFORMED ABOUT THIS EAR-
lier?" Steve Abbott asked quietly.

It was Monday afternoon. Abbott had insisted on accom-
panying Jimmy to a meeting with Detectives Sloane and
Mars in the 19th Precinct station house.

"I want to know what's going on!" Jimmy had said to
him that morning, the anger in his voice reflected in his
face. "Something's up. The cops have to know where Lacey
Farrell is. She can't have just disappeared. She's a witness
to a murder!"

"Did you call them?" Steve had asked.

"You bet I did. But I ask about her and they just tell me
to have Parker and Parker assign another agent to handle
the sale of the apartment. That's not what I called about. Do
they think that's what's bugging me, that this is about
money? That's nuts! I told them I was coming to see them,
and *I wanted answers.*"

Abbott knew that painting Heather out of the restaurant

murals had if anything increased Jimmy Landi's anger and depression. "I'm going with you," he had insisted.

When they had arrived, Detectives Sloane and Mars brought them into the interrogation room off the squad room. They had admitted reluctantly that Lacey Farrell had been placed in the federal witness protection program because an attempt had been made on her life.

"I asked why Mr. Landi hadn't been informed earlier about what happened to Ms. Farrell," Abbott repeated. "I want an answer."

Sloane reached for a cigarette. "Mr. Abbott, I have assured Mr. Landi that the investigation is continuing, and it is. We're not going to rest until we find and prosecute Isabelle Waring's murderer."

"You gave me a cock-and-bull story about some guy whose racket is getting into expensive apartments as a potential buyer and then coming back to burglarize them," Jimmy said, his anger exploding once again. "At that point you told me you thought Isabelle's death was just a matter of having been at the wrong place at the wrong time. Now you're telling me that the Farrell woman is in the witness protection program, *and* you're admitting that Heather's journal was stolen from under your noses right here in this station. Don't play games with me. This was no random killing, and you've known it from day one."

Eddie Sloane saw the anger and disgust that flared in Jimmy Landi's eyes. I don't blame him, the detective thought. His ex-wife is dead; we lose something intended for him that may be crucial evidence; the woman who brought the killer into his ex-wife's apartment has disappeared. I sympathize because I know how *I'd* feel.

For both detectives it had been a lousy four months since that October evening when the 911 call from 3 East Seventieth had been received in the station house. As the case developed, Eddie was grateful that the district attorney had gone toe to toe with U.S. Attorney Baldwin's office. The DA had been adamant that the NYPD was not signing off on this one.

"A murder occurred in the 19th Precinct," he had told Baldwin, "and like it or not, we're in it for the duration. We'll share information with you, of course, but you've got to share it with us. When Savarano is collared, we'll cooperate in a plea bargain if you can cut a deal with him. But we'll cooperate only, and I repeat *only,* if you don't try to upstage us. We have a very real interest in this case, and we intend to be involved."

"It wasn't a cock-and-bull story, Mr. Landi," Nick Mars said heatedly. "We want to find Mrs. Waring's killer just as much as you do. But if Ms. Farrell hadn't taken that journal from Isabelle Waring's apartment, apparently with the idea of giving it to you, we might be a lot further along in this investigation."

"But I believe that it was after it arrived here that this journal was stolen," Steve Abbott said, his voice dangerously quiet. "And are you now suggesting that Ms. Farrell may have tampered with the journal?"

"We don't think she did, but we can't be sure," Sloane admitted.

"Be honest with us, Detective. You can't be sure of very much except that you botched this investigation," Abbott snapped, his anger now evident. "Come on, Jimmy. I think it's time we hire our own investigator. With the police in charge, I don't think we'll ever find out what's going on."

"That's what I should have done the minute I got the call about Isabelle!" Jimmy Landi said, getting to his feet. "I want the copy of my daughter's journal I gave you before you lose that one too."

"We ran off extras," Sloane said calmly. "Nick, get the set Mr. Landi gave us."

"Right away, Eddie."

While they waited, Sloane said, "Mr. Landi, you told us very specifically that you read the journal before you gave it to us."

Jimmy Landi's eyes darkened. "I did."

"You told us that you read the journal *carefully*. Thinking back, would you say that's true?"

"What's carefully?" Jimmy asked rather irritably. "I looked through it."

"Look, Mr. Landi," Sloane said, "I can only imagine how difficult all this is for you, but I'm going to ask you to read it carefully now. We've gone through it as thoroughly as we know how, and except for a couple of ambiguous references in the early pages about something involving an incident that happened on the West Side, we can't find anything even *potentially* helpful. But the fact is that Mrs. Waring told Lacey Farrell that she'd found something in those pages that might help prove your daughter's death was not an accident—"

"Isabelle would have found something suspicious in the Baltimore catechism," Jimmy said, shaking his head.

They sat in silence until Nick Mars returned to the interrogation room with a manila envelope which he held out to Landi.

Jimmy yanked it from him and opened the envelope. Pulling out the contents, he glanced through them, then stopped at the last page. He read it, then glared at Mars. "What are you trying to pull now?" he asked.

Sloane had the sickening feeling that he was about to hear something he didn't want to know.

"I can tell you right now that there were more pages than this," Landi said. "The last couple of pages in the set I gave you weren't written on lined paper. I remember because they were all messed up. The originals of those pages must have had bloodstains . . . I couldn't stand the sight of them. So where are they? Did you lose those too?"

29

Upon arrival at the Minneapolis–St. Paul airport, Sandy Savarano went directly from the plane to the baggage area where he picked up his heavy black suitcase. Then he found a men's room and locked himself in a stall. There, he placed the suitcase across the toilet and opened it.

He took out a hand mirror and a zippered case containing a gray wig, thick gray eyebrows, and round glasses with a tortoiseshell frame.

He removed his contact lenses, revealing his charcoal brown eyes, then with deft movements placed the wig on his head, combed it so that it covered part of his forehead, pasted on the eyebrows, and put on the glasses.

With a cosmetic pencil he added age spots to his forehead and the backs of his hands. Reaching into the sides of the suitcase he took out orthopedic oxfords and exchanged them for the Gucci loafers he had been wearing.

Finally he unpacked a bulky tweed overcoat with heavily

padded shoulders, placing in the bag the Burberry he had worn getting off the plane.

The man who left the stall looked twenty years older and totally different from the man who had entered it.

Sandy next went to the car rental desk where a car had been reserved for him in the name of James Burgess of Philadelphia. He opened his wallet and took out a driver's license and a credit card. The license was a clever fake; the credit card was legitimate, an account having been set up for him using the Burgess name.

Cold, bracing air greeted him as he exited the terminal and joined a group of people waiting at the curb for the jitney to take them to the car rental area. While he waited he studied the map the clerk had marked for him and began to memorize the routes that led in and out of the city and to estimate the length of time each should require. He liked to plan everything out carefully. No surprises—that was his motto. Which made the unexpected arrival of that Farrell woman at Isabelle Waring's apartment all the more irritating. He had been surprised and had made a mistake by letting her get away.

He knew that his attention to detail was the main reason he was still a free man, while so many of his fellow graduates of reform school were off serving long prison terms. The very thought made him shiver.

The clanging of a cell door . . . Waking up and knowing that he was trapped there, that it would never be any different . . . Feeling the walls and ceiling close in on him, squeezing him, suffocating him . . .

Underneath the strands of hair he had so carefully combed over his forehead, Sandy could feel beads of sweat forming. It won't happen to me, he promised himself. I'd rather die first.

The jitney was approaching. Impatiently, he raised his arm to be sure the vehicle stopped. He was anxious to get started, anxious to begin the task of finding Lacey Farrell. As long as she was alive, she remained a constant threat to his freedom.

As the jitney stopped to admit him, he felt something slam against the back of his legs. He spun around and found himself facing the young woman who had been his seatmate on the plane. Her suitcase had toppled over against him.

Their eyes met, and he took a deep breath. They were standing only inches apart, yet there was no trace of recognition in her expression. Her smile was apologetic. "I'm so sorry," she said.

The jitney door was opening. Savarano got on, knowing that this clumsy woman had just confirmed that with his disguise he would be able to get close to Farrell without fear of recognition. This time she would have no chance to escape him. That was a mistake he would not repeat.

30

WHEN MILLICENT ROYCE AGREED TO TRY HER OUT ON A
volunteer basis, Lacey suggested that she spend the rest
of the afternoon familiarizing herself with the files in the
computer and going through the mail that was stacked on
the reception desk.

After four months away from an office, it was pure pleasure to be at a desk, going through listings, familiarizing
herself with the price range of homes in the area covered by
the agency.

At three o'clock, Mrs. Royce took a potential buyer
to see a condominium and asked Lacey to cover the
phone.

The first call was a near disaster. She answered, "Royce
Realty, Lace—"

She slammed down the receiver and stared at the phone.
She had been about to give her real name.

A moment later the phone began to ring again.

149

She had to pick it up. It was probably the same person. What could she say?

The voice on the other end sounded slightly irritated. "I guess we got cut off," Lacey said lamely.

For the next hour the phone continued to ring, and Lacey carefully managed each call. It was only later, when she was jotting down the message that the dentist's office called to confirm Millicent Royce's appointment for the following week, that she realized being back in her own milieu could be a trap. As a precaution she went through all the messages she had taken. A woman had phoned to say that her husband was being transferred to Minneapolis and that a friend had suggested that she call the Royce agency to help her find a house.

Lacey had asked the usual real estate broker questions: price range? how many bedrooms? any limits on the age of a house? was school district a factor? would purchase be contingent on sale of present home? She had even put the answers in real estate shorthand: "min. 4BR/3b./fpl/cen air/."

I was proud of myself, she thought as she copied the woman's name and phone number on a different sheet of paper, careful to disguise her working knowledge of the business. At the end she added the message, "good potential prospect due to immediate relocation." Maybe even that sounded too knowledgeable, she thought, but let it stand when she looked up to see that Millicent Royce was on her way in.

Mrs. Royce looked tired and was obviously pleased to get the messages and to see how efficiently Lacey had separated the mail for her. It was nearly five o'clock. "I *will* see you in the morning, Alice?" There was a hopeful note in her voice.

"Absolutely," Lacey told her. "But I do have a lunch date I can't break."

* * *

As she drove back into the city, Lacey felt a letdown setting in. As usual, she had no plans for the evening, and the thought of going back to the apartment and preparing another solitary meal was suddenly repugnant to her.

I'll go to the gym and work out for a while, she decided. At least between that exercise and the run this morning, I may be tired enough to sleep.

When she got to the gym, Ruth Wilcox beckoned her over. "Guess what?" she said, her tone conspiratorial. "Tom Lynch was really disappointed when you didn't show up this afternoon. He even came over and asked if you'd been here earlier. Alice, I think he likes you."

If he does, he likes someone who doesn't really exist, Lacey thought with a trace of bitterness. She stayed in the gym for only a half hour, then drove home. The answering machine was blinking. Tom had phoned at four-thirty. "Thought I might see you at the gym, Alice. I enjoyed Friday night. If you pick this up by seven and feel like having dinner tonight, give me a call. My number is—"

Lacey pushed the STOP button on the machine and erased the message without waiting to hear Tom's phone number. It was easier to do that than to spend another evening lying to someone who in different circumstances she would have enjoyed dating.

She fixed herself a BLT on toast for dinner. Comfort food, she thought.

Then she remembered—this was what I was eating the night before Isabelle Waring died. Isabelle phoned, and I didn't pick up. I was tired and didn't want to talk to her.

Lacey remembered that in the message she had left on the answering machine, Isabelle said she had found Heather's journal and declared that something in it made her think she might have proof that Heather's death hadn't been an accident.

But the next morning, when she phoned me at the office, she wouldn't talk about it, Lacey recalled. Then she stayed in the library reading the journal when I brought Curtis Caldwell in. And a few hours later she was dead.

Mental images suddenly threatened to close her throat as she finished the last bite of the sandwich: Isabelle in the library, weeping as she read Heather's journal. Isabelle with her last breath begging Lacey to give that journal to Heather's father.

What is it that's been bothering me? Lacey asked herself. It was something about the library that last afternoon, something I noticed when I spoke to Isabelle in there. What *was* it? She mentally revisited that afternoon, struggling to make the elusive image come into focus.

Finally she gave up. She simply couldn't remember.

Let it go for now, Lacey told herself. Later I'll try to put my mind in the search-and-retrieve mode. After all, the mind *is* a computer, isn't it?

That night in her dreams she had vague visions of Isabelle holding a green pen and weeping as she read Heather's journal in the last hours of her life.

31

AFTER CHECKING INTO THE RADISSON PLAZA HOTEL, HALF a block from the Nicollet Mall, Sandy Savarano spent the rest of his first day in Minneapolis poring over the phone book and making a list of the health clubs and gyms in the metropolitan area.

He made a second list of all the real estate agencies, putting in a separate column the ones whose ads indicated they were geared to commercial sales. He knew that Lacey Farrell would have to try to find a job without benefit of references, and the odds were those agencies would be unwilling to hire anyone without some kind of background check. He would start calling the others tomorrow.

His plan was simple. He would just say that he was conducting an informal survey for the National Association of Realtors because there was growing evidence that adults in the twenty-five to thirty-five age group were not entering the real estate field. The survey would ask two questions: Had the agency hired anyone in that age group as an agent, secretary, or receptionist in the last six months, and if so, were they a male or female?

He'd need another plan for checking out health clubs and gyms. Those survey questions wouldn't work there, since most of the people who joined them were in that age group. It meant that locating Farrell through the clubs would be riskier.

He would have to actually go to them, pretend he was interested in joining, then flash Farrell's picture. It was an old photo, cut from her college yearbook, but it still looked like her. He would claim that she was his daughter and had left home after a family misunderstanding. He was trying to find her because her mother was sick with worry about her.

Checking out the health clubs would be a long shot, but fortunately there were not too many in the metro area, so it wouldn't take him too long.

At five of ten, Sandy was ready to go out for a walk. The mall was dark now, the windows of the toney stores no longer glittering.

Sandy knew that the Mississippi River was within walking distance. He turned right and headed in that direction, a solitary figure who to a casual viewer would appear to be a man in his sixties who probably ought not to be walking alone at night.

A casual observer would have no idea how misdirected that concern was, since on that walk, Sandy Savarano began to experience the curious thrill that came to him whenever he began to stalk a victim and sensed that he was approaching the habitat of the hunted.

32

On Tuesday morning, Lacey was waiting in front of Royce Realty when Millicent Royce arrived at nine o'clock.

"The pay isn't *that* good," Millicent Royce said with a laugh.

"It's what we agreed on," Lacey said. "And I can tell I'll like the job."

Mrs. Royce unlocked and opened the door. The warmth of the interior greeted them. "A Minnesota chill in the air," Royce said. "First things first. I'll put the coffee on. How do you like yours?"

"Black, please."

"Regina, my assistant who just left to have a baby, used two heaping teaspoonsful of sugar and never gained an ounce. I told her it was serious cause for simple hatred."

Lacey thought of Janey Boyd, a secretary at Parker and Parker, who always seemed to be munching a cookie or a chocolate bar but remained a size six. "There was a girl like that at—" She stopped herself. "At the doctor's office," she finished, then quickly added. "She didn't stay long. Just as well. She was setting a bad example."

Suppose Millicent Royce had picked up on that and suggested calling a coworker for a personal reference. Be careful, Lacey told herself, *be careful.*

The first phone call of the day came right then and was a welcome interruption.

At twelve Lacey left for the luncheon date with Kate Knowles. "I'll be back by two," she promised, "and after this, I'll have a sandwich at the desk so if you want to make outside appointments, I'll be here."

She arrived at the Radisson at 12:25 to find that Kate was already at the table, munching on a roll. "This is breakfast and lunch for me," she told Lacey, "so I started. Hope you don't mind."

Lacey slid into the seat opposite her. "Not at all. How's the show going?"

"Great."

They both ordered omelets, salads, and coffee. "The necessaries out of the way," Kate said with a grin. "I have to admit I'm getting curious. I was talking to Tom this morning and told him we were having lunch. He said he wished he could join us and sent his best to you."

Kate reached for another roll. "Tom was telling me that you just decided to pick up and move here, that you'd only been here once on a visit as a kid. What makes a place stick in your mind like that?"

Answer the question with a question.

"You're on the road a lot with shows," Lacey said. "Don't you remember some cities better than others?"

"Oh, sure. The good ones, like here, and the not-so-good ones. Let me tell you about the all-time not-so-good one . . ."

Lacey found herself relaxing as Kate told her story, her timing perfect. So many show business people are like that, Lacey thought nostalgically. Dad had the same talent; he could make a grocery list sound interesting.

Over a second cup of coffee she managed to steer the conversation to the friend named Bill that Kate had mentioned. "You talked the other night about someone you're dating," she began. "Bill something, wasn't it?"

"Bill Merrill. Nice guy. Could even be Mr. Right, although the way things are going I may never know. I'll keep trying, though." Kate's eyes brightened. "The trouble is that I'm on the road so much, and he travels all the time too."

"What does he do?"

"He's an investment banker and practically commutes to China."

Don't let him be in China now, Lacey prayed. "Which bank is he with, Kate?"

"Chase."

Lacey had learned to watch for the flicker of curiosity that signaled she was being studied. Kate was smart. She sensed now that she was being probed for information. I've got what I need to know, Lacey thought. Get back to letting Kate do the talking.

"I guess the best of all possible worlds for you is to get a Broadway hit that runs for ten years," she suggested.

"Now you're talking," Kate said with a grin. "That would be having my cake and eating it too. I'd love to be able to stay put in New York. Primarily because of Bill, of course, but there's no question that Tom's going to end up there in the next few years. He's clearly headed for success, and New York will be where he lands. That really would be the icing on the cake for me. We're both only children, so we've been more like siblings and best friends than cousins. He's always been there for me. Plus Tom's just naturally the kind of guy who seems to sense when people need help."

I wonder if that's why he asked me out last week and called me last night? Lacey thought. She signaled for a check. "I've got to run," she explained quickly. "First full day on the job."

A t a pay phone in the lobby, she called and left a message for George Svenson. "I have new information concerning the Heather Landi case that I must give directly to Mr. Baldwin at the U.S. Attorney's office."

When she hung up, she hurried through the lobby, aware she was already late getting back to the agency.

Less than a minute later, a hand with brown age spots picked up the receiver that was still warm from her touch.

Sandy Savarano never made phone calls that could be traced. His pockets were filled with quarters. His plan was to make five calls here, then go to a different location and make five more until his list of local real estate offices was exhausted.

He dialed, and when someone answered, "Downtown Realty," he began his spiel. "I won't take much of your time," he said. "I'm with the National Association of Realtors. We're conducting an informal survey . . ."

33

As U.S. Attorney Gary Baldwin told NYPD Detective Ed Sloane, he did not suffer fools gladly. He had been infuriated by the phone call from Sloane the previous afternoon, informing him that several pages of Jimmy Landi's copy of his daughter's journal apparently had vanished while it was in the police station. "How is it you managed to not lose the whole thing?" he had raged. "That's what happened to the original."

When Sloane phoned again twenty-four hours later, it gave Baldwin a second chance to air his grievances: "We're busting our chops going over the copy of the journal you gave us, and we find that we don't have several pages that obviously were of some importance, since someone took the risk of stealing them from under your nose! Where'd you leave the journal when you got it? On the bulletin board? Where'd you leave the copy? On the *street?* Did you hang out a sign on it? *'Evidence in a murder case. Feel free to take'?"*

As he listened to the tirade, Detective Ed Sloane's thoughts about what he would like to do to Baldwin yanked him back to his Latin 3 Class at Xavier Military Academy. When he preached on a grave sin, St. Paul had cautioned, *"Ne nominatur in vobis"*—Let it not be named among you.

It fits, Sloane thought, because what I'd like to do to you would be better off unnamed. But he too was incensed by the fact that the original journal, as well as possibly several pages from the copy, had disappeared from *his* locked evidence box in *his* cubby, which was located in the squad room.

Clearly it was *his* fault. He carried the keys to the box and the cubby on the heavy key ring that he kept in his jacket pocket. And he was always taking off his jacket, so virtually anybody could have taken the key ring out of his pocket, made duplicates, then returned the keys before he had even noticed that they were missing.

After the original journal vanished, the locks had been changed. But he hadn't changed his habit of forgetting to take his keys out of the jacket that was draped on the back of his desk chair.

He focused once more on the phone conversation. Baldwin had finally run out of breath, so Sloane grabbed the opportunity to get in a word. "Sir, I reported this yesterday because you should know about it. I'm calling now because, frankly, I'm not at all sure Jimmy Landi is a reliable witness in this instance. He admitted yesterday that he barely even scanned the journal when Ms. Farrell gave it to him. Plus he only had it a day or so."

"Oh, the journal's not that long," Baldwin snapped. "It could be read carefully in just a few hours."

"But he didn't, and that's the point," Sloane said emphatically, as he nodded his thanks to Nick Mars, who had just placed a cup of coffee on his desk. "He's also threatening to be difficult, saying he's going to bring in his own investigator. And Landi's partner, Steve Abbott, came to the meeting with him and was throwing his weight around on Jimmy's behalf."

"I don't blame Landi," Baldwin snapped. "And another investigator on this case could be a good idea, especially since you don't seem to be getting anywhere."

"You know that's not so. He'd just get in the way. But at this point it looks like it's not going to happen. Abbott just called me," Sloane said. "In a way, he apologized. He said that thinking it over, it's possible that Landi was mistaken about the pages he thinks are missing. He said the night Jimmy got the journal from Lacey Farrell, it was so tough on him to try to read it that he put it aside. The next night he got smashed before he looked at it. Then a day later we took his copy from him."

"It's possible he's mistaken about the missing pages, but we'll never know, will we?" Baldwin said, his voice cold. "And even if he *is* wrong about the missing unlined pages, the original journal clearly was taken while in your possession, which means you've got someone in the precinct who's working both sides of the street. I suggest you do some housecleaning up there."

"We're working on it." Ed Sloane did not think it necessary to tell Baldwin that he had been setting traps for the culprit by talking cryptically around the station house about new evidence in the Waring case that he had stored in his cubby.

Baldwin concluded the conversation. "Keep me posted. And try to hang on to any other evidence that may come up in the case. Think you can do that?"

"Yes, I do. And as I remember it, sir, *we* were the ones who found and identified Savarano's fingerprint on the door to Farrell's apartment after the break-in," Sloane shot back. "I think *your* investigators were the ones who certified that he was dead."

A click of the phone in the U.S. Attorney's office proved to Detective Ed Sloane that he had succeeded in getting to the thin-skinned Baldwin. Score one for the good guys, he thought.

But it was a hollow victory, and he knew it.

For the rest of the afternoon, Gary Baldwin's staff endured the fallout from his frustration over the bungled investigation. Then his mood changed suddenly when he received word that the secured witness, Lacey Farrell, had new information for him. "I'll wait as long as it takes, but make sure you get her call through to me tonight," he told George Svenson in Minneapolis.

Following the call, Svenson drove to Lacey's apartment building and waited for her in his car. When she got home from work, he didn't even give her a chance to go inside. "The man is jumping up and down waiting to talk to you," he said, "so we're going to do this *now*."

They drove off in his car. Svenson was a quiet man by nature, and he did not seem to find the need to make small talk. During her indoctrination period in the safe site in Washington, Lacey had been tipped off that federal marshals hated the witness protection program, hated dealing with all those misplaced persons. They felt they had been stuck with what was, in essence, a baby-sitting job.

From day one in Minneapolis, Lacey had decided that while it was not pleasant to be dependent on a stranger, she was determined not to give him cause to consider her anything more than a minimal nuisance. In the four months she had been there, her single extraordinary request to Svenson had been for permission to do her furniture shopping at garage sales rather than at department stores.

Lacey now had a feeling that she had earned Svenson's

grudging respect. As he drove through the gathering evening traffic to the secure phone, he asked her about her job.

"I like it," Lacey told him. "I feel like a whole person when I'm working."

She took his grunt as a sign of approval and agreement.

Svenson was the only person in the entire city to whom she could have talked about how she had almost burst into tears when Millicent Royce showed her a picture of her five-year-old granddaughter, dressed in a ballet recital costume. It had reminded her so much of Bonnie, and she had suffered an almost overwhelming wave of homesickness. But of course she *wouldn't* tell him.

Looking at the picture of a child Bonnie's age had made Lacey long to see her niece again. An old, turn-of-the-century song had been playing in her head since she saw the picture: *My bonnie lies over the ocean, my bonnie lies over the sea . . . bring back, bring back, oh bring back my bonnie to me . . .*

But Bonnie isn't over the ocean, Lacey told herself. She's about a three-hour flight away, and I'm about to give the U.S. Attorney information that may help get me on a plane home soon.

They were driving past one of the many lakes that were dotted throughout the city. The latest snow was nearly a week old but still appeared pristine white. Stars were beginning to come out, clear and shining in the fresh evening air. It *is* beautiful here, Lacey thought. Under different circumstances, I could very well understand why someone would choose to live here, but I want to go home. I *need* to go home.

For tonight's call they had set up a secure line in a hotel room. Before he put the call through, Svenson told Lacey that he would wait in the hotel lobby while she was talking to Baldwin.

Lacey could tell that the phone at the other end was picked up on the first ring; she could even hear Gary Baldwin identify himself.

Svenson handed her the phone. "Good luck," he murmured as he left.

"Mr. Baldwin," she began, "thank you for getting back to me so quickly. I have some information that I think may be very important."

"I hope so, Ms. Farrell. What is it?"

Lacey felt a stab of resentment and irritation. It wouldn't hurt to ask how it's going with me, she thought. It wouldn't hurt to be civil. I'm not here because I want to be. I'm here because *you* haven't been able to catch a killer. It's not *my* fault I wound up a witness in a murder case.

"What it is," she said, forming her words deliberately and slowly, as though otherwise he might not understand what she was telling him, "is that I have learned that Rick Parker—remember him? he was one of the Parkers of the Parker and Parker I used to work for—was in the same ski lodge as Heather Landi only hours before Heather died, and that she seemed frightened, or at least very agitated, when she saw him."

There was a long pause; then Baldwin asked, "How did you possibly come by that information in Minnesota, Ms. Farrell?"

Lacey realized suddenly that she had not thought this revelation through before making the phone call. She had never admitted to anyone that she had made herself a copy of Heather Landi's journal before she turned it over to Detective Sloane. She already had been threatened with prosecution because she had taken the original journal pages from Isabelle's apartment. She knew they never would believe that she had made a secret copy of it only to honor her promise to Isabelle to read it.

"I asked you how you came by that information, Ms. Farrell," Baldwin said, his voice reminding Lacey of a particularly prickly principal she had once had at school.

Lacey spoke carefully, as though wending her way through a minefield. "I have made a few friends out here, Mr. Baldwin. One of them invited me to a party for the road company production cast of *The King and I*. I chatted with Kate Knowles, an actress in the group, and—"

"And she just *happened* to say that Rick Parker was in a skiing lodge in Vermont just hours before Heather Landi died. Is *that* what you're telling me, Ms. Farrell?"

"Mr. Baldwin," Lacey said, knowing that her voice was rising, "will you please tell me what you are suggesting? I don't know how much you know about my background, but my father was a Broadway musician. I've attended, and enjoyed, many, many musicals. I know the musical theater, and I know theater people. When I spoke to Kate Knowles, it came up that she had been in a revival of *The Boy Friend* that ran off-Broadway two years ago. We talked about it. I saw that show, with Heather Landi in the lead."

"You never told us that you knew Heather Landi," Baldwin interrupted.

"There was nothing to tell," Lacey protested. "Detective Sloane asked me if I knew Heather Landi. The answer I gave him, which happens to be the truth, is that, no, I didn't *know* her. I, like hundreds and perhaps thousands of other theatergoers, saw her perform in a musical. If I see Robert De Niro in a film tonight, should I tell you that I *know* him?"

"All right, Ms. Farrell, you've made your point," he said without a trace of humor in his voice. "So the subject of *The Boy Friend* came up. Then what?"

Lacey was gripping the phone tightly with her right hand. She pressed the nails of her left hand into her palm, reminding herself to stay calm. "Since Kate was in the cast, it seemed obvious to me that she must have known Heather Landi. So I asked her, and then got her to talk about Heather. She freely told me that Isabelle Waring had asked everyone in the cast if Heather had seemed upset in the several days before she died, and if so, did they have any idea what the cause could have been."

Baldwin sounded somewhat mollified. "That was smart of you. What did she say?"

"She said the same thing that I gather Isabelle heard from all Heather's friends. Yes, Heather was troubled. No, she never told anyone *why* she was troubled. But then—and this is the reason for my call to you—Kate told me that she was thinking of calling Heather's mother with one thing she had remembered. Of course, she's been on the road and didn't know that Isabelle was dead."

Once again Lacey spoke slowly and deliberately. "Kate Knowles has a boyfriend. He lives in New York. His name is Bill Merrill. He's an investment banker with Chase. Apparently he is a friend of Rick Parker, or at least knows him. Bill told Kate he had been chatting with Heather in the après-ski bar of the big lodge in Stowe the afternoon before she died. When Rick came in, though, she apparently broke off their conversation and left the bar almost immediately."

"He's sure this was the afternoon before Heather died?"

"That's what Kate said. Her understanding is that Heather was very upset when she spotted Rick. I asked if she had any idea why Heather would react so strongly, and Kate told me that apparently Rick had pulled something on Heather when she first moved to New York, four years ago."

"Ms. Farrell, let me ask you something. You worked for Parker and Parker for some eight years. With Rick Parker. Is that right?"

"That's right. But Rick was in the West Side office until three years ago."

"I see. And through this whole thing with Isabelle Waring, he never communicated to you that he knew, or might have known, Heather Landi?"

"No, he did not. May I remind you, Mr. Baldwin, that I'm where I am because Rick Parker gave me the name of Curtis Caldwell, who supposedly was from a prestigious law firm? Rick is the only one in the office who spoke, or *supposedly* spoke, to that man who turned out to be Isabelle Waring's killer. Wouldn't it have been natural in the weeks I was showing that apartment, and telling Rick about Isabelle Waring and her obsession over her daughter's death, for him to have said he knew Heather? I certainly think so," she said emphatically.

I turned the journal over to the police the day after Isabelle died, Lacey thought. I told them at the time that I had given a copy to Jimmy Landi, as I promised. Did I say anything about Isabelle asking me to read it? Or did I say I'd glanced at it? She rubbed her forehead with her palm, trying to force herself to remember.

Don't let them ask me who my date for the show was, she thought. Tom Lynch's name is in the journal, and they're sure to recognize it. It won't take them long to learn that all this wasn't a coincidence.

"Let me get this straight," Baldwin said. "You say the man who saw Rick Parker in Stowe is an investment banker named Bill Merrill who works for Chase?"

"Yes."

"Was all this information just volunteered at this casual meeting with Ms. Knowles?"

Lacey's patience snapped. "Mr. Baldwin, in my effort to get this information for you I manipulated a luncheon with a very nice and talented actress whom I would enjoy having as a friend. I've lied to her as I have to every living soul I've met in Minneapolis, other than George Svenson, of course. It's in my best interests to pick up any information I can that might lead to my having the chance to become a

normal, truthful human being again. If I were you, I think
I'd be much more concerned with investigating Rick Parker's link to Heather Landi than acting as if I'm making
things up."

"I wasn't suggesting anything of the sort, Ms. Farrell.
We'll follow up on this information immediately. However,
you must admit that not too many witnesses in the protection
program manage to bump into the friend of a dead woman
whose mother's murder was the cause of their being in the
program."

"And not too many mothers get murdered because
they're not convinced their daughter's death was an accident."

"We'll look into this, Ms. Farrell. I'm sure you've been
told this already, but it's very important. I insist that you be
extremely careful not to let your guard down. You say you
have new friends, and that's fine, but watch what you say to
them. Always, always, *just be careful.* If even *one* person
knows where you can be reached, we will have to relocate
you."

"Don't worry about me, Mr. Baldwin," Lacey said, as
with a sinking heart she thought again about telling her
mother she was in Minneapolis.

As she hung up the phone and turned to leave the room,
she felt as though the weight of the world was pressing on
her shoulders. Baldwin had practically dismissed what she
told him. He had seemed not to believe there was any significance to Rick Parker having had a connection to Heather
Landi.

There was no way Lacey could have known that the moment he replaced the receiver, U.S. Attorney Gary Baldwin
said to his assistants, who were monitoring the phone call,
"The first real break! Parker is in this up to his neck." He
paused, then added, "And Lacey Farrell knows more than
she's telling."

34

I GUESS I WAS WRONG ABOUT ALICE, TOM LYNCH THOUGHT as he showered after working out at the Twin Cities Gym. Maybe she *was* sore that I didn't stick by her at the party. For the second day in a row she had not shown up at the gym. Nor had she returned his phone call.

But Kate had called to tell him about her lunch with Alice, and Alice had been the one who made the date, so at least she likes *somebody* in the family, he told himself.

But why didn't she call me back, even if it was to say she couldn't make it, or that she didn't get the message in time to make dinner last night? he wondered.

He stepped out of the shower and vigorously toweled himself dry. On the other hand, Kate also mentioned that Alice was starting a new job. Maybe *that's* why she hadn't gotten back to him, he decided.

Or maybe there was another guy in the picture?

Or maybe she was sick?

Knowing that Ruth Wilcox missed nothing, Tom stopped

at her office on the way out. "No sign of Alice Carroll again today," he said, trying to sound casual. "Or maybe she comes in at a different time now?"

He saw the spark of interest in Ruth's eyes. "As a matter of fact, I was just about to give her a call to see if something was wrong," she said. "She's been so faithful, coming in every day for two weeks, that I figure something must be up."

Ruth smiled slyly. "Why don't I call her right now? If she answers, should I tell her you're asking for her, and put you on?"

Oh boy! Tom thought ruefully. It'll be all over the gym that something's brewing between Alice and me. Well, you started it, he reminded himself. "You're a regular Dolly Levi, Ruth," he said. "Sure, if she answers, put me on."

After four rings, Ruth said, "What a shame. She must be out, but the answering machine is on. I'll leave a message."

Her message was that she and a certain very attractive gentleman were wondering where Alice was keeping herself.

Well, at least that will smoke her out, Tom thought. If she's not interested in going out with me, I'd like to know it. I wonder if there is some kind of problem in her life?

When he went out, he stood on the street for a few minutes, debating what he wanted to do. Had he run into Alice at the gym, he would have asked her to go to dinner and a movie, or that at least had been his plan. The film that had been awarded first prize at the Cannes Film Festival was playing at the Uptown Theatre. He knew he could always go alone, but he just didn't feel like seeing it by himself.

He was getting cold, standing on the sidewalk, trying to decide. Finally he shrugged and said aloud, "Why not?" He would drive over to where Alice lived. With luck she would be there and he would ask her if she wanted to go to the movie with him.

From his car phone he tried her number again and got the answering machine. She wasn't home yet. He parked at the curb outside her building and studied it, remembering that Alice lived on the fourth floor and her windows were directly over the main entrance.

Those windows were dark. I'll wait awhile, Tom decided, and if she doesn't show up, I'll get something to eat and skip the movie.

Forty minutes passed. He was about to leave when a car pulled into the semicircular driveway and stopped. The passenger door opened, and he saw Alice get out and dart into the apartment building.

For a moment the car was illuminated by the overhead light. Tom could see that it was a dark green Plymouth; it appeared to be five or six years old, the very essence of nondescript. He caught a glimpse of the driver and was pleased to note that he obviously was an older man. Certainly he would be an unlikely romantic partner for Alice.

The intercom was in the foyer. Tom pushed 4F.

When Alice answered, she obviously thought it was the man who had just dropped her off. "Mr. Svenson?"

"No, Alice, it's Mr. Lynch," Tom said, his tone one of mock formality. "May I come up?"

When Lacey opened the door, Tom could see that she looked drained, even stunned. Her skin was pale, almost alabaster white. The pupils of her eyes seemed enormous. He did not waste time on preliminaries. "Obviously something's terribly wrong," he said, alarm in his voice. "What is it, Alice?"

The sight of his tall, rangy figure filling the doorway, the concern in his eyes, in his whole expression, the realization that he had sought her out when she ignored his call, almost unhinged Lacey.

It was when he called her Alice that she managed to rein herself in, to regain at least a modicum of control. In the twenty-minute ride from the secure phone back to the apartment, she had exploded at George Svenson. "What is the *matter* with that Baldwin? I give him information that *has* to be useful in this case, and he treats me as if I'm a criminal! He just dismissed me, treated me like a child. For two cents I'd go home and walk down Fifth Avenue with a sign on me saying 'Rick Parker is a no-good, spoiled jerk who must have done something terrible to Heather Landi when she was a twenty-year-old kid just arriving in New York, because four years later she was still obviously spooked by him. Anyone with any information please come forward.' "

Svenson's response had been, "Take it easy, Alice. Calm down." And in fact he had the kind of voice that could soothe a lioness, let alone Lacey. It came with the job, of course.

During the drive home a new fear had hit Lacey. Suppose Baldwin had someone on his staff talk to her mother or Kit to be sure she hadn't told them where she was living. They would see through Mom in a minute, she thought. She would never be able to fool them. Unlike me, she's never learned to be an accomplished liar. If Baldwin thought Mom knew, he would relocate me, I know it. I can't go through the whole business of starting over again.

After all, here in Minneapolis she had a semblance of a job, and at least the beginnings of something resembling a personal life.

"Alice, you haven't invited me in. You might as well. I have no intention of leaving."

And it was here that she had met Tom Lynch.

Lacey attempted a smile. "Please come in. It's nice to see you, Tom. I was just about to pour myself a much needed glass of wine. Will you join me?"

"I'd be glad to." Tom took off his coat, and tossed it on

a chair. "How about I do the honors?" he asked. "Wine in the refrigerator?"

"No, as a matter of fact it's in the wine cellar. That's just beyond my state-of-the-art kitchen."

The Pullman kitchen in the tiny apartment consisted of a small stove and oven, a miniature sink, and a bar-sized refrigerator.

Tom raised his eyebrows. "Shall I lay a fire in the great room?"

"That would be nice. I'll wait on the verandah." Lacey opened the cabinet and poured cashews into a bowl. Two minutes ago I was within an inch of going to pieces, she thought. Here I am, actually joking with someone. Clearly Tom's presence had made the difference.

She sat in a corner of the couch; he settled in the over-stuffed chair and stretched out his long legs. He lifted his glass to her in a toast, "Good to be with you, Alice." His expression became serious. "I have to ask you a question, and please be honest. Is there another man in your life?"

Yes, there is, Lacey thought, but not the way you're thinking. The man in my life is a killer who's stalking me.

"*Is* there someone, Alice?" Tom asked.

Lacey looked at Tom for a long minute. I could love you, she thought. Maybe I've already started to love you. She remembered the bullets whistling past her head, the blood spurting from Bonnie's shoulder.

No, I can't risk that. I'm a pariah, she thought. If Caldwell, or whatever his name is, learns where I am, he'll follow me here. I can't expose Tom to danger.

"Yes, I'm afraid there *is* someone in my life," she told him, struggling to keep her voice steady.

He left ten minutes later.

35

Rick Parker had taken more than a dozen prospective buyers to look at the Waring apartment. A few times he had seemed to be on the verge of a sale, but each time the potential buyer had pulled back from making an offer. Now he had another strong possibility, Shirley Forbes, a fiftyish divorcée. She had been to see the place three times, and he had arranged to meet her there again at ten-thirty.

This morning, as he had walked in the door of the office, his phone was ringing. It was Detective Ed Sloane. "Rick, we haven't talked in a couple of weeks," Sloane said. "I think you'd better come in and see me today. I just want to see if maybe by now your memory has improved a little."

"I have nothing to remember," Rick snapped.

"Oh yes you do. Twelve o'clock. Be here."

Rick jumped as Sloane abruptly broke off their connection. He sat heavily in his chair and began rubbing his forehead, which increasingly seemed to be covered with icy beads of perspiration. The savage pounding going on inside his head made him feel as though his skull was about to explode.

I'm drinking too much, Rick told himself. I've got to slow down.

He had made the rounds of his favorite bars last night. Did something happen? he wondered. He vaguely remembered that he had ended up at Landi's for a nightcap, although it wasn't on his usual circuit. He had wanted to see Heather's portraits in the murals.

I had forgotten they were painted out, he thought. Did I do something stupid while I was there? Did I say anything to Jimmy about the paintings? *Did I say anything about Heather?*

The last thing he needed this morning was to go back into Heather's apartment just before he had to go talk to Sloane, but there was no way he could postpone the appointment. Shirley Forbes had made a point of telling him she would be coming there from a doctor's appointment. He knew that all his father would need to hear was that he had let another potential sale of that apartment slip through his fingers.

"Rick."

He looked up to see R. J. Parker Sr. standing over his desk, scowling at him. "I was in Landi's for dinner last night," his father told him. "Jimmy wants that apartment sold. I said you had someone coming back this morning who's definitely interested. He said he'd gladly settle for a hundred thousand less than the six hundred he's been asking, just to get rid of it."

"I'm on my way to meet Mrs. Forbes now, Dad," Rick said.

My God! he thought. *R. J. was in Landi's last night. I could have bumped into him!* The very idea of such a disastrous encounter increased the pounding in his head.

"Rick," his father said, "I don't think I have to tell you that the sooner that place is off our hands, the less chance Jimmy has of finding out—"

"I know, Dad, I know." Rick pushed his chair back. "I've got to go."

"I'm sorry. It's exactly what I want, but I just know I'd never spend a comfortable moment alone here. I'd keep thinking of the way that poor woman died, trapped and defenseless."

Shirley Forbes announced her decision as she and Rick stood in the bedroom where Isabelle Waring had died. The apartment had been left with everything still in place. Forbes looked around the room. "I looked up all the newspaper accounts of the murder on the Internet," she said, dropping her voice as though confiding a secret. "From what I understand, Mrs. Waring was propped up against *that* headboard."

Her eyes unnaturally wide behind oversized glasses, Mrs. Forbes pointed to the bed. "I've read all about it. She was resting right here in her own bedroom, and someone came in and shot her. The police think she tried to get away, but her killer was blocking the door, so she shrank back on the bed and put her hand up to protect herself. That's why her hand was so bloody. And then that real estate agent came in, just in time to hear her beg for her life. Just think, that agent could have been killed too. That would have been two murders in this apartment."

Rick turned abruptly. "Okay. You've made your point. Let's go."

The woman followed him through the sitting room and down the stairs. "I'm afraid I've upset you, Mr. Parker. I'm so sorry. Did you know either Heather Landi or Mrs. Waring?" Rick wanted to rip off those idiotic glasses and grind them under his feet. He wanted to push this stupid woman, this voyeur, down the stairs. That's all she was, he decided—a voyeur, wasting his time, churning up his guts. She probably had looked at this place *only* because of the murder. She had no intention of buying.

He had other listings to offer her, but to hell with them, he decided. She saved him the trouble of telling her to get out by saying, "I really must rush now. I'll call you in a few days to see if anything else has come up."

She was gone. Rick went into the powder room, opened the door of the linen closet, and extracted a bottle from its hiding place. He carried the bottle into the kitchen, got out a glass, and half filled it with vodka. Taking a deep sip, he sat down on a bar stool at the counter that separated the kitchen from the dining area.

His attention became riveted on a small lamp at the end of the counter. The base was a teapot. He remembered it all too well.

"It's my Aladdin's lamp," Heather had said that day when she spotted it in a secondhand store on West Eightieth. "I'll rub it for luck," she had said. Then, holding it up, she had closed her eyes, and chanted in a somber voice: "Powerful genie, grant me my wish. Let me get the part I auditioned for. Put my name up in lights." Then in a worried voice she had added, "And don't let Baba be too mad at me when I tell him I bought a co-op without his permission."

She had turned to Rick with a frown and said, "It's my money, or at least he told me I could use it for whatever I wanted, but at the same time I know he wanted to have a say in where I live here. He's worried enough as it is about my deciding to leave college early and move here and be on my own."

Then she had smiled again—she had a wonderful smile, Rick remembered—and rubbed the lamp once more. "But maybe he won't mind," she had said. "I bet finding this 'magic' lamp is a sign that everything will be fine."

Rick looked at the lamp, now sitting on the counter. Reaching for it, he yanked out the cord as he picked it up.

The next week, Heather had begged him to cancel the sale and give back her deposit. "I told my mother on the phone that I'd seen a place I loved. She was so upset. She told me that as a surprise my father had already bought an apartment for me on East Seventieth at Fifth Avenue. I can't let him know that I've bought another one without his permission. You just don't know him, Rick," she pleaded. "Rick, please, your family *owns* the agency. You can help me."

Rick aimed the lamp at the wall over the sink and threw it with all the force he could muster.

The genie in the lamp had gotten Heather the part in the show. After that he hadn't helped her very much.

Undercover detective Betty Ponds, the woman Rick Parker knew as Shirley Forbes, reported to Detective Sloane at the 19th Precinct. "Parker's so jumpy that he's twitching," she said. "Before too long, he'll crack like a broken egg. You should have seen the look in his eyes when I described how Isabelle Waring died. Rick Parker is scared silly."

"He has a lot more to be worried about," Sloane told her. "The Feds are talking right now to a guy who can place Parker in Stowe the afternoon before Heather Landi died."

"What time do you expect him?" Ponds asked.

"Noon."

"It's almost that now. I'm out of here. I don't want him to see me." With a wave she left the squad room.

Twelve-fifteen and twelve-thirty came and went. At one o'clock Sloane phoned Parker and Parker. He was told that Rick had not returned to the office since leaving for a ten-thirty appointment.

By the next morning it was clear that Rick Parker had disappeared, voluntarily or otherwise.

36

IT HAD BECOME CLEAR TO LACEY THAT SHE COULD NOT
continue to go to the Twin Cities Gym, because she would
just keep running into Tom Lynch. Even though she had
told him there was someone else in her life, she was sure
that if they saw each other day after day at the gym, inevita-
bly they would end up going out together, and there was
just no way she could tolerate the constant fabrication and
the web of lies she would have to spin.

There was no question she liked him, and no question
that she would like to get to know him. She could imagine
sitting across a table from him, and over a plate of pasta and
a glass of red wine, telling him about her mother and father,
about Kit and Jay and the children.

What she could *not* imagine was inventing stories about
a mother who supposedly lived in England, about the school
she never attended, about her nonexistent boyfriend.

Kate Knowles had said that Tom loved New York and
would end up there eventually. How *well* did he know it?

Lacey wondered. She thought of how much fun it would be to take him on one of the Jack Farrell tours of the city, "East Side, West Side, all around the town."

In the days that immediately followed Tom's visit to her apartment, Lacey found that when she finally got to sleep, she had vague dreams of him. In those dreams, the doorbell of her apartment would ring and she would open the door and he would say, just as he had on the intercom that last night, "No, Alice, it's Mr. Lynch."

But on the third night, the dream changed. This time, as Tom came down the corridor, the elevator door opened and Curtis Caldwell stepped out, the pistol in his hand aimed at Tom's back.

That night Lacey awoke with a scream, trying to warn Tom, trying to pull him into the apartment, to bolt the door so they both could be safe inside.

Given her generally distressed state, the job with Millicent Royce was a lifesaver. At Millicent's invitation, Lacey had been out with her on several sales calls, either to show houses to a prospective client or to obtain new listings.

"It will be more interesting for you if you get to know the area well," Mrs. Royce told her. "Did you ever hear it said that real estate is all about location?"

Location, location, location. In Manhattan a park or river view dramatically increased the price of an apartment. Lacey found herself longing to swap stories with Millicent about some of the eccentric clients she had dealt with over the years.

The evenings were the hardest times. They stretched long and empty in front of her. On Thursday night she made herself go to a movie. The theater was half empty, with rows of unoccupied seats, but just before the film began, a man came down the aisle, went past her row, turned, looked around, and chose the seat directly behind her.

In the semidarkness she could only tell that he was of medium height and slender. Her heart began to race.

As the credits rolled on the screen, Lacey could hear the creaking of the seat behind her as he settled into it, she could smell the popcorn he was carrying. Then suddenly she felt his hand tap her shoulder. Almost paralyzed with fright as she was, it took what felt to be a superhuman effort to turn her head to look at him.

He was holding a glove. "This yours, ma'am?" he asked. "It was under your chair."

Lacey did not stay to see the film. She found it impossible to concentrate on what was happening on the screen.

On Friday morning, Millicent asked Lacey what she would be doing over the weekend.

"Mostly hunting for a gym or health club," Lacey said. "The one I joined is fine, but it doesn't have a squash court, and I really miss that."

Of course, that's not the *real* reason I won't go to Twin Cities Gym anymore, she thought, but for once, it isn't a totally dishonest answer.

"I've heard there's a new health club in Edina that's supposed to have a great squash court," Millicent told her. "Let me find out about it."

In a few minutes she came back to Lacey's desk with the smile of someone who has achieved a goal. "I was right. And because they're new, there's a discount for joining right now."

When Millicent left later for her appointment, Lacey called George Svenson. She had two requests for him: she wanted to speak to U.S. Attorney Gary Baldwin again. "I deserve to know what's happening," she said.

Then she added, "People are getting too curious at the

Twin Cities Gym. I'm afraid I've got to ask you to advance the registration fee for a different one."

Beggar, she thought despairingly as she waited for his answer. I'm not only a liar but a beggar!

But Svenson did not hesitate: "I can okay that. The change will do you good."

37

LOTTIE HOFFMAN READ THE NEW YORK PAPERS EVERY morning over her solitary breakfast. For forty-five years, up until a little over a year ago, she and Max had shared them. It was still unreal to Lottie that on that day in early December, Max had gone out for his usual early morning walk and never returned.

An item on page three of the *Daily News* caught her eye: Richard J. Parker Jr., wanted for questioning in the murder of Isabelle Waring, had disappeared. What had happened to him? she wondered nervously.

Lottie pushed her chair back and went to the desk in the living room. From the middle drawer, she took out the letter Isabelle Waring had written Max the very day before she had been murdered. She read it once again.

Dear Max,
    I tried to phone you today, but your number is un-listed, which is why I am writing. I am sure that you

must have heard that Heather died in an accident last December. Her death was a tremendous loss to me, of course, but the circumstances of her death have been especially troublesome.

In clearing out her apartment I have come across her journal, and in it she refers to her intention of meeting you for lunch. That was only five days before her death. She does not mention either you or the lunch date after that. Instead the next two entries in the journal indicate that she was clearly distraught, although there is no indication of what was actually bothering her.

Max, you worked at Jimmy's restaurant for the first fifteen years of Heather's life. You were the best captain he ever had, and I know how much he regretted your leaving him. Remember, when Heather was two and you did magic tricks to make her sit still for the artist who was painting her into the mural? Heather loved and trusted you, and it is my hope that she may have confided in you when you saw her.

In any event, will you please phone me? I'm staying in Heather's apartment. The number is 555-2437.

Lottie returned the letter to the drawer and went back to the table. She picked up her coffee cup, then realized that her right hand was trembling so much that she had to steady the cup with the fingers of her left hand. Since that terrible morning, when she had answered the doorbell to find a policeman standing there . . . well, ever since that terrible morning she had felt every one of her seventy-four years.

She thought back to that time. I called Isabelle Waring, she remembered nervously. She was so shocked when I told her that Max had been killed by a hit-and-run driver only two days before Heather's death. At that time, I still thought his death was an accident.

She remembered that Isabelle had asked if she had any idea what Max and Heather might have talked about.

Max had always said that in his business you heard a lot, but you learned to keep your mouth shut. Lottie shook her head. Well, he must have broken that rule when he talked to Heather, she decided, and now I know it cost him his life.

She had tried to help Isabelle. I told her what I knew, she thought. I told her that I'd never met Heather, although I had gone with my senior citizen group to see the production of *The Boy Friend* when she was appearing in it. Then sometime soon after that, Lottie had gone on a day outing with the same group to Mohonk Mountain House, the resort in the Catskills. She had seen Heather there a second—and last—time. I took a walk along the trails, she remembered, and I saw a couple in ski clothes with their arms around each other. They were in a gazebo, all lovey-dovey. I recognized Heather, but not the guy she was with. That night she had told Max about it.

He asked about Heather's boyfriend, she remembered. When I described him, Max knew who I was talking about and became terribly upset. He said that what he knew about that man would curl my hair. He said the man had been very careful, that there wasn't a breath of suspicion against him, but Max said he was a racketeer and a drug dealer.

Max didn't tell me the man's name, Lottie thought, and before I could describe him to Isabelle Waring when she had called that night, Isabelle had said, "I hear someone downstairs. It must be the real estate agent. Give me your number. I'll call you right back."

Lottie remembered how Isabelle had repeated the number several times, then hung up the phone. I waited for the call all evening, Lottie thought, and then I heard the eleven-o'clock news.

It was only then that the full impact of what must have happened had hit her. Whoever had come in while she and Isabelle were on the phone must have been Isabelle Waring's murderer. Isabelle was dead because she would not stop looking for the reason for Heather's death. And now Lottie was convinced that Max was dead because he had warned Heather away from the man she was seeing.

And if I saw that man, I could identify him, she thought, but thank the Lord no one knows that. If there was one thing Lottie was sure of, it was that whatever Max told Heather when he cautioned her, he had not involved Lottie. She knew Max would never have put her in danger.

Suppose the police should ever come to her, she wondered suddenly. What would Max want her to do?

The answer was very calming, and it came to her as clearly as if he were sitting across the table from her. "Do absolutely nothing, Lottie," he cautioned. "Keep your mouth shut."

38

SANDY SAVARANO WAS FINDING HIS SEARCH WAS TAKING
more time than he had expected. Some real estate agencies
answered his questions willingly. The ones that told him
they had hired young women between the ages of twenty-
five and thirty-five all had to be checked out, which meant
on-site surveillance. Other agencies refused to give him information on the phone, which meant they had to be
checked out too.

In the mornings he would drive to the agencies and look
them over, giving the most attention to the small mom-and-
pop businesses. Usually they were storefront offices where
he could walk past and by merely looking inside see what
was going on. Some were obviously two-person operations.
To the ones that turned out to be more elaborate, prosperous-
looking setups, he gave scant attention. They wouldn't be
the kind to take on someone without a thorough background
check.

The late afternoons he spent covering the health clubs

and the gyms. Before he went into one of them, he would park for a time outside, looking at the people who were going in and out.

Sandy had no doubt that eventually he would find Lacey Farrell. The kind of job she would probably look for, and the kind of recreation she would rely on, were more than enough to lead him to her. A person didn't change her habits just because she changed her name. He had tracked down his quarry in the past with a lot less to go on. He would find her. It was just a matter of time.

Sandy liked to think about Junior, an FBI informant he had tracked to Dallas. The one good clue he had was that the guy was a nut for sushi. The problem was that sushi had become very trendy, and a lot of Japanese restaurants had opened in Dallas recently. Sandy had been parked outside a restaurant named Sushi Zen, and Junior had come out.

Sandy liked to remember the look on Junior's face when he had seen the car's tinted window slide down and had realized what was going to happen. The first bullet had been aimed at his gut. Sandy wanted to wake up all those raw fishies. The second had been directed at his heart. The third, to his head, had been a mere afterthought.

Late Friday morning, Sandy drove to check out Royce Realty in Edina. The woman he had spoken to on the phone had seemed one of those firm, schoolmarm types. She had answered his initial questions freely enough. Yes, she had a young woman working for her, age twenty-six, who was planning to take her Realtor certification test but had left to have a baby.

Sandy had asked if that young woman had been replaced.

It was the pause that interested him. It indicated neither denial nor confirmation. "I have a candidate in mind," was what Mrs. Royce finally told him. And yes, she was in the twenty-five to thirty-five age category.

When he reached Edina, Sandy parked his car in the supermarket lot across the street from the Royce office. He sat there for about twenty minutes, taking in details of the area. There was a delicatessen, next door to the agency, which had a fair amount of traffic. A hardware store halfway down the block also looked busy. He saw no one, however, either going into or coming out of Royce Realty.

Finally Sandy got out of the car, crossed the street, and sauntered past the agency, casually glancing inside. Then he stopped as though to examine the contents of a flyer prominently displayed in the agency window.

He could see that there was a desk in the reception area. Neatly stacked papers suggested that it was usually occupied. He could see beyond to where a largish woman with gray hair was sitting at a desk in a private office.

Sandy decided to go in.

Millicent Royce looked up as the door chimes signaled the arrival of a visitor. She saw a conservatively dressed gray-haired man in what she judged to be his late fifties. She went out to greet him.

His story was simple and direct. He said he was Paul Gilbert, visiting the Twin Cities on business for 3M —"That's Minnesota Mining and Manufacturing," he explained with an apologetic smile.

"My husband worked there all his adult life," Millicent answered, not quite understanding why it should irritate her that this stranger had assumed she would not understand what 3M stood for.

"My daughter's husband is being transferred here, and my daughter was told that Edina is a lovely place to live," he told her. "She's pregnant, so I thought that while I'm here I could do a little house hunting for her."

Millicent Royce dismissed her feeling of pique. "Aren't you the good father!" she said. "Now let me just ask you a few questions so I can get some idea of what your daughter is hoping to find."

Sandy smoothly gave appropriate answers about his supposed daughter's name, address, and family needs, which included "a kindergarten for her four-year-old, a good-sized back yard, and a large kitchen—she loves to cook." He left half an hour later with Millicent Royce's card in his pocket, and her promise to find just the right house. In fact, she told him she had one just coming on the market that might be perfect.

Sandy went back across the street and again sat in the car, his eyes fixed on the entrance to the agency. If there was someone using the reception desk, she was probably at lunch, he figured, and would return soon.

Ten minutes later, a young blond woman in her twenties went into the agency. Customer or receptionist? Sandy wondered. He got out of the car and again crossed the street, taking care to stay out of view of anyone inside the real estate office. For several minutes he stood in front of the delicatessen, reading the lunch specials. From the corner of his eye he could glance from time to time into the Royce agency.

The young blond woman was sitting at the reception desk, talking animatedly to Mrs. Royce.

Unfortunately for Sandy, he could not read lips. Had he been able to, he would have heard Regina saying, "Millicent, you have no idea how much easier it was to sit behind this desk than to take care of a colicky baby! And I have to admit that your new assistant keeps it a lot neater than I did."

Irritated at having wasted so much time, Sandy walked

quickly back to his car and drove away. Another washout, he thought. Since there were other possibilities to track down in the area, he decided to continue to make the rounds of suburban agencies. He wanted to be back in downtown Minneapolis by late afternoon, though. That was a good time to look into the health clubs.

The next club on his list was the Twin Cities Gym on Hennepin Avenue.

39

"Now Bonnie, don't be like that. You know you do *so* like Jane to mind you," Kit said persuasively. "Daddy and Nana and I are just going to dinner in New York. We won't be late, I promise. But now Mommy has to finish getting dressed."

Heartsick, she looked at her daughter's woebegone face. "Don't forget, Nana promised that next week, when Lacey phones, you can talk to her."

Jay was putting on his tie. Kit's eyes met his over Bonnie's head. Her look implored him to think of something to say to their daughter.

"I've got an idea for Bonnie," he said cheerfully. "Who wants to hear it?"

Bonnie did not look up.

"I want to hear it," Kit volunteered.

"When Lacey comes home, I'm going to send her and Bonnie—just the two of them—to Disney World. How does that sound?"

"But when is Lacey coming home?" Bonnie whispered.

"Very soon," Kit said heartily.

"In time for my birthday?" There was the sound of hope in the little girl's voice.

Bonnie would be five on March 1st.

"Yes, in time for your birthday," Jay promised. "Now go on downstairs, sweetheart. Jane wants you to help her make brownies."

"My birthday isn't that far away," a much happier Bonnie said, as she sprang up from beside Kit's dressing table.

Kit waited until she heard Bonnie's footsteps going down the stairs. "Jay, how *could* you . . . ?"

"Kit, I know it was a mistake, but I had to say *something* to cheer her up. We can't be late for this dinner. I don't think you understand how I've sweated this order for Jimmy Landi's casino. For a long time I've been closed out there completely. As it is, I got underbid on some of the biggest orders. Now that I'm back in with them, I can't let anything go wrong."

He pulled on his jacket. "And, Kit, remember that Jimmy just found out from some private detective he hired that Lacey is my sister-in-law. In fact, Alex said that's why Landi called him to set up the dinner."

"Why Alex?"

"Because he also found out that Alex is dating your mother."

"What *else* does he know about us?" Kit asked angrily. "Does he know that my sister could have been killed if she'd gone into that apartment five minutes earlier? Or when she was shot at on our doorstep? Does he know that our child is recovering from a bullet wound and is under treatment for depression?"

Jay Taylor put his arm around his wife's shoulders. "Kit, please! It'll be okay, I promise. But we have to go. Don't forget, we've got to pick up your mother."

* * *

Mona Farrell had carried the phone to the window and was looking outside when she saw the car pull up. "They're here, Lacey," she said. "I'm going to have to go."

They had been talking for nearly forty minutes. Lacey knew that Deputy Marshal Svenson would be getting impatient, but she had been especially reluctant to break the connection tonight. It had been such a long day, and the weekend stretched endlessly before her.

Last Friday at this time she had been looking forward to her date with Tom Lynch. There was nothing for her to look forward to now.

When she had asked about Bonnie, she could tell from her mother's overly cheerful reassurances that Bonnie was still not doing well.

Even less reassuring had been the news that her mother, Kit, and Jay were having dinner tonight with Jimmy Landi at Alex Carbine's restaurant. As she started to say good-bye, Lacey cautioned, "Mom, for heaven's sake, be careful not to tell anyone where I am. You've got to *swear* to me—"

"Lacey, don't you think I understand the danger I'd put you in? Don't worry. No one will learn anything from me."

"I'm sorry, Mom, it's just—"

"It's all right, dear. Now I really do have to go. I can't keep them waiting. What have you got on for tonight?"

"I'm signed up at a new gym. It has a great squash court. Should be fun."

"Oh, I know how much you love to play squash." Mona Farrell was genuinely pleased as she murmured, "Love and miss you, dear. Good-bye."

She hurried down to the car, thinking that at least she could tell Kit and Jay and Alex what Lacey was doing for recreation.

40

On Friday evening, Tom Lynch was planning to have an after-theater drink with his cousin, Kate. Her show was completing its Minneapolis engagement, and he wanted to say good-bye to her. He was also hoping that she might pick up his spirits.

Ever since Alice Carroll had told him that there was another man in her life, he had been depressed, and as a result everything seemed to be going wrong. The producer of his radio program had had to signal him several times to pick up his delivery, and even he was aware that he had sounded downright flat during several author interviews.

A touring production of *Show Boat* was opening at the Orpheum on Saturday night, and Tom's fingers itched to dial Alice's number and invite her to see it with him. He even found himself planning what he would say to her: "This time *you* can have the extra slice of pizza."

On Friday evening he decided to go over to the gym and work out for a while. He wasn't meeting Kate until eleven o'clock, and there was absolutely nothing else he could think of to do with his time.

He admitted to himself that he actually was harboring the secret hope that Alice might come into the gym, that they would start talking, and she would admit that she had serious doubts about this man in her life.

When he came out of the men's locker room, Tom looked around, but it was clear that Alice Carroll wasn't there, and, in fact, he already knew that she hadn't been there all week.

Through the glass that surrounded the manager's office, he could see Ruth Wilcox in deep conversation with a gray-haired man. As he watched, Ruth shook her head several times, and he thought he detected a slight expression of distaste on her face.

What does he want, a discount? Tom asked himself. He knew he should start to jog, but he had to ask Ruth if she had heard anything from Alice.

"Have I got news for you, Tom!" Ruth confided. "Close the door. I don't want anyone else to hear this."

Somehow Tom knew that the news had to do with Alice and the gray-haired man who had just left.

"That guy is looking for Alice," Ruth told him, her voice snapping with excitement. "He's her father."

"Her father! That's crazy. Alice told me her father died years ago."

"Maybe that's what she told you, but that man is her father. Or at least he says he is. He even showed me her picture and asked if I'd seen her."

Tom's instincts as a newsman were aroused. "What did you tell him?" he asked cautiously.

"I didn't say anything. How do I know he wasn't a bill

collector or something? I said that I couldn't be sure. Then he told me that his daughter and his wife had had a terrible misunderstanding, and that he knew his daughter had moved to Minneapolis four months ago. His wife is very sick and desperate to make amends before she dies."

"That sounds phony as hell to me," Tom said flatly. "I hope you didn't give him any information."

"No way," Ruth said positively. "All I told him was to leave his name and if I happened to find that young lady was among our clients I'd ask her to call home."

"He didn't give you *his* name, or tell you where he's staying?"

"No."

"Didn't you think that was strange?"

"The gentleman said that he'd appreciate it if I didn't tell his daughter he was looking for her. He doesn't want her to disappear again. I felt so sorry for him. He had tears in his eyes."

If there's one thing I know about Alice Carroll, Tom thought, it is that no matter how big a misunderstanding, she's not the kind who would turn her back on a terminally ill mother.

Then another possibility occurred to him, one that he found enticing. If she wasn't telling the truth about her background, maybe the man she claimed to be involved with doesn't exist, he thought. He felt better already.

41

DETECTIVE ED SLOANE WORKED THE EIGHT-TO-FOUR DAY
shift, but at five-thirty on Friday evening he was still in his
office at the 19th Precinct, with Rick Parker's file spread
out on his desk. He was glad that it was Friday. He hoped
that at least over the weekend, he might have some peace
from the Feds.

It had been a grueling last couple of days. Since Tuesday,
when Rick Parker had not shown up for his appointment,
the rocky relationship between the NYPD and the U.S. Attorney's office had become openly hostile.

It drove Sloane nuts that it was only when two federal
agents showed up, looking for Parker, that Gary Baldwin
finally admitted they had a witness who could place Rick at
a ski lodge in Stowe the afternoon before Heather Landi
died.

Baldwin didn't share that information, Sloane thought,
but when he learned that I was putting heavy pressure on
Parker, he had the nerve to complain to the district attorney.

Fortunately the DA stood by me, Sloane thought grimly. In a face-to-face confrontation, the DA had reminded Baldwin that the NYPD had an unsolved homicide that had occurred in the 19th Precinct, and it was their intention to solve it. He also made it clear that if the federal law enforcement officials wished to cooperate and share information, they might all be better off, but the NYPD was running the case, not the Feds.

The fact that the DA had gone to bat for him, even though he had had to sit and listen as Baldwin reminded him that vital evidence had disappeared from Sloane's locked cubby, had given Sloane a driving need to be the one who eventually pulled Rick Parker in.

Unless he was already dead, of course, Sloane reminded himself, which was a distinct possibility.

If not, Rick's disappearance was a sure sign that they were on the right track. It certainly cast in a new light the fact that he had never been able to explain how Isabelle Waring's murderer was able to pass himself off so easily as a lawyer with a prestigious law firm that just *happened* to be a major Parker and Parker client.

Now they knew that Parker had been at the ski lodge, and that Heather Landi was spooked when she had seen him there, only hours before her death.

In the four months since Isabelle Waring's murder, Sloane had put together an extensive curriculum vitae on Rick Parker. I know more about him than he knows about himself, Sloane thought, as once again he read through the thick file.

Richard J. Parker Jr. Only child. Thirty-one years old. Kicked out of two prestigious prep schools for possession of drugs. Suspicion, but no proof, of selling drugs—witness probably paid off to recant. Took six years to finally finish college at age twenty-three. Father paid for damages to fraternity house during wild party.

Always plenty of spending money through school years, Mercedes convertible as a 17th birthday present, Central Park West apartment as college graduation gift.

First and only job at Parker and Parker. Five years in the West 67th Street branch office, three years to present in East 62nd Street main office.

It hadn't been hard for Sloane to learn that Rick's coworkers on the West Side had despised him. One former employee of Parker and Parker told Sloane, "Rick would be out partying all night, show up with a hangover or still high on coke, and then start throwing his weight around in the office."

Five years ago Rick's father had elected to settle a sexual assault complaint brought against Rick by a young secretary, rather than have a public scandal. Following that episode, Parker Sr. had pulled the rug out from under his son.

The income from Rick's trust fund had been frozen, and he had been put on exactly the same base salary plus sales commission as his fellow employees.

Papa must have taken a course on tough love, Sloane thought with a touch of sarcasm. There was one problem with that scenario, however: Tough love doesn't support a cocaine habit. Once again he skimmed through the file. So where's Rick been getting his money for drugs, and if he's still alive, who's paying for him to hide out?

Sloane pulled another cigarette from the ever-present pack in his shirt pocket.

The curriculum vitae for Richard J. Parker Jr. revealed one consistent pattern. For all his bluster and desk pounding, Parker Sr. always came through in the end when his son was in real trouble.

Like now.

Ed Sloane grunted and got up. Theoretically he was off for the weekend, and his wife had big plans for him to clean out the garage. But he knew that those plans would have to be changed; the garage would have to wait. He was going to drive up to Greenwich, Connecticut, and have a little chat with R. J. Parker Sr. Yes, it definitely was time for him to visit the palatial estate where Rick Parker had been raised, and had been given everything that money could buy.

42

ON FRIDAY EVENINGS, THE TRAFFIC FROM NEW JERSEY into New York City was as heavy as the commuter traffic headed in the other direction. It was a dinner-and-theater night for many people, and Kit could see the strained expression on her husband's face as they inched their way across the George Washington Bridge. She was glad he had not said anything to her mother about how they should have left earlier.

Lacey had once asked her, "How can you stand it when he snaps at you for something that isn't your fault?"

I told Lacey that I didn't let it bother me, Kit remembered. I understand. Jay is a world-class worrier, and that's his way of expressing it. She glanced at him again. Right now he's worried because we are going to be late for dinner with an important client, she thought. I know he's worried sick about Bonnie, and by now he's churning about the fact that he's made a promise to her that he can't keep.

Jay sighed heavily as they finally turned off the bridge

and onto the ramp leading to the West Side Highway. Kit was relieved to see that the cars ahead of them seemed to be moving downtown in a steady flow.

She put a comforting hand on her husband's arm, then turned to look in the backseat. As usual after speaking with Lacey, her mother had been on the verge of tears. When she got in the car, she had said, "Let's not talk about it."

"How's it going, Mom?" Kit asked.

Mona Farrell attempted a smile. "I'm all right, dear."

"Did you explain to Lacey why I wasn't able to talk to her tonight?"

"I told her we were going into New York and you wanted to be sure Bonnie had her dinner before you left. She certainly understood."

"Did you tell her we were meeting Jimmy Landi?" Jay asked.

"Yes."

"What did she say?"

"She said—" Mona Farrell stopped herself before she blurted out that Lacey had cautioned her not to tell where she was living. Kit and Jay did not know that Lacey had confided that information to her.

"She said that she was surprised," Mona finished lamely, feeling uncomfortable.

"So Alex has made you a captain, Carlos?" Jimmy Landi greeted his former employee as he sat down at the reserved table in Alex's Place.

"Yes, he did, Mr. Landi," Carlos said with a big smile.

"If you'd waited a while, Jimmy would have promoted you," Steve Abbott said.

"Or maybe I wouldn't," Jimmy said shortly.

"In any case it's a moot point," Alex Carbine told him.

"Jimmy, this is your first time here. Tell me what you think of the place."

Jimmy Landi looked around him, studying the attractive dining room with its dark green walls brightened by colorful paintings in ornate gold frames.

"Looks like you got your inspiration from the Russian Tea Room, Alex," he commented.

"I did," Alex Carbine agreed pleasantly. "Just as you paid homage to La Côte Basque when you opened *your* place. Now, what are you having to drink? I want you to try my wine."

Jimmy Landi isn't the kind of man I had anticipated, Kit thought as she sipped a glass of chardonnay. Jay had been so worried about not keeping him waiting, but he certainly didn't seem upset that we were a couple of minutes late. In fact, when Jay apologized, Landi said, "In my place I *like* people to be late. Whoever's waiting has another drink. It adds up."

Despite his apparent good humor, Kit sensed that Jimmy Landi was extremely tense. There was a drawn look to his face, along with an unhealthy pallor. Perhaps it's just that he's grieved so much for his daughter, she decided. Lacey had told them that Heather Landi's mother had been heart-broken over their daughter's death. It made sense that Heather's father would have the same reaction.

When they had been introduced, Mona had said to Jimmy, "I know how much you've been through. My daughter—"

Alex interrupted, holding up his hand. "Why don't we wait until later to talk about that, dear?" he said smoothly.

Kit instinctively liked Jimmy's partner, Steve Abbott. Alex had told them that he had become something of a surrogate son to Jimmy, and that they were very close. Not in appearance, though, Kit decided. Abbott is *really* good-looking.

As dinner progressed, Kit could see that Steve and Alex were deliberately keeping the conversation away from any mention of either Lacey or Isabelle Waring. Between them they got Landi to tell some amusing stories about encounters with some of his celebrity clients.

Landi was, in fact, a first-class raconteur, a trait that Kit decided combined with his earthy, peasant appearance to make him oddly attractive. He also seemed genuinely warm and interested in them.

On the other hand, when he noticed a waiter looking impatiently at a woman who was obviously hemming and hawing over her entrée selection, his face darkened.

"Fire him, Alex," he said sharply. "He's no good. He'll never be any good."

Wow! Kit thought. He *is* tough! No wonder Jay is afraid of stepping on his toes.

Finally it was Jimmy who abruptly began to discuss Lacey and Isabelle Waring. As soon as coffee was served he said, "Mrs. Farrell, I met your daughter once. She was trying to keep her promise to my ex-wife by delivering my daughter's journal to me."

"I know that," Mona said quietly.

"I wasn't very nice to her. She'd brought me a copy of the journal instead of the original, and at the time I thought she had a hell of a nerve to decide to give the original to the cops."

"Do you still feel that way?" Mona asked, then didn't wait for an answer. "Mr. Landi, my daughter has been threatened with prosecution for withholding evidence because she tried to fulfill Isabelle Waring's dying wish."

Dear God, Kit thought. Mom is ready to explode.

"I learned about this only two days ago," Landi said brusquely. "I finally had the brains to hire a private detective when I saw that I'd been given the runaround by the cops. He's the one who found out that the cock-and-bull story they'd given me about a professional thief unintentionally killing Isabelle was so much hogwash."

Kit watched as Landi's complexion darkened to beet red.

It was obvious that Steve Abbott had noticed too. "Calm down, Jimmy," he urged. "You'll make a lousy patient if you have a stroke."

Jimmy shot a wry glance at him, then looked back at Mona. "That's just what my daughter used to tell me," he said. He swallowed the rest of the espresso in his cup. "I know your daughter's in that witness protection plan," he said. "Pretty lousy for her and for all of you."

"Yes, it is," Mona said, nodding in agreement.

"How do you stay in touch with her?"

"She calls once a week," Mona said. "In fact the reason we were a few minutes late is because I was talking to her until Jay and Kit picked me up."

"You can't call her?" Jimmy asked.

"Absolutely not. I wouldn't know where to reach her."

"*I* want to talk to her," Jimmy said abruptly. "Tell her that. The guy I hired tells me she spent a lot of time with Isabelle in the days before she died. I have a lot of questions I want to ask her."

"Mr. Landi, that request would have to be made through the U.S. Attorney's office," Jay said, breaking his silence on the matter. "They talked with us before Lacey went into the program."

"What you're saying is they'll probably turn me down," Jimmy growled. "All right, maybe there's another way. You ask her this question for me. Ask her if she remembers if there were a couple of unlined pages with writing on them at the end of Heather's journal."

"Why is that important, Jimmy?" Alex Carbine asked.

"Because if there *were,* it means that none of the evidence delivered to that precinct is going to be safe; it's going to be doctored or disappear. And I gotta find a way to do something about it."

Jimmy waved away Carlos, who was standing behind him with the coffee carafe. Then he stood and extended his hand to Mona. "Well, that's it, I guess. I'm sorry for you, Mrs. Farrell. I'm sorry for your daughter. From what I hear she was very nice to Isabelle, and she tried to be helpful to me. I owe her an apology. How is she doing?"

"Lacey is a trouper," Mona said. "She never complains. In fact she's always trying to cheer me up." She turned to Kit and Jay. "I forgot to tell you two in the car that Lacey just joined a brand-new health club, apparently one that has a fabulous squash court." She turned back to Landi. "She's always been a demon for exercise."

43

AFTER COMPLETING HER CALL TO HER MOTHER AND HANG-
ing up, Lacey met George Svenson in the lobby of the motel
and walked wordlessly with him to the car.

She thought briefly about what she would do for the rest
of the evening that stretched out ahead of her. One thing
was certain—she simply could not spend all that time alone
in the empty apartment. But what should she do? She was
not particularly hungry and didn't like the idea of going to a
restaurant alone. After the experience at the movie Thursday
night, she also could not bear the idea of sitting alone in a
darkened movie theater.

In a way, she would have enjoyed seeing the final Minneapolis performance of *The King and I,* if she could get a
ticket, but was sure that the overture would completely unravel her. She had a mental image from years ago of looking
down into the orchestra pit for her father.

Dad, I miss you, she thought as she got into Svenson's
car.

But a voice inside her head came back with a reply.

Be honest, Lacey, my girl, you're not grieving for me at the moment. Face it—you've met someone you want, but you're using my image to block out his. Admit it. It's not my face you're chasing, and not my image you're running away from.

Svenson was silent the entire drive, leaving her to her thoughts. Finally Lacey asked him if he had heard anything more from Gary Baldwin.

"No, I haven't, Alice," he replied.

It irritated Lacey that the one human being with whom she had even this much honest contact would not call her by her own name.

"Then kindly pass the word to the Great One that I want to know what is going on. I gave him some important information Tuesday night. As a simple courtesy, he could keep me informed of developments. I don't think I can live like this much longer."

Lacey bit her lip and slumped back in the seat. As always when she vented her anger on Svenson, she felt embarrassed and childish. She was sure he wanted to be home with his wife and three teenage daughters, not out dragging her around to motels to make phone calls.

"I had money put in your account, Alice. You can join the new health club tomorrow morning."

It was Svenson's way of telling her that he understood how she felt.

"Thanks," she murmured, then realized she wanted to shout, *"Please, just once, call me Lacey! My name is Lacey Farrell!"*

When they reached her apartment building, she went into the lobby, still undecided about what to do. For several long moments she stood irresolutely in front of the elevator, then turned abruptly. Instead of going upstairs, she went out again, but this time got into her own car. She drove around aimlessly for some time, finally turning in the direction of Wayzata, the community in which she had attended the *King and I* cast party. Once there she looked for a small restaurant she remembered passing that night, and took some comfort in the fact that despite her less than sterling sense of direction, she found it easily. Maybe I'm finally getting the feel and sense of this area, she thought. If I'm going to be in the real estate business out here for any length of time, I'll definitely need it.

The restaurant she had chosen might have been on West Fourth Street in New York's Greenwich Village. As soon as she opened the door, she smelled the welcoming aroma of baking garlic bread. There were about twenty tables, each covered with a red-and-white-checked tablecloth, and each sporting a candle.

Lacey glanced around. The place was clearly crowded. "It looks like you're full," she said to the hostess.

"No, as a matter of fact, we just got a cancellation." The hostess led her to a corner table that had not been visible from the desk.

As she waited to be served, Lacey nibbled at warm, crunchy Italian bread and sipped red wine. Around her, people were eating and chatting, obviously enjoying themselves. She was the only solitary diner.

What was different about this place? she wondered. Why did she feel different in here?

With a start, Lacey realized she had put her finger on something she had either been avoiding or not recognizing. Here, in this small restaurant, where she could see whoever came in the door without being immediately seen herself, she felt safer than she had all week.

Why was that? she wondered.

It's because I told Mom where I am, she admitted to herself ruefully.

The warnings she had received in the safe site echoed in

her head. *It's not that your family would knowingly give you away,* she was told. *It's remarks they might unconsciously make that could jeopardize your safety.*

She remembered how her dad had always joked that if Mom ever wrote her memoirs, they ought to title it *In Deepest Confidence,* because Mom never *could* keep a secret.

Then she thought of how shocked her mother had sounded when Lacey warned her not to drop anything to Jimmy Landi about where she was living. Maybe it will be okay, Lacey thought, praying that her mother had taken the warning seriously.

The salad greens were crisp, the house dressing tangy, the linguine with clam sauce delicious, but the feeling of safety was short-lived, and when Lacey left the restaurant and drove home, she was haunted by the sense that something or someone was closing in on her.

Tom Lynch had left her a message. "Alice, it's imperative that I see you tomorrow. Please call me back." He left his number.

If only I could call him, Lacey thought.

Ruth Wilcox had phoned as well: "Alice, we miss you. Please come in over the weekend. I want to talk to you about a gentleman who was inquiring about you."

Ruth, still playing the matchmaker, Lacey thought wryly.

She went to bed and managed to fall asleep, but then drifted promptly into a nightmare. *In it she was kneeling beside Isabelle's body. A hand touched her shoulder . . . She looked up and saw Isabelle's murderer, his pale blue eyes staring down at her, the pistol he was holding pointed at her head.*

She bolted up in bed, trying to scream. After that, it was no use. There was no more sleep for the rest of the night.

* * *

Early in the morning Lacey made herself go out for a jog but found she could not resist casting frequent glances over her shoulder to make certain she was not being followed.

I'm turning into a basket case, she acknowledged when she got back to the apartment and bolted the door.

It was only nine o'clock in the morning, and she had absolutely no plans of any kind for the rest of the day. Millicent Royce had said that often on weekends she had appointments to show houses and Lacey was welcome to go along with her. Unfortunately, though, there were none scheduled this weekend.

I'll have some breakfast, then try the new club, Lacey decided. At least it will be something to do.

She got to the Edina Health Center at ten-fifteen and was waved to a seat in the business office. She fished in her tote bag for her completed registration forms as the manager wound up a phone call by saying, "Yes, indeed, sir. We're a brand-new facility and have a wonderful squash court. Do come right over and take a look."

44

ON SATURDAY MORNING, DETECTIVE ED SLOANE DROVE
from his home in the Riverdale section of the Bronx to the
meeting he had insisted on having with Richard J. Parker
Sr., in Greenwich, Connecticut. On the way, he noted that
the snow, which had been so picture perfect only a few days
ago, was already disintegrating into piles of graying slush.
The sky was overcast, and rain was predicted, although the
forecast said it would turn into sleet as the temperatures
dropped.

It's just another lousy winter day, the kind when the smart
people who could afford it became snowbirds and flew
south, Sloane told himself.

Or to Hawaii. That was the trip he was saving for. He
planned to take Betty there on their thirtieth anniversary,
which was two years away.

He wished they were leaving tomorrow. Maybe even
today.

Although with what was going on at the precinct, he

knew he couldn't have gotten away. It haunted Sloane that evidence that might have been crucial to solving the murder of Isabelle Waring had been lost. It was bad enough, he thought, that Lacey Farrell had originally taken the journal from the crime scene. Infinitely worse was the fact that some still unknown perpetrator—most likely a "bad cop"—had stolen the journal from his own cubby. And probably had stolen pages from the copy that Jimmy Landi had turned over, he reminded himself.

The thought that he might be working, eating, and drinking with a cop who worked both sides of the street disgusted him physically.

As he turned off the Merritt Parkway at Exit 31, Ed thought about the sting he had set into motion in the squad room, aimed at catching whoever had been taking things out of the evidence box. He had begun to make a production out of taking his keys out of his suit jacket and locking them in his desk.

"I'm damned if I'll lose anything else out of my cubby," he had announced grimly to whoever happened to be in the squad room. With the captain's help, he had concocted the story that a piece of evidence locked in his cubby just *might* turn out to be the key to solving Isabelle Waring's murder. His entry describing the supposed evidence in the precinct's evidence log was deliberately ambiguous.

A hidden ceiling camera was now trained on his desk. Next week he would start reverting to his old habit of leaving his keys in his jacket on the back of his desk chair. He had a feeling that with the kind of fake information he was passing around, there was a good chance he would smoke out his quarry. Surely whoever killed Isabelle Waring had to be behind the thefts from the squad room and would be seriously worried about potential new evidence. Sloane found it hard to believe, though, that someone like Sandy Savarano would be behind the thefts himself. He was just a trigger man. No, he thought, chances were there was somebody with clout and lots of money who was calling the shots. And when he heard about this new evidence, he would order it destroyed.

Ed Sloane's dilemma was that, much as he wanted to expose a bad cop, he knew it might well turn out to be one of the guys who over the past twenty-five years had at one time or another pulled him out of a tight spot. This kind of thing was never easy.

The Parker estate was situated on Long Island Sound. The handsome pale-red-brick mansion was turreted at either end, and old enough to have acquired a mellow patina, set off by the patches of snow still covering the extensive grounds.

Sloane drove through the open gates and parked to the side of the semicircle at the main entrance, thinking as he did so that he doubted too many five-year-old Saturns had stopped there.

As he went up the flagstone walk, his eyes darted from one window to another, half hoping to catch Rick Parker looking out at him.

A very attractive young woman in a maid's uniform admitted him, and when he gave his name, told him he was expected. "Mr. Parker is waiting for you in his study," she said. There was a hint of intimacy in the way she spoke. Ed had the feeling she had just left the study.

As he followed her down a wide, carpeted foyer, he reviewed what he knew of Parker Sr. He had heard that he had the reputation of being a womanizer, and wondered as he looked at the attractive young woman ahead of him if Parker was fool enough to try anything in his own home.

He just might be that damned foolish, Sloane decided a few minutes later. He found Mr. Parker sitting on a leather couch, sipping coffee; there was another cup beside his, half filled.

Parker neither got up to greet him nor did he offer him coffee. "Sit down, Detective Sloane." It was not so much an invitation as an order.

Sloane knew that the next thing he would hear was that Parker was very busy, so this couldn't take more than a few minutes.

He heard exactly that.

Noticing that the maid was still in the room, Sloane turned to her. "You can come back as soon as I leave, miss," he said crisply.

Richard Parker jumped up, his expression one of indignation. "Who do you think—"

Sloane interrupted him. "I think, Mr. Parker, that you should know from the outset that I'm not one of your lackeys. This is not some real estate transaction, some big deal that you're running. I am here to talk to you about your son. He is well on the way to being considered a suspect in not one, but *two* murder cases."

He leaned forward and tapped the coffee table for emphasis. "Isabelle Waring did not believe that her daughter's death was an accident. Evidence points to the fact that Mrs. Waring died at the hands of a professional killer, one known to us, and known as well to have worked for a drug cartel. That, by the way, isn't general knowledge, yet, but I'm letting you in on it. You are certainly aware that your son was the one who cleared the way for the killer to get into Isabelle Waring's apartment. That alone makes him an accessory before the fact. A bench warrant on that charge is about to be issued for his arrest.

"But here's another piece of information you should know about your son, or perhaps you know it already. Rick was in Stowe the afternoon before Heather Landi died, and we have an eyewitness who can testify that she appeared to be frightened of him and ran out of the ski lodge when he showed up." Sloane stopped and looked at the man sitting tensely before him.

Red patches mottled Parker's face, revealing his agitation, but his voice was icy calm when he said, "Is that all, Detective?"

"Not quite. Your pride and joy, Richard J. Parker Jr., is a drug addict. You've apparently stopped paying his bills, but he's still getting the drugs somehow. Chances are, that means he owes someone a lot of money. That could be a very dangerous situation. My advice to you is to hire a criminal lawyer for him and tell him to surrender to us. Otherwise you might face charges yourself."

"I don't know where he is." Parker spat out the words.

Sloane stood up. "I think you do. I warn you. He's potentially in great danger. He wouldn't be the first person who got in over his head, and who paid the price by disappearing. Permanently."

"My son is in a drug rehabilitation clinic in Hartford," Priscilla Parker said.

Detective Sloane turned, startled by the unexpected voice.

Priscilla Parker was standing in the doorway. "I drove him there last Wednesday," she said. "My husband is being honest when he says he doesn't know where his son is. Rick came to me for help. His father was otherwise occupied that day." Her eyes rested on the second coffee cup, then she looked at her husband, contempt and loathing written clearly on her face.

45

AFTER SHE HAD GIVEN THE MANAGER AT THE EDINA Health Club the completed registration forms and her check, Lacey went directly to the squash court and began hitting balls against the wall. She quickly realized that the combination of the previous sleepless night and an earlier long jog had left her exhausted. She kept missing easy returns, and then she fell, badly wrenching her ankle, all in an attempt to connect with a ball she had no chance of hitting. It was typical of her life right now.

Disgusted with herself and close to tears, she limped off the court and collected her coat and tote bag from the locker.

The door to the manager's office was partially open. Inside, a young couple was sitting at the manager's desk, and a gray-haired man was waiting to speak to her.

Lacey could feel her ankle swelling already. For a moment she paused in front of the open door, debating whether to ask the manager if the club kept elastic bandages in its medical supply kit. Then she decided to go straight home and put ice on her ankle instead.

As much as she had wanted to get out of her apartment this morning, Lacey realized that all she wanted now was to be back inside, with the door locked and bolted.

Earlier that morning, when Lacey had gone out jogging, a smattering of clouds dotted the sky. Now they were filling it, moving so close together as to be seamless. Driving from Edina to Minneapolis, Lacey could tell that a heavy snowfall was imminent.

She had a designated parking spot behind her apartment building. She pulled into the space and turned off the engine. She sat for a moment in the silence. Her life was a total mess. Here she was, hundreds of miles away from her family, living an existence that could not be called a life, alone and lonely. She was trapped in a lie, having to pretend to be someone other than herself—and why? Why? Just because she had been a witness to a crime. Sometimes she wished the killer had seen her there in the closet. She had no desire to die, but it would have been easier than living this way, she thought desperately. I've got to do something about this.

She opened the door and got out of the car, careful to favor her throbbing right ankle. As she turned to lock the door, she felt a hand on her shoulder.

It was the same emotion she experienced in the nightmare, life moving in slow motion as she tried to scream, but no sound would come. She lunged forward, trying to break away, then gasped and stumbled as a flash of pain like the sting of a hot branding iron seared her ankle.

An arm went around her, steadying her. A familiar voice said contritely, "Alice, I'm sorry! I didn't mean to frighten you. Forgive me."

It was Tom Lynch.

Limp with relief, Lacey sagged against him. "Oh Tom

... Oh God ... I ... I'm all right, I just ... I guess you startled me."

She started to cry. It was so good to feel herself firmly encircled and protected by his arm. She stood there for several moments, not moving, feeling a sense of relief wash over her. Then she straightened and turned to face him. She couldn't do this—not to him, not to herself. "I'm sorry you bothered to come, Tom. I'm going upstairs," she said, making herself breathe normally, wiping away the tears.

"I'm coming with you," he told her. "We have to talk."

"We have nothing to talk about."

"Oh but we do," he said. "Starting with the fact that your father is looking all over Minneapolis for you because your mother is dying and wants to make up with you."

"What ... are ... you ... talking ... about?" Lacey's lips felt rubbery. Her throat constricted to the point where she could barely force the words out of her mouth.

"I'm talking about the fact that Ruth Wilcox told me yesterday afternoon some guy had showed up at the gym with your picture, looking for you and claiming to be your father."

He's in Minneapolis! Lacey thought. *He's going to find me!*

"Alice, look at me! Is it *true?* Was that your father looking for you?"

She shook her head, desperate now to be free of him. "Tom, please. Go away."

"I will *not* go away." He cupped her face in his hands, forcing her to look up at him.

Once again, Jack Farrell's voice echoed in Lacey's mind: *You put my face in front of the one you want,* he said. *Admit it.*

I admit it, she thought, looking up at the firm line of Tom's jaw, the way his forehead was creased with concern for her—the expression in his eyes.

The look you give someone special. Well, I won't let anything happen to you because of it, she promised.

If Isabelle Waring's murderer had been able to coax my address out of Ruth Wilcox at Twin Cities Gym, I probably wouldn't be alive right now, she thought. So far, so good. But where else was he showing her picture?

"Alice, I know you're in trouble, and no matter what it is, I'll stand by you. But I can't be in the dark anymore," Tom's voice urged. "Can't you understand that?"

She looked at him. It was such a strange sensation, seeing this man in front of her who clearly had special feelings for her—love? Maybe. And he was exactly the person she had hoped to meet someday. But not now! Not here! Not in this situation. *I cannot do this to him,* she thought.

A car drove into the parking area. Lacey's instinct was to pull Tom down, to hide with him behind her car. I have to get away, she thought. And I have to get Tom away from me.

As the approaching car came into full view she saw that the driver was a woman whom she recognized as living in the building.

But who would be driving the next car to come into the parking lot? she wondered angrily. It could be him.

The first flakes of snow were beginning to fall.

"Tom, please go," she begged. "I have to call home and talk to my mother."

"Then that story is true."

She nodded, careful not to look at him. "I have to talk to her. I have to straighten some things out. Can I phone you later?" Finally she looked up.

His eyes, troubled and questioning, lingered on her face.

"Alice, you will call me?"

"I swear I will."

"If I can help you, you know—"

"Not now, you can't," she said, interrupting him.

"Will you honestly tell me just one thing?"

"Of course."

"Is there another man in your life?"

She looked into his eyes. "No, there is not."

He nodded. "That's all I need to know."

Another car was driving into the parking area. *Get away from me,* her mind screamed. "Tom, I have to call home."

"At least let me walk you to the door," he responded, taking her arm. After they had gone a few steps, he stopped. "You're limping."

"It's nothing. I stumbled over my own feet." Lacey prayed her face wasn't showing the pain she felt when she walked.

Tom opened the door to the lobby for her. "When will I hear from you?"

"In an hour or so." She looked at him again, forcing a smile.

His lips touched her cheek. "I'm worried about you. I'm worried *for* you." He clasped her hands and looked intently into her eyes. "But I'll be waiting for your call. You've given me some great news. And a whole new hope."

Lacey waited in the lobby until she saw his dark blue BMW drive away. Then she rushed to the elevator.

She did not wait to take off her coat before she called the health club. The gratingly cheerful voice of the manager answered. "Edina Health Club. Hold on, please."

A minute, then a second minute went by. Damn her, Lacey thought, slamming her hand down to break the connection.

It was Saturday. There was a chance her mother was home. For the first time in months Lacey dialed the familiar number directly.

Her mother picked up on the first ring.

Lacey knew she could not waste time. "Mom, who did you tell I was here?"

"Lacey? I didn't tell a soul. Why?" Her mother's voice went up in alarm.

Didn't *deliberately* tell a soul, Lacey thought. "Mom, that dinner last night. Who all was there?"

"Alex and Kit and Jay and Jimmy Landi and his partner, Steve Abbott, and I. Why?"

"Did you say *anything* about me?"

"Nothing significant. Only that you'd joined a new health club with a squash court. That was all right, wasn't it?"

My God, Lacey thought.

"Lacey, Mr. Landi wants very much to talk to you. He asked me to find out if you knew whether the last few pages of his daughter's journal were written on unlined paper."

"Why does he want to know that? I gave him a complete copy."

"Because he said that if they were, somebody stole those pages from the copy while it was at the police station, and they stole the *whole* original copy. Lacey, are you telling me that whoever tried to kill you knows you're in Minneapolis?"

"Mom, I can't talk. I'll call you later."

Lacey hung up. Once again she tried the health club. She did not give the manager a chance to put her on hold this time. "This is Alice Carroll," she interrupted. "Don't—"

"Oh, Alice." The manager's voice became solicitous. "Your dad came in looking for you. I took him to the squash court. I thought you were still there. I didn't see you leave. Someone told us you gave your ankle a nasty wrench. Your dad was so worried. I gave him your address. That was all right, wasn't it? He left just a couple of minutes ago."

* * *

Lacey stopped only long enough to jam the copy of Heather Landi's journal into her tote bag before she half ran, half hopped to the car and headed for the airport. A sharp wind slapped snow against the windshield. Hopefully he won't figure out right away that I've left, she told herself. I'll have a little time.

There was a plane leaving for Chicago twelve minutes after she reached the ticket counter. She managed to get on it just before the gates closed.

Then she sat in the plane for three hours on the runway, while they waited for clearance to take off.

46

Sandy Savarano sat in his rental car, the street map of the city unfolded in front of him, the thrill of the chase warming him.

He could feel his pulse quicken. He would have her taken care of soon.

He had found 520 Hennepin Avenue on the map. It was just ten minutes from the Radisson Plaza, where he had been staying. He took the car out of PARK and stepped on the accelerator.

He shook his head, still irritated that he had come so close to catching her at the health club. If she hadn't fallen on the squash court, she would still have been inside while he was there, cornered, an easy target.

He felt adrenaline pumping through his body, accelerating his heartbeat, quickening his breath. He was close. This was the part he liked most.

The attendant said he had noticed that Farrell was limping when she left the club. If she had hurt herself badly enough to limp, chances were she went directly home.

Alice Carroll was the name she had taken—he knew that now. Shouldn't be too difficult to find out the number of her apartment—probably would be on her mailbox in the lobby.

Last time she had slammed the door before he could get to her, he reminded himself grimly. This time she wouldn't get the chance.

The snow was getting heavier. Savarano frowned. He didn't want to have to deal with any weather problems. His suitcase was open in the hotel room. When he finished with Farrell, he planned to pack and be checked out in ten minutes. A guest who didn't check out and left his luggage behind invited questions. But if the airport closed down and the roads got bad, he would be trapped, which was of concern only if anything went wrong.

Nothing *would* go wrong, he told himself.

He glanced at the street sign. He was on Hennepin Avenue in the 400 block.

The other end of Hennepin was near Nicollet Mall with all its fancy stores. The hotels and new office building were there too. This end wasn't much of a neighborhood, he noted.

He found 520. It was a nondescript corner building, seven stories high, not large, which was better for him. Savarano was sure the building would have little in the way of security.

He drove around the side and through the parking lot. It had numbered spaces for residents, with only a few off to the side marked for visitors. They were all occupied. Since he had no intention of drawing notice by taking a resident's spot, he drove back out, parked across the street, and walked to the building entrance. The door to the small vestibule was unlocked. The names and apartment numbers of the residents were on the wall above the mailboxes. Alice Carroll was in apartment 4F. Typical of such buildings, in order to gain admittance to the lobby, it was necessary to either have a key or to use the intercom to get a resident to buzz down and release the lock.

Savarano waited impatiently until he saw someone coming up the walk, an elderly woman. As she opened the outer door, he dropped a key ring on the floor and bent down to retrieve it.

When the woman unlocked the door that opened to the lobby, he straightened up and held it for her, then followed her in.

She gave him a grateful smile. He followed her to the elevator, then waited until she had pushed the button for the seventh floor before he pushed four. A necessary precaution, the kind of attention to detail that made Sandy Savarano so good—and so successful. He didn't want to find himself getting off the elevator with Farrell's next-door neighbor. The less he was seen, the better.

Once on the fourth floor, he turned down the corridor, which was quiet and poorly lighted. All to the good, he thought. Four F was the last apartment on the left. Sandy's right hand was in his pocket, holding his pistol, as he rang the bell with his left hand. He had his story ready if Farrell wanted to know who was there before she opened the door. "Emergency Services, checking a gas leak," he would say. It always had worked for him.

There was no answer.

He rang the bell.

The lock was new, but he had never seen a lock he couldn't take apart. The necessary tools were in a kit he kept around his waist. It looked just like a money belt. It had always amused him that the night when he went to the Waring apartment, he had been able to let himself in with the key she had kept on a table in the foyer.

In less than four minutes of working with the lock on the door to 4F, he was inside, the lock securely back in place. He would wait for her here. It was better that way. Somehow he didn't think that she would stay out long. And wouldn't she be surprised!

Maybe she's gone to have her ankle x-rayed, he thought.

He flexed his fingers; they were encased in surgical gloves. He had been uncharacteristically careless that night he had been in Farrell's apartment in New York, and he had left a fingerprint on the door. That night he hadn't noticed that the index finger of the right glove had split. That was a mistake he wouldn't make a second time.

He had been told to search Farrell's apartment to be sure she hadn't made a copy of Heather Landi's journal for herself. He started toward the desk to begin the search.

Just then the phone rang. With swift, catlike steps he crossed the room to stand beside it, glad to see that the answering machine was turned on.

Farrell's voice on the tape was low and reserved. "You have reached 555-1247. Please leave a message," was all it said.

The caller was a man. His voice was urgent and authoritative. "Alice, this is George Svenson," he said. "We're on the way. Your mother just phoned the emergency number in New York to report you were in trouble. Stay inside. Bolt your door. Don't let anyone in until I get there."

Savarano froze. *They were on the way!* If he didn't get out of there immediately, he was the one who would be trapped. In seconds he was out of the apartment, down the corridor, and onto the fire stairs.

Safely back in his car, he had just joined the light traffic on Hennepin Avenue when police cars, lights flashing, roared past him.

That had been as near a miss as any he had ever had. For a few moments he drove aimlessly, forcing himself to calm down, to think carefully.

Where would Farrell go? he asked himself. Would she be hiding at a friend's place? Would she hole up in a motel somewhere?

Wherever she was, he figured she wasn't more than thirty minutes ahead of him.

He had to try to figure out how she would be thinking. What would *he* do if he were in the witness protection program and had been tracked down?

I wouldn't trust the marshals anymore, Sandy told himself. I wouldn't move to another city for them and wonder how long it would take to be found again.

Usually people who left the witness protection program voluntarily did so because they missed their families and friends. They usually went back home.

Farrell hadn't called the Feds out here when she realized she had been traced. No, she had called her mother.

That's where she was headed, he decided. She was on her way to the airport and New York. Sandy was sure of it.

He was going there too.

The woman had to be scared. She wouldn't trust the cops to protect her. She still had a New York apartment. Her mother and sister lived in New Jersey. She would be easy enough to find.

Others had evaded him for a while, but no one had ever really gotten away. In the end he always found his prey. The hunt was always fun, but the actual kill was the best.

H e went to the Northwest Airlines counter first. From the number of agents there, it was obviously the busiest carrier in Minneapolis. He was told that at present all flights were grounded by the snow. "Then maybe I'll be able to join my wife," he said. "She left about forty minutes ago. Her mother was in an accident in New York, and I imagine she took whatever flight she could get. The name is Alice Carroll."

The ticket agent was warmly helpful. "No direct flight to

the New York airports left in the last hour, Mr. Carroll. She might have made a connection through Chicago, though. Let's check the computer."

Her fingers tapped the keys. "Here we are. Your wife is on Flight 62 to Chicago, which departed at 11:48." She sighed. "Actually, it only pulled away from the gate. Her plane is sitting right out there on the runway. I'm afraid I can't put you on it, but would you want to meet her in Chicago? There's a plane boarding right now. Chances are, they'll end up arriving only minutes apart."

47

Detective Ed Sloane and Priscilla Parker sat together as they waited for her son, Rick, to appear. The Harding Manor sitting room was exceptionally comfortable. The estate was a private home that had been donated as a rehabilitation center by a couple whose only son died of a drug overdose.

The cheerful blue-and-white-chintz sofa and matching chairs, complemented by the Wedgwood blue walls and carpet, were clear evidence to Sloane that these were the original furnishings and that those who could afford to pay to come here to kick their habits were being charged a fortune.

On the drive from Greenwich, however, Mrs. Parker had told him that at least half the clients paid nothing.

Now, as they waited for Rick Parker, she nervously explained, "I know what you must think of my son. But you don't realize how much goodness and promise there is in him. Rick could still do so much with his life. I *know* he could. His father has always spoiled him, taught him to think of himself as above any discipline, or even any sense of decency. When he got into trouble over drugs in prep school, I *pleaded* with my husband to make him face the consequences. But instead he bought people off. Rick ought to have done well in college. He's smart, but he just never took time to apply himself. Tell me what seventeen-year-old kid needs a Mercedes convertible? What kid that age needs unlimited spending money? What young man learns about a sense of decency when his father puts a maid's uniform on his mistress of the month and brings her into his own home?"

Sloane looked at the Italian-marble fireplace, admiring the delicate carving. "It seems to me that you have put up with a lot for a long time, Mrs. Parker. More than you should have, maybe."

"I didn't have much choice. If I had left, I would have lost Rick altogether. By staying, I think I accomplished something. The fact that he's here and willing to talk to you bears me out."

"Why did your husband change his mind about Rick?" Sloane asked. "We know that about five years ago he cut off his income from his trust fund. What brought that on?"

"Let Rick tell you," Priscilla Parker replied. She tilted her head, listening. "That's his voice. He's coming. Mr. Sloane, he's in a lot of trouble, isn't he?"

"Not if he's innocent, Mrs. Parker. And not if he cooperates. . . . It's up to him."

Sloane repeated those words to Rick Parker as he waited for him to sign a Miranda warning. The younger Parker's appearance shocked him. In the ten days or so since he had last seen him, Rick's appearance had changed dramatically. His face was thin and pale, and there were dark circles under his eyes. Kicking a drug habit isn't fun, Sloane reminded himself, but I suspect there's more to the change than the rehabilitation program.

Parker handed him the signed release. "All right, Detective," he said. "What do you want to know?" He was seated next to his mother on the sofa. Sloane watched as her hand reached for and covered his.

"Why did you send Curtis Caldwell—and I'll call him that since it's the name he was using—to Isabelle Waring's apartment?"

Beads of perspiration appeared on Parker's forehead as he spoke. "At our agency . . . " He stopped and looked at his mother. "Or as I should say, at my father's agency, there's a policy of not showing an apartment unless we check out potential buyers. Even then you still get window-shoppers, but at least they'll be qualified."

"Meaning they can afford to buy a place you show them?"

Rick Parker nodded. "You know the reason I'm here. I have a drug habit. In fact I've got an *expensive* habit. And I simply haven't been able to cover it. I've been buying more and more on credit. In early October I got a call from my dealer, the one I owe the money to, saying that he knew someone who wanted to see the apartment. He also said he knew this guy might not meet our standards, but if he liked it, things could be straightened out."

"Were you threatened in case you didn't go along with that?" Sloane asked.

Parker rubbed his forehead. "Look, all I can tell you is I *knew* what I had to do. It was clear to me that I wasn't being asked for a favor; I was being told what to do. So I made up a story. In the office, we'd just finished selling several co-ops to some lawyers the firm of Keller, Roland, and Smythe had transferred to Manhattan, so I made up the name Curtis Caldwell and said he was from that firm. No one questioned it. That's all I did," he burst out. *"Nothing more.* I figured the guy could be a little shady, but I had no idea he was that bad. When Lacey Farrell told me that guy was the one who killed Heather's mother, I didn't know what to do."

Sloane noted immediately the familiar way in which Rick Parker referred to Heather Landi.

"Okay. Now, what had been going on between you and Heather Landi?"

Sloane saw Priscilla Parker squeeze her son's hand. "You've got to tell him, Rick," she said softly.

Parker looked directly at Ed Sloane. The misery in his eyes seemed genuine to the detective. "I met Heather nearly five years ago, when she came to our office looking for a West Side apartment," he said. "I started taking her around. She was . . . she was beautiful, she was vivacious, she was fun."

"You knew Jimmy Landi was her father?" Sloane asked, interrupting him.

"Yes, and that was part of what made me enjoy the situation so much. Jimmy had barred me from going into his place one night because I was drunk. It made me angry. I wasn't used to being denied anything. So when Heather wanted to get out of her contract for a co-op on West Seventy-seventh Street, I saw my chance to have some fun, at least indirectly, at Jimmy Landi's expense."

"She signed a contract?"

"An airtight one. Then she came back to me in a panic. She found out her father had already bought her a place on East Seventieth. She begged me to tear up the contract."

"What happened?"

Rick paused and looked down at his hands. "I told her I would tear it up, if I could take it out in trade."

You bastard, Sloane thought, she was a kid, new to New York, and you pulled that.

"You see," Rick Parker said, and now it seemed to Sloane that he was almost talking to himself, "I didn't have the brains to realize what I really felt for Heather. I had been able to crook my finger, and any number of girls would come running. Heather had ignored my attempts to seduce her. So in the deal we made over the co-op contract, I saw a chance to get what I wanted and to even the score with her father. But the night she came to my apartment, she was clearly terrified, so I decided to back off. She really was a sweet kid, the kind I could actually fall in love with. In fact, maybe I *did.* I do know that I found *myself* suddenly very uncomfortable having her there. I teased her a little bit, and she started crying. So then I just told her to grow up, and to leave, that I was too old for babies. I guess I succeeded in humiliating her enough to scare her away from me for good. I tried to call her, to see her after that, but she wouldn't have any part of it."

Rick got up and walked to the fireplace as if he needed the warmth of the flames there. "That night, after she had been to my apartment, I went out drinking. When I left a bar on Tenth Street in the Village, I was suddenly hustled into a car. Two guys worked me over good. They said if I didn't tear up that contract and stay away from Heather, I wouldn't live to see my next birthday. I had three broken ribs."

"Did you tear up the contract?"

"Oh, *yes,* Mr. Sloane, I had torn it up. But not before my father got wind of it and forced me to tell him what had happened. Our main office had sold the East Side apartment to Jimmy Landi, for Heather, but that deal was peanuts compared to another deal that I found out was in the works. At that same time, my father was brokering the sale of the Atlantic City property to him. If Landi had found out what I pulled on Heather, it could have cost my father millions. That's when Daddy told me to make all this go away, or get out. Don't forget, for my father, if there's a business deal involved, it doesn't matter that I'm his son. If I interfere, I will be punished."

"We have an eyewitness who claims that Heather ran from the après-ski lounge in Stowe the afternoon before she died because she saw you there," Sloane told him.

"I never saw her that day," Rick Parker said, shaking his head. He seemed sincere. "The few times I had run into her, that was the reaction I got: She couldn't get away from me fast enough. Unfortunately nothing would have changed that."

"Heather obviously confided in someone, who ordered you roughed up. Was it her father?"

"Never!" Rick almost laughed. "And tell him she had signed that contract! Are you kidding? She wouldn't have dared."

"Then who?"

Rick Parker exchanged glances with his mother. "It's all right, Rick," she said, patting his hand.

"My father has been a regular at Landi's for thirty years," Rick said. "He always made a fuss over Heather. I think Dad was the one who set the goons on me."

48

WHEN HER PLANE FINALLY TOOK OFF AT 3:00 P.M., LACEY did not join in the spontaneous cheering and applause that erupted from the other passengers. Instead she leaned back and closed her eyes, sensing that the choke collar of terror she had felt tightening around her neck was easing. She was in a middle seat, trapped between an elderly man who had napped—and snored—for most of the wait, and a restless young executive–type who spent the time working on his laptop computer, but had tried several times to start a conversation with her.

For three hours she had been terrified that the flight would be canceled, that the plane would taxi from the runway back to the gate, that she would find Curtis Caldwell waiting for her.

Finally they were in the air. For the next hour or so—at least until they reached Chicago—she was safe.

She was still wearing the same sweat suit and sneakers she had worn to the Edina Health Club earlier that morning.

She had loosened the sneaker on her right foot as much as she could, but had not taken it off for fear she would not be able to get it back on again. Her ankle was now swollen to twice its normal size, and the throbbing pains from her injury were shooting up as far as her knee.

Forget it, she told herself. You can't let it stop you. You're lucky you're alive to *feel* pain. You've got to *plan*.

In Chicago she would get on the first available flight to New York. *But what do I do when I get there?* she asked herself. *Where do I go? Certainly not to my apartment. And I could never go to Mom's place or Kit's house—I would only be putting them in danger.*

Then where?

She already had put one full-fare coach flight on her Alice Carroll credit card. Now she would have to book a second full-fare flight to New York. Her card had a three-thousand-dollar limit, and there might not be enough left to cover a hotel room in Manhattan. Besides, she was sure that when the U.S. Attorney's office became aware she was missing, a trace would be put on that card. If she registered in a hotel, Gary Baldwin would have his agents there before midmorning. And then she would be trapped again. He had the power to hold her as a material witness in flight.

No, she had to find a place to stay, one where she wouldn't be putting anyone in danger, and where no one would think to look for her.

As the plane flew over the snow-covered Midwest, Lacey considered her options. She could call Gary Baldwin and agree to go back into the witness protection program. The marshals would whisk her away again, she would stay in a safe house for a few weeks before being sent to another unfamiliar city, where she would emerge as a newly created entity.

No way, she vowed silently. *I'd rather be dead.*

Lacey thought back to the chain of circumstances that

had led her to this point. If only she had never received the call from Isabelle Waring, leading to the exclusive listing on Heather Landi's apartment. If only she had picked up the phone and talked to Isabelle when she had called the night before she was murdered.

If I had talked to Isabelle that night, she might have given me a name, Lacey thought. She might have told me what she'd discovered in Heather's journal. Man . . . that was her last word. What man? But I'm getting closer to whoever is behind all this. That's obvious. One of two things had happened. Either Mom somehow gave me away, or someone is getting inside information from the police about me. Svenson may have had to get an okay from New York for me to get another fifteen hundred dollars to register at the Edina Health Club. If there was a leak in the U.S. Attorney's office, that information might have been passed on. That scenario seemed unlikely, though. There were many people in the program; surely those who were in charge were carefully selected and closely monitored.

What about her mother? Mom had dinner last night at Alex Carbine's restaurant, Lacey thought. I like Alex a lot. He was especially wonderful the night Bonnie was injured. But what do we really know about him? The first time I met him, when he came to dinner at Jay and Kit's, he told us that he'd met Heather.

Jay may have known Heather too, a voice whispered to her. *He denied it. But for some reason when her name came up he was upset and tried to change the subject.*

Don't even think that Kit's husband might be involved in this, Lacey told herself. Jay may have his quirks, but he's basically a very good and solid person.

What about Jimmy Landi? No, it couldn't be him. She had seen the grief in his eyes when he took the copy of Heather's journal from her.

What about the cops? Heather's handwritten journal disappeared after I gave it to them, Lacey thought. Now Jimmy Landi wants to know if there were entries written on unlined paper at the end of the journal. I remember those three pages. They had spatters of blood on them. If the copies of those three pages disappeared while they were in police custody, then there had to be something important on them.

Her copy of the journal was in her tote bag, pushed under the seat in front of her. Lacey was tempted to take it out and look at it but decided to wait until she could study the unlined pages undisturbed. The guy on her right, with the computer, seemed to her the kind who would comment on them, and she had no intention of talking to anyone about all this. Not even complete strangers. *Especially* not complete strangers!

"We are beginning our descent . . ."

Chicago, she thought. Then New York. *Home!*

The flight attendant finished the speech about seats upright in a locked position and buckling up, then added, "Northwest apologizes for the weather-related delay you encountered. You may be interested to learn that the visibility lowered immediately after we took off. We were the last plane to leave the airport until flights were resumed only a few minutes ago."

Then I'm at least an hour or so ahead of anyone who may be following me, Lacey told herself.

Whatever comfort that thought provided, however, was driven away by another possibility. If someone was following her and thought she was planning to go to New York, wouldn't it be smart for him to have taken a direct flight and be waiting for her there?

49

EVERY NERVE IN TOM LYNCH'S BODY HAD SHOUTED AT HIM not to leave Alice alone. He drove five miles in the direction of his apartment in St. Paul before he made a fast U-turn and headed back. He would make it clear to her that he had no intention of getting in her way while she spoke to her mother and whatever other family members might be involved in their rift. But, he reasoned, surely she could have no objection to his waiting in the lobby of her building, or even in his car, until she was ready for him to come up. Clearly she's in trouble, and I want to be there for her, he thought.

Having made the decision to go back, Tom became wildly impatient with the overly cautious drivers who, because of the blowing snow, were moving at a snail's pace.

His first indication of trouble came at the sight of police cars parked to the front and side of Alice's building, their lights flashing. A cop was there directing traffic, firmly prodding rubbernecking drivers to keep moving.

A sickening sense of inevitability warned Tom that the police presence had to do with Alice. He managed to find a parking spot a block away from her building and jogged back. A policeman stopped him at the entrance to the building.

"I'm going up," he told the cop. "My girlfriend lives here, and I want to see if she's all right."

"Who's your girlfriend?"

"Alice Carroll, in 4F."

The change in the police officer's attitude confirmed Tom's suspicion that something had happened to Alice. "Come with me. I'll take you upstairs," the officer told him.

In the elevator, Tom forced himself to ask the question he dreaded to put in words. "Is she all right?"

"Why don't you wait till you talk to the guy in charge, sir?"

The door to Alice's apartment was open. Inside he saw three uniformed cops taking instructions from an older man whom he recognized as the one who had driven Alice home the other evening.

Tom interrupted him. "What's happened to Alice?" he demanded. "Where is she?"

He could see from the surprise on the other man's face that he had been recognized, but there was no time wasted in greeting him. "How do you know Alice, Mr. Lynch?" George Svenson asked.

"Look," Tom said, "I'm not going to answer your questions until you answer mine. Where is Alice? Why are you here? Who are you?"

Svenson responded succinctly. "I'm a deputy federal marshal. We don't know where Ms. Carroll is. We do know that she had been getting threats."

"Then that guy at the gym yesterday who claimed to be her father was a phony," Tom said heatedly. "I thought so, but when I told Alice about him she didn't say anything except that she had to go and call her mother."

"*What* guy?" Svenson demanded. "Tell me everything you know about him, Mr. Lynch. It may save Alice Carroll's life."

When Tom finally got home, it was after four-thirty. The flashing light on the answering machine indicated he had received four messages. As he had expected, none of them was from Alice.

Not bothering to take off his jacket, he sat at the table by the phone, his head in his hands. All Svenson had told him was that Ms. Carroll had been receiving threatening phone calls and had contacted his office. She had apparently had a bad fright this morning, which was why they were there. "She may have gone out to visit a friend," Svenson told him, his tone unconvincing.

Or she may have been abducted, Tom thought. A child could see that they were avoiding telling him what was *really* going on. The police were trying to find Ruth Wilcox from Twin Cities Gym, but she was off duty over the weekend. They said they hoped to get a fuller description of the man claiming to be Alice's father.

Tom had told Svenson that Alice had promised to call. "If you hear from her, tell her to call me—immediately," Svenson ordered sternly.

In his mind, Tom could see Alice, quiet and lovely, standing at the window of the banker's home in Wayzata only a week ago. *Why didn't you trust me?* he raged at that image. *You couldn't wait to get rid of me this morning!*

There was one possible lead that the police had shared with him. A neighbor reported that she thought she had seen Alice getting in her car around eleven o'clock. I only left her at quarter of eleven, Tom thought. If that neighbor was right, then she left only ten minutes after I did.

Where would she go? he wondered.

Who was she, really? he asked himself.

Tom stared at the old-fashioned black rotary-dial phone. *Call* me, Alice, he half demanded, half prayed. But as the hours ticked by, as the morning light made its dim appearance, and the snow continued its steady fall, the phone did not ring.

50

Lacey arrived in Chicago at four-thirty. From there she took a five-fifteen plane to Boston. Once again she used her credit card, but she planned to pay cash for the Delta shuttle from Boston to New York. That plane landed at Marine Terminal, a mile from the main terminals at La Guardia Airport. She was sure anyone who followed her to New York wouldn't look for her there, and by not using her credit card for the shuttle, she might lead Baldwin's office to think she had stayed in the Boston area.

Before she boarded the plane from Chicago she bought a copy of *The New York Times*. Midway through the flight she glanced through the first section of the paper. Realizing that she was absorbing nothing of what she was reading, she began to fold the remaining sections. Suddenly she gasped. Rick Parker's face was looking up at her from the first page of Section B.

She read and reread the account, trying to make sense of it. It was an update on an earlier story about Rick. Last seen on Wednesday afternoon, when he brought a prospective buyer to see the apartment of the late Isabelle Waring, Richard J. Parker Jr., police now confirmed, was a suspect in Waring's death.

Was he in hiding? Lacey wondered. Was he dead? Had the information she passed on to Gary Baldwin Tuesday night played a part in this? She remembered that when she had told him about Rick being in Stowe hours before Heather Landi's death, Baldwin had offered no reaction. And now the police were naming Rick as a suspect in Isabelle's murder. There *must* be a connection, she decided.

It was only as the plane was landing in Boston that Lacey realized she had finally figured out the one place she could stay in New York where no one would ever think of looking for her.

It was 8:05 local time when she got off the plane at Logan Airport. With a silent prayer that he would be home, Lacey made a phone call to Tim Powers, the superintendent of Isabelle Waring's building.

Four years ago, when she was leaving 3 East Seventieth after showing an apartment, Lacey had been instrumental in preventing what surely would have been a terrible accident, and one for which Tim Powers would have been blamed. It had all happened so quickly. A child broke free from his nanny and raced into the street, thanks to the fact that Tim had left the building's front door open while he worked on it. Lacey's quick action had kept the child from being hit by a passing delivery truck.

Tim, trembling from the shock of the near disaster, had vowed, "Lacey, it would have been my fault. If you ever need *anything*—anything at all—you can count on me."

I need it now, Tim, she thought as she waited for him to answer.

Tim was astonished to hear from her. "Lacey Farrell," he said. "I thought you'd disappeared off the face of the earth."

That's almost exactly what I've done, Lacey thought.
"Tim," she said, "I need help. You once promised—"
He interrupted her. "Anything, Lacey."
"I need a place to stay," she said, her voice barely above
a whisper. She was the only one at the bank of phones. Even
so she looked around, fearful of being overheard.
"Tim," she said hurriedly, "I'm being followed. I think
it's the man who killed Isabelle Waring. I don't want to put
you in danger, but I can't go to either my apartment or my
family. He'd never look for me in your building. I want to
stay, at least for tonight, in Isabelle Waring's apartment.
And please, Tim—this is *very* important—don't tell anyone
about this. Pretend we never spoke."

51

THE DAY CLEARLY WAS NOT OVER FOR DETECTIVE ED Sloane. After leaving Rick Parker at the rehabilitation center in Hartford, he rode with Priscilla Parker to her Greenwich estate, where he picked up his own car.

On the drive to Manhattan, he phoned the precinct to check in. Nick Mars was there. "Baldwin's been calling for you, practically every few minutes," he told Sloane. "He wants to see you ASAP. He couldn't reach you on your car phone."

"No," said Sloane, "I'm sure he couldn't." Wonder what he would say if he knew I'd been riding around in a chauffeured limousine, he thought. "What does he want now?"

"All hell is breaking loose," Mars told him. "Lacey Farrell almost got nailed in Minneapolis, where the Feds had her stashed. She's disappeared, and Baldwin thinks she's headed for New York. He wants to coordinate with us to find her before she gets nailed here. He wants to take her into custody as a material witness." Then he added, "How did you make out, Ed? Any luck finding Parker?"

"I found him," Sloane said. "Call Baldwin and arrange a meeting. I'll join you at his office. I could be there by seven."

"Better than that. He's in midtown. He'll talk to us here at the precinct."

When Detective Sloane arrived at the 19th Precinct, he stopped at his desk and took off his jacket. Then, with Nick Mars in tow, he went in to see U.S. Attorney Gary Baldwin, who was waiting in the interrogation room.

Baldwin was still angry that Lacey Farrell had disappeared but took time from his anger to congratulate Sloane on finding Rick Parker. "What did he tell you?" he asked.

Glancing only once or twice at his notes, Sloane gave a full report.

"Do you believe him?" Baldwin asked.

"Yeah, I think he's telling the truth," Sloane said. "I know the guy who sells Parker drugs. If he was the one who told Parker to set up that appointment that got Savarano into Isabelle Waring's apartment, it was nothing he actually planned himself. He was just a messenger. Somebody passed the word to him."

"Meaning we won't get the big boys through Parker," Baldwin said.

"Exactly. Parker's a jerk, but he's not a criminal."

"Do you believe that his father ordered him roughed up when he tried to hit on Heather Landi?"

"I think it's possible," Sloane said. "If Heather Landi went to Parker Sr. to complain about Rick, it's even *probable*. On the other hand, that doesn't seem likely, because I'm not sure she would trust Parker Sr. I think she'd be afraid he might say something to her father."

"All right. We'll pick up Rick Parker's supplier and lean on him, but I suspect you're right. Chances are he's only a link, not a player. And we'll make damn sure that Rick Parker doesn't set foot outside that rehabilitation center without one of us alongside him. Now to Lacey Farrell."

Sloane reached for a cigarette, then frowned. "They're in my jacket. Nick, would you?"

"Sure, Ed."

The round trip took Mars about a minute. He plunked the half-empty cigarette pack and a grimy ashtray on the table in front of Sloane.

"Has it ever occurred to you to give up smoking?" Baldwin asked, eyeing both cigarettes and ashtray with disdain.

"Many times," Sloane responded. "What's the latest on Farrell?"

As soon as Baldwin opened his mouth it was obvious to Ed Sloane that he was furious with Lacey. "Her mother admits she knew Farrell was in Minneapolis, but she swears she didn't tell anyone. Although I don't believe *that* for a minute."

"Maybe there was a leak somewhere else," Sloane suggested.

"There was no leak from my office or from the federal marshal's office," Baldwin said, his tone icy. "We maintain security. Unlike this precinct," he added.

I let myself in for that one, Sloane acknowledged silently. "What's your game plan, sir?" he asked. It gave him a fleeting sense of satisfaction to know that Baldwin would not be sure if his addressing him as "sir" was meant as sarcasm or a sign of respect.

"We've flagged the credit card we gave Farrell. We know she used it to fly to Chicago, then to Boston. She's got to be on her way to New York.

"We have a tap on the phone in her apartment, not that I think she'd be stupid enough to go there," Baldwin continued. "We've got that building under surveillance. We have taps on her mother's phone, her sister's phone, and Monday there'll be taps on the phones in her brother-in-law's office. We've got a tail assigned to each family member, in case they try to meet her somewhere."

Baldwin paused and looked at Sloane appraisingly. "It also occurred to me that Lacey Farrell just might try to call you directly," he said. "What do you think?"

"I seriously doubt it. I didn't exactly treat her with kid gloves."

"She doesn't deserve kid gloves," Baldwin said flatly. "She concealed evidence in a murder case. She gave away her location when we had her protected. And now she's putting herself in an extremely risky position. We've invested a hell of a lot of time and money in keeping Ms. Farrell alive, and we've gotten nothing much back for it except complaints and lack of cooperation on her part. Even if she doesn't have any common sense, you'd think she'd at least be grateful!"

"I'm sure she's eternally grateful," Sloane said as he got up. "I'm also sure that even if you *hadn't* spent all that time and money, she'd probably like to stay alive."

52

As they had agreed, Lacey called Tim Powers from the Marine Terminal. "I'm getting in a cab," she told him. "Traffic should be light, so at this hour, I should be there in twenty minutes, a half hour at the most. Be watching for me, please, Tim. It is very important that nobody else sees me come in."

"I'll give the doorman a coffee break," Tim promised, "and I'll have the key ready to hand you."

It feels so strange to be back in New York, Lacey thought, as the cab sped over the Triborough Bridge into Manhattan. When the plane had made its final approach before landing, she had pressed her face against the window, drinking in the New York skyline, realizing how much she had missed it.

If only I could just go home to my own apartment, she thought. I'd fill the Jacuzzi, send out for something to eat, phone my mother and Kit. And Tom.

What was Tom thinking? she wondered.

As she had hoped, the traffic was light, and in minutes

they were headed south on the FDR Drive. Lacey felt her body growing tense. Let Tim *be* there, she thought. I don't want Patrick to see me. But then she realized that in all likelihood Patrick wouldn't be around. When she had last seen the doorman, it was his plan to retire on January 1st.

The driver got off the FDR Drive at Seventy-third Street and headed west to Fifth Avenue. He turned left on Fifth, then left again on Seventieth and stopped. Tim Powers was standing outside the building, waiting for her. He opened the door and greeted her with a smile and a pleasant, "Good evening, miss," but he showed no sign of recognition. Lacey paid the driver and hobbled out of the cab, thankful that finally she would be able to stop moving around. It was just in time, because she could no longer deny the pain of her wrenched ankle.

Tim opened the door to the lobby for her, then slipped her the key to the Waring apartment. He assisted her to the elevator, put his master key in the control, and pushed 10.

"I fixed it so you'll go straight up," he said. "That way there'll be no risk of running into anyone who knows you."

"And I certainly don't want to, Tim. I can't tell you how much—"

He interrupted her. "Lacey, get upstairs fast and lock the door. There's food in the fridge."

Her first impression was that the apartment had been kept in pristine order. Then Lacey's eyes went to the closet in the foyer where she had hidden the night Isabelle Waring died. She had the feeling that if she opened the door, she would see her briefcase still sitting there, with the blood-stained pages from the journal stuffed inside.

She double-locked the door, and then remembered that Curtis Caldwell had stolen the key Isabelle kept on the foyer table. Had the lock been changed? she wondered. She even fastened the safety chain, although she knew how ineffective a safety chain was when someone really wanted to get in.

Tim had drawn all the drapes and turned on lights for her, a potential mistake, she thought, if the draperies weren't usually kept closed. Someone watching the apartment, either from Fifth Avenue or Seventieth Street, might realize someone was there.

On the other hand, if the drapes *have* been kept closed, it would be sending a signal to open them. Oh God, she thought, there's no sure way to be safe.

The framed pictures of Heather that had been scattered through the living room were still there. In fact everything seemed to be much as Isabelle had left it. Lacey shivered. She almost expected to see Isabelle walk down the stairs.

She realized that she had not yet taken off her down jacket. The casualness of the jacket and her sweats was so far removed from the way she had dressed the other times she had been in this apartment that they added to her feeling of displacement. As she unfastened the jacket, Lacey shivered again. She suddenly felt as if she were an intruder, moving in with ghosts.

Sooner or later she had to force herself to walk upstairs and to look in the bedroom. She didn't want to go near it, but she knew that she had to see it just to be rid of the feeling that Isabelle's body was still there.

There was a leather sofa in the library that converted into a bed, and adjacent to the library was the powder room. Those were the rooms she would use. There was no way that she could ever sleep in the bed in which Isabelle had been shot.

Tim had said something about there being food in the fridge. As Lacey hung her jacket in the foyer closet, she remembered hiding there and watching as Caldwell rushed past.

Get something to eat, she told herself. You're hungry, and the irritation from that is just making everything else worse.

Tim had done a good job of putting together a meal for her. There was a small roast chicken, salad greens, rolls, and a wedge of cheddar cheese and some fruit. A half-empty jar of instant coffee was sitting on a shelf. She remembered that she and Isabelle had shared coffee from that same jar.

"Upstairs," Lacey said aloud. "Get it out of the way." She half hopped her way to the staircase, then held on to the wrought-iron railing for support as she climbed the steps to the bedroom suite.

She went through the sitting room to the bedroom and looked in. The draperies were drawn here as well, and the room was dark. She turned on the light.

The place looked exactly the same as it had the last time she had stood there with Curtis Caldwell. She could still picture him as he looked around, his expression thoughtful. She had waited in silence, believing he was debating about whether or not to make an offer on the apartment.

What he had been doing, she now realized, was making sure there was no way Isabelle could escape him when he attacked her.

Where was Caldwell now? she wondered suddenly, a feeling of panic and resignation washing over her. Had he followed her to New York?

Lacey looked at the bed and visualized Isabelle's bloodied hand, trying to pull the journal pages from under the pillow. She could almost hear the echo of Isabelle's dying plea:

Lacey . . . give Heather's . . . journal . . . to her father . . . Only to him . . . Swear . . .

With sickening clarity, Lacey remembered the gasps and harsh choking breaths between each painfully uttered word.

You . . . read it . . . show him where . . . Then Isabelle had made one last effort to breathe and speak. She'd died as she exhaled, whispering, *man . . .*

Lacey turned and hobbled through the sitting room and eased her way down the stairs. Get something to eat, take a shower, go to bed, she told herself. Get over your jumpiness. Like it or not, you know you've got to stay here. There's no place else to go.

Forty minutes later she was sitting wrapped in blankets on the couch in the library. The copy she had made of Heather Landi's journal was lying on the desk, the three unlined pages spread out side by side. In the dim light from the foyer, the bloodstains that had smeared Heather's handwriting on the original pages resembled a Rorschach test blot. What does this mean to you? it seemed to ask.

What do you see in it? Lacey asked herself. As exhausted as she was, she knew she was not going to fall asleep anytime soon. She turned on the light and reached for the three unlined pages. They were the hardest to read because of the bloodstains.

A thought came to her. Was it possible that Isabelle had been making a special effort to touch these particular pages in her last moments of life?

Once again Lacey began to read these pages, searching for some clue as to why they were so important that someone had stolen the only other copies that existed. She had no doubt that these were the pages that Caldwell had found it worth killing for, but *why?* What was the hidden secret in them?

It was on these pages that Heather had written about being caught between a rock and a hard place, about not knowing what to do.

The last entry that seemed upbeat was the one at the top of the first unlined page, where Heather wrote that she was going to have lunch with Mr. or Max or Mac Hufner, it was impossible to tell. She had added, "It should be fun. He says he's grown old and I've grown up."

It sounds like she was going to meet an old friend, Lacey

thought. I wonder if the police have talked to him to see if Heather dropped any hint to him? Or did she have their reunion lunch *before* things went so drastically wrong for her?

The original journal had been stolen from the police. Had they made a list of the people mentioned in it before it was taken? Lacey wondered.

She looked around the room, then shook her head. If only I had someone I could talk to about this, she thought, someone to bounce ideas off of. But, of course, there is not, she told herself. You are completely alone, so just get on with it.

She looked at the pages again. Neither Jimmy Landi nor the police have these three pages now, she reminded herself. Mine is the only copy.

Is there any way I can find out who this man is? Lacey wondered. I could look in the phone book, she thought, make some calls. Or maybe I could simply phone Jimmy Landi himself.

Again she paused. She knew she had to get to work on trying to solve the mystery hidden in those pages. If anyone was going to unravel the secret, clearly it would have to be her. But could she do it in time to save her own life?

53

WHEN FLIGHTS FROM THE MINNEAPOLIS AIRPORT WERE RE-
sumed, Sandy Savarano took the first available direct flight
to New York. He reasoned that Lacey Farrell must have
grabbed the first plane she could get on, which was the only
reason she had gone to Chicago. He was sure that from there
she would connect to New York. Where else would she go?

While he waited for his flight, he got a list of scheduled
departures of major airlines from Chicago to New York. His
bet was that Lacey Farrell would stick with Northwest. It
would make sense that when she deplaned she would go
directly to the nearest Northwest agent and make inquiries.

Even though his instinct told him she would be on that
airline, Sandy managed to cover most of the areas through
which passengers deplaning from Chicago would have to
pass.

Finding and gunning down Lacey Farrell had become
more than a mere job for him. At this point, it was consum-
ing him. The stakes had become higher than he wanted to

play for. He liked his new life in Costa Rica; he liked his new face; his young wife intrigued him. The money he was being paid to get rid of Lacey Farrell was impressive but not necessary to his lifestyle.

What *was* necessary to him was not having to live with the knowledge that he had botched his final job—that, and eliminating someone who could send him to prison for life.

After checking all the New York flights for a stretch of five hours, Sandy decided to call it quits. He was afraid that he would only draw attention to himself if he hung around any longer. He took a cab to the brownstone apartment on West Tenth Street that had been rented for him. He would wait there for further information on Lacey Farrell.

He did not have the slightest doubt that by midafternoon tomorrow he would once again be closing in on his quarry.

54

JIMMY LANDI HAD INTENDED TO GO TO ATLANTIC CITY FOR
the weekend to see for himself that everything was in
readiness for the opening of the casino. It was an exciting
time for him, and he found it difficult to stay away. There
were millions to be made, plus there was the genuine thrill
of glad-handing the movers and shakers, the excitement,
and the noise of the slot machines ringing as a hundred
bucks' worth of quarters gushed out from them, making the
players feel like big-time winners.

Jimmy knew that real gamblers were contemptuous of
people who played the one-armed bandits. He was not. He
was only contemptuous of people who played with other
people's money. Like people who gambled away salaries
that were supposed to pay the mortgage or keep a kid in
college.

But the people who could afford to gamble—let them
spend as much as they wanted in his place. That was the
way he saw it. His boast was quoted and requoted in articles

about the new casino: "I'll give you better rooms, better service, better food, better entertainment than you'll find anywhere else, whether in Atlantic City, Vegas, or even Monaco." The opening weeks were booked solid. He knew that some people were coming just to pounce on anything they could find not to like, to complain about anything they could. Well, they would change their tune. He had vowed that.

He felt it was always important for a person to have a challenge, but it was never more important to him than now, Jimmy acknowledged. Steve Abbott was taking care of the day-to-day routine of running the operation, which freed him for the big picture. Jimmy didn't want to know who printed the menus or ironed the napkins. He wanted to know what they cost and how they looked.

But he didn't seem to be able to keep his mind on the casino, no matter how hard he tried. The problem was that since he had gotten back the copy of Heather's journal last Monday, he had become obsessed with it and was spending too much time reading and rereading it. It was like a gateway to memories he wasn't sure he wanted to revisit. To him, the crazy thing about it was that Heather only started the journal when she moved to New York to try for a show business career, but throughout it she referred to times in the past when she had done something with either him or her mother. It was like an ongoing diary and a memory book.

One thing in the journal that had bothered him was a suggestion that Heather had been afraid of him. What did she think she had to be afraid of? Oh sure, he had bitten her head off a couple of times, just like he always had with anyone who stepped out of line, but surely that wasn't enough for her to be *afraid* of him. He hated to think that.

What had happened five years ago that she was so anxious to keep from him? he wondered. He couldn't help dwelling on that part of her journal. The thought that somebody had pulled something on Heather and gotten away with it was driving him crazy. Even after all this time, he still needed to get to the bottom of it.

The question of those unlined pages from the journal was also gnawing at him. He could *swear* he had seen them. Admittedly he had only glanced at the journal the night Lacey Farrell brought it over, and the next night when he had actually tried to read it, he had gotten drunk for the first time in years. Still, he retained a hazy impression of seeing them.

The cops claimed they never got any unlined pages. Maybe they didn't, he told himself, but assuming that I'm not wrong, and that the pages were there originally, then chances are they wouldn't have disappeared unless someone thought they were important. There was only one person who might be able to tell me the truth, he thought: Lacey Farrell. When she made the copy of the journal for me, surely she would have noticed if some of the last pages were different from the others.

There were stains on them—he vaguely recalled that. Jimmy decided to go ahead and call Lacey Farrell's mother and again ask her to pass on to Lacey the question he needed to have answered: *Did those pages exist?*

55

LACEY GLANCED AT THE CLOCK WHEN SHE WOKE UP. SHE must have been asleep for about three hours. When she opened her eyes, she felt as she always had when she was in the dentist's chair and under light sedation. She experienced a sensation of something hurting, although now it was her ankle rather than her teeth. She also felt out of it, but not so much so that she was unaware of what was going on. She could remember hearing faint street sounds, an ambulance, a police car or fire engine.

They were the familiar Manhattan sounds that always had elicited mixed emotions from her—she felt concerned for the injured but was aware of a sense of being protected. *Someone is out there ready to come if I need help,* she had always told herself.

I don't feel that way now, she thought as she pushed back the blankets and sat up. Detective Sloane had been furious because she had taken Heather's diary; U.S. Attorney Baldwin must have gone ballistic when he learned that she had told her mother where she was staying and then had run away.

In fact, he had threatened to take her into custody and hold her as a material witness if she didn't abide by the rules of the witness protection program, and she was sure that was exactly what he *would* do—*if* he were able to locate her. She stood up, automatically putting most of her weight on her left foot, biting her lip at the throbbing discomfort of the swollen right ankle.

She put her hands on the desk to steady herself. The three unlined pages still lay there, commanding her immediate attention. Once again she read the first line of the first page. "Lunch with Mr."—or was it Max or Mac?—"Hufner. It should be fun. He says he's grown old and I've grown up."

That sounds like Heather was referring to someone she had known for a long time, Lacey thought. Who could I ask? There was only one obvious answer: Heather's father.

He's the key to all this, Lacey decided.

She had to get dressed, get something to eat. She also had to remove any trace of her presence here. It was Sunday. Tim Powers said that he would warn her if a real estate agent intended to bring a potential buyer to see the apartment, but still she worried that someone might show up unannounced. She looked around, making a mental inventory. The food in the refrigerator would be a dead giveaway that the apartment was being used. So would the damp towel and washcloth.

She decided that a quick shower now would help to wake her up. She wanted to get dressed, to get out of the nightshirt that had belonged to Heather Landi. But what do I wear? she asked herself, hating the fact that she was once again going to have to find something in Heather's clothes closet.

Shortly after she had arrived there she had showered, then she had wrapped the big bath towel around her and made herself go upstairs again, to find something to sleep in. She had felt ghoulish opening the doors of the walk-in closet off the bedroom. Even though she only wanted to grab something to wear to bed, she couldn't help but notice that there were two different styles of clothes on the hangers. Isabelle had dressed conservatively, in flawless taste. It was easy to tell which were her suits and dresses. The rest of the rack and open shelves contained a collection of mini and long skirts, funky shirts, grandmother dresses, cocktail dresses that probably didn't consist of more than a yard of material, baggy oversized sweaters, and at least a dozen pairs of jeans, all of it obviously Heather's.

Lacey had grabbed an oversized nightshirt with red-and-white stripes that must have belonged to Heather.

If I go out, I can't wear my sweat suit and jacket, she thought. *I was wearing them yesterday. I might be too easy to spot.*

She fixed herself coffee and a toasted roll, and then showered. The underwear she had rinsed out earlier was dry, but her heavy socks were still wet. Once again she had to go through the personal belongings of two dead women in order to get dressed.

At eight o'clock, Tim Powers called on the apartment intercom. "I didn't want to use the telephone in the apartment," he said. "Better that the kids and even Carrie don't know that you're here. Can I come up?"

They had coffee together in the library. "How can I help you, Lacey?" Tim asked.

"Obviously, you already have," she replied with an appreciative smile. "Is Parker and Parker still handling the sale of the apartment?"

"As far as I know. You've heard that Junior is missing?"

"I read that. Has anyone else from their office brought somebody in to look at the place?"

"No, and Jimmy Landi phoned the other day and asked about that. He's getting pretty disgusted with Parker. Wants the apartment sold, and soon. I told him straight that I thought it would have a better chance if we cleared everything out."

"Do you have his personal number, Tim?"

"His personal office number, I guess. I was out when he called and had to call him back. He picked up the phone himself."

"Tim, give me that number, please."

"Sure. You know this phone is still on. They never bothered to disconnect it. I spoke to Parker a couple of times when I saw the bill come in, but I think he liked having it in case he wanted to make a call. He came in and out of here on his own sometimes."

"Which means he might still do it," she said. She knew it would cost Tim his job if she were discovered using this place, so she couldn't risk staying much longer. Still, there was one other thing she had to ask him to do. "Tim, I've got to get word to my mother that I'm all right. I'm sure her phone is tapped so they can trace any call I might make to her. Would you go to a public phone and call her? Don't identify yourself, and don't stay on for more than a few seconds, or they'll be able to trace the call, although even if they do, at least it won't be coming from here. Just tell her I'm fine and safe and will call her as soon as I can."

"Sure," Tim Powers said as he stood. He glanced at the pages on the desk, then looked startled. "Is that a copy of Heather Landi's journal?"

Lacey stared at him. "Yes it is. How do you know that, Tim?"

"The day before Mrs. Waring died, I was up here changing the filters in the radiators. You know how we change them around October 1st, when we go from air-conditioning to heat. She was reading the journal. I guess she'd just found it that day, because she was very emotional and clearly upset, especially when she read the last couple of pages."

Lacey had the feeling that she might be on the brink of

learning something important. "Did she talk to you about it, Tim?" she asked.

"Not really. She got right on the phone, but whoever she tried to call has an unlisted number."

"You don't know who it was?"

"No, but I think I saw her circle the name with her pen when she came across it. I remember it was right near the end. Lacey, I've gotta get going. Give me your mother's phone number. I'll call on the intercom and give you Landi's."

When Tim left, Lacey went back to the desk, picked up the first of the unlined pages, and brought it to the window. Blotched as the page was, she could detect a faint line around the name Hufner.

Who *was* he? How could she find out?

Talk to Jimmy Landi, she decided. That was the only way.

On the intercom from the lobby, Tim Powers gave Landi's phone number to Lacey, then went out for a walk, looking for a public phone. He had a supply of quarters with him.

Five blocks away, on Madison Avenue, he found a phone that worked.

Twenty-seven miles away in Wyckoff, New Jersey, Mona Farrell jumped at the sound of the telephone. *Let it be Lacey,* she prayed.

A hearty, reassuring man's voice said, "Mrs. Farrell, I'm calling for Lacey. She can't talk to you but she wants you to know that she's okay and will get in touch with you herself as soon as she can."

"Where is she?" Mona demanded. "Why can't she talk to me herself?"

Tim knew that he should break the connection, but Lacey's mother sounded so distraught he couldn't just hang up on her. Helplessly, he let her pour out her anxiety as he kept interjecting, "She's okay, Mrs. Farrell, trust me, she's okay."

Lacey had warned him not to stay on the phone too long. Regretfully, he replaced the receiver, Mona Farrell's voice. still pleading for him to tell her more. He started home, deciding to walk back on Fifth Avenue. That decision made him unaware of the unmarked police car that raced to the phone booth he had just used. Nor did he know that the phone was immediately dusted for his fingerprints.

Every hour that I'm here doing nothing means that I'm an hour closer to being tracked down by Caldwell or taken into custody by Baldwin, Lacey thought. It was like being caught in a spider's web.

If only she could talk to Kit. Kit had a good head on her shoulders. Lacey walked over to the window and pulled the curtains back just enough to peer into the street.

Central Park was crowded with joggers, in-line skaters, people strolling, or pushing carriages.

Of course, she thought. It was Sunday. Almost ten o'clock on Sunday morning. Kit and Jay would be in church now. They always went to the ten-o'clock Mass.

They always went to the ten-o'clock Mass.

"I *can* talk to her!" Lacey said aloud. Kit and Jay had been parishioners at St. Elizabeth's for years. Everyone knew them. Her spirits suddenly buoyed, she dialed New Jersey Information and received the number of the rectory.

Somebody be there, she prayed, but then she heard an answering machine click on. The only thing she could do was to leave a message and hope that Kit would get it before they left the church. Leaving her phone number, even at a rectory, would be too great a risk.

She spoke clearly and slowly. "It is urgent that I speak with Kit Taylor. I believe she is at the ten-o'clock Mass. I'll call this number again at eleven-fifteen. Please try to locate her."

Lacey hung up, feeling helpless and trapped. There was another hour to kill.

She dialed the number for Jimmy Landi she'd gotten from Tim. There was no answer, and when the machine picked up, she decided not to leave a message.

What Lacey did not know was that she already had left a message. Jimmy Landi's Caller ID showed the phone number from which a call to him had been placed, as well as the name and address of the person to whom the phone was registered.

The message on the ID indicated that his caller had dialed from 555-8093, a number registered to Heather Landi, at 3 East Seventieth Street.

56

DETECTIVE SLOANE HAD NOT PLANNED TO GO TO WORK ON Sunday. He was off duty, and his wife, Betty, wanted the garage cleaned. But when the desk sergeant at the precinct phoned to say that a friend of Lacey Farrell's had called her mother from a pay phone on Seventy-fourth and Madison, nothing could have kept him home.

When he reached the precinct, the sergeant nodded toward the captain's office. "The boss wants to talk to you," he said.

Captain Frank Deleo's cheeks were flushed, usually a warning sign that something or someone had incurred his wrath. Today, however, Sloane saw immediately that Deleo's eyes were troubled and sad.

He knew what that combination meant. The sting had worked. They had pinned down the identity of the rogue cop.

"The guys in the lab sent over the tape late last night," Deleo told him. "You're not going to like it."

Who? Ed wondered, as faces of longtime fellow officers became a picture gallery in his mind. Tony . . . Leo . . . Adam . . . Jack . . . Jim W. . . . Jim M. . . .

He looked at the TV screen. Deleo pressed the POWER button, then PLAY.

Ed Sloane leaned forward. He was looking at his own desk with its scarred and cluttered surface. His jacket was on the back of the chair where he had left it, the keys deliberately left dangling from the pocket, in an effort to tempt the thief who was removing evidence from his cubby.

On the upper left section of the screen he could see the back of his own head as he sat in the interrogation room. "This was filmed last night!" he exclaimed.

"I know it was. Watch what happens now."

Sloane stared intently at the screen as Nick Mars scurried out of the interrogation room and looked around. There were only two other detectives in the squad room. One was on the phone with his back to Nick, the other was dozing.

As they watched, Mars reached into Sloane's coat pocket and slid out his key ring, cupping it in his palm to conceal it. He turned toward the cabinet containing the locked private cubbies, then spun swiftly around, quickly replacing the keys. He then pulled a pack of cigarettes out of the breast pocket of Sloane's jacket.

"This is where I made my untimely entrance," Deleo said dryly. "He went back to interrogation."

Ed Sloane was numb. "His father's a cop; his grandfather was a cop; he's been given every break. Why?"

"Why *any* bad cop?" Deleo asked. "Ed, this has to remain between you and me for now. That piece of film alone isn't enough to convict him. He's your partner. He could argue convincingly that he was just checking your pocket because you were getting careless and he was wor-

Ma

ried that you'd be blamed if anything else disappeared. With those baby-blue eyes of his, he'd probably be believed."

"We have to do something. I don't want to have to sit across the table from him and work a case together," Sloane said flatly.

"Oh yes you do. Baldwin's on his way here again. He thinks Lacey Farrell is in the neighborhood. There's nothing I'd like better than for us to be able to crack this case and rub Baldwin's face in it. Your job, as you well know, is to be damn sure Nick doesn't get the chance to lift or destroy any more evidence."

"If you promise me ten minutes alone with the jerk once we nail him."

The captain stood up. "Come on, Ed. Baldwin will be here any minute."

I t's a day for show-and-tell, Ed Sloane thought bitterly as an assistant U.S. Attorney prepared to replay the conversation they had taped between Lacey Farrell's mother and her unknown caller.

When the recording began to play, Sloane's raised eyebrows were the only sign of the shock he was experiencing. He knew that voice from the countless times he had been in and out of 3 East Seventieth. It was Tim Powers, the superintendent there. He was the caller.

And he's hiding Farrell in that building! Sloane thought.

The others sat silently, listening intently to the conversation. Baldwin had a cat-who-ate-the-canary expression. He thinks he's showing us what good police work is all about, Sloane thought angrily. Nick Mars was sitting with his hands folded in his lap, frowning—Dick Tracy incarnate, Sloane said to himself. Who would that rat tip off if he got wind that Powers was Lacey Farrell's guardian angel? he wondered.

Ed Sloane decided that for now, at least, only one person beside Tim Powers was going to know where Lacey Farrell was staying.

Himself.

57

TIM POWERS TAPPED ON THE APARTMENT DOOR AT TEN-
thirty, then let himself in with his master key. "Mission
accomplished," he told Lacey, with a smile, but she could
see that something was wrong.

"What is it, Tim?"

"I just got a call from a real estate agent with Douglaston
and Minor. Jimmy's listed the apartment with them, and the
agent told me he wants her to dispose of all the furniture
and personal items in it as soon as possible. She's coming
at eleven-thirty with someone to look the place over."

"That's only an *hour* from now!"

"Lacey, I hate to—"

"You can't keep me here. We both know that. Get a box
and clean out the refrigerator. I'll put the towels I used in a
pillowcase, and you take them to your place. Should the
draperies be open or closed?"

"Open."

"I'll take care of it. Tim, how did my mother sound?"

"Pretty shook up. I tried to tell her you're okay."

Lacey experienced the same sinking feeling she had had when she revealed to her mother that she was living in Minneapolis. "You didn't stay on the phone too long?" she asked.

Despite his reassurances, she was sure that by now the police were scouring this neighborhood, searching for her.

After Tim left, carrying the telltale evidence that the apartment had been used, Lacey stacked the pages of Heather's journal together and put them in her tote bag. She would make one more attempt to reach Kit at St. Elizabeth's rectory, but then she had to get out of there. She looked at her watch. She had just enough time to try Jimmy Landi's number once more.

This time he answered on the fourth ring. Lacey knew she could not waste time. "Mr. Landi, this is Lacey Farrell. I'm so glad I reached you. I tried a little while ago."

"I was downstairs," Jimmy said.

"I know there's a lot to explain, Mr. Landi, but I don't have time, so just let me talk. I know why you wanted to talk to me. The answer is yes, there were three unlined pages at the end of Heather's journal. Those pages were filled with her worries about hurting you. Heather referred repeatedly to being trapped 'between a rock and a hard place.' The only happy reference was right at the beginning, where she wrote about having lunch with some man who sounds like he must have been an old friend. Heather wrote that he said something to her about her growing up and his growing old."

"What's his name?" Jimmy demanded.

"It looks like Mac or Max Hufner."

"I don't know the guy. Maybe he's someone her mother knew. Isabelle's second husband was quite a bit older." He paused. "You're in a lot of trouble, aren't you, Miss Farrell?"

"Yes, I am."

"What are you going to do?"

"I don't know."

"Where are you now?"

"I can't tell you."

"And you are certain that there were unlined pages at the end of the journal? I was pretty sure I'd seen them in the copy you gave me, but I couldn't be absolutely positive."

"Yes, they were in that copy, I'm sure. I made a copy for myself as well, and those pages are in it. Mr. Landi, I'm convinced Isabelle was onto something and that's why she was killed. I'm sorry; I've got to go."

Jimmy Landi heard the click as Lacey hung up. He laid down the receiver as Steve Abbott came into his office. "What's up? Did they close down Atlantic City? You got back early."

"Just got back," Abbott said. "It was quiet down there. Who was that?"

"Lacey Farrell. I guess her mother got my message to her."

"Lacey Farrell! I thought she was in the witness protection plan."

"She was, but not anymore, I guess."

"Where is she now?"

Jimmy looked at his Caller ID. "She didn't say, and I guess I didn't have this on. Steve, did we ever have a guy with a name like Hufner work for us?"

Abbott considered for a moment, then shook his head. "I don't think so, Jimmy, unless it was a kitchen helper. You know how they come and go."

"Yeah, I know how they come and go." He glanced toward the open door that led to the small waiting room. Someone was pacing outside. "Who's that guy out there?" he asked.

"Carlos. He wants to come back. He says working for Alex is too quiet for him."

"Get that bum out of here. I don't like sneaks around me."

Jimmy stood up and walked to the window, his eyes focused on the distance, as if Abbott weren't there. "A rock and a hard place, huh? And you couldn't turn to your baba, could you?"

Abbott knew Jimmy was talking to himself.

58

AT TEN PAST ELEVEN, LACEY PHONED THE RECTORY OF ST. Elizabeth's in Wyckoff, New Jersey. This time the phone was answered on the first ring. "Father Edwards," a voice said.

"Good morning, Father," Lacey said. "I called earlier and left a message asking that Kit Taylor be—"

She was interrupted. "She's right here. Just a moment."

It had been two weeks since Lacey had spoken to Kit, going on five months since she had seen her. "Kit," she said, then stopped, her throat tight with emotion.

"Lacey, we miss you. We're so scared for you. Where are you?"

Lacey managed a tremulous laugh. "Trust me. It's better you don't know. But I *can* tell you that I have to be out of here in five minutes. Kit, is Jay with you?"

"Yes, of course."

"Put him on, please."

Jay's greeting was a firm pronouncement. "Lacey, this

278

can't go on. I'll hire an around-the-clock bodyguard for you, but you've got to stop running and let us help you."

Another time she probably would have thought Jay sounded testy, but this morning she could hear clearly the concern in his voice. It was the way Tom Lynch had spoken to her in the parking lot. Was that only yesterday? Lacey thought fleetingly. It seemed so long ago.

"Jay, I have to get out of here, and I can't call you at home. I'm sure your line is tapped. I just can't go on living like I have been. I won't stay in the witness protection program, and I know the U.S. Attorney wants to take me into custody and hold me as a material witness. I'm sure now that the key to this whole terrible mess is to find out who was responsible for Heather Landi's death. Like her mother, I'm convinced she was murdered, and the clues to who did it have got to be in her journal. Thank God I kept a copy, and I've been studying it. I've got to find out exactly what caused Heather Landi to be so troubled during the last few days of her life. The clues are there in the pages of the journal, if I can just figure them out. I think Isabelle Waring tried to find out what happened, and that's why she died."

"Lacey—"

"Let me finish, Jay. There's one name I think is important. About a week before she died, Heather had lunch with an older man whom she'd apparently known for a long time. My hope is that he was somehow connected to the restaurant business and that you may know him, or could ask around about him."

"What's his name?"

"It's so blurred that it's hard to make it out. It looks like Mr. or Mac or Max Hufner."

As she said the name "Hufner," she could hear the rectory door chimes ringing loudly.

"Did you hear me, Jay? Mr. or Mac or Max Huf—"

"Max Hoffman?" Jay asked. "Sure I knew him. He worked for Jimmy Landi for years."

"I didn't say Hoffman," Lacey said. "But oh, dear God, that's it . . ."

Isabelle's last words . . . "read it . . . show him . . ." then that long shuddering gasp, ". . . man."

Isabelle died trying to tell me his name, Lacey realized suddenly. She was trying to separate those pages from the others. She wanted Jimmy Landi to see them.

Then Lacey realized what Jay had just said, and it sent a sudden chill through her. "Jay, why did you say you *knew* him?"

"Lacey, Max died over a year ago in a hit-and-run accident near his home in Great Neck. I went to his funeral."

"How *much* over a year ago?" Lacey asked. "This could be very important."

"Well, let me think," Jay said. "It was just about the time I bid on the job at the Red Roof Inn in Southampton, so that would have made it about fourteen months ago. It was the first week in December."

"The first week in December—fourteen months ago! That's when Heather Landi was killed," Lacey exclaimed. "Two car accidents within days of each other . . ." Her voice trailed off.

"Lacey, do you think that—" Jay began.

The apartment intercom was buzzing, a series of soft quick jabs. Tim Powers was signaling her to get out. "Jay, I've got to leave. Stay there. I'll call you back. Just one thing, was Max Hoffman married?"

"For forty-five years."

"Jay, get her address for me. I *have* to have it."

Lacey grabbed her tote bag and the black hooded coat she had taken from Isabelle's closet. Hobbling, she left the apartment and went down the corridor to the elevator. The indicator showed that the elevator was at the ninth floor and ascending. She managed to reach the safety of the fire stairs just in time to avoid being seen.

Tim Powers met her inside the staircase at the lobby level. He pressed folded bills into her hand and dropped a cellular phone in her pocket. "It will take them a while to trace any calls you make on this."

"Tim, I can't thank you enough." Lacey's heart was pounding. The net was closing. She knew it.

"There's a cab waiting out in front with the door open," Tim said. "Keep that hood up." He squeezed her hand. "Six G is having one of their family brunches. There are a lot of people coming in at once. You may not be noticed. Get going."

The cabdriver was obviously annoyed at having to wait. The cab leaped forward into the traffic, slamming Lacey backward. "Where to, miss?" he demanded.

"Great Neck, Long Island," Lacey said.

59

"I HOPE MOM GETS HERE BEFORE LACEY CALLS BACK," KIT said nervously.

They were having coffee with the pastor in the rectory study. The phone was at Kit's elbow.

"She should only be ten minutes or so," Jay said reassuringly. "She was going to meet Alex in New York for brunch and was just ready to walk out the door."

"Mom is a basket case over all this," Kit explained to the priest. "She knows the U.S. Attorney's office blames her for the leak, which is ridiculous. She didn't even tell *me* where Lacey was living. She'd have a fit if we didn't give her a chance to talk to Lacey now."

"*If* she calls back," Jay cautioned. "She may not get the chance, Kit."

*   *   *

Had she been followed? Lacey wondered. She couldn't be sure. There was a black Toyota sedan that seemed to be maintaining a constant distance behind the cab.

Maybe not, she thought, breathing a slight sigh of relief. The car had turned off the expressway at the first exit after they came out of the Midtown Tunnel.

Tim had taped the unlock code to the back of the cellular phone he had lent her. Lacey knew Kit and Jay were waiting in the rectory for her call, but if she could get the information she needed another way, she would rather do it. She had to get the street address where Max Hoffman had lived, and where, please God, his wife still lived. She had to go there and talk to her and get from her anything she might know about her husband's conversation with Heather Landi.

Lacey decided first to try to get Mrs. Hoffman's address from the telephone information operator. She dialed and was asked what listing she required.

"Max Hoffman, Great Neck. I don't have his address."

There was a pause. "At the request of the customer, that number cannot be given out."

The traffic was fairly light, and Lacey realized that they were getting close to Little Neck. Great Neck was the next town. What would she do if they arrived there and she didn't have an address to give this driver? She knew he hadn't wanted to make the drive so far out of Manhattan in the first place. If she *did* get to where Mrs. Hoffman lived and the woman wasn't home or wouldn't open the door, what would she do then?

And what if she was being followed?

She called the rectory again. Kit answered immediately. "Mom just got here, Lacey. She's dying to talk to you."

"Kit, please . . ."

Her mother was on the phone. "Lacey, I didn't tell a soul where you live!"

She's so upset, Lacey thought. It's so hard for her, but I just can't talk to her about all this now.

Then mercifully her mother said, "Jay has to speak to you."

They were entering Great Neck. "What's the address?" the driver asked.

"Pull over for a minute," Lacey told him.

"Lady, I don't want to spend my Sunday out here."

Lacey felt her nerves tingle. A black Toyota sedan had slowed down and driven into a parking lot. She *was* being followed. She felt her body go clammy. Then she allowed herself a sigh of relief as she saw a young man with a child get out of that car.

"Lacey?" Jay was saying, his tone questioning.

"Jay, did you get the Hoffmans' street address in Great Neck for me?"

"Lacey, I haven't a clue where to get it. I'd have to go into the office and make phone calls to see if anyone knows. I did call Alex. He knew Max very well. He says he has the address in a Christmas-card file somewhere. He's looking for it."

For the first time in her horrible months-long ordeal, Lacey felt *total* despair. She had gotten *this* close to what she was sure was the information she needed, and now she was stuck. Then she heard Jay ask, "What can you do, Father? No, I don't know which funeral home."

Father Edwards took over. While Lacey talked again with her mother, the pastor called two funeral homes in Great Neck. Using only a slight ruse, he introduced himself and said that one of his parishioners wanted to send a Mass card for Mr. Max Hoffman who had died a year ago December.

The second funeral home acknowledged having made the arrangements for Mr. Hoffman. They willingly furnished Mrs. Hoffman's address to Father Edwards.

Jay passed it to Lacey. "I'll talk to all of you later," she said. "For God's sake, don't tell anyone where I'm going."

At least I *hope* I'll talk to you later, she thought as the cab pulled out from the curb on its way to a gas station for directions to 10 Adams Place.

60

It made Detective Ed Sloane's flesh crawl to be sitting next to Nick Mars, having to act as if everything were fine—"brothers all are we," as the hymn went, he thought bitterly.

Sloane knew he had to be on guard against sending out some hostile signals that Nick might pick up, but he promised himself that he would have his full say when everything was finally out in the open.

They began their vigil of watching the apartment building at 3 East Seventieth Street at about eleven-fifteen, immediately after the meeting with Baldwin broke up.

Nick, of course, didn't understand. As he parked halfway down the block, he complained, "Ed, we're wasting our time. You don't really think Lacey Farrell got her old job back selling co-ops here, do you?"

Very funny, Junior, Sloane thought. "Just call it an old dog's hunch, okay, Nick?" He hoped he sounded genial.

They were there only a few minutes when a woman in a

long hooded coat walked out of the building and got into a
waiting cab. Sloane couldn't see the woman's face. The coat
was one of those bulky wraparounds, with a lot of loose
material, so he also couldn't see her shape, but as he
watched her move he sensed something familiar about her
that raised the hairs on the back of his neck.

And she was favoring her right leg, he realized. The report from Minnesota mentioned that Farrell had apparently
injured her ankle at a gym yesterday.

"Let's go," Sloane told Mars. "She's in that cab."

"You're kidding! Are you psychic, Ed, or just holding
back on me?"

"Just a hunch. The phone call to her mother was made
five blocks from here. Maybe she picked up a boyfriend in
that building. She was there often enough."

"I'll call it in," Nick said.

"Not yet, you won't."

They followed the cab through the Midtown Tunnel onto
the L.I.E. It was one of Nick Mars's little witticisms that the
initials for the Long Island Expressway told it all: LIE. He
laughed as he repeated his observation.

Sloane wanted to tell Nick that those initials described
him perfectly. Instead he said, "Nick, you're the best tail in
the business."

It was true. Nick could manipulate a car in any kind of
traffic; he was never obvious, never too close, sometimes
passing and then getting in a slower lane and letting the
other guy pass him. It was a talent, and a terrific asset for a
good cop. And for a crook, Sloane thought grimly.

"Where do you think she's going?" Nick asked him.

"I don't know any more than you do," Sloane replied.
Then he decided to lay it on: "You know, I've always
thought that Lacey Farrell might have made a copy of
Heather Landi's journal for herself. If so, she may be the
only one with the complete journal, the whole thing. Maybe

there's something important in those three pages that Jimmy Landi says we're missing. What do you think, Nick?"

He saw Nick's eyes shift toward him suspiciously. Knock it off, Sloane warned himself. Don't make him nervous.

It was Nick's turn to respond. "I don't know any more than you do."

In Great Neck the cab pulled over to the curb. Was Farrell getting out? Sloane wondered. He got ready to follow her on foot, if necessary.

Instead she stayed in the cab. After a few minutes, it pulled out and two blocks later stopped at a gas station, where the cabby asked for directions.

They followed her through town, past some obviously expensive houses. "Which one do you want?" Nick asked.

Is that what you're about? Sloane wondered. A cop's salary not good enough for you? All you had to do was to get out, kid, he thought. You could have changed jobs. You didn't need to change sides.

Gradually the neighborhood they were driving through changed. The houses were much smaller, closer together, but well kept, the kind of neighborhood Ed Sloane felt comfortable in. "Take it easy," he cautioned Nick. "He's looking for a house number."

They were on Adams Place. The cab stopped in front of number 10. There was a parking spot across the street, about five car lengths down, behind an RV. Perfect, Sloane thought.

He watched as Lacey Farrell got out of the cab. She seemed to be pleading with the driver, reaching back through the window, offering money. He kept shaking his head. Then he rolled up the window and drove away.

Farrell watched the cab until it was out of sight. For the first time he could fully see her face. Sloane thought she looked young and vulnerable and very scared. She turned and limped up the walk. Then she rang the bell.

It didn't look as if the woman who had answered the door, opening it only a crack, was going to let her in. Lacey Farrell kept pointing to her ankle.

"My foot hurts. Please let me in, nice lady. Then I'll mug you," Nick simpered.

Sloane looked at his partner, wondering why he had ever found him amusing. It was time to call in a report. He found it very satisfying that he would be the one to bring Lacey Farrell in, even though it meant turning her over to Baldwin's custody.

He did not know that an amused and equally satisfied Sandy Savarano was watching him from a second-story bedroom in 10 Adams Place, where he had been patiently awaiting Lacey Farrell's arrival.

61

MONA FARRELL WENT BACK HOME WITH KIT AND JAY. "I can't go into New York and have brunch while I'm worrying like this," she said. "I'll call Alex and ask him to come out here."

Kit's two boys, Todd and Andy, had gone skiing at Hunter Mountain with friends for the day. A baby-sitter was minding Bonnie, who was starting with another cold.

Bonnie rushed to the door when she heard them arriving.

"She told me all about how she's going to Disney World for her birthday with her Aunt Lacey," the sitter said.

"My birthday is coming *very* soon," Bonnie said firmly. "It's next month."

"And I told her February is the shortest month of the year," the sitter said as she put on her coat and got ready to leave. "That *really* made her feel good."

"Come with me while I make a phone call," Mona said to Bonnie. "You can say hello to Uncle Alex."

She picked up her granddaughter and hugged her. "Did

you know that you look just like your Aunt Lacey did when she was *almost* five years old?"

"I like Uncle Alex very much," Bonnie said. "You like him too, don't you, Nana?"

"I don't know what I'd have done without him these past months," Mona said. "Come on, sweetheart, let's go upstairs."

Jay and Kit looked at each other. "You're thinking the same thing I am," Jay said after a moment of silence. "Mona admits that Alex encouraged her to make Lacey tell her where she was living. She may not have told him where Lacey actually was, but there are other ways to give it away. Like the way Mona announced at dinner the other night that Lacey had joined a new health club with a great squash court. Less than twelve hours later somebody followed Lacey from that health club, probably intending to kill her. It's hard to believe this was just coincidence."

"But Jay, it's also hard to believe that Alex would be involved with all this," Kit said.

"I hope he isn't, but I told him where Lacey was going, and now I'm calling the U.S. Attorney at the emergency number and telling him too. She may hate me for it, but I'd much rather see her held in custody as a material witness than dead."

62

"WHY DID YOU COME HERE?" LOTTIE HOFFMAN DE-manded, after reluctantly admitting Lacey into her home. "You can't stay here. I'll call another cab for you. Where do you want to go?"

Now that she was face to face with the one person who might be able to help her, Lacey felt as though she were bordering on hysteria. She still wasn't sure whether or not she had been followed. At this point it didn't matter. All Lacey was certain of was that she couldn't keep running.

"Mrs. Hoffman, I haven't *got* any place to go," she declared passionately. "Someone is trying to kill me, and I think he's been sent by the same person who ordered your husband, Isabelle Waring, and Heather Landi killed. It has to stop, and I think you're the one who can *make* it stop, Mrs. Hoffman. *Please help me!*"

Lottie Hoffman's eyes softened. She noticed Lacey's awkward stance, how she clearly favored one foot. "You're in pain. Come in. Sit down."

The living room was small but exquisitely neat. Lacey sat on the couch and slipped off the heavy coat. "This isn't mine," she said. "I can't go to my own home or reach into my own closet. I can't go near my family. My little niece was shot and almost killed because of me. I'm going to live like this for the rest of my life if whoever is behind all this isn't identified and arrested. Please, Mrs. Hoffman, tell me—did your husband know who was behind it?"

"I'm afraid. I can't talk about it." Lottie Hoffman kept her head down, her eyes on the floor, as she spoke in a near whisper. "If Max had kept his mouth shut, he'd still be alive. So would Heather. So would her mother." She finally raised her head and looked directly at Lacey. "Is the truth worth all those deaths? I don't think so."

"You wake up scared every morning, don't you?" Lacey asked. She reached over and took the elderly woman's thin, heavily veined hand. "Tell me what you know, please, Mrs. Hoffman. Who is behind all this?"

"The truth is I don't know. I don't even know his name. Max did. Max was the one who worked for Jimmy Landi. He was the one who knew Heather. If only I hadn't seen her that day at Mohonk. I told Max about it and described the man she was with. He got so upset. He said that the man was a drug dealer and a racketeer but that no one knew it, that everyone thought he was respectable, even a good guy. So Max made the lunch date with Heather to warn her— and two days later, he was dead."

Tears welled in Lottie Hoffman's eyes. "I miss Max so much, and I'm so scared."

"You're right to be," Lacey told her gently. "But keeping your door locked isn't the solution. Someday, whoever this person is, he'll decide that you're a potential threat too."

*　*　*

Sandy Savarano attached the silencer to his pistol. It had been child's play to get into this house. He could leave the same way he had come in—through the back window of this bedroom. The tree outside was like a staircase. His car was on the next street, directly accessible through the neighbor's yard. He would be miles away before the cops sitting outside even suspected something was wrong. He looked at his watch. It was time.

The old woman would be first. She was only a nuisance. What he wanted most was to see the expression in Lacey Farrell's eyes when he pointed the pistol at her. He wouldn't give her time to scream. No, there would be just long enough for her to make that whimpering little sound of recognition that was so thrilling to hear, as she realized that she was about to die.

Now.

Sandy put his right foot on the first step of the staircase, then with infinite caution, began his descent.

63

ALEX CARBINE CALLED LANDI'S RESTAURANT AND ASKED to speak to Jimmy. He waited, then heard Steve Abbott's voice. "Alex, is there anything I can do for you? I hate to bother Jimmy. He's feeling awfully down today."

"I'm sorry about that but I need to talk to him," Carbine said. "By the way, Steve, has Carlos come to you guys looking for a job?"

"As a matter of fact, he has. Why?"

"Because if he's still there you can tell him he doesn't have one here anymore. Now put me through to Jimmy."

Again he waited. When Jimmy Landi picked up his phone it was clear from his voice that he was under immense strain.

"Jimmy, I can tell something's wrong. Can I help?"

"No, but thanks."

"Well, look, I'm sorry to bother you, but I've figured out something and wanted to pass it on to you. I understand

Carlos is sniffing around for a job from you. Well, listen to me: don't take him back!"

"I don't intend to, but why not?" Jimmy responded.

"Because I think he's on the take somehow. It's been driving me nuts that Lacey Farrell was tracked down by this killer to where they had her hiding in Minneapolis."

"Oh, is that where she was?" Jimmy Landi remarked. "I hadn't heard."

"Yes, but only her mother knew it. She got Lacey to tell her. And since I was the one who told her to make Lacey tell her where she was living, I feel responsible."

"That wasn't too smart of you," Jimmy Landi said.

"I never pretended to be smart. All I could see was that Mona's guts were being torn out. Anyway, the night she learned that Lacey was in Minneapolis she bought a copy of the *Minneapolis Star Tribune* and had it with her at dinner. I saw her slip it back in the bag when I came to the table, but I never asked her about it, and I never saw it again. But here's what I'm getting at: I noticed that at one point, when Mona was off to the powder room and I was glad-handing a customer, Carlos was over at our table, supposedly straightening our napkins. I saw him move the bag, and it's entirely possible that he looked inside."

"It's just the sort of thing Carlos would do," Landi replied. "I never liked the guy in the first place."

"And then he was our waiter again on Friday night when Mona talked about Lacey joining a new health club. One with a squash court. It seems to me more than a coincidence that somebody showed up at that club looking for her a few hours later. You just have to put two and two together, right?"

"Hmmm," Jimmy murmured, "it sounds like maybe Carlos was working to earn more than a tip Friday night. I gotta go, Alex. Talk to you soon."

64

Ed Sloane could tell that something was spooking his partner. Even though it was cold in the car, Nick Mars was giving off an acrid odor of perspiration. Shiny droplets of sweat covered the forehead of his babyish face.

The instinct that had never failed him told Sloane that something was going terribly wrong. "I think it's time we go in and collect Ms. Farrell," he said.

"Why do that, Ed?" Mars asked, surprised. "We'll pick her up when she comes out."

Sloane opened the door of the car and drew his pistol. "Let's go."

Lacey wasn't sure if she actually heard a sound on the staircase. Old houses seem sometimes to have a life of their own. She was aware, however, that the atmosphere in the room had changed, like a thermometer suddenly plummeting. Lottie Hoffman felt it too; Lacey could see it in her eyes.

Later she realized that it was the presence of evil, creeping, insidious, enveloping her, so real it was almost tangible.

She had felt this same chill when she hid in the closet as Curtis Caldwell came down the stairs after killing Isabelle.

Then she heard it again. The faintest of sounds, but still very real. It wasn't her imagination! She knew that for certain now, and her heartbeat accelerated at the realization. There was someone on the staircase! I'm going to die, she thought.

She saw terror creep into Mrs. Hoffman's eyes, so she put a warning finger to her own lips, urging her to remain quiet. He was coming down the stairs so slowly, playing cat and mouse with them. Lacey looked around the room—there was only one door, and it opened just next to the stairs. There was no way out. They were trapped!

Her eyes fastened on a glass paperweight on the coffee table. It was about the size of a baseball, and it appeared to be heavy. She couldn't reach it without getting up, something she was afraid to risk. Instead, she touched Mrs. Hoffman's hand and pointed to the paperweight.

The staircase became exposed to Lacey's view halfway down. That's where he was now. Through the wooden spindles, she could see his one well-polished shoe.

A frail and trembling hand grasped the paperweight and slid it into Lacey's hand. Lacey stood up, swung her arm back, and, as the assassin she knew as Caldwell came into full view, threw the paperweight with all the strength she could muster, at his chest.

The heavy piece of glass struck him right above the stomach, just as he prepared to move quickly down the remaining steps. The impact caused him to stumble and drop the pistol. Lacey immediately lunged to try to kick it away from his reach, just as Mrs. Hoffman, with faltering steps, made her way to the front door and flung it open. She screamed.

Detective Sloane rushed past her into the entry hall. Just as Savarano's fingers were closing on the pistol, Sloane lifted his foot and smashed it down on Savarano's wrist. Behind him, Nick Mars aimed his pistol at Savarano's head and started to pull the trigger.

"Don't!" Lacey screamed.

Sloane whirled and slapped his partner's hand, causing the bullet intended for Savarano's head to go through his leg instead. He let out a howl of pain.

Dazed, Lacey watched as Sloane handcuffed Isabelle Waring's murderer, the sound of approaching sirens shrilling outside. Finally she looked down into the eyes that had haunted her these past few months. Ice blue irises, dead black pupils—the eyes of a killer. But suddenly she realized she was seeing something new in them.

Fear.

U.S. Attorney Gary Baldwin appeared suddenly, surrounded by his agents. He looked at Sloane, at Lacey, then at Savarano.

"So you beat us to him," he said, grudging respect evident in his voice. "I was hoping to beat you to him, but no matter—it's a job well done. Congratulations."

He leaned over Savarano. "Hi, Sandy," he said softly. "I've been looking for you. I'm preparing a cage that's got your name on it—the darkest, smallest cell at Marion, the roughest federal prison in the country. Locked down twenty-three hours a day. Solitary, of course. Chances are you won't like it, but you never know. Some people don't stay sane long enough in solitary for it even to matter. Anyway, you think about it, Sandy. A cage. Just for you. A tiny, little cage. All your own, for the rest of your life."

He straightened up and turned to Lacey. "You all right, Miss Farrell?"

She nodded.

"Someone isn't." Sloane went over to Nick Mars, whose

face was chalk white. He took his pistol, then opened his partner's jacket and took out his handcuffs. "Stealing evidence is bad enough. Attempted murder is a lot worse. You know what to do, Nick."

Nick put his hands behind his back and turned. Sloane snapped Nick's own cuffs on him. "Now they're really yours, Nick," he said with a grim smile.

65

JIMMY LANDI DID NOT EMERGE FROM HIS OFFICE ALL AFTER-
noon. Steve Abbott looked in on him several times. "Jimmy,
you okay?" he asked.

"Never better, Steve," he said shortly.

"You don't look it. I wish you'd stop reading Heather's
journal. It's just getting you down."

"I wish you'd stop telling me to stop reading it."

"*Touché*. I promise I won't bother you again, but remember this, Jimmy—I'm always here for you."

"Yes, you are, Steve. I know."

At five o'clock, Landi received a phone call from Detective Sloane. "Mr. Landi," he said, "I'm at headquarters. I
felt we owed it to you to fill you in. Your ex-wife's murderer
is in custody. Ms. Farrell has positively identified him. He's
also being charged with the death of Max Hoffman. And we
may be able to prove that he was the one who ran your
daughter's car off the road, too."

"Who is he?" Jimmy Landi had the fleeting thought that

he wasn't feeling anything—not surprise, not anger, not even grief.

"Sandy Savarano is his name. He's a paid hit man. We expect him to cooperate fully in the investigation. He doesn't want to go to prison."

"None of them do," Jimmy said. "Who hired him?"

"We expect to know that very soon. We're just waiting for Sandy to come to Jesus. Of much less magnitude, by the way, we have a suspect in the theft of your daughter's journal."

"Suspect?"

"Yes, in the legal sense, even though he admitted it. But he swears he didn't take the three unlined pages you thought we lost. I guess your partner was right. We never had them."

"You never had them," Jimmy agreed. "I realize that now. My partner seems to have a lot of the answers."

"Miss Farrell is here making a statement, sir. She'd like to talk to you."

"Put her on."

"Mr. Landi," Lacey said, "I'm awfully glad this is over. It's been an ordeal for me, and I know it's been terrible for you as well. Mrs. Max Hoffman is with me. She has something to tell you."

"Put her on."

"I saw Heather at Mohonk," Lottie Hoffman began. "She was with a man, and when I described him to Max, he was so upset. He said the guy was a racketeer, a drug dealer, and that no one suspected him, least of all Heather. She had no idea that . . ."

Even though she had heard it all before, it was chilling to Lacey to consider the appalling crimes committed after Max Hoffman warned Heather away from the man she was dating.

She listened as Mrs. Hoffman described the man she had seen that day. Clearly it was no one *she* knew, Lacey thought with relief.

Sloane took the phone from Mrs. Hoffman. "Does the man she described sound like anyone you know, sir?"

He listened for a moment, then turned to Lacey and Mrs. Hoffman. "Mr. Landi would be very appreciative if you'd stop by his office now."

All Lacey wanted to do was to get home to her own apartment, get in her own Jacuzzi, dress in her own clothes, and go to Kit's house to see everyone. They were having a late dinner, and Bonnie was staying up for it. "As long as it's just a few minutes there," she said.

"That's all," Sloane promised. "Then I'll drive Mrs. Hoffman home." Sloane was called to the phone as they were leaving the station house. When he returned, he said, "We're going to have company at Landi's. Baldwin is on his way."

The receptionist took them upstairs to where Jimmy was waiting. When Lottie Hoffman admired the handsome furnishings, Jimmy said, "The restaurant used to be half this size. When Heather was a baby this was her room."

Lacey thought that there was something in Landi's even, almost indifferent, tone that made her think of an unnaturally calm ocean—one in which an underwater current was threatening to turn into a tidal wave.

"Describe again exactly the man you saw with my daughter, please, Mrs. Hoffman."

"He was very handsome; he . . ."

"Wait. I'd like my partner to hear this." He turned on the intercom. "Steve, got a minute?"

Steve Abbott came into the office smiling. "So, you're out of your cocoon at last, Jimmy. Oh. Sorry, I didn't realize you had company."

"*Interesting* company, Steve. Mrs. Hoffman, what's wrong?"

Lottie Hoffman was pointing at Abbott. Her face was ghastly white. "You're the one I saw with Heather. You're the one Max said was a drug dealer and a racketeer and a thief. You're the reason I'm alone . . ."

"What are you talking about?" Abbott said, his brows knitting fiercely, the mask of geniality momentarily fallen from his face. All of a sudden, Lacey thought it was possible to imagine this handsome, debonair man as a killer.

Accompanied by a half dozen agents, U.S. Attorney Gary Baldwin came into the room.

"What she is saying, Mr. Abbott, is that you are a murderer, that you ordered her husband killed because he knew too much. He quit working here because he had seen what you were doing and knew his life wouldn't be worth a plug nickel if you knew. You've been dropping the old suppliers like Jay Taylor and buying from mob-owned businesses, most of the stuff stolen. You've done it in the casino, too. And that's only one of your activities.

"Max had to tell Heather what you are. And she had to decide whether to let you keep cheating her father or tell him how she found out about you.

"You didn't take the chance. Savarano told us you called Heather and said Jimmy had had a heart attack and she should get right home. Savarano was waiting for her. When Isabelle Waring wouldn't stop looking for reasons to prove Heather's death wasn't an accident, she became too dangerous."

"That's a lie," Abbott shouted. "Jimmy, I never . . ."

"Yes, you did," Jimmy said calmly, "you killed Max Hoffman and you did the same to my daughter's mother. And to Heather. You killed her. Why did you need to mess with her? You could have had any woman you wanted." Jimmy's eyes blazed with anger; his hands formed into giant fists; his cry of agony exploded through the room. "You let my baby burn to death," he howled. "You . . . you . . . ."

He lunged across the desk and wrapped his powerful hands around Abbott's throat. It took Sloane and the team of agents to pry his fingers loose.

Jimmy's racking sobs echoed throughout the building as Baldwin took Steve Abbott into custody.

Sandy Savarano had completed his bargaining from his hospital bed.

At eight o'clock, the driver Jay had sent to pick up Lacey at her apartment called to say he was downstairs. Lacey was frantic to see her family, but there was a phone call she still had to make. There was so much to tell Tom, so much to explain. Baldwin, now suddenly her friend and ally, had told her, "You're out of the loop now. We've plea-bargained with Savarano, so we won't need your testimony to get Abbott. So you'll be okay. But keep a low profile for a while. Why not take a vacation until things settle down?"

She had replied only half jokingly, "You know I *do* have an apartment and a job in Minnesota. Maybe I should just go back there."

She dialed Tom's number. The now familiar voice sounded strained and anxious. "Hello," he said.

"Tom?"

A whoop of joy. "Alice, where *are* you? Are you all right?"

"Never better, Tom. And you?"

"Worried sick! I've been going out of my mind since you disappeared."

"It's a long story. You'll hear it all." She paused. "There's just one thing. Alice doesn't live here anymore. Do you think you could possibly get used to calling me Lacey? My name is Lacey Farrell."

**POCKET
BOOKS**

Also by

MARY HIGGINS CLARK
You Belong To Me

Regina Clausen was forty-three, successful in her career but insecure and unfulfilled in her personal life. Travelling alone on the luxury liner *Gabrielle*, she disembarked in Hong Kong saying she would rejoin the ship when it docked in Japan. She was never seen again . . .

Five years later, radio presenter Susan Chandler does a series about vanishing women on her radio talk show. When a caller, who refuses to identify herself, tells of meeting a man on a cruise who gave her a ring inscribed 'You Belong to Me', but then disappeared when she refused to leave the ship with him, she thinks little of it. But then Regina's mother appears at Susan's office with a ring bearing the same inscription which was found amongst her daughter's belongings, and Susan begins to suspect that they are on the trail of something dangerously sinister . . .

ISBN 0-7434-8432-0

PRICE £6.99

**POCKET
BOOKS**

MARY HIGGINS CLARK
On The Street Where You Live

In 1892, in the seaside resort town of Spring Lake, New Jersey, a young woman disappears and the house in which she grew up is immediately sold.

Now, more than a century later, Emily Graham buys back her ancestral home. Recovering from the bitter break up of her marriage, with a new position as criminal defence attorney in a major law firm, Emily begins renovating the Victorian house. In the backyard, the skeleton of a young woman is found, and identified as that of Martha Lawrence, the girl who disappeared from Spring Lake over four years ago. Within her skeletal hand is the finger bone of another woman, adorned with a ring – a family heirloom, Emily's family heirloom.

Seeking desperately to find the link between her forebear's past amd this recent murder, Emily herself becomes a threat to the killer. Devious and seductive, he has chosen her as his next victim . . .

PRICE £6.99

ISBN 0 7434 1499 3

**POCKET
BOOKS**

These books and other **Mary Higgins Clark** titles are available from your bookshop or can be ordered direct from the publisher.

☐ 0 7434 6773 6	**Second Time Around**	£6.99
☐ 0 7434 4937 1	**Daddy's Little Girl**	£6.99
☐ 0 7434 1499 3	**On the Street Where You Live**	£6.99
☐ 0 671 01039 5	**Before I Say Goodbye**	£6.99
☐ 0 7434 8427 4	**The Cradle Will Fall**	£6.99
☐ 0 7434 8430 4	**Moonlight Becomes You**	£6.99
☐ 0 7434 8428 2	**Stillwatch**	£6.99
☐ 0 7434 8429 0	**Let Me Call You Sweetheart**	£6.99
☐ 0 7434 8431 2	**We'll Meet Again**	£6.99
☐ 0 7434 8432 0	**You Belong To Me**	£6.99
☐ 0 7434 8433 9	**Pretend You Don't See Her**	£6.99
☐ 0 7434 4099 4	**He Sees You When You're Sleeping**	£4.99
☐ 0 7434 1501 9	**Deck the Halls**	£6.99
☐ 0 671 02284 9	**All Through The Night**	£6.99

Please send cheque or postal order for the value of the book, free postage and packing within the UK.

Please debit this amount from my:

VISA/ACCESS/MASTERCARD ....

CARD NO ....

EXPIRY DATE..

AMOUNT £ ....

NAME..

ADDRESS..

....

SIGNATURE..

Send orders to: SIMON & SCHUSTER CASH SALES
PO Box 29, Douglas, Isle of Man, IM99 1BQ
Tel: 01624 675137, Fax 01624 670923
www.bookpost.co.uk
Please allow 14 days for delivery.
Prices and availability subject to change without notice.

Published by Accent Press Ltd 2019

www.accentpress.co.uk

Copyright © Lorraine Mace 2019

ISBN 9781786156815
eISBN 9781786156808

Printed and bound in Great Britain by Clays Ltd,
Elcograf S.p.A

CHAPTER 1

6th October (early morning)

Joey held the blade against Edona's neck. A tiny line of red trickled down, collecting on the edge of her blue sweatshirt. He didn't want to kill her. She'd always been one of his best money earners, still looking like a schoolgirl even though she was almost twenty.

"Make the call," he whispered. "Make the call and you can live."

He could feel her trembling against his body as he pulled her closer.

"Make the call," he repeated.

She nodded and dialled. Her fingers shook so much Joey wondered if she'd hit the right buttons. He'd know when the call was answered. His head was close enough to hers to hear the ringing tone and then the copper's sleepy voice.

"Sterling."

The call had obviously woken him. Not surprising. It was five in the morning.

1

Joey released the knife just enough to enable Edona to speak. If she tried anything stupid, he'd put an end to her before she had chance to betray him again.

"It's me. I…"

Joey touched the knife gently against Edona's neck; a reminder of what they'd agreed.

"I'm listening," Sterling said. "What have you got for me?"

"Some girls, they come tonight."

"Where? What time?"

"I not know what time, but they bring them to motorway. Change van in car park outside restaurant and shop."

"Tell me who is bringing them in. Who are you working for? I can protect –"

Joey took the phone and ended the call.

"What a kind man! He wants to protect you. It's a bit too late for that, Edona. I wonder what else you've told him. I don't suppose I'll ever find out. Not that it matters to you now, but I've always been very fond of you. What I have to do to you breaks my heart."

"No hurt me. Please no. You say me, I make call, you forgive."

"And you believed me? Shame on you, Edona. I could never forgive such a betrayal. You've been working against me for too long now. I've heard you telling the young ones that they'd get free, someday." He laughed. "You're such a fool. For girls like you, someday never comes."

He felt her tears dripping onto his hand.

"Ah no, don't cry. I don't like to have my girls crying. No more tears."

He pulled the knife across her throat. As the blood spurted, he pushed her away, smiling as her body tumbled into the foundation pit.

"Edar, Bekim!" he called to the two men waiting by the car. "Cover her up."

They moved forward and began shovelling rubble and sand. Joey watched for a while, but soon got bored. He went and leaned against the car until Bekim signalled for him to come back and approve what they'd done.

He looked down into the pit and smiled. There was no trace of Edona. He glanced at his watch. It was now five-thirty. The concrete was due to be poured in three hours' time. Perfect.

"That's cleared up that loose end. I'd wondered how Sterling seemed to know so much, but without you two pointing her out, I'd never have guessed it was Edona. Good work," he said, smiling at the two men. He passed her phone to one of them. "Get rid of that, Bekim. Make sure it can't be traced back to us. Right, let's get everything in place for tonight's delivery. Now that we know Sterling will be on the other side of town, the transfer will be, as the Brits like to say, a piece of cake. I wonder what the fuck that means, a piece of cake." He grinned. "Talking of cake, it's time for breakfast."

***

3

Detective Inspector Paolo Sterling's foot had gone to sleep, but that was the least of his worries. Staying awake after spending several hours in a parked car, listening to Dave Johnson, his detective sergeant, list the reasons he was in love, was a bigger issue. The darkened car they were in, partially hidden behind bushes, faced the entrance to the car park of Bradchester Motorway Services. Paolo felt as if he'd been there half his life.

He moved about on the seat, trying to get the circulation going in his foot. It felt like a lump of dead meat on the end of his leg.

"Rebecca isn't like any other girl I've known," Dave said.

Paolo smiled in the dark. That must be the hundredth time Dave's said that tonight, he thought. But he didn't really mind. It was nice listening to Dave saying positive things these days. It wasn't that long ago Paolo would have classed his DS as a misogynist.

Giving up on trying to coax his foot back to life, Paolo shifted his position again and almost screamed as pain shot the length of his spine. They should get medical compensation for stake-outs, he thought. Wear and tear on muscles forced to stay in one place for too many hours.

"I think it's her hair I love the most," Dave said. "Or maybe it's her smile. Yes, that's what it is."

Paolo thought about the list Dave had given over the last few hours and felt as if he knew more about Rebecca than she did herself. He peered out into the night. No sign of the lorry they were waiting for. He checked his watch. It was no longer night. The time was just after five in the morning. A full twenty-four hours since the call had come in. Maybe his tip off had got the day wrong. Paolo decided to give it another couple of hours until the sun came up at and then tell the teams scattered around the car park to go home and get some sleep.

Paolo wouldn't have that luxury. He had the joy of a meeting with his ex-wife and his daughter's psychiatrist to look forward in only a few hours' time. Another couple of turns of his ankle and suddenly the circulation was back in his foot. The pins and needles were agony, but at least he could feel both feet once more.

"Do you think we've been given duff information, sir?"

It took Paolo a moment to realise Dave had stopped talking about Rebecca and was back into police mode.

"It's beginning to look that way, Dave, but I don't want to give up too soon just in case the tip off was a good one. I can't bear to think of more kids being smuggled in. If they're being transferred here, we need to get to them before they're handed over and put to work."

Through the gloom, Paolo could just make out Dave's head nodding in agreement. They settled back into silence and Paolo wondered about the series of phone calls that had led to this point. It had been the first break they'd had. Albanian girls were turning up on the Bradchester streets. Someone was smuggling them in, getting them hooked on drugs and then putting them out to work to earn enough to pay for their addiction.

They'd picked up many of these kids and placed them in social services, but not one of them could, or would, tell them who was behind the trafficking. Terrified and addicted, they all told the same story. They'd been abducted and kept prisoner in Albania, then sent here. What happened to them once they arrived remained a mystery. Paolo hadn't been able to discover any connection to the Albanian community in Bradchester.

Then came the tip off. It seemed the girls came in elsewhere and were shipped to Bradchester in various vehicles, often hidden behind false panels. The caller, a woman, had sounded terrified and was only on the phone for a few minutes each time, but managed to give enough information for Paolo to set up this operation. Now it looked as if they'd camped out all night for nothing. There'd been a procession of various vans and cars, but none of them had done anything even remotely suspicious.

Paolo felt himself dozing off and jerked awake just as a van drove past and parked in the darkest corner of the car park, diagonally opposite their car.

"Dave, I think this might be our man. Let's see what he does next."

As they watched, the driver climbed out and lit a cigarette. Leaning against the van, he took out a mobile phone and made a short call. When he'd finished, he slipped the phone back in his pocket. He looked around

6

the car park, as if searching for something, then turned and climbed back into the van.

"What do we do now, sir? It looks as if he might be pulling out again."

"We'll watch for a bit. If he drives off one of the teams out on the road can follow at a safe distance. At least until we're sure this isn't our man. But he hasn't started the engine, so maybe he's waiting for someone."

Twenty minutes later a dark van swept past Paolo's and pulled up next to the lorry. Both drivers got out of their vehicles and embraced. Then the first driver took the second man to the rear of his vehicle and unlocked it. From where they were parked, Paolo couldn't see into the van, so signalled to Dave to wait.

The second van driver returned to his vehicle and manoeuvred it so that the two ends faced each other, blocking any view of what was being transferred between the two vans.

"Now," Paolo said into his phone.

The car park lit up as several police vehicles switched on their lights and moved forward, blocking any chance of the vans making a getaway. The two men took off, one towards the services and the other towards the motorway.

Paolo jumped out and ran after the one aiming for the motorway. He was almost past him when Paolo threw himself at the man and brought him down with a flying rugby tackle. As the air whooshed out of Paolo's lungs, he forced himself to hang on to the man's legs.

Panting, he held the man down and waited for Dave to arrive. Between them, they got the man handcuffed and dragged him to his feet. They handed him over to the uniformed officers to put into a squad car. The other man was already sitting in one of the other cars.

It took Paolo a while to get his breath back and he realised how unfit he was. He'd turn forty later this month; too old to be throwing himself about the place like a kid.

"Right, let's see what they've got hidden in those vans," Paolo said when he had enough air in his lungs to be able to speak again.

He and Dave walked over to the open doors of the first van. Cartons of cigarettes filled the entrance floor to ceiling like a wall.

"Pull them all out," Paolo ordered the uniformed officers. "There might be kids hidden behind there."

An hour later both vans had been stripped bare. A fortune in stolen cigarettes filled the area around the vans, but there was no sign of any children. Paolo swore, but it didn't relieve his frustration. Whoever was bringing the girls in had taken him for a mug.

CHAPTER 2

6th October (night) / 7th October (morning)

Pete played back the track, not quite happy with the mix. The session musicians had done well, but the heavy beat thundered against the guitar melody. He tweaked a bit and listened again.

"Të më ndihmojë, nënë. Të më ndihmojë, nënë," a child's voice, sweet and plaintive, whispered behind his vocals. That was better.

Help Me, Mama was the best thing he'd ever recorded – better than any of the hits he'd had with The Vision Inside. If this didn't get him back at the top of the charts there was no justice in the world. Fuck those bastards, all his so-called mates. They'll be green when they hear *Help Me, Mama*. As the song filled the studio he realised he was glad now that they'd said no to getting back together again. He didn't need them. There were too many other bands reforming and singing their tired old crap. Wankers, all of them. With this as his first solo track he'd be out there riding high on his own. No longer just Gunnar Tate Reed, lead vocalist for The Vision Inside.

Maybe he should reinvent himself completely. Go for a new name. Say something like Zak Babcock or Maxx Payne. He shrugged as the song came to an end. Time enough to decide about names when the album was ready. He had plenty to do before that day came round.

Through the glass partition separating the mixing area from the rest of the studio, Pete watched the child struggle to her feet and stagger across the room, eyes unfocused, as if sleepwalking. She looked like she needed another fix. Was he up for it though? Nah, he could screw her anytime, the music was more important right now. Besides, she wasn't going anywhere. Judging by the way she was falling over the furniture, she'd be out soon.

He continued mixing. Altering pitch and tone until he couldn't bear to listen to the track even one more time. He glanced through the glass. The girl had fallen in a heap in the corner behind the sofa. Time to wake her up.

As he wandered through from the recording area, picturing his name in the headlines once more, his cock throbbed at the memory of the young chicks who'd thrown themselves at him in, back in the glory days. He hadn't had to buy them then. Not like now where that bastard Joey upped the charges every time he brought a new girl over. He undid his belt. Time to rock and fucking roll.

The kid normally scrambled behind the furniture as soon as she heard him coming, but not this time. The stupid bitch was just lying there, waiting for him; ruining his fun. He liked a bit of foreplay; enjoyed the chase when she tried to get away.

"Hey, come on. I'm ready. Get up."

She lay on her stomach with her arms covering her head, leaving her bare arse on show. Did he want her that way? Nah, not this time.

"Turn over," he said and nudged her with his foot. Nothing. Not a flicker of movement. Sighing, he flipped open his phone and hit speed dial. While the number rang he tried nudging the brat again. Nada, zilch, fuck all. The phone rang on and on. Why was it taking so long for the bastard to pick up? When the voicemail message kicked in, he ended the call and tried again. This time it was answered almost immediately.

"At last. Where the fuck you been, Joey?"

"I had someone with me. Couldn't talk with her listening."

Pete wandered into the centre of the room and flopped down on the couch. Shit, he was tired. What time was it? He shrugged his sleeve back and managed to focus on his Rolex. Nearly midday. He'd started working on the track well before midnight. No wonder he was whacked. All he wanted was to get laid and then he'd go over to the house and sleep.

He glanced at the unmoving girl. What a waste of space. He needed someone able to keep up with him. "I want you to pick up this piece of shit. She's stopped moving; passed out or something. Bring me a new one. Make sure she's got more go in her than this one."

"What do you mean, not moving? She's not dead, is she?"

11

Pete peered over his shoulder and studied the girl's back. "Nah, I think she's still breathing. Hard to tell though. Might not be."

"Fuck it, Pete, what did I tell you? Huh? What did I say? Don't overdo it, that's what I said. Do what you want, but leave them fit for work. If she's dead, that's money down the fucking drain, man."

Stretching to pick up the whisky bottle, Pete fell forward, just managing to slop some liquid into his glass. Shit, he was more tired than he'd realised. He struggled back up onto the couch and listened to the voice droning on. Eventually Joey ran out of steam and Pete was able to get a word in.

"So what if she's dead? I pay you enough to cover any future earnings. You said I can do what the fuck I like with them. Anyway, this one's batteries've run down. Whatcha got for me this time?"

He heard a long drawn-out sigh, as if the idiot wanted to say no to him. Yeah, like that was ever going to happen. He grinned. It didn't matter what he did to the girls, his money would always buy him more. Thank you, God, for royalty payments. The gift that keeps on giving.

"I had a delivery last night," Joey said. "I've got two that haven't yet been taken that might suit you. Just arrived in the country, untouched. Very fresh, just as you like them. One fair, one dark. Which one you want?"

Pete swallowed another mouthful of whisky before answering; wondering if he should take both. He was tired, but could always keep one for tomorrow. "How much for the pair? One to watch while I do the other one could be fun. Hang on, though, they street kids? I don't want no gutter stuff."

"I've just told you, they're both fresh. You don't need to know their backgrounds, but these two are from good families. We picked them up on their way to school and shunted them off to the home. They were only in there for two days and they've been in transit since."

"School? That mean they speak English? You know it freaks me out if I can understand them when they start jabbering on."

"The dark one does a little, just a few words."

"Knowing my luck she'll start spouting when I'm at it. Can't stand that. Don't mind if I don't know what they're saying, but can't stand it when they speak English."

"Then you'd better just take the blonde. She speaks only Albanian."

"Pity. Two would've been neat. She a natural blonde?"

"She's ten, not likely to be dyeing her hair."

"No, but you wouldn't think twice about bleaching it to suit a punter. So, I'll ask again. She a natural blonde?"

"You know, Pete, you are getting close to being scratched from my list."

Pete laughed and reached again for the bottle. "Yeah, right. I pay way over the odds and you know it. I keep you in business, my friend. Now, let's cut the crap and talk money. How much and how soon can you get here? I'm up for it and having that useless piece of shit on the floor is pissing me off."

"I'll be there in an hour."

"I'll be in the studio. Call me from the side gate. I've got decorators in the main house and I don't want them seeing I've got visitors. You can't trust any of the fuckers not to spot something and decide to sell a story to the redtops."

Pete disconnected the call and cleared a space on the coffee table. As he cut a line of coke he cursed his boring sex life. Whatever he did these days, nothing seemed to give him the buzz he got from his music. Whether he took them up the arse, or thrust his prick down their throats, it all felt the same. Pity he couldn't have had both girls, though. That might have done the trick. Then it hit him. Shit, he could gag the dark one. In fact, that's what he'd do. Shove something in her mouth to keep her quiet. He could tie her up and make her watch her mate on the job. That would add a bit of spice.

He picked up the phone again. Fuck, he deserved some excitement in his life. In fact, after all the work he'd done on the new track, he owed himself a bit of a treat.

CHAPTER 3

7ᵗʰ October (morning)

Paolo could barely keep his eyes open. His body craved sleep, but there was little chance of that until much later. He glanced over at Lydia, his ex-wife, and wondered if it was worth trying just one more time to start a conversation. Somehow she must have felt his eyes on her, because she looked up from the magazine she clearly wasn't reading and glared. She held his gaze for a few seconds. He felt her disgust and anger wash over him in a torrent and was relieved when she went back to pretending to read the magazine. Okay, maybe reaching out wasn't such a good idea, he decided.

Every time they came to one of these conferences with their daughter's psychiatrist, they sat in complete silence in the waiting room. Lydia couldn't even seem to bring herself to greet him without snarling. He looked at the clock for what seemed like the thousandth time, but it was only five past ten. How could it be possible that only five minutes had passed since he'd sat down?

Eternity dragged on and on and then, finally, the door to Jessica Carter's office opened. Before the psychiatrist could speak, Paolo was on his feet and moving towards her.

"Good afternoon, Dr Carter."

"Good afternoon, Detective Inspector. Please come through."

Lydia took her time replacing the magazine on the table next to the chair. She stood up and Paolo felt guilty at how frail she looked. Her hollow cheeks and drawn face emphasised her weight loss. Something else to lay at his door. Maybe one day, if he stayed alive long enough, he'd be able to forgive himself.

He waited for Lydia to enter the office and then followed her in. He prayed today would be the day they heard some good news about Katy. Maybe, just maybe, she'd break through her silence. He might be able to get over his guilt regarding Lydia, but he knew if he lived forever he'd never, *never* forgive himself for what had happened to Katy. Sighing, he took the seat next to Lydia's. Please, he begged silently, please let the news be better than last week.

Dr Carter moved behind her desk and sat down. Paolo tried to gauge what she might have to tell them by the expression on her face but, as always, she gave nothing away. She leaned back and smiled. Paolo hated this part. This was where the hopes and prayers he'd built up all week came crashing back down again. He could sense it. Surely if the news was good Jessica Carter would show it in some way?

16

"Thank you both for coming," she began and Paolo's heart sank. Her voice told him all he needed to know, but he still held out a tiny hope. Her next words crushed it. "I'm sorry; there has been no change in Katy's mental and emotional state." She turned to Lydia. "I know you are anxious to do so, but I'm afraid I have to advise against taking her home."

"Why?" Lydia demanded and Paolo winced at the anger in her voice. "It's been three months since the attack. She looks fit enough now. I'm sure if she came home, back to her old life, she'd start talking again. It can't be good for her, stuck away with... with... *real* nutcases."

"Mrs Sterling, if I felt she would get better by going home, then that is exactly what I would recommend. I agree with you that physically she has recovered remarkably well, but she remains locked in her head and won't communicate with anyone outside of therapy sessions. As I've explained before, this is purely trauma related and she will recover, but the recovery process cannot be forced." She turned her head slightly, so that she was no longer just addressing Lydia. "I'm sure you both want her to be discharged, but when I mentioned the possibility of going home, she became so agitated she had to be sedated. I really don't feel she is ready yet to face the outside world."

Lydia leaned forward. Her distress was almost physical. Paolo wished there was something he could do to help her, ease her pain in some way, but knew anything he said would just make matters worse.

"With all due respect, Dr Carter, I don't agree with you. Her home, *my* home, is exactly where she should be. I want a second opinion."

"That is your right, of course, but..."

"There's no but about it," Lydia hissed.

Paolo put his hand on her arm. "Sorry, Lydia, I don't agree. I think getting someone new in to see Katy would upset her too much."

She shrugged off his touch as if burnt. "What do *you* know? It's your fault she's in this state. If you'd kept your work to yourself, none of this would have happened."

Paolo felt that old familiar punch to the guts. He couldn't argue with the facts.

Lydia brushed away tears. "I'd stop you seeing her if I could. I'd..."

"Mrs Sterling! Please, this isn't doing anyone any good, least of all Katy. In fact, this constant blaming of her father is one of the reasons Katy doesn't want to leave the hospital."

Lydia sat back as if she'd been slapped. "No, that's not true. How can you say that when Katy doesn't even speak to you?"

Jessica rested her arms on the desk and leaned forward, her face showing only concern.

"I talk to her every day," Jessica said, "and her body language tells me quite a lot. Depending on the questions I ask, she lets me know how she's feeling about a wide range of emotionally difficult subjects."

"Such as the attack?" Paolo asked.

"Yes, I talk to her about that, amongst other things. One of the topics that upsets her greatly is knowing how much blame you carry." She turned her head and looked directly at Lydia. "Katy doesn't blame her father, Mrs Sterling. I feel it's important for you to know that."

"Katy may not, but I do and I always will. Whether Paolo agrees with me or not, I *am* going to take steps to get a second opinion on the best way forward for Katy. Now, if you'll excuse me, I'm going to the hospital to visit my daughter."

She grabbed her bag from the floor and stood up, glaring first at the psychiatrist and then at Paolo. "You haven't heard the last of this, either of you."

Paolo waited until Lydia had slammed the door, then shrugged. "In fairness to Lydia, she has good reason for the way she feels. She cannot possibly blame me more than I blame myself."

"Mr Sterling, you've said that before and I'm going to repeat the same advice I gave you last week. You have to forgive yourself. You were not at fault. You specifically told Katy that you would see her at home and that she was not to involve herself in your case. She disobeyed you and, as a direct result, was picked up and viciously attacked by someone she had good reason to trust. How could you possibly have foreseen that would happen? No, don't answer, that was a rhetorical question. The attack Katy sustained has damaged her, I'm not disputing that, but she *will* recover. She is a very strong young woman. However, her recovery will take longer if you don't allow her to accept responsibility for her own actions."

"But..." Paolo began.

"No buts," Jessica said. "You didn't cause her attack and there was nothing you could have done to prevent it, short of locking her in her bedroom until you'd solved the case. I'm quite sure you'll always feel a degree of guilt. That is a natural reaction. But the more you walk around in sackcloth and ashes, the more Katy feels responsible for *your* distress. Do you understand what I'm saying?"

"I think so. You want me to hide my guilt over failing to protect my daughter. Forget somehow that every waking moment I carry the image in my head of that bastard on top of Katy as he's about to kill her?"

"No, I'm not asking for that. I'm asking for you and Mrs Sterling to stop adding to the guilt that *Katy* feels. She is blaming herself for the fact that you two cannot even be in the same room without war breaking out. She needs to be able to come to terms with what happened to her, without also feeling responsible for the way you and her mother react to each other."

Paolo walked outside into the early October sunshine and shrugged off his suit jacket. It was unseasonably warm, but he wasn't complaining. The weather people had promised another week like this before a cold front was due to arrive. He hoped they were right. As he made his way to the car park behind the office block, he mulled over the psychiatrist's words. Maybe she was right. Maybe he and Lydia were putting additional strain on their daughter. He wondered how to get through to Lydia that they had to stop fighting in front of Katy. Sighing, he thought that might be impossible, given how his ex-wife felt about him. He was almost at his car when a movement further down the line of parked vehicles caught his attention. Lydia was standing with her back to him. From her arm and head movements she was clearly having an animated conversation with someone.

He waited until she'd finished her call and then walked over.

"Lydia, wait up. I need to talk to you."

She spun round, looking furtive, almost guilty. "Paolo! What do you want?"

He stopped at the car next to hers, desperately trying to frame the right sentence so that he didn't put her back up again – something he was so good at, without even trying.

"I wanted to talk to you about what the psychiatrist said... about how our arguing is affecting Katy."

"Really?" Lydia said, her eyes narrowing. "Funnily enough, I've just been talking about exactly the same thing and have put steps in place to do something about it."

Paolo felt a massive wave of relief. This might be easier than he'd hoped.

Lydia moved towards him. "You see, Paolo, I think the doctor is right. Katy shouldn't have to listen to you apologising, or hear me blaming you for what happened to her. She needs peace and quiet so that she can get better. Do you agree?"

Paolo nodded, stunned by Lydia's change of heart.

"Good," Lydia said. "I'm glad you agree. I've just been speaking to my solicitor."

"Solicitor? What? Why?"

"To get a restraining order, stopping you from visiting Katy until she's well again."

He felt like he'd wandered into a twilight world. Not be able to see his daughter? He'd never let that happen. "Are you mad? On what grounds? You'll never get a restraining order. I'll fight you all the way."

His phone rang. He ignored it while his fevered brain tried to put words together that would get through to Lydia. One of the tunes Katy had chosen for him, so that he'd know who was calling, played on endlessly. It was Dave Johnson, his detective sergeant. It stopped briefly and then started again. He wanted to ignore it, sort something out with Lydia, but Dave had been given strict instructions not to call this afternoon unless it was urgent. He had to take the call. Turning his back to Lydia, he flipped the phone open.

"Dave, your timing stinks. This had better be important."

"It is, sir. We've found the body of a young girl, about ten or eleven. Dressed like a hooker, it's almost certain she'd been forced to work on the streets. Barbara Royston says the girl had been sexually active for some time."

"Cause of death?"

"Looks like an overdose, but you know Dr Royston. She won't commit herself until after the autopsy."

"No, I know. Where are you?"

"Heading back to the station."

"Okay, I'm on my way."

22

He snapped the phone shut and turned back to Lydia. "I have to go. A child's body has been found. Please don't go through with this, Lydia. Trying to cut me out of Katy's life will make it harder for her to recover, not easier."

Lydia looked at him as if he'd crawled out of a drain. "You don't care about Katy. You only care about your precious work. Look at you, raring to get back to the office to weep over some unknown brat when your own daughter is... is..." she broke off as tears streamed down her face.

Paolo took a step forward, reaching for her, but she moved away.

"Don't come near me. Don't touch me. Your bloody work killed one of our girls and destroyed our marriage. Now you've allowed your job to put our other daughter in hospital. I'll never forgive you. Never. I hate you."

She wrenched open her car, slipped into the driver's seat, and slammed the door. The engine roared into life and Paolo had to jump out of the way as the car shot out in reverse. He watched helplessly as Lydia manoeuvred out of the parking space and turned the car, the tyres chucking up gravel as she ground the gears and sped off towards the parking barrier. The car screeched to a halt just before the bar and then stalled.

Paolo thought about how distressed Lydia must be to drive so badly and realised he'd managed to achieve exactly the opposite of what he'd hoped.

Well done, me, he thought, I really handled that well.

CHAPTER 4

Pete drank in the screams of his young fans as he strutted across the stage. Their mothers had done pretty much the same thing twenty-odd years before. He leant forward as he belted out the song, trying to find the one girl he would choose for tonight, but it was like setting a starving dog loose in an abattoir, there was too much choice. Kids of ten and eleven dressed up to look years older. How could he screw just one when there would be twenty or thirty ready to drop their pants if he so much as smiled at them? He felt his erection pulsing. God, he could get his rocks off right here on the stage. What a buzz, what a fucking buzz! Then he spotted her – the one he'd been searching for. What was she – nine, ten? Certainly no older. She looked sweet and innocent. No makeup, nothing to make her come across as anything other than what she was, a kid out with the grownups and having a great time. Was that her big sister with her? She'd have to go.

24

He sashayed across the stage, getting ever higher on the adulation of his fans, until he was right in front of the girl. Locking eyes with her, he sang himself straight into her heart. He could feel the connection. Shit, he was horny as hell. He could come right now, just from knowing he'd be inside her later. He pictured her sweet little face scrunched up. Pleasure or pain, it didn't matter which.

Suddenly a different tune cut across the music on the stage, competing with *Help me, Mama*. What the fuck was going on? He took his hands off the guitar and looked around. The crowds of eager girls had disappeared. The other music continued, driving him insane. It just kept on and on and on and on and...

He shook himself awake. The intercom played that irritating tune over and over, ruining the best dream he'd had in months. Dragging himself up, he staggered over to the box on the wall and pressed the button.

"What?" he barked as the bloody awful noise finally stopped.

"Pizza delivery."

"I didn't order any. Fuck off."

"It's me. Joey. I've got a special order for you. Double crust."

Pete laughed. "Why didn't you say? Come on in."

He pressed the button to open the side gates and went to stand outside. Shit, was it still daytime? He shook his head, trying to clear his muddled brain. Within minutes a white van drew up and reversed in the drive so that the rear doors were close up against the stable block housing the recording studio. The van had Domingo's Pizzas – We're the Best! emblazoned on the side.

Joey jumped out from the driver's side and went to the back of the van. He opened one of the rear doors and dragged out two young girls; they both had their arms tied behind and were gagged with gaffer tape. Joey pushed them into the studio, shut the van door and followed the girls in. Pete's heart beat faster. This was more like it. These two might be worth a few nights at least. Smiling, he went back inside and shut the door.

"Well, what do you think of my latest method of delivery? Pizza vans go everywhere and no one ever notices them. When you said you had people in the main house I thought I'd better make sure they couldn't spot the girls arriving."

"Smart thinking," Pete said as he walked around the two girls who'd crawled to the centre of the room. They pushed up against each other. Big eyes pleading. One pair blue and the other brown. Not bad, he thought, not bad at all. The blonde was a bit scrawny, but pretty enough to do the job. The dark one, though, was a real looker. And she wasn't showing any fear either. He'd soon change that. What a pity he couldn't use her face on the new album cover, she'd have been ideal. Still, she'd be perfect for other things instead.

"You've done well, Joey. I'll take 'em both. How much?"

"Five hundred each."

Pete spun round. "Are you fucking mad? I'll give you five hundred for the pair, you robbing bastard."

26

Joey grinned at him. "Pete, you won't get fresher than this, my friend. Not unless you went out and caught them yourself and you can't do that, now can you? Be reasonable. I have transportation costs and other expenses. But I'm a fair man; let's say eight hundred for the pair."

"Six hundred and it's a deal."

"Seven-fifty and we can shake on it."

Pete walked over and held out his hand. "Done!" He pointed at the girl in the corner. "She hasn't moved for a while. You can take her away with you when you go."

Joey walked to the naked child and crouched down next to her. He reached out and felt for a pulse. "She seems to be alive. What did you give her?"

"I can't remember. A bit of everything, I think. Why has she gone all zombie on me? None of the others did."

Joey stood. "Maybe she had a bad reaction. Who knows? This is gonna cost you, Pete. Loss of earnings from her is going to hit me hard."

Pete laughed. "You must be joking. You think I don't know you supply all the weirdoes around here? I bet you've got a queue of them just waiting to fuck a zombie. Go on, tell me I'm wrong." Joey didn't answer. "See, I knew I was right. You should be paying me, not the other way round. I've turned her into an asset. You can charge extra for her from now on."

He pulled out his wallet and counted out the money. "Best if you push off now. It's going to look odd if the van stays outside too long. Pity you didn't bring some pizza with you. I'm hungry." He grinned at the girls.

"Never mind. I'll eat later. These two can take my mind off food."

He waited while Joey scooped up the unconscious child and then opened the door. He scanned the grounds, but no one seemed to be around. Opening the van doors, he nodded to Joey to bring the brat out.

"Don't forget to hoot when you reach the gates," he said as Joey climbed into the van. "Last time the gates stayed open all day. Any fucker could've wandered in."

As soon as Joey drove off, Pete went back inside and closed the door. Pulling the blonde one to her feet, he undid the knots tying her hands.

"Come and make friends with me, baby."

CHAPTER 5

7ᵗʰ October (late morning)

Paolo walked into the station with Lydia's words hammering in his head. No way could she stop him from seeing Katy. No way. But a tiny seed of doubt wormed its way to the top. What if she could? What if her solicitor managed to convince the courts that he was holding back Katy's recovery in some way? Was it possible? No, he told himself, over and over, but that didn't stop him fearing that Lydia might, just *might*, find a legal loophole that would keep him away from his daughter.

He passed through the main room, nodding to his team, but not really seeing them. Dave Johnson stood up and followed Paolo into his private office, closing the door behind them. His body working on autopilot, Paolo moved to his desk and sat down, barely aware of Dave settling himself in one of the visitor's chairs.

"The girl's body has been taken for post mortem. Dr Royston said she'd be doing it tomorrow morning if we wanted to attend."

Paolo forced his mind away from Lydia's threat.

"Thanks, Dave. I think we should both go. Poor kid deserves that someone cares about what happened to her. We've got to find out who's bringing these girls in. They're getting younger and younger. How old was that one uniform picked up last week?"

Dave checked his notes. "The interpreter said fourteen, but she'd been working the streets for at least a year, so must have been put on the game no older than twelve or thirteen. From what we can work out she'd been abused in a private paedophile ring from about eight or nine and then put to work on the streets when she was too old for the perverts. I'd like to get the bastards in a private room and –"

"And then they would be able to claim police brutality," Paolo interrupted, "and most probably end up being seen as victims instead of the scum they are. Keep your temper in check, Dave. You can't want to see them put away more than I do, but we have to work by the book on this. Okay?"

Dave nodded, but Paolo wasn't sure if that was just to shut him up. He decided to keep an eye on his DS if, no, *when* they found out who was behind the influx of teenage prostitutes flooding the Bradchester streets.

"What did the doctor have to say about Katy, sir? Any improvement?"

Paolo shook his head, trying to shrug off his fears over Lydia's threat. "Not really. The psychiatrist is convinced Katy will recover fully in time, but she still hasn't said a word since she came out of her coma and that was nearly three months ago." He knew if he thought too long about how she'd ended up in a coma he'd go out of his mind. "Sorry, Dave, not a good day to talk about it." He smiled, trying to ease the tension he felt whenever he pictured Katy being strangled. If he and Dave had arrived just two minutes later, his daughter would have been dead. He shivered. "Anyway, back to the case. Where was the girl found?"

"Curled up in a shop doorway on Zephyr Road. You know that section of boarded up shops near the station end? She was found by one of the older hookers who called for an ambulance. By the time they arrived the kid was dead."

"Do we know who called it in?"

Dave shook his head. "I'm on my way over there when I leave you, sir, but you know what they're like, not liable to tell me anything worthwhile."

"No, but some of the older women do at least try to keep an eye on the young girls. You might hit lucky and discover who the kids are working for. See if you can find a few of the old-timers to talk to."

"Will do, sir." Dave picked up his files and made for the door.

"Dave!"

"Yes, sir?" he said, turning back to face Paolo.

"I meant to tell you, I saw Rebecca the other day in town. She was getting tickets for the Pete Carson concert on New Year's Eve and asked if I wanted to go with the two of you. You'll be pleased to hear I declined."

Dave laughed. "I wish I could decline."

"Why? Not your type of music?"

"Not really, but Rebecca reckons we should support the local talent. Talent? He might have been good twenty-odd years back, but too many of these old rockers are making comebacks and most of them would be better off drinking cocoa and dreaming of the good old days."

Paolo smiled. "My ex-wife and I went to see The Vision Inside before we were married. Pete Carson, or Gunnar Tate Reed as he was then, was really good, great voice, but his real genius was in song writing. He's written for many of the top names over the years. As for The Vision Inside, they sold millions back in the day. That's how he was able to buy that massive place out near Bradchester Woods. When he first moved in the locals were up in arms, fearing he'd be having wild parties and so on, but you never hear a peep from him. I believe he converted his stable block into recording studios. They must be expecting a big turnout as his comeback gig is being held in the football stadium. If his voice hasn't broken down, you'll enjoy the concert."

"You reckon? Listening to some old bloke who should have stayed retired isn't exactly my idea of the best way to see in the New Year."

Paolo laughed at the look on Dave's face. "That's the price you pay for true love."

Dave grinned back. "Yeah, right. I'd best get over to Zephyr Road."

"Good. Ask George to tell CC to come in here when she gets back, would you? She's been to the social services hostel with the interpreters to see if we can get anything more out of the girls we've taken off the streets.

32

When you get back we'll have a meeting in the general office about last night's, or rather, this morning's arrests. I don't know about you, but I can barely keep my eyes open."

Half an hour later, a tap on the door signalled the arrival of Cathy Connor. She stuck her head into the room and Paolo thought he was hallucinating. Her cropped hair stood up in luminescent green spikes. He thought he'd seen every conceivable style over the last few months, but this one took his breath away. He wondered if she'd chosen the colour just to annoy those who felt women police officers should blend into the background.

"My God," he said. "Not planning to go undercover any time soon, hey?"

She laughed and closed the door. "No, sir. Do you like it? I thought I'd give our local thugs a sporting chance and let them see me coming."

"Give them time to run away?"

"Exactly, sir. Can you believe it? The last pimp I picked up has put in a complaint against me. Me! I ask you, do I look like I could hurt a six foot ex-rugby player?"

"No," Paolo said, grinning back. "I expect that's why he didn't give himself up when you went to arrest him. Did you break anything?"

"Just hurt his pride, sir. No broken bones."

Paolo signalled for CC to sit down. "Were you able to get anything from the Albanian girls this time?"

"Nothing. Not a fecking word. They are shit scared of all men, even our interpreter, and you know how gentle Gazmend is with them. They don't even open up when he leaves the room and it's only his wife talking to them. I suppose it's not really surprising when you consider what they've been through. Most of them will be fighting a drug addiction for the rest of their lives."

Paolo sighed. "They're all Albanian. You'd think we'd be able to get some sort of hint about who smuggled them in."

"I asked Gazmend about that. He seemed to think whoever it is must have a hold over the girls' families back in Albania, which is why they won't tell us how they came to be in the UK."

"Did he give any clue as to who we should watch?"

Cathy shrugged. "Not really. According to Gazmend, the entire Albanian community is ashamed of what is happening, but no one knows anything. Of course, it's possible that even if someone knew who was involved they might keep it to themselves. Who knows what might happen to those back home if they upset the Albanian Mafia here? From what I can understand, it's very easy to make enemies disappear over there. I mean, sir, would you put your family in danger if... oh shit, sorry, sir. I didn't mean... I wasn't thinking..."

"I know you didn't, CC. Don't worry, I didn't take it the wrong way." Paolo rubbed his face. God, he was tired. "I've heard the same stories about the families of informers being wiped out. I have no idea how we'll do it, yet, but we need to get the local Albanians to shop the bastards trafficking the kids."

"Let's hope Gazmend can get through to them. He says he's working on some of the best connected families to see if he can get them to encourage others to cooperate with us."

Paolo nodded. "Good. What do social say about getting the girls home again?"

Cathy scowled. "No fecking joy there, sir. The girls won't say who they are, so the Albanian authorities won't accept them. Apparently, the best we can hope for is that an Albanian orphanage will take them in, but I'm worried they'll end up in a worse case over there. I mean, some of their institutions look dodgier than being out on the street."

"I know," Paolo said. "I saw that documentary too. Those poor kids were in a desperate state. Let's hope the girls will be allowed to stay here. I know our system has flaws, but at least we do something about it when the stench is uncovered."

She rose to leave. "Dave tells me they found a dead kid. One of ours?"

"I don't know for sure yet, CC, but it looks like it. She was dressed for business. Seems she might have taken an overdose of whatever she was on. We'll know more tomorrow after the post-mortem."

"Well, whatever happens to the girls I saw today, they're better off with social than they were a few weeks ago on the streets. I'm off to sort out some tickets for the Pete Carson concert."

"You too? At this rate I'm going to be the only person in Bradchester not going."

"You should go. Give yourself a bit of a break. You shouldn't be stuck at home on New Year's Eve."

Paolo looked at the kindness in Cathy's eyes and felt his chest tighten. He had to get rid of her before he ended up in tears. Wouldn't that be great? Breaking down like an idiot just because someone was being nice. He managed to pull himself together.

"I might just do that." He smiled. "Pull down the blind and close the door on your way out, CC. I need to work on these reports and don't want to be disturbed."

As the door closed, he felt the first tear trickle down his cheek. Dropping his head, he let the tears flow. It was time to let out the emotions he'd been holding back. Time to move on and take control of his life again.

He was alive and so was Katy, which was more than he could say about the poor kid waiting on Barbara Royston's slab. He'd find out who put her on the streets and make sure the bastard paid for every child he'd ruined.

CHAPTER 6

7th October (early evening)

Pete stood up. The blonde lay on her back, a glazed look in her eyes. He just needed a hit and he'd be ready for the dark one. He flopped down on the sofa and sighed. It was a pity the blonde hadn't put up more of a fight. She'd been a bit too passive. Too roll over and give in to make it fun.

He reached forward for the coke, glancing over at the dark one as he did so. Ah, that was better. She looked as if she had a bit more fight in her than the blonde who'd now dragged herself off to the corner and was snivelling. What was it with that corner? They all ended up there.

He finished cutting the coke and rolled a twenty. As the drug hit his system the world righted itself once more. Yes! Now he was ready to go again. Standing up, he moved over to where he'd tied up the dark-haired brat and was delighted to see the look on her face. Terror and defiance mixed. That was the best combination. He could almost smell the fear coming off her; it added spice that she was trying to hide it by glaring at him.

But the sobbing from the blonde was distracting. He picked up a box of tissues from a side table and threw it towards the kid in the corner.

"For fuck's sake shut up. And get yourself clean while you're at it," he said, using mime to show she should wipe between her legs. The blonde made no attempt to touch the box, but at least she stopped whimpering. Was that a bit of hatred he could see in her face? Great. She might be more fun next time.

He turned back to the dark-haired girl and stood directly in front of her, stroking his prick until he was hard again. He grinned. This felt so good.

"Look what's coming your way, little one."

Her eyes widened in horror. No sign of defiance now, just pure fear.

"You're giving me a better high than the fucking coke, baby. You are going to love me inside you, I promise," he whispered as the bliss of anticipation washed over him. It was time.

Blood throbbing through his veins, he knelt down and reached for the ropes tying her to the chair. He wanted her now. Now, fuck it! Why couldn't he get the knots undone? As he struggled, he heard a scrambling noise and turned his head. The blonde stood right behind him. She raised her hand.

"What the –?"

Pete came round wondering what shit he'd taken. Whatever it was, it must have been bad. His head felt like it had been split open. As he sat up, nausea hit and he retched, spewing his guts onto the polished wood covering the studio floor.

When the heaving finally stopped, his memory returned. The blonde had whacked him with something. The bitch. She'd pay for that. He looked around for her. Where was she hiding? And where was that draft coming from? He managed to focus on its direction. The studio door was wide open. That couldn't be right. Why was it...? Then it hit him.

Shit, the girls were gone.

He hauled himself to his feet, wave after wave of nausea making him want to throw up again. Staggering towards the door, he tripped and fell over the shattered remains of something ceramic. He put his hands out to break his fall, screaming as one of the larger pieces sliced into his left palm. The bitch had hit him with a fucking ornamental bowl! Cursing, he got up again, pulling the shard free and wiping the blood off on his leg.

Where could they have gone? His head was throbbing fit to bust. Concentrate, Pete. Come on, man, pull yourself together. Then he remembered the decorators over at his house. They might see the bitches running around.

"Oh no, fuck, fuck, fuck," he whispered, running outside, surprised to find it was already night.

Thank God for the full moon, at least he was able to see. What time was it? He glanced at his watch, just after seven. What about the decorators? Would they still be around? He looked over towards the main house. Thank fuck for that, their van was gone. At least he didn't have to worry about them finding the bitches. But what about his staff? His housekeeper might not have left yet. Would the girls have gone over there? Mrs Baxter would have a fit. He stopped to think about it. Nah, they wouldn't know it was safe. So where would they go? Come on, Pete. Think!

He scanned the grounds and drive. Not a sign of life. They must be here somewhere. Without someone to open the gates there was no way out. Forcing himself to breathe normally, he tried to think what he should do next.

Phone Joey, that was it! Reaching down automatically towards his pocket, he realised he was naked. Shit! He had to put some clothes on. Turning back towards the studio, a movement caught his eye. One of the brats was climbing over the side gate. There was no time to worry about getting dressed. He had to stop her. He took off, sprinting towards the gate, keeping to the edge of the drive under cover of the bushes. The last thing he needed was someone in the main house to see him and call the police thinking he was an intruder. He had to grab the girls and get them back in the studio.

As he neared the gates, desperate for breath, he saw the dark one was about halfway to the top. Where was the blonde? He reached the gates just in time to grab the girl's leg and drag her down. She hit her head on the drive and cried out. Pete instinctively looked over at the house. Did anyone hear her? When he looked back, the girl hadn't moved. She must have knocked herself out. Good, one less to worry about. But where was the other one?

Through the ornamental bars Pete saw the blonde running for the woods. Shit! Fuck! Joey! He had to call

Joey. He scooped up the unconscious child and headed back to the studio as fast as his shaking legs could carry him.

Slamming the door shut with his heel, he slung the girl on the floor. Where was his phone? Where? Great, he fumed, chucking clothes across the room. This is all I need with the concert promotion about to hit the national papers. Where is the fucking phone? He spotted it finally under the coffee table and snatched it up.

As he listened to the ringing tone, he began to shake. Head to toe, he quivered uncontrollably. "Come on, Joey, come on," he whispered. "Answer."

Pete shifted from foot to foot, sweat pouring down his back. The kid on the floor still hadn't moved. He didn't think she was even breathing. What should he do now? Why was that bastard never around when he needed him? He cut the connection and dialled again. Once again it rang and rang. With shaking hands he redialled. This time it only rang once.

"Fuck me, but you're an impatient bastard," Joey snarled. "What's wrong this time? Too old? Too young? Too –"

"The blonde's gone."

"Gone? What do you mean gone?"

"The bitch hit me with a bowl. Knocked me out and now she's gone."

"Are your decorators still around?"

"What? No! What's that got to do with anything?"

"I'm asking," Joey said, as if speaking to a child, "because if they are still there they might see her. If

41

they've gone you can relax. We know she'll be in your grounds somewhere. I'll come over and help you look."

"Joey! Will you just fucking listen? She's gone. *Gone*. I saw her through the gates. She ran into the woods. She's stark naked and escaped from my house. She'll bring the police here. And it's not just my balls on the line. If I go down, you're going with me. Now get your arse into gear and get over here. We've got to find her before someone else does."

"Oh shit. Right, I'm on my way. What about the other one?"

Pete looked down at his feet. The child lay perfectly still, her head at an impossible angle to her body. "She's here and she's not going anywhere in a hurry. I think she might have broken her neck."

CHAPTER 7

7ᵗʰ October (late afternoon / early evening)

Paolo glared at the mound of papers covering his desk, all waiting for his signature – none of which he could sign until he'd read them. Every new government promised they'd cut down on bureaucracy and then, as soon they'd got their pick installed in number ten, they all decided more reports, more forms, more tables, more bloody paperwork was needed to cut down on crime. He seemed to spend more time reading about his job than actually doing it.

He reached for the top report, ignoring the pain throbbing in his temples. The headache would pass eventually, but the paper stack would keep growing unless he did something about it.

An hour and a half later, Paolo would have cheerfully added to the crime figures by murdering whoever it was who'd thought money spent recording statistics was more important than having coppers on the beat.

A knock dispelled his murderous thoughts. As he looked up, Dave stuck his head round the door.

"You busy, sir?"

Grateful for the interruption, Paolo shoved the papers to one side and signalled for Dave to come in and sit down.

"What have you found out?"

"Nothing we didn't already know, unfortunately. The kids on the streets are Albanian, some of them as young as ten when they are first put out." Dave paused, and Paolo could see the younger man was fighting not to explode. "You're right about the older women taking care of them. You can tell they are all sick about how young these girls are, but no one is prepared to say who the pimps are or where the girls might be kept during the day."

Paolo sighed. "So we're no further forward? A kid takes an overdose, probably to escape the shit life she's leading, and no one will tell us anything."

"I did see someone who might help us, sir, but she won't speak to me."

"Really? Who?"

"Do you remember that older prostitute you spoke to when we were working the serial killer case? The woman didn't know anything about the killer, but seemed to know who was dropping the kids off and picking them up. At the time she was too scared, or stoned, to tell us. I looked for her today, but she's no longer on the streets. It seems your words about going into rehab did the trick. She's been clean for a few months and is helping out at the soup kitchen on Donald Street. I went and had a chat, but she says she'll only tell you and no one else what she knows."

Dave grinned. "In her eyes you're the closest she's ever going to get to God."

Paolo scanned the papers screaming at him, thought about the hours he would need to spend after the meeting with his team just to make a dent in them, looked back at Dave and nodded.

"Let's get the debrief over and done with and then we'll go chat to her," he said, getting to his feet. "I've never had a fan club before, so I think I'd better do what I can to make sure the only member doesn't leave it."

Dave held the door open for him and then followed him to the main office. Paolo scanned the room. Only a couple of chairs were vacant. Everyone he needed was there. Normally he stood when addressing his team, but his legs felt like they'd give out at any moment. God, he had to get some sleep. Taking one of the vacant chairs and turning it to face the room, he sank down on it.

"Right, as you all know, we arrested a couple of men in the act of handing over stolen cigarettes in the early hours of this morning. Which is good, of course, but that wasn't why we were there. Our informant has been feeding me scraps of information about the child trafficking, all of which has been spot on, which is why we've been able to pick up so many of the girls and take them into care. My fear is that she's been found out and was forced to give us the run-around last night." A few officers whispered to colleagues. He waited until the murmuring stopped. "Two things arise from that assumption. Firstly that she is in danger, but as I have no idea who she is or where to find her there is nothing we can do to help her. Secondly, I think we were deliberately sent to the motorway services last night to keep us occupied while children were brought in and delivered elsewhere."

CC called out. "Sir, each time we ran a check on the mobile she used to call you, it was a prepaid throwaway job. Same with yesterday morning's call."

Paolo nodded. He already knew that, but CC was putting the information out there for the rest of the team.

"The two men in custody are both Albanian, which leads me to suppose they are known in some way to whoever is running the trafficking ring. They claim to know nothing about that, but we'll keep questioning them. Maybe we'll get a break."

"The important thing here is that there are most probably a number of children about to be handed over to perverts. We've got to find them. Our informant was our only link to those kids and I don't think I'll be hearing from her again, so we need to find a new source of information. I want all of you to get in touch with any contacts you have. Most criminals won't have anything to do with child sex crimes and might be prepared to help put the bastards away. See what you can find out."

He glanced at the clock. Nearly half past six. Where did the bloody time go?

"Okay, everyone, home time. I know half of you are dead on your feet from last night, so get a good night's sleep."

Over the murmurs of good nights and see you tomorrows, Paolo called to Dave.

"No rest yet for us. Let's go and see my one and only fan."

Dave drove the car into the tiny parking area behind the old St Peter's church. Paolo got out. By the light of the full moon, the back of the church looked romantic, like something out of a Disney film, but Paolo knew how much of an illusion it was. There was nothing romantic, no hint of fairy-tales, about this part of town. He couldn't help comparing the area as it was now with his childhood memories. He'd been an altar boy in this church, with the priest celebrating mass to a packed congregation. Now the building was deconsecrated and used as a soup kitchen and shelter for the homeless. He smiled; maybe there was more godliness in the building's new role than there had ever been in the old one.

Paolo waited for Dave to lock the car and then the two strolled round to the shelter's main entrance in Donald Street. As they walked in, Paolo was nearly knocked backwards by the stench of unwashed bodies, stale urine and boiling vegetables. The last time he'd been in the building was during a mass and he'd almost passed out from the smell of incense. Wishing he could wave some incense around now, he looked over at Dave, who seemed to be trying to breathe without opening his mouth.

"You okay?"

Dave nodded. "When I was here earlier the place was virtually empty, so the smell wasn't so bad. How do they cope with it day after day?" he asked, indicating the people at the back of the building, standing behind a long trestle table. They were ladling soup and handing out bread rolls as if they couldn't smell the people shuffling along in front of them.

"I suppose after a while you'd stop noticing it," Paolo said, but he wasn't convinced by his own words. Surely no one could ever get used to it? Mind you, he thought that about autopsies as well and yet Barbara Royston appeared not even to notice the odour of decay while she was working.

He glanced up at the workers, trying to pick out the former prostitute and addict they'd come to see.

"Where is she, Dave? I can't spot her up there."

"You won't, Inspector, because I'm behind you," said a slightly out of breath voice.

Paolo spun round and was confronted by a massive sack which virtually obscured the speaker. He could hardly believe what he saw when she put the sack down. The woman was dressed in jeans and a sweat shirt. The last time he'd seen her she'd been wearing a halter neck top and short skirt in the middle of a freezing cold spell. She looked twenty years younger than the woman he remembered on the streets waiting for customers.

She pointed to the sack. "Bread rolls. Today's leftovers donated by the local bakery. Excuse me while I take them up front. I won't be long."

"Can I help you with them?"

The woman smiled and aged ten years as her decayed teeth appeared. "No, best if you stay back here. Most of our people are a bit uncomfortable around you lot. You wanna wait for me outside?"

48

Paolo nodded and Dave followed him out into the relatively fresh night air. They'd barely settled on the low stone wall separating the shelter's grounds from the pavement when the woman came out to join them. She lit a cigarette.

"They'll kill you," Paolo said with all the zeal of a reformed smoker.

"I've given up drugs, booze and sex. A girl's gotta have one vice," she said, waving the smoke away from them.

"You're looking good, Alice. I wouldn't have recognised you if we'd passed in the street."

She grimaced. "Not Alice, not any more. You can call me Michelle. That's also not my real name, but it's a good one to start over with."

Paolo noted the educated voice, completely at odds with the way she'd spoken when he'd last seen her. "You've also lost your foreign accent," he said.

Michelle laughed. "I'd been pretending to be *exotic* for so long, I'd forgotten how to speak normally." She looked down and shrugged. "I'd forgotten lots of things."

When she looked up again Paolo could see she was battling tears. He waited while she fought to control her emotions.

"You saved my life," she said. "That day, when you were asking about that maniac who was killing prostitutes, reminded me how I came to be on the streets and I remembered, just for a few minutes, who I used to be. It was enough. A few days later I found myself here,

49

in desperate need of a fix, but John, that's the guy who runs the place, helped me into rehab instead."

Paolo smiled. "Then it's John who saved you, not me."

Michelle shook her head. "No, it was because of the things you'd said that I listened to John. Your words started me thinking again. Anyway, you're not here to listen to my life story. What do you want to know?"

"Well, who it is that's putting kids out on the streets would be a start."

Michelle sighed. "I wish I could give you a name, but I don't know it. All I do know is that they are vicious. Everyone, even the pimps, are terrified of them. They are Albanian and well connected, it seems. We used to wonder if the police were taking backhanders from them. Is that true?"

She looked up from under her lashes and Paolo could see a glimpse of the girl she must have been before her life took a turn for the worse.

"Not as far as I know, but I promise if I find out that is the case, I won't rest until the buggers are brought down – and that's no matter how high up they might be. So, what *can* you tell me?"

Michelle lit another cigarette from the glowing end of the first and dragged the smoke deep into her lungs. "It's a well-run people trafficking organisation. The kids are picked up in Albania and brought over here. They have no money or passports and no way of getting in touch with their families. They're farmed out to paedoes to be broken in and passed around until they reach an age where they're considered too old. Or the drugs have made them *look* too old. After that, they're put on the streets."

Paolo nodded. "That's pretty much what we suspected. We need to find out who's bringing them in. If we can do that, it's a short step to finding out who is in the paedo ring. The poor kids we've taken into care won't, or can't, tell us anything."

"I'm amazed some of them can walk, let alone talk. They've been passed around and fed drugs for years by the time they're put out on the streets," Michelle said. "Poor little cows are like robots. I don't know the people at the top, but I can point you in the direction of a couple of men lower down who drop off the kids for work and pick up them up again when they've earned enough for their keep. I don't know the men's names, but I can describe them."

"Any chance you can remember the car registration?"

She shook her head. "No, sorry. I didn't know anyone would come asking me for it so didn't make a point of looking. But I did get a good look at the two pigs running the girls. I'm sure I can give you a good enough description to do one of those identikit things they're always showing on *Crimewatch*."

"That would be great, Michelle. Can you come to the station tomorrow? I'll make sure our artist is available to spend some time with you."

Michelle nodded and got to her feet. "I have some stuff I need to do here tomorrow morning. The breakfast shift. I'll come down after that." She looked up at the church clock. "I must get back inside; they'll be needing another

51

pair of hands to dish out the food. I wish I knew more, but I don't. Still, I'll ask around and pass on whatever I find out. If anyone can help those kids, it's you. I know *you* won't let them down."

She glanced over at Dave as if she thought he *would* let people down, nodded at Paolo, and went back inside.

"Bloody hell," said Dave, "she doesn't think much of me, but she believes you can walk on water."

Paolo stood up and brushed bits of debris from the wall off his trousers. "Then I'd better not fail her or the kids," he said. "Walking on water? I wouldn't mind getting my ankles wet, but I'd be more likely to drown."

CHAPTER 8

7th October (evening)

Pete waited outside the gates, peering through the early evening gloom into the distant woods, hoping to catch a glimpse of the child. Thank fuck the house was miles from anywhere. At least he didn't have close neighbours to worry about. But Joey needed to get his arse over here in a hurry. Who knew how far the kid would be able to run. He checked his watch again. Fifteen minutes he'd been standing out here like an arsehole. Where the fuck was Joey?

Five minutes later a black BMW screeched to a halt in front of the gates. Joey lowered the window. "Get in," he yelled. "I'll drive as far into the woods as I can. Then we'll have to walk."

Pete climbed into the passenger's seat and shut the door. Ignoring Joey's two heavies in the back, he smacked the dashboard in frustration. "She could be anywhere by now. What took you so long?"

"I had people with me. It took me a while to shake them off."

Pete turned to watch Joey's profile. "Not part of your organization then?"

"No. It's no sweat, but I had to be careful, that's all. I couldn't just take off. What did you do with the dark-haired one?"

Pete shrugged. "I left her in the studio. What else was I going to do with her? Bring her body along for the ride?"

The car screeched to a halt. "Are you mad?" Joey yelled. "We'll have to go back. What if someone goes into your studio?"

"No one will go in for another three days. It only gets cleaned when I tell Mrs Baxter I need someone to do it and the cleaner knows better than to go in if I'm not there."

"As far as you know," Joey said.

"You must think I'm stupid. I change the numbers on the security code on the door every week. I have to tell Mrs Baxter the code each time she has to let someone in."

"At least you do something right. It's good to know you're not always a fuck up. Now stop yakking and start looking."

Pete peered through the window as the car slowly made its way along the dirt track. When they reached a picnic site Joey pulled into the parking area next to it.

"I'll park up here. We'll split up and search. You come with me, Pete, and you two can work together," he ordered, nodding at the other men.

Pete didn't recognise either of them and Joey made no attempt at introductions.

"You two search that side. If you find her, shut her up and bring her back to the car. Put her in the boot. We'll meet back here in an hour. Okay?"

The two men nodded and set off, soon disappearing from Pete's sight. "Not very chatty, are they? Friends of yours?"

Joey laughed. "Not exactly. You don't need to know who they are. We need to find the kid *you* lost. Let's get on with it."

Half an hour later and Pete was fed up to the back teeth. His head was throbbing fit to bust where the bitch had clouted him. The bottoms of his jeans and his trainers were covered in mud. God only knew what sort of shit he'd walked through. He had scratches on his face from the brambles he'd walked into and they still hadn't so much as caught a sniff of the girl.

It was only fear of someone else finding her that drove him on. With his comeback concert planned for New Year's Eve, the last thing he needed was reporters banging on about his private life.

Joey had virtually ignored him since they'd set out. The stupid fucker was acting like he'd lost the brat on purpose. So he was really surprised when Joey grabbed his arm and pulled him to a stop.

"Ssh," Joey hissed and pointed ahead.

Pete heard it then. Voices.

They crept towards the sound and stopped just before a clearing in the woods. Peering through bushes they could see a large travellers' camp. There were a variety of brightly painted traditional wagons, interspersed with prosaic white vans and campervans.

The raised voices they'd heard came from a group of women huddled together outside one of the traditional wagons. It was clear an argument was in progress. It wasn't possible to make out the words, but from the way they were yelling Pete thought it looked as though half of them wanted one thing and the other half wanted nothing to do with it.

He glanced over at Joey and raised his eyebrows in a question. Joey shook his head and waved his hand in a signal to wait.

Suddenly the group appeared to have settled their differences and the small crowd dispersed, leaving the object of the discussion huddled in a blanket on the steps of the wagon with two women watching over her. Pete gasped out loud at the sight of the small blonde figure. Joey punched his arm.

"Sorry," Pete whispered. "It was a shock seeing the brat there. What do we do now?"

"We wait," Joey whispered back. "As soon as we get the chance, we snatch her back again."

"Look!" Pete hissed. "There's something going on."

A group of men came towards the wagon and another debate started up, with the two women seemingly pitted against the rest of the camp. Pete noticed an older man standing quietly, leaning on a stick as he watched the argument flying back and forth. Suddenly the man struck the ground with his stick and everyone fell silent. He said something in a language Pete couldn't understand, but it

56

soon became obvious what he'd ordered his people to do because they all scurried off to the various wagons and vans. The child was pushed into the wagon behind her and within minutes the entire camp was on the move.

"Shit! Now what do we do? They're taking her with them. Do you think they can understand her? What if she tells them about me?"

"Pete, just shut up a minute. Let me think." Joey grabbed Pete's arm. "Come on, we need to get back to the car. We'll follow them. Wherever they pitch camp next, I'm sure we'll be able to grab the girl."

"What about your two men?"

Joey snapped open his phone. "I'll get them to meet us back at the car."

Pete sighed. He needed to piss and he needed a fix. They seemed to have been in the car for hours, but when he looked at his watch only twenty minutes had passed since they'd left the woods and began to follow the travellers' procession.

"Where the fuck do you suppose they're going, Joey? We're heading towards town. I'd expected them to set off towards the motorway. Don't you think it's odd?"

"The only thing I find odd is that you can't shut up. Your mouth never stops."

Pete swallowed the insult, but promised himself if he ever got the chance, he'd repay Joey for treating him like shit. Okay, so the brat escaped, but how the fuck was he supposed to know she'd smack him over the head with his own ornament? He hadn't even enjoyed her as much as he'd hoped. She'd been too passive, not put up much of a fight, and then what? Out of the blue she'd turned into a fucking Amazon warrior. How unfair was that?

As the procession reached the outskirts of Bradchester, the vehicles as one pulled over the side of the road. Joey drove past for a few hundred yards and eased the car into a parking bay.

"Do you think they've seen us?" Pete asked, peering over his shoulder. "What if they have? They might be getting ready to –"

"Pete! Shut the fuck up!" Joey yelled. "Look, no one's coming this way. I don't know what's going on, but they aren't interested in us."

Pete turned in his seat to get a better view, looking past the two backseat passengers. The door to the wagon holding the girl opened and she came down the steps, half pushed by the two women who'd seemed to be guarding her at the camp. The women and the girl, now dressed in jeans and a sweatshirt, climbed into a white van, which then drove off.

"They're taking her into Bradchester. Fuck it, Joey, they're taking her into town. Where do you think they're going with her? I bet it's the police. If she tells them about me, that's my comeback screwed."

"We'd better follow and find out where they go then, hadn't we," Joey said as he turned the key in the ignition. "But you'd better hope they aren't going to the police with her. If they do, I'll have to organise someone to deal with her and that'll be the third worker you'll have lost for me. If that happens you won't need to worry about your comeback concert, Mr Rock Star, because you'll be dead."

"Just fuck off, Joey. Don't think you can threaten me…"

"I don't think it and I'm not threatening. I'm stating a fact. You'd better hope we get to the girl before the police do, because if she leads them to you, I'll make sure *you* won't be able to lead them to *me*."

Pete shut his eyes. How had it come to this? All he'd wanted was a bit of fun. Now it seemed everything he'd worked so hard for was in danger. The little bitch had messed up his life for him. Why'd she have to ruin everything just when it was all going so well? Life was so fucking unfair.

CHAPTER 9

8th October (morning)

Paolo watched as Barbara Royston concluded the autopsy. It made him sick to realise she was treating the child's body with more respect in death than it had received in life. He vowed yet again to destroy whoever was trafficking these kids. Sometimes he wished he lived in a world where certain criminals were punished in a way that *really* fitted their crimes. Child traffickers, for example, could have their –

"Are you with us, or off in some world of your own?"

He jumped, brought out of his daydream, back to the real world where evil bastards rarely got what they deserved.

"Sorry, Barbara, I was just thinking about justice. What did you say?"

"I said I'll have the report for you tomorrow, but I haven't found anything we hadn't expected. She's about thirteen or fourteen, been subjected to continual sexual abuse over an extended period of time, both vaginally and anally, and she died from an overdose. We won't know the full details of that until the tox reports are back." She frowned. "You'd think in my line of work I'd get used to sights like this, but when you know the life a child has been subjected to –"

She didn't finish, but she didn't need to. Paolo was thinking the same thing. When you know what the child has been through before this point, it's so much harder to bear.

"Do you have any leads?"

Paolo signalled to Dave to answer.

"A witness came in early this morning and gave our artist some excellent information. As we've finished here, I'm off to the area this child was found to show the identikit images of two men we'd like to interview. Apparently they drop off and pick up the kids, so someone must know who they are." He nodded to Barbara. "See you back at the station, Paolo."

Paolo watched Barbara's face as Dave left. "You look surprised."

"I am," she said. "That's the first time I've seen him in months. What happened? Did aliens take over his body?"

Paolo laughed. "No. It's love that's done the trick."

"Good grief. Who'd have thought an out and out misogynist could turn into a decent person."

"It was all an act, Barbara. Putting on a brave front to hide the soft centre."

"Hmm, like someone else I know. Have you got time for a coffee?"

Paolo checked his watch. Ten-fifteen and he hadn't yet started on the paperwork mountain. "Sure. I'd love one."

He waited while she cleaned up and then walked by her side the few yards along the corridor to her office. An image of the child's lifeless body came to him and he shivered. They are just kids, he thought; they should be playing and having fun, not servicing bloody perverts.

"How's Katy?" Barbara's voice cut across the unwelcome pictures in his head.

"The same. Her doctor thinks she's making progress, but it's so slow that we, Lydia and I, can't see it."

Mention of his ex-wife's name brought to mind the previous morning's threat to stop him seeing Katy. Surely she wouldn't carry through with it. God, he hoped not. Putting that fear out of his mind along with all the other unpleasant things his brain felt stuffed with, he settled himself into one of Barbara's comfortable chairs. A strange noise from behind made him look round.

"Very snazzy," he said as Barbara slipped a capsule into what was clearly a fancy new machine. "I haven't seen that before."

Barbara grinned. "You know me and my love of a perfect cup of coffee. This was a present from a friend who was fed up with my constant complaints about the coffee we get from the vending machines here."

Paolo looked at the expression on Barbara's face. Yes, she loved good coffee, but that glint of excitement was a bit over the top.

"Friend?" he asked.

"Friend," she said firmly, placing a cup on the low table in front of him.

But the blush that crept over her face, almost blending with the livid birthmark covering her neck, made him think friend might be too mild a word. He felt as though someone had punched him in the stomach, which was stupid. He had no right to feel anything where Barbara was concerned. He was the one who'd turned down any chance of a relationship, so why shouldn't she have someone in her life?

Barbara had no sooner fixed her own coffee and sat in the opposite chair than her phone rang.

"No rest for the wicked," she said, picking up the receiver. "Royston speaking. Oh, hi, how are you? No, I'm fine, just having a coffee from my wonderful new machine. Yes, tonight would be lovely. Yes, usual place. I'll try not to be late this time."

As she replaced the receiver Paolo noted her blush had gone several shades darker.

"The coffee machine friend?" he asked.

She nodded. "One and the same."

His phone began playing a tune, another of Katy's choices, signalling CC was calling. Grateful for the interruption before he could say something he would definitely regret, he flipped the cover to answer.

"What's up, CC?"

"I've picked up a report that I think might interest us, sir. A young girl, maybe ten or thereabouts, who doesn't speak English has turned up at Bradchester Central. She's a rape victim and the doctors over there reported it to the station."

"Do we know what nationality the girl is?"

"The report doesn't say, sir, but I wondered if we should arrange for Gazmend and his wife to meet you at the hospital, just in case the child is Albanian."

"That's not a bad idea. Although, if she isn't, then that means we have other sick bastards bringing in girls from abroad. Jesus, that doesn't bear thinking about. Dave's gone to show the suspects' images over in Zephyr Road, where the overdose girl was found, so you'd better come with me to the hospital." He checked his watch. "I'll come over and pick you up. Ask Gazmend to meet us there in an hour."

Glad of the excuse to leave, he swallowed the hot liquid, trying not to wince as it scalded his throat.

"Sorry, Barbara, must run. Thanks for the coffee," he said, halfway to the door.

He was already in the corridor when he heard her answer. What the hell was wrong with him? Barbara had made it clear for months that she liked him and wanted to get closer and he'd pushed her away. Now she had a new man in her life he was behaving like an idiot. He should be happy for her. He *was* happy for her.

So why did he feel as if he'd lost something precious?

Shaking his head, he raced down the corridor and out to the car park. His tangled love life, or lack of one, could wait. The child in Bradchester Central couldn't.

Paolo filled in CC on the autopsy results during the short drive from the station to the hospital.

"Poor kids," CC said. "The ones in social won't tell me anything. They huddle together as if expecting to be dragged away again at any minute."

"Not surprising," Paolo said, "when you consider how they must have ended up in this country. Living a normal life one minute and trafficked into the sex trade the next."

Paolo drove into the restricted parking area and pulled into the space marked for the head of hospital administration.

"We're not supposed to park here, sir."

"I know, but please note I haven't taken a doctor's bay." He grinned. "It won't hurt a pen pusher to park a bit further away and walk. It will do him good. Healthy exercise and all that."

Paolo climbed out and waited for CC. Pressing the key fob to lock the car, he looked around the car park. "You know, it looks to me like there are as many admin spaces as there are spaces for doctors. How can that be right?"

"You want me to answer that? Really?"

He laughed. "No. I was just commenting. I've got this thing about admin people and paperwork at the moment."

CC grinned. "I know, sir. I've seen it all over your desk."

They walked into the hospital and headed for reception, manned by a formidable looking grey-haired woman who reminded Paolo a bit too much of his primary school headmistress. Resisting the urge to duck in case she swiped the top of his head, as Miss Fletcher had been apt to do, he flashed his badge.

"We're here to see Doctor Peters about the child brought in during the early hours of this morning," Paolo explained. "Could you call him for us, please?"

The woman nodded and picked up the phone. After a brief conversation, she replaced the receiver with the same precision Miss Fletcher had used for everything she did. Paolo once again had to fight off the feeling of being six years old and in trouble for some minor misdemeanour.

"Doctor Peters will meet you on Rutland ward, where the child has been admitted. Take the lift to the third floor and turn right. It's the second door on the left. You can't miss it."

"Do you have any record of who brought her in?"

The woman consulted her computer. "No, I'm afraid not. Apparently she was discovered outside, next to the laundry delivery depot. When they opened up this morning, one of the porters found her propped against the wall."

Paolo turned to CC. "I wonder if whoever put her there was hoping she'd get medical attention. There are CCTV cameras all around this hospital. I would have thought the person dropping her off must have known that. But we might get lucky, maybe they weren't local. Before we leave we'll take a detour to hospital security."

He turned back to the woman. "We are expecting two interpreters to arrive shortly. Gazmend and Diellza Dushku." He spelled out the names and waited while the woman wrote it down. "When they get here, would you ask them to come up to the ward?"

She nodded, almost regally, and Paolo knew they had been dismissed.

CC pressed the button to call the lift. As the doors opened, a man who'd been studying the board displaying the wards and floor numbers came rushing over and got in behind them. The man stood back so that CC could press the button for the third floor before reaching forward and pressing number two.

When the man got out, CC, who'd been staring straight ahead, turned towards Paolo. The mirrored wall reflected the full glory of her appearance. Green spiky hair, a stud through one eyebrow, and enough make up to launch her own cosmetics company, Paolo wondered how much was stating 'here I am' and how much was camouflage. He knew many of the men on the force were intimidated by her. Perhaps that's what she'd set out to do. What better way to stop people from picking on her than by flaunting her personality? And there would have been quite a few coppers in line to do just that: all those who felt threatened by a woman – and a woman only interested in her own sex, no less.

"What is it, sir? Have I got dirt on my face?"

He laughed. "Sorry, was I staring? I'm still trying to come to terms with the green hair."

She grinned. "I'm just waiting for the day you no longer notice it and then I've got another colour in mind. One that will really stand out."

"As opposed to this one, that just blends nicely into the background, you mean?"

She nodded, an impish grin spreading across her face. Paolo wondered what shade her hair would be next week. Not that it mattered one iota. She could dye it purple with pink stripes as far as he was concerned. CC was one of the best detectives on his team. He wished he had another ten just like her.

The lift doors opened and they followed the directions they'd been given. A sign on the wall next to double swing doors told them they'd reached Rutland ward. Pushing through the doors, they came into another, narrower, corridor with doors leading off on both sides. A little way along the corridor, set back on the left, was a nurses' station, at present unoccupied.

"We'd better wait here," Paolo said.

After a few minutes one of the doors opened and a nurse appeared.

"Have you come to see Doctor Peters?" she asked.

"Yes," Paolo answered, showing her his identification.

"Could you follow me, please? I'll take you to him."

"We have interpreters coming along shortly. Will there be someone here to show them where to go?"

The nurse hesitated. "Possibly not. What with the flu epidemic and cut backs, we're all rushed off our feet."

"You go with the nurse, sir," CC said. "I'll wait here for Gazmend and Diellza. You can come back for us after you've seen the doctor."

"That sounds like a plan," Paolo said. "Lead on, nurse."

He followed her almost to the end of the corridor before she stopped and showed him into a tiny waiting room.

"Doctor Peters is just finishing his ward rounds. He'll be along in a few minutes."

"Thank you," Paolo said sitting down on a less than comfortable plastic chair, resigning himself to a long wait. But he'd barely had time to register just how hard the seat was before the door opened again and a man came in.

Without the white coat and stethoscope hanging from the man's neck, Paolo would never have placed the man as a doctor. In his mid to late thirties, he looked more like a lumberjack. He stood at least six foot five, with massive shoulders, bushy hair and a beard that could have won competitions for healthy growth.

"Detective Inspector Sterling?"

Paolo stood up. "That's me. You must be Doctor Peters," he said.

"Sit, sit," Doctor Peters said as he lowered himself onto a chair facing Paolo. "You've come to see that poor child we found outside. To be honest, I'm not sure you'll get much out of her. She's in a terrible state."

"Physically?"

"Yes, that too, but I was thinking more along emotional lines. She's been badly traumatised. Whoever raped her was extremely rough. By the time we brought her into the hospital she'd lost a fair amount of blood where she'd been torn on penetration. She's scared to death, poor thing. Doesn't seem to speak or understand English, so it's been difficult to deal with her fears."

Paolo nodded. "Sadly, Doctor Peters, we see too many cases where young girls, children who should be safely at home with their families, have been repeatedly traumatised in such a way. We know where she was found, but is there anything else you can tell me that might help catch the people who did this to her?"

"Unfortunately, no. I've stitched her up and tried to calm her down, but being a man, the gender she sees as the source of her troubles, isn't helping. She seems to be more at ease with the nurses, so I'm staying out of sight as much as possible."

"We think she might be Albanian. Would it be possible for our interpreters to try talking to her?"

"You can, of course, but I'm not sure how far you'll get. I'll get one of the nurses to show you into the child's room, but I'll be on hand, just in case she reacts badly to your visit."

They walked back to the nurses' station where CC was chatting to Gazmend and another man. Paolo only caught a glimpse of the man before he turned away to read something on the notice board, but guessed he must a relative of the interpreter's. Apart from being almost the same height, build and colouring, the other man moved in the same fluid way as Gazmend.

CC and Gazmend came forward, leaving the other man on his own. He held out his hand to Paolo, who shook it before making introductions.

"Gazmend, this is Doctor Peters. Doctor Peters, Gazmend Dushku, our interpreter. And this is Detective

Sergeant Connors," he said, enjoying the look of surprise on the doctor's face as he took in CC's appearance.

He turned to Gazmend. "Where's Diellza?"

"She went out early this morning to visit her sister and won't be back for several hours. Detective Sergeant Connor said it was urgent, so I came over as soon as I could. Should I have waited for my wife?"

Paolo looked at Dr Peters. "What do you think?"

"It would, of course, be better for a woman to speak to her, but I think the sooner someone communicates in her own language, the better. We can't get through to her at all."

Dr Peters pointed down the corridor. "Our patient is in room 14, just along there on the right. Please don't stay too long or tire her out. Let one of the nurses know if you need me for any reason."

Paolo let CC lead the way to the room. As CC opened the door, the child looked up and screamed. Yelling and crying, she scrambled up and climbed onto the pillow, trying to pull the drip from her arm. Paolo felt himself being shoved to one side as Doctor Peters rushed into the room.

"Get out!" the doctor shouted. "Shut the door so that she can't see you."

Paolo quickly pulled the door closed, shaken to the core at the poor kid's reaction. What must she have gone through? After several minutes the door opened and the doctor emerged.

"I've sedated her. You'll have to come back tomorrow, but I don't think she should be interviewed by men. In

71

fact, as her doctor, I am forbidding any males from entering her room."

Paolo nodded. "Gazmend, will your wife be available tomorrow?"

"Yes. I'm sure she'll be happy to put herself at your disposal."

"CC," Paolo said, "will you make arrangements with Mrs Dushku to meet you here? I have no intention of subjecting that child to more trauma; only you will interview her. I won't go into her room again."

"Yes, sir."

"Gazmend, I'm sorry to have dragged you all the way over here for nothing."

"It is not a problem. I will leave you now and tell Diellza to expect a call from Detective Sergeant Connor."

Paolo waited until Gazmend caught up with the other man and they disappeared through the double doors before turning once again to the doctor. "Forgive me for asking, but in view of what we've just seen, shouldn't the child be treated by a female doctor?"

Doctor Peters sighed. "She should, of course, but with the flu outbreak we are so short staffed that I'm her only option at the moment. As soon as one of my female paediatric colleagues is available, I'll be handing over to her. In the meantime, as I said, I'm staying out of sight as much as I can."

Paolo smiled in sympathy. "It must be very difficult for you when a patient cannot bear you to be in the room. I'm going to place a WPC outside her door. We need to make sure no one has access to her apart from medical staff."

Doctor Peters nodded. "Yes, of course."

"One last thing before we go, Doctor, we'd like to take the clothes she was wearing when she was admitted. We might be able to get some idea of where she'd been from forensic testing."

"Yes, of course. I'll get a nurse to bring them out to you, but I don't think they were actually her clothes. They seemed to be at least two sizes too big for her."

"That could be good news for us, doctor," Paolo said. "If they belonged to someone else we might get traces of the original owner from them."

"Good point. I hope you catch whoever did this. I'd hate to see another child in this state."

The doctor walked over to the nurses' station to explain what was required. He nodded farewell to Paolo and CC before disappearing into one of the side rooms.

"Was that a relative with Gazmend? They look so alike, I thought it might be his brother," Paolo asked.

"Not a brother, a cousin, Jeton. Gazmend's car is in for service and Jeton gave him a lift over. I see him with Gazmend quite often. I think they're very close. In fact, if I remember rightly, Jeton is staying with Gazmend at the moment. Marriage problems."

"Is he also an interpreter? I'm beginning to think the more people we have who can speak Albanian and English, the easier it might be to flush out our traffickers."

"I don't think he is on any official list, but his English is even better than Gazmend's, so maybe we should suggest he takes the test?"

"Good idea." Paolo looked at his watch. "CC, I'm going to call for a WPC to sit outside the girl's room. Would you wait here until she arrives? When she does, collect the clothes, then go down to security and pick up the CCTV coverage from last night. Get everything you can – all cameras, all entrances and exits. The child didn't walk here, so someone dropped her off. Odd though, I wouldn't have thought the people we're hunting would have brought her here, so maybe she's not connected to our case after all." He sighed. "Whether she is or she isn't, we need to get the bastard who did this to her."

"I agree, sir. I take it you're going to see Katy?"

"Yes, as I'm here, I thought I'd pop in for a few minutes. I'll come back again this evening as usual, but…"

"I know, sir. Take as long as you need. I'll wait for you downstairs."

Paolo could never suppress a shudder when he entered the psychiatric ward. He'd visited Katy every day for months and yet he still hadn't come to terms with her being here. He made his way to her room and stood outside, steadying his emotions. The reaction of the young girl had shaken him badly and he didn't want his daughter to see his distress. Katy had already had more than enough trauma in her life without him adding to it. He was about to open the door when a friendly voice called out.

"Hello, we don't usually see you here during the day."

He looked up to find Jessica Carter walking towards him.

He smiled. "No, but I was here on business so thought I'd drop in. I hope that's okay."

"Yes, of course. Katy will be pleased to see you. I take it you're here regarding our poor young rape victim?"

"You know about her?"

"The entire hospital knows. Collective rage is the dominant emotion in Bradchester Central at the moment."

Paolo nodded. "I can imagine. She's going to need counselling. Will she be in your care?"

"I think so, although a lot depends on language issues."

"Yes, I can see that would be a problem," Paolo said. "Have you already seen Katy this morning?"

"Yes, and before you ask, there is no change. Please don't mention your reason for being here to Katy." She smiled. "I'm sorry, that was unnecessary. I know you won't." She touched his arm in apology. "Enjoy your visit."

She walked on towards the lifts, leaving Paolo trying to remember the last time a woman had touched him. It had been Barbara, the best part of a year ago. He hadn't had any female contact since their brief affair. No wonder he felt so alone. Pushing that thought to one side, he plastered on a smile and opened the door to his daughter's room.

Katy was standing with her back to him, staring out of the window. Paolo came in and closed the door, but Katy remained absolutely still. He could see her reflection in the glass. Dark hair and eyes, olive skin and delicate features, she looked so much like his mother. Katy used to have his mother's fiery Italian personality as well, but now she was always so passive it was like being with a different person.

His little girl wasn't so little anymore. She'd be sixteen on Christmas Day, just over two months away. He prayed she wouldn't be spending the day in here. Surely she'd be well enough to go home by then. But if Lydia carried through on her threat, how often would he be allowed to see Katy? Better not to worry about that now.

"Hi, baby, how are you doing today? I was in the area, so thought I'd drop in early."

Katy spun round.

"Dad!" she screamed and threw herself into his arms, sobbing as if she would never be able to stop.

Paolo stroked her back and made soothing noises, trying to remain calm in the face of her hysteria, but he was stunned. She'd spoken! For the first time in months she'd called to him!

She pulled away, her mouth moving, clearly desperate to say more. Pain and rage filled her face as she tried to force words out, but none escaped.

"What is it, baby? What's happened? Tell me."

But the effort proved too much, she began to howl. Paolo pulled her back into his arms and manoeuvred them closer to the wall so that he could reach for the buzzer.

Katy needed more help than he could give. And she needed it now.

CHAPTER 10

8th October (midday)

Pete glared at the clock. Midday already and still no word from Joey. What the fuck was taking him so long to come over? He jumped when the intercom finally played. His nerves were shot to shit. He hadn't been able to calm down since Joey had dropped him off the night before. Hands shaking, he pressed the button.

"Who is it?"

"Pizza delivery."

"Thank fuck for that, Joey. Where you been?"

"You want to have this conversation over the intercom, or you going to open the gates and let me in?"

"Fuck, you're right. I'm not thinking straight."

He pressed the key button and then went to open the studio door. He stood outside, barely able to keep still as he watched for the pizza van to appear. Joey manoeuvred the vehicle so that the back doors were close to the studio's entrance. The van had hardly stopped before Pete was reaching for the driver's door.

"What have you found out?" he asked as Joey climbed out.

"Let's get inside, shall we? Stop asking questions out here like a moron."

"Don't you speak to me like that," Pete said as Joey pushed past and disappeared into the studio. Pete followed him in and slammed the door. Joey was already sprawled in Pete's favourite chair. Fucking bastard was acting like he was somebody important instead of just a pimp.

"Screw you, Joey. Where do you get off telling me I'm a moron?"

"Well now, let's look at this, shall we? In the last three days you've totally fucked up the mind of one girl, killed another and lost me a third. In my eyes that makes you a moron."

Pete swallowed the insults he wanted to hurl. Right now he needed to find out what was happening and Joey was the only one who could tell him.

"Have you got people in the hospital?"

Joey nodded. "Yes, but the kid is being watched 24/7. We can't get close to her just yet. Fortunately, she doesn't speak a word of English, so can't do us any harm at the moment, but the cops have already been sniffing around. We can't take the chance on there being no one in the hospital who can speak Albanian. I need to get rid of her today, before she can spill her guts."

Pete shook his head. "You should have picked her up last night when the travellers dumped her at the hospital. I told you that."

"And I told you there are too many cameras around the place. If we'd been caught on CCTV that would have been the end of everything. Anyway, I'm not here to talk over old ground. I'm here to clean up after you, yet again. What have you done with the girl's body?"

Pete pointed. "She's through there. I put her in the bath, out of the way."

Joey stood up. "I'll go get her."

"What will you do with her body? What if she's found?"

"Pete, believe me, where she's going, no one will ever find her. I've hidden more bodies than you want to know about. Remember that," Joey said, glaring at Pete with enough venom to make him wish he'd kept his mouth shut. Joey grinned and then headed off to the bathroom.

He soon reappeared with the child in his arms. "Open the door and make sure it's safe, will you."

Pete peered out. No one was in sight. His staff over at the house would all be busy at this time of day, although what they did he couldn't imagine. Not that he cared enough to find out, but sometimes he wondered what exactly he was getting for his huge wage bill.

He opened the rear van doors and signalled to Joey. The girl was slung in the back and the doors locked. Joey headed for the driver's door.

"Wait," Pete hissed. "I need a replacement."

Joey turned and pushed Pete back into the studio, shutting the door behind him.

"Are you out of your tiny mind? Do you think I'm bringing in more girls before this shit is cleared up? Shit, let me remind you, caused by you and you alone. You're obviously off your trolley, but let me make this clear, Mr Fuck Up, the next girl is going to cost you far more than what you've paid for three of the others put together. You're a liability, Pete, and liabilities have to pay." He patted Pete's cheek. "And if you mess up again, the price trebles. Every screw up from now on triples the previous price. Got that?"

Pete wanted to punch Joey in the face, but, instead, he nodded. He'd accept the insults and pay whatever Joey asked, for now, but he swore to himself, if he ever got the chance to fuck up Joey's life in some way, he'd jump at it.

"As long as we understand each other, everything will be just fine," Joey said.

Pete watched, silently fuming, as Joey left. He wished he could find himself a new supplier of brats, but that bastard was the only one he could trust not to sell him out to the press.

Fuck it. Fuck, fuck, fuck!

He'd have to do without for the time being. At least the concert tickets were selling well. Not everything in his life had gone down the drain.

CHAPTER 11

8th October (afternoon)

Lunchtime came and went and still Paolo sat at his desk, trying to work out why Katy had reacted as she had that morning. After he'd pressed the buzzer for the nurses, everything seemed to happen in slow motion and yet, looking back, he saw events in double speed.

A young nurse had responded almost immediately. When she came in and tried to prise Katy out of Paolo's arms, Katy screamed as if possessed. The nurse then tried to calm Katy, but only succeeded in making her worse.

"We need her doctor," Paolo yelled and the nurse fled from the room. He'd felt like crying himself, with relief, when the nurse returned with Jessica Carter.

"I'll need to sedate her. Hold her steady for me," Jessica said.

Within moments, Katy's screaming softened to a whimper and she'd slumped against Paolo. He'd picked her up and carried her over to the bed.

"What happened?" Jessica asked.

Paolo hadn't been sure if she was speaking to him or the nurse, but he'd answered anyway.

"When I came in, Katy was standing over by the window, looking out. I called out to her and she ran at me." Waves of nausea swept over him. "I don't know what I did. I don't know why…"

"Come outside," Jessica said. "Katy will sleep for a few hours now."

Paolo followed the psychiatrist into the corridor.

"Can you recall anything, no matter how small, that might have caused Katy's reaction?"

Paolo had images revolving in his head: Katy trying to speak, but not being able to get the words out,.

"She called out to me. She actually spoke and wanted to say more, but the more she tried to force words out, the more upset she'd become, until she was as you saw her. I don't know what set her off, but I think it must have been me."

"Blaming yourself again?"

Paolo looked up, surprised at Jessica's tone. The psychiatrist sounded as if she was mocking him. But there was only kindness in her eyes.

"As I explained to you yesterday, you are not to blame for everything that is wrong with Katy. It seems to me that she must have been upset before you entered her room. The fact that she clung to you shows she was seeking your protection or support. She would not have done that had you been the cause of her upset."

Paolo was relieved, but a tiny voice had persisted. Maybe Lydia was right. Maybe he was holding back Katy's progress.

"It's encouraging that she spoke," Jessica said, "even if it was just the one word. It's even more encouraging that she wanted to say more. That's the first time she has tried to break through her silence. I suggest you go now. I will call you if I am able to find out the catalyst, but I sincerely doubt it was anything you did or said."

Paolo shook off the memories. The shot the psychiatrist gave Katy would put her out for a few hours, so he knew he wouldn't hear from Jessica Carter until this evening and only then if she'd discovered something. So there was really no point in staring at the phone, willing it to ring, but he did it anyway.

It would be better to stop wasting time and get the paperwork under control, he thought. He picked up a report, read the first line and put it back down again. Then he glanced at a sheet covered in numbers. None of them made any sense. Come on, Paolo; pull yourself together, he ordered, but his inner Paolo stuck two fingers up.

He was still staring at the phone half an hour later when Dave knocked and came into the office. Grateful for the interruption, Paolo signalled for him to sit down.

"What have you found out?"

"Not a great deal more than we knew already. I showed the pictures around and the reactions I got told me all I needed to know about the kind of men we're looking for. Everyone seems scared of them, prostitutes, shopkeepers, even some of our local street thugs lost much of their swagger when they realised who I wanted to talk about."

"And no one told you where we could find them?"

Dave shook his head. "Nope. Here's the interesting bit, though. No one knew anything about them. They had never seen them, never heard about the car they drove or the kids they managed, but they all looked sick when they saw the photos, then clammed up and sang the same tune – seen nothing, know nothing. I know that's par for the course over in that area, but I don't usually get such a sense of an entire community as scared to speak as this one is."

Paolo drummed his fingers on the desk. "Any thoughts on what hold the men might have?"

"Only one thing stood out. One of the older women, who'd also claimed not to know the men, said something under her breath as I was leaving, but it doesn't really help us as it doesn't seem connected to our case."

"What did she say?"

"It was difficult to make out. As I say, she whispered as I went past, but it sounded like, 'an older one has disappeared.' When I turned back, she'd moved off with the other women. Bearing in mind how scared they all were, I didn't want to chase her down and ask questions in front of the others, so thought I'd go back later and see if I can get her on her own. It might mean something, it might not."

Paolo nodded. "Good idea. I'll come with you. At this stage we can't afford to pass up anything that might help.

In the meantime, CC has dropped the girl's clothes off at the lab. She's now watching the footage of the CCTV film from the hospital. George questioned the porter who found the girl, but she'd already been there for a while when he discovered her, so couldn't tell us anything new."

"Yeah, I saw CC on my way in. She was staring at the screen as if it might escape if she glanced away. I didn't want to disturb her concentration to ask her about your visit to the hospital. How did it go?"

Paolo studied Dave and wondered if there was more behind his words than he was letting on. He knew Dave was a touch jealous of their partnership and didn't like it when Paolo picked one of the other detective sergeants to accompany him. Deciding Dave was simply asking to be brought up to speed, Paolo told him about the child's reaction when they'd gone into her room.

"We're going to have to wait until Dr Peters feels she's ready to see CC and Mrs Dushku, but we can't wait too long. If this child has been brought into the country by the traffickers, and it seems likely, then she's our best chance of finding out who they are. The other girls we've taken off the streets are too far gone on drugs, or too scared, to tell us anything. The ones who can talk are convinced if they speak out either they will die, or their families back in Albania will suffer. They've been brainwashed into thinking they have no value and that whoever ran them on the streets can reach in and get them, even in the social services hostel."

As he spoke, something in the back of his mind raised a red flag. Something had been said today that was out of place, something not quite right. What was it? Dave's voice faded into the background as Paolo tried to tease whatever it was to come to the forefront of his mind, but it remained just out of reach. And yet, somehow he knew the tiny scrap of information was important.

The phone rang, interrupting Paolo's thoughts. His heart did a summersault. Please let it be Jessica Carter with some positive news about Katy, he prayed.

"Sorry, Dave, I need to take this." Paolo picked up the phone. "Sterling."

But his luck was out. It wasn't the voice he'd been hoping to hear.

"This is Doctor Peters. We met this morning."

Forcing his mind into work mode, he responded. "How can I help you, Doctor?"

"Detective Inspector, you need to get over here to Bradchester Central immediately."

"What's happened? Is it the child? Does she want to speak?"

Paolo heard a deep sigh and then the doctor's voice came back.

"I'm afraid not. She'll never be able to speak again. She has been murdered."

CHAPTER 12

8th October (afternoon)

Pete paced up and down the studio, kicking out at the sofa each time he passed. He craved a hit, but didn't dare touch his stuff until he'd heard from Joey. What was taking him so long? He'd said he'd be able to deal with the kid now they knew which ward she was on, so why hadn't he sorted her out?

He stopped pacing and threw himself down on the couch. Staring at the stuff on the coffee table, the craving intensified. Maybe just one line. Surely that would be okay. His head would still be clear enough if he just had the one line. His hand reached out, but he changed his mind and jumped up again.

He'd go into the recording area. That's the way to make time pass. He'd work on the next track of the album. His agent had been bugging him about getting it released before the concert, but what with one thing and another, he was a few weeks behind. The latest brats had really fucked up his timing. He wished now he'd just taken one of them. Maybe the cock up had been his fault

88

for being greedy. Maybe he was being punished for wanting too much from life. From now on he'd settle for one at a time.

But even the music failed to take his mind off what might be happening at the hospital. Giving up, he moved back into the lounge area. What was taking Joey so long?

Deciding to take a hit after all, he headed back towards the couch. His phone rang as he sat down. Relief made him clumsy and he dropped it as he tried to answer it. Snatching it back up, he hit the button.

"Pete here. What's up?"

"You can relax. The problem has been dealt with."

"Thank fuck for that. Joey, I owe you."

Pete heard Joey laugh, so wasn't completely surprised by what came next.

"Yes, you do. You owe me five grand."

"What for?"

"Expenses, my friend. Expenses and loss of income. As I said to you, liabilities have to pay and you have become a major liability."

"Go screw yourself, Joey. I'm not paying that much. I don't mind coughing up a bit towards expenses, but..."

Joey cut across his words. "You pay, Pete, or the tabloids you fear so much will be getting an anonymous tip off about your choice in sexual partners."

Pete went cold. "That's blackmail."

"No, it's business. I've incurred a great deal of expense importing commodities that no longer exist. You should be grateful I'm not demanding more. I'll be round tomorrow to collect."

Pete sighed. He'd have to pay. What choice did he have?

"Okay. When will you have some fresh stuff in? I'm going through withdrawal here."

"You'll have to take a few cold showers, my friend. I'm holding off on imports until this current situation dies down. I'll let you know when we start up again, but you'd better start taking care of my stock or pretty soon the price will be so high you'll need to sell your fancy mansion to buy a single night's fun."

The line went dead. Pete slung the phone across the room, and it hit the sofa on the other side of the room, falling to the floor. Joey had him by the balls – literally. What would he do if the royalty cheques dried up? Right now, people were still playing the old stuff from The Vision Inside, but that wouldn't go on forever. If Joey carried through on his threat, even a single brat was going to cost him a fortune each time he bought one. His comeback concert had to be a success. He was going to need the money.

He reached forward and sorted himself a line of coke. As he hoovered it up, his head cleared. No problem, no problem at all. Of course his concert was going to be successful. He'd nail it. He fell to his knees and crawled over to his phone. Time to make sure his agent was on the fucking ball.

Scrolling through his contacts, Pete realised how few of his so-called friends had kept in touch over the years. They'd all be sniffing round when he was back at the top where he belonged. Where was his agent's number? Ah, there it was. Stuart Windham.

He pressed call and waited. His agent didn't always answer. Pete was sure the bastard saw his name on the phone and pretended to be in a meeting or some fucking thing, but this time he heard Stuart's voice.

"Hi Pete, what's up?"

"How's things with the concert? We got everything covered?"

"Pete, I've told you over and over. The ground says ticket sales are going well, but we need to get the new album out and played ahead of that. You know how it works. You're gonna be playing all new stuff and no one will know any of it if it hasn't already had some air time."

"I'm nearly done with it."

"Good. As soon as it's ready I'll do my best to get you on breakfast TV to talk about it. Get…"

"On what? I'm not a fucking jungle survivor. I'm a serious musician. What do I want to go on breakfast TV for? Get me on some decent music shows."

"Breakfast TV is important. It's not like back in the day when *Top of Pops* was the show to be seen on. Nowadays, you have to go on the chat show circuit."

"Screw that. My music can do the talking for me."

"Really? You think so? Let me give you the facts of life as they are now, Pete. To get anyone to listen to your music, you've first got to remind them you're even alive. You haven't recorded anything new in over twenty years. Today's music buyers don't know you exist."

"They will when —"

91

"Pete, will you please just shut up for five seconds and listen? I've been pushing your name down the throats of anyone I can pin in a corner and it's not been easy. The ones who remember you aren't exactly thrilled to hear you're still alive. The ones who don't remember you think you're another washed up ex-star desperate to get on stage before you die. You seem to think all I have to do is mention your name and people will be falling over themselves to play your stuff, but it's not that simple. That's why I booked the local stadium for the concert. At least people in Bradchester know who you are."

Pete felt as if his entire life was fucked up. First the brats, now his agent sounded as if he had to climb Everest just to sell a few albums. It wasn't fair. He worked hard. He was a good musician. Fuck, he was a *great* musician. It was time Stuart remembered just who was paying for his nice office and car.

"Stuart, stop whining. You think I don't know all of that? Why do you think I started my own record label? It wasn't to help out other musicians, that's for sure. It was to make sure my stuff was out there to be played. You said the concert tickets are selling. The album's nearly done. I've got the session musos and backing singers coming over here in the week between Christmas and New Year to practice for the concert and we'll do a full rehearsal at the stadium during the afternoon of New Year's Eve. I'm prepared, Stuart. I really am, and I'm ready to give this comeback my best shot. All I'm saying is that early mornings don't suit me. I don't look my best before midday."

Pete expected to hear Stuart laugh, but all he got was a sigh.

"Grow up, Pete. I've finally got a bit of mainstream interest for you and you need to take advantage of it. We've got to tell them when the album is coming out and release at least one track ahead of that date. So, come on, are you ready to let one of your new songs out into the world?"

"I think so, yeah. I'll get a demo over to you tomorrow." But not *Help Me, Mama*, Pete thought. He'd keep that one for the concert. He wanted to feel the rush when the fans went wild over it.

"Okay," Stuart said. "That's more like it. I'll chat to the radio people; get it some air time, then follow up with breakfast TV and a few chat shows. You are clean, aren't you? Promise me you're not using, cos if you are, I'm out of this."

Pete glanced over at the table, littered with his stuff.

"I'm not using. Haven't touched anything in years. I told you after my last stint in rehab there was no way I was ever gonna get fucked up like that again. What are you asking me for? You know the answer."

Stuart sighed again. Pete was beginning to hate that sound even more than Joey's laugh.

"I'm asking you, Pete, because we can't afford any negative publicity. None at all. It's not like the old days when it was taken for granted rock stars would be high as a kite in interviews. Now you've got to be clean and look it. You screwed up big time when you crashed and burned

93

so publicly. That's why the rest of The Vision Inside won't reform."

"Yeah, well, when I'm back at the top those fuckers needn't think they're gonna come and hitch a ride on my success cos they can just fuck off."

He thought back over the nightmare of the last couple of days. At least with the brat dead, he didn't need to worry about her pointing fingers at him, but as it hit home just how close he'd come to losing his chance at the big time, he almost threw up.

"I've worked hard for this, Stuart. I deserve whatever comes my way and I'm not sharing it with those losers."

CHAPTER 13

8th October (late afternoon / early evening)

Paolo looked down at the child's body and felt rage surge through him. She looked even younger than the girl he'd seen at yesterday's autopsy. Violated and killed at such a young age. What sick bastards would do such a thing? But he knew he had to let the rage pass or it would cloud his judgement and he might miss some small clue that could lead him to the traffickers.

Forcing the anger to the background, he turned to the waiting hospital staff.

"Who found her?"

"I did," a young nurse said and stepped forward. Fighting back tears, her voice was almost inaudible.

"Can you tell me exactly what happened," Paolo said. "Take your time."

The nurse took a deep breath and managed to stop the tears from falling. "We've been so busy; we're all behind in our work. If the hospital hadn't brought in agency nurses we wouldn't have been able to cope. It was my turn to check the patients' blood pressure and temps, but I was late. Normally, I'd have finished and been back at the nurses' station. If I had been I'd have seen the woman before she went in and maybe asked who she was. I might have been able to stop her."

She stopped speaking and wiped her eyes. The sudden silence highlighted the sound of Dave's pen scratching on his pad as he took notes.

"You're doing well," Paolo said. "Tell me what you saw."

"I was working my way down the ward when I saw a nurse in our uniform leave the girl's room. I didn't recognise her, but assumed she'd been sent from one of the other wards to fill in. The policewoman was outside the door, so I didn't think there could be anything wrong. You know? It just didn't register that there might be a reason to worry. It took me another half an hour or so to get to this end of the ward and then when I came in, I saw the pillow over... I saw... I... I'm sorry. I can't..."

Paolo waited until the nurse had composed herself.

"Could you describe the nurse to us?"

"Dark hair. She was too far away for me to see her face clearly, but olive skin."

"Height?"

"Taller than average. Taller even than me, I think."

"How tall are you?" Paolo asked, guessing at about 5ft 10in.

"I'm 5ft 11."

"So the fake nurse could have been about 6ft? Maybe an inch or two more?"

The nurse nodded. "It's difficult to tell from the other end of the corridor, but I think she was about that."

"Anything else you can remember?"

"Nothing. I'm sorry, I was so behind on my round, I wasn't really paying attention. That's all I can recall."

Paolo smiled. "You've done very well. You've certainly given us enough to look for on the CCTV. With a bit of luck we might see her as she leaves, or getting into a car, or at least see which direction she took when she left the hospital."

He turned to the WPC who'd been standing by while the nurse had been speaking.

"How did you come to let her in?"

The WPC looked haggard, as well she might, Paolo thought. She had been placed there for one reason only – to stop anyone hurting the child.

"Sir, I'm so sorry. She seemed to be part of the hospital staff."

"I realise that," Paolo said. "I'm aware you were tricked. What I want to know is how it happened."

"The nurse, sorry, the woman dressed as a nurse came through the double doors with a blood pressure machine on a trolley. The same as the real nurse. She started at that end of the ward, going into three rooms before she reached this one. She looked and acted like a nurse. She'd been in the other rooms first, and went into two others afterwards before she left the ward. It didn't occur to me there might be anything wrong with her." She hung her head. "I'm so sorry, sir. She seemed genuine."

"Did you get a good look at her face?"

"Not really. Maybe enough for an identikit image, but..." She took a deep breath. "I'm afraid I didn't look too closely, sir. I'm so sorry."

"It's no good getting upset over it now. Go back to the station and see if you can work with our artist. Maybe we can get a good enough image to put out to the media."

"Yes, sir."

Paolo watched as the WPC left, then turned to Dave.

"Smart move by the killer," he said. "If the fake nurse had come directly to the child's room, alarm bells would have rung in the WPC's mind. By going to the other rooms first, she made it look like she belonged on the ward. I'm not sure I wouldn't have fallen for it as well."

Dave shook his head. "I don't believe you would have, sir. I've never known anyone as suspicious as you."

Paolo sighed. "I wish our WPC had been more suspicious, but it's too late to cry over what can't be changed. Now we've got a murder inquiry on our hands. Let's stop these bastards before they destroy anyone else." He took out his phone. "Before we go down to collect the CCTV footage I need to arrange for uniform to run a search and interview."

Paolo and Dave left the hospital nearly an hour later, with Dave holding copies of yet more CCTV film from the hospital security cameras.

"One problem we might have is if the killer was aware of the cameras. If she was, all she needed to do was ditch the uniform and we won't pick her up on the film as she left," Dave said.

"I know, but let's hope she hadn't taken the cameras into account. But if she has ditched the clothes, let's hope uniform find them in the overall search of the hospital. We could do with a break on this."

They walked through to the parking area where Dave had left the car.

"It gets dark so early now," Paolo said. "And it's bloody cold at nights, but still feels like spring during the day. No wonder everyone's going down with flu." He groaned. "I do believe I have now officially turned into my father. He always blamed flu outbreaks on unseasonal weather."

Dave laughed. "Not just *your* father. We all do that, don't we?"

"I suppose we do. Right, let's make sure we've covered everything before we head off home. Uniform are questioning everyone left in the hospital and conducting a room by room search. Not that I think we'll glean much from that. I would imagine the woman left as soon as she'd done what she came to do." Paolo clenched his fists. "I'm pretty pissed off with myself."

Dave stopped next to the car and began his usual patting of pockets looking for the keys. "Why, sir?"

Paolo walked to the passenger side and peered through the gloom over the top of the car. "Because I should have realised she was in danger."

"I don't see that, sir," Dave said as he finally located the keys and unlocked the door. "Even though you left someone outside to protect her, there was no reason to believe anyone, other than whoever left her at the hospital, even knew where she was."

Paolo waited until they were in the car before answering. "You're right, of course, but clearly someone did know. What I'd like to find out is who dropped her outside. I mean, if the people who brought her to the hospital were the traffickers, why did they bother? Why didn't they simply kill her in the first place?"

"But they came back to do it, sir," Dave said, looking at Paolo as if he'd lost the plot.

"Yes, I know that, but it doesn't make sense to do it that way. I don't think it *was* the traffickers who left her at the hospital. I think someone else found her and brought her here. Then, somehow, the traffickers found out where she was and covered their tracks by killing her. Which makes me wonder how the hell they knew where she was."

Dave started the car and reversed out, doing a three point turn and heading towards the station.

"I'll tell you another thing, Dave. We've been looking at this trafficking thing from the wrong angle. We've been concentrating on the streets, trying to pick up the pimps. Okay, so we might get lucky and discover the two men Michelle described, but even if we do, they aren't likely to be the ones actually bringing the kids in. I think we need to start investigating the Albanian business community." He pulled a notepad and pen from his pocket. "Tomorrow morning we'll get together a complete list of all those businesses that could be used as a cover." He scribbled down his thoughts as he spoke. "Import/export companies, language schools, overseas haulage, employment agencies specialising in finding work for Albanians and so on. There has to be a definite connection between Albania and Bradchester. The girls don't arrive here by magic. We've got to find the routes and the people making it possible to use those paths. Maybe they are shipped in from other cities, as the mysterious tip-off woman said, but someone is putting them to work here." He nodded, feeling more positive than he had for a long time. "There's a link, Dave, and we're going to find it if we have to work overtime every day from now until Christmas."

Dave pulled up outside the station and Paolo got out.

"See you tomorrow, sir," Dave said, but didn't immediately drive away. As Paolo closed the door, the window slid down and Dave leaned over towards the passenger side. "Would you like to join a few of us later? I'm meeting Rebecca in the Nag and Bag and then we're heading off to the Indian in the High Street. There's about ten of us going. You'd be more than welcome."

Paolo was tempted. It would be nice to spend an evening in company, but the bloody paperwork had stopped simply calling to him. It was now screaming through a loud hailer. If he didn't tackle at least some of it tonight, he'd never get to sleep.

"Thanks for the invite, Dave, but I'll pass this time. Maybe next, hey?"

He watched as Dave's car disappeared into the night. When was the last time he'd gone out for the evening? God, it was so long ago he couldn't even remember. I'll get this case put to bed and then fix up some sort of social life, he promised himself. It was his birthday in eight days. Maybe he should go out for a celebratory drink after work with his team. He did a quick calculation. The seventeenth of October fell on a Thursday this year. Thursdays weren't such great nights to go out.

Maybe someone else's birthday would be a better event to begin his new social life, he decided, as he walked into the station. But he would be damned if he'd work late on the seventeenth, he thought, going into his office. He flicked the light switch and groaned, convinced there was double the number of files there'd been when he left to go to the hospital earlier.

Two hours later he switched off the light and headed for home.

As he walked into the apartment he couldn't help but remember the excitement of choosing it with Katy earlier in the year, only a few days before she'd been picked up and attacked. Don't think about that, he told himself, but his inner voice only went a bit quieter. He had no idea how to switch it off completely. Maybe he needed Jessica Carter's help as much as Katy.

He slung his jacket on his bed and wandered into the second bedroom, flicking on the bedside light. This was supposed to be Katy's for the weekends when she stayed with him. She'd chosen the colour scheme and Paolo had decorated – red and black dominated. Not his choice, but he'd wanted Katy to feel the room was hers. He picked up the photo frame from the dressing table. The picture had been taken four years earlier, back in the days when he and Lydia had been the contented parents of two lovely, healthy girls. In the photo he had his arms around Katy and Sarah, with Lydia standing next to Sarah. He could almost feel the warmth of his daughters' bodies as they snuggled into him. They were all laughing and Lydia looked radiantly happy.

Paolo remembered the day it had been taken. It was towards the end of their holiday in Wales. One of those rare magical moments where the weather was perfect, no one was upset with anyone else, the girls were having one of their best friends with each other days and Lydia had held tightly to his hand as they walked, almost as if she couldn't bear to let it go. Katy had gone up to a complete stranger and asked him to take a picture. The man had turned into a David Bailey clone, insisting on taking several photos from different angles until Katy said she was happy with the result.

And now Sarah was dead, wiped out in a hit and run that had been targeting him. And Katy was in hospital, again because of him. No wonder Lydia couldn't bear to be in the same room. In her place, he doubted he'd want to be in the same country.

He put the photo back on the dressing table and switched off the light. It hurt too much to be reminded of all he'd lost.

Paolo switched on the television. He needed noise, any kind, to block out his thoughts. Settling himself down in the armchair, he tried to empty his mind and relax. The news came on. A photograph of a pretty blonde child, only six years old, holding a baby doll and grinning happily at the camera, filled the screen. As the image faded, the camera panned to a young couple, clearly distraught begging for news of their daughter who'd disappeared the day before.

The woman was crying and shaking her head. "I was watching her through the window while she played in the garden. The phone rang and I went to answer it. I came back with the phone in my hand. Seconds. I was only gone seconds and Lucy... my baby... she wasn't... I couldn't see... I ran outside."

She pulled herself together and pointed at the doll in the picture she was holding.

"She loved her baby doll. It went everywhere... everywhere..."

As she collapsed again, her husband put his arm round her and faced the cameras.

"We found her doll in the flowerbed of our front garden," he said. "Lucy wouldn't have gone outside the gate without it."

The screen filled once again with the image of the six-year-old clutching her doll. A number came up and a voice asked viewers to call with any information relating to the disappearance of Lucy Bassington.

Paolo felt sick. What sort of world were they living in?

CHAPTER 14

9th October (morning)

After another all-night session on the new album, Pete knew he needed to get some sleep or he'd collapse. He could catnap here in the studio, but now that the decorators had finished, he fancied stretching out on his king-size bed over in the main house.

He shut up the studio, changing the number sequence on the lock. Until he'd had chance to get rid of all the evidence in there, he didn't want anyone coming over to clean. He strolled across to his mansion, enjoying the warmth of the sun on his face and the glint of sunlight on the lake in the distance. Acres and acres of land and all his.

God, he loved his place. Who would have guessed a council estate boy like him would end up lord of the fucking manor. As he approached the wide stone stairway leading up to the massive oak door, he wished his mum was still alive. She'd have loved living here. His dad briefly cast a shadow over his pleasure, but Pete shoved his memory to one side. No way was he going to waste time dwelling on that bastard. He'd been dead for fifteen years and still Pete couldn't think about him without wanting to run and hide. Even at the height of his fame with The Vision Inside he'd been scared of his dad. Scared to go home and visit his mum and scared his dad would show up at one of the places the group were performing. The fact that he'd never shown any interest in Pete's music or career, and wasn't likely to turn up, hadn't stopped Pete from crapping himself whenever he was told he had a visitor.

Memories of the beatings he'd had as a kid made him shake, which was stupid because the man was long buried and couldn't hurt him anymore. Stupid prick, he swore silently, shrugging off the memories.

He opened the front door and looked around. He'd been living in the house for years, and yet every time he came in he got that same sense of awe. A Jacobean staircase stretched out in front of him and split at the top to lead up to the two wings of the house.

"Ah, there you are, Mr Carson. I wanted to have a word, if you've got a moment."

He turned to see his housekeeper coming towards him, her usually cheerful face looking very serious for once.

"Problem, Mrs Baxter?"

"Not now, but I think there might have been one."

Pete sat on one of the hall chairs and pointed at the one next to him.

"Take a seat and tell me what's up."

Mrs Baxter sat on the very edge of the seat. Pete wondered if she was scared of it breaking. It looked very flimsy, but had been hanging around the place for a couple of hundred years, so must be sturdier than it looked.

"We've had an intruder," she said.

"What, here in the house?"

"No, nothing like that. It's a bit weird," she said. "Tony, the gardener's assistant, came through the side entrance today. He usually comes via the main gate, but apparently his wife dropped him at the side gate for some reason. Anyway, the whys and wherefores aren't important. What is important is that Tony spotted blood on the drive and there was also some on the gate. It was almost as if someone had climbed over it while bleeding."

Waves of nausea swept over Pete as he listened. Oh no, oh fucking no. He tried desperately to come up with some plausible explanation, but his mind refused to operate. All he could do was picture that brat as she climbed. She must have been bleeding, the little cow. He waited for the blow to fall – for Mrs Baxter to say she knew what he'd been doing over in the stable block.

"I realised straight away what had happened," she said, nodding fiercely, her usually placid face screwed in disgust. "Someone must have climbed the gates to break in and cut themselves as they scrambled over. There are some very sharp points in the wrought ironwork."

Sick with relief, Pete could only nod. No words came out.

"I had Tony search the grounds, but he couldn't find anyone. The blood on the gates was dried up, so it couldn't have happened today. It must have been yesterday or the day before. Do you think there's any point in still calling the police?"

Pete forced himself to speak. "N... no, I don't think so, do you?"

Mrs Baxter nodded. "I doubt they'd even send anyone out. It's not as if whoever it was managed to break into the house. At least, I don't think he did. Nothing seems to be missing at any rate."

"I'm sure you're right, Mrs Baxter."

She stood up. "I'm glad you agree with me. I'll get Tony to clean up the drive and gates with the power hose. Are you okay? You look a bit peaky."

Pete shook his head. "I'm fine, just a bit shaken by the thought of someone wandering around without our knowing."

"You should get some dogs, Mr Carson. They are the best deterrent and good companions, too."

Pete clambered to his feet and tried to control his shaking legs. "I'll give that some thought, but right now I'm going to have a lie down. I spent most of last night in the recording studio and I'm whacked."

Mrs Baxter patted his arm in her usual motherly fashion. "You work too hard. You need to take better care of yourself. I'm off home shortly. I hope you get some sleep. See you tomorrow."

"Yes, tomorrow," Pete said and turned for the stairs. How close a call was that? His heart couldn't take too many more shocks. The last few days had aged him about a hundred years.

He was so shaken he passed the treasures he'd collected over the years, paintings, sculptures, bronzes and tiny ceramics, without even seeing them. Normally he stopped and admired his collections, gloating on them. If he was honest with himself, he didn't even like most of them, but he'd wanted to own stuff that proved he was rich. To show anyone who came that he had so much money they needn't bother looking down their fucking noses at him.

None of that mattered today. What if someone had been able to question that brat before Joey had her silenced? What if she'd been able to lead the police here? He'd have lost everything. Was it worth the fuck she'd given him? He knew the answer to that. No, it wasn't. But even as he threw himself on his bed, promising that he wouldn't touch another brat, that it wasn't worth the chance of getting caught, his body betrayed him. Just thinking about that young flesh made him hard.

As he drifted off to sleep, he decided he didn't have to give them up; he just needed to be careful. That was the answer. He'd been a bit greedy, that's why everything had gone so wrong. He'd learned his lesson now, though.

His last thought before oblivion claimed him was that Joey would have a new batch arriving soon. He wondered how much it would cost him to make sure he got the pick of the bunch.

CHAPTER 15

9th October (morning)

Paolo stood in front of the white board and scribbled.

"Right, listen up, everyone. We're not giving up on our search for the two pimps, but we are going to widen our field of attack."

He turned back to his team. "George, I want you to get in touch with the Chamber of Commerce. We need a list of all Albanian-owned businesses. We're looking for any set up with links to Albania. Any enterprise that imports goods, has people who regularly travel to Albania, anything really that might be used as a cover for people trafficking. But we also need to uncover any businesses regularly dealing with other cities with large Albanian groups living there. The girls might arrive here directly, or they might be transported via another town. We have to keep our options open."

Paolo waited until George had finished taking notes before moving on to the next item he'd listed on the whiteboard.

"CC, what's the situation with the film footage from outside the hospital?"

"I've found the section where the child was left, sir. It's not that clear, but it's fairly obvious that a woman is carrying what looks like a child and leaving her in the spot the porters found her. So I've assumed it must be the same girl."

"Good work," Paolo said. "Were you able to see which vehicle the woman arrived and left in?"

"Yes, sir. A white transit van. I couldn't make out the full registration, but I've got enough to work with. I'm running it through the DVLA database. Unless the plates are fake, we should have details on it shortly."

Paolo checked his list on the whiteboard. "Sorry to do this to you, CC, but we have more footage for you to go through. This time it includes internal feed as well as external."

CC groaned before grinning up at Paolo. "What am I looking for this time?"

"Our murder suspect. The only description we have of her is dark hair and wearing a nurse's uniform."

CC looked up. "You're joking me. Looking for a nurse in a hospital?"

"I wish I was joking," Paolo said, passing CC the drawing the artist had composed with the WPC. "This might help, but it isn't that clear. Sadly, our WPC wasn't as observant as we would have liked. Mind you, even if it had been a perfect likeness, if the killer knows her way around the hospital, she'll know where the cameras are, so might have managed to avoid them. One good thing, we're looking for a nurse quite a bit taller than the average. I know it's a thankless task, CC, but I need you to go through every inch of film, just in case she stopped and smiled for the camera." He raised his hands in surrender. "I know. You hate me because I've landed you with a crap job, but you're the best when it comes to spotting things on film."

CC grinned. "Never mind the soft soap, sir. Just remember this when it comes to my birthday. I'll want an extra big cake to make up for it."

Paolo grinned back. "That's a promise. Uniform are still questioning the hospital staff. If they get anything to help your search they've been told to contact you directly. Dave, you and I are going over to Zephyr Road. I'm hoping we might strike it lucky with the woman who whispered to you as you passed her yesterday. Picking up the two men controlling the girls has to be a top priority. Second only to taking the kids off the streets."

Paolo watched as they dispersed. He was lucky with his people. Remembering past teams he'd worked with, both as officer in command and as one of those being told what to do, he knew how fortunate he was not to have any of the cocky shits out for personal glory.

The only one who worried him slightly was George. Quiet and often withdrawn, George didn't offer much about his private life. All Paolo knew about him was the fact that he was divorced with no children. He wondered what George did outside of his working day and then wondered why he was even thinking along those lines.

But, in truth, he knew the answer to that. It was because he was questioning his own lack of any kind of social life.

Let me just get this case solved and I'll do something about that, he promised that persistent inner voice pushing him to get back into the human race.

"I'll see you at your car, Dave," he said, heading to his office to pick up his jacket. As he opened the door the phone on his desk began to ring. He contemplated letting it go to voicemail, but he hadn't yet heard from Jessica Carter about Katy's outburst.

Snatching up the receiver, he answered the call, trying to keep the anxiety out of his voice. "Sterling," he said as he sat down.

"Good morning, Detective Inspector. I hope I'm not calling at a bad moment, but I need to set up an appointment with you for this afternoon."

He felt a mixture of fear and relief on hearing the psychiatrist's voice. A meeting meant something to report, but that could be good or bad.

"Of course," he said. "What time?"

"That depends on Mrs Sterling. I haven't yet been able to contact her and it's extremely important that you are both available. Let's set a time now and I'll get back to you if Mrs Sterling cannot make it. Shall we say three this afternoon?"

"At your office, or the hospital?" he asked.

"My office. I have other appointments before and after yours."

Paolo put the time and place into his i-Phone. "Is this to do with what happened with Katy yesterday?"

"Yes, it is, but I really cannot go into details over the phone, or, indeed, without Mrs Sterling being part of the discussion."

He promised to be there in plenty of time unless he heard from her to the contrary and replaced the receiver. His hands were shaking. The psychiatrist had sounded more serious than he'd ever heard her. Shaking his head, he got up and fetched his jacket. No point in painting the devil on the wall, as his mother used to say. The devil would appear in person if and when he was good and ready.

Paolo shook his head, trying to get rid of negative thoughts. He'd find out what Katy's problem was when he saw Jessica and Lydia this afternoon.

Dave drove into the station forecourt and manoeuvred the car into a spot only just vacated by another car.

"Yet again you're lucky," Paolo said. "That's why I get you to drive. No one ever leaves a space for me to drive into."

"Yeah, but the only thing I'm lucky with is finding places to park," Dave said as he turned off the ignition. "I never win on the lottery or raffles and sweepstakes."

"Yes, but you can virtually guarantee finding a parking space. You drive in, someone else drives out." Paolo laughed. "You could set up as a parking space finder in your spare time. You'd make a fortune round here."

Dave grinned, dropping the keys into his pocket. "I'd rather win millions on the lottery, but I suppose I should be grateful I'm lucky with something."

"Let's hope we're both lucky enough to find your prostitute. Come on, let's go."

Station Road wasn't exactly the best part of town, but the place looked respectable. Paolo was pleased to see that most of the businesses he remembered from his youth were still operating. This was one of the few communities that still had a drycleaners, newsagent, old-fashioned fruit and veg, alongside a mini-supermarket, hairdressers and a bank. He glanced up. Even the flats above the businesses looked lived in and cared for. Nice nets and curtains framed the windows and many of the street doors had been painted in recent history.

They walked a couple of hundred yards before turning into Zephyr Road. It was like turning into another country. Here, most of the shops they passed were boarded up and the few remaining open for business seemed to Paolo to concentrate on ways to transform goods into cash. Pawnbrokers, gold for cash, payday cheque converters. It seemed as though all the dregs of the financial service industry had found their way into this street. This time when he glanced up, Paolo saw the flats above the shops were likewise either boarded up or had dirty nets hiding whatever was going on up there.

Paolo knew the council were trying to clean up the area, but from what he could see today, they hadn't been very successful. Even this early in the day groups of women were gathered, clearly waiting for customers. Many of them walked off when they saw Paolo and Dave approaching.

"Any sign of your contact?" Paolo asked.

"I'm not sure," Dave replied. "I think that might be her down by the wrecked phone box."

Paolo looked where Dave had indicated. Sure enough there was one of the old red boxes, but all the glass was missing from the windows and there was no sign of the phone that used to be there.

Leaning against the frame was a woman, possibly in her forties, but she might have been much younger. Paolo knew that a few years on the streets tended to age people much faster than normal. Add to that a drug habit and a twenty-five year old could end up looking closer to fifty.

They carried on walking until they were a few yards short of the box.

"Is that her?"

"Yes," said Dave, "but she's got those other two with her. I doubt she'll say anything in front of them."

"Well, we don't need to worry about one of them. She's taken off," Paolo said as a woman in a dirty red leather skirt and skimpy blue top peeled away from the other two and disappeared down one of the many alleyways leading off from Zephyr Road. Paolo wondered if that was why the place was so popular with prostitutes – plenty of dark places for quickies day or night.

"Which one is your contact?" Paolo asked.

"The one in hot pants."

"Okay, I'll have a chat with her friend and keep her occupied for as long as you need."

But it wasn't necessary for them to split up. Both women stood facing them, almost as if they'd been waiting for this moment.

"I know you," the woman next to Dave's contact said. "You caught that mad bastard."

"Yes," he said, "we got him in the end. It's a pity we weren't able to catch him before he'd killed so many."

"You make that sound like you cared." She laughed, but there was no humour in it. "We know what you lot think of us, so don't try playing the sympathy card here. It won't work."

Her friend nudged her. "Alice says he's okay."

"It's okay for her. She's off the game. What the fuck does she care about us now?" She turned back to Paolo. "The only reason we're telling you anything is because it's kids involved. It's not right, what they do to the kids. Barely old enough to cross the fucking street on their own, some of them are, but they're servicing the pervs like there's no fucking tomorrow. And you know why? Cos the bastards running them have them so fucking hooked they'd suck off a leper if they were told to. And then, when they get to be teenagers, they're put out here to work."

She stopped and glared at Paolo and Dave as if it was their fault.

"We want to get these bastards," Paolo said. "But we need help. No one will tell us anything about their pimps, but someone here must know who they are."

The two women looked at each other. Dave's contact nodded.

"We don't want to get involved in any court case nor nothing," she said. "We'll tell you what we know, but don't come back expecting us to sign nothing, cos we

ain't getting in shit with anyone. Especially not that lot."
She shuddered. "Those pictures you showed us," she
continued, turning to Dave, "they work for someone
called Joey."

The other woman spoke up again. "We've never seen
this Joey bloke down here, but the two men sometimes
mention his name to the girls as a threat. Makes them fall
apart every time, so he must be pretty fucking bad. You
got the pictures with you?"

Dave pulled them from an inside pocket of his jacket
and passed them over to the two women.

They studied them for a few seconds. "This one here,"
Dave's contact said, "is called Bekim and his mate is
Edar. Right pair of shits they are. The girls are terrified of
them, but when they mention this Joey's name it turns
them to fucking jelly."

Dave made a note and looked up. "I don't suppose
you'd care to give us your names?"

"Oooh, get him, Mr Posh himself," Dave's contact
said, mimicking his voice. "You don't suppose right,
sonny. We've already told you, we're not getting involved
in no court case and we don't want it known we've told
you nothing. There was one girl, bit older than the others,
used to take care of them, she did. Reckoned she was
going to find a way to get the young ones out. Anyway,
she disappeared a few days back. We think she got done
in and we're not looking to go the same way."

"Did she say how she was planning to rescue them?"
Paolo asked.

"She'd phone someone and then you lot would turn up and take the kid away." The women looked at each other. "She must have been caught. Those two blokes most probably cottoned on to what she was up to. Now, if you don't mind, we'd like you to fuck off. We've got work to do and you're interfering with trade."

"Thank you for giving us the names," Paolo said, handing each of them his card. "If you remember anything else that might help the girls, please call me. Anytime. Day or night."

"We've told you all we know," Dave's contact said, stuffing the card in her bra. "But we'll keep your nice shiny cards, just in case."

Paolo and Dave watched as the two women sauntered off. "Come on, Mr Posh," Paolo said. "I don't think we'll learn anything more here. Time to get back to the station."

Dave nodded. "You're not going to call me that from now on, are you?"

Paolo laughed at the horrified look on Dave's face. "Only on Wednesdays and Fridays, or any day you piss me off," he said.

Dave grinned. "That's all right then. It was worth the trip down here. At least we've got some names to go with the pictures."

"Yep," said Paolo, "but what's even better is we know there's someone called Joey higher up the food chain. We want them all, but to put them out of business, we need to find out who this Joey character is. I'll get CC to have a chat with Gazmend. He might be able to point us towards Bekim and Edar, but Joey isn't an Albanian name.

119

Strange the Albanian connection doesn't go all the way through the ranks. I'd expected another ethnic name."

They retraced their steps to the car and Paolo watched in amusement as Dave went through his usual ritual of finding his keys, as always, patting all pockets barring the right one.

"Have you thought of having them hanging from a string round your neck?" he said as Dave finally found them and unlocked the car.

"Very funny, sir. You should be a comedian in your spare time."

All desire to laugh left Paolo. Spare time? Not much of that going at the moment. Somehow he had to find a couple of hours to get over to Jessica Carter's office this afternoon and he was already behind today.

Images of the two dead girls came into his head, one in the morgue and one in the hospital. He could almost hear them begging him not to forget them. He silently promised them justice – and vowed to himself that he'd deliver on that promise. All he had to do now was find a way to make each day a few hours longer.

CHAPTER 16

9th October (early afternoon)

They arrived back at the station to find George and CC high-fiving in the main office.

"That looks very positive," Paolo said, taking off his jacket.

CC and George spun round.

"Sorry, sir, didn't hear you come in," CC said. "We've both got news for you."

"Great. Come through to my office and fill me in. Dave and I will bring you up to date with what we've found out. Judging by your celebrations, you've got more to tell us than we've got to tell you."

Paolo opened his office door and stepped back to allow the other three in. While George pulled a third chair up to the desk, Paolo hung his jacket on the hook and then walked round to take his place behind the desk.

"Right," he said as he sat down. "Who's going first?"

"I will, sir," CC said. "I've got less to report."

"Okay, let's hear it."

"I've got a fix on the transit van's registration. It belongs to a Shadrack Faa listed with a Rochester address."

"Unusual name," Paolo said. "Is it Albanian?"

"No, sir, I've been on the net to check and it turns out it's Romani in origin. Seems our van might be registered to a traveller. I've been on to the Rochester police, but they tell me the address is a derelict building. It hasn't been inhabited for at least three years, so although our Mr Faa used it to register his van, he didn't actually live there. Unless, of course, he was squatting. That's always a possibility. Rochester say it has been used as a squat in the past."

"Travellers? Maybe just passing through and not familiar with the hospital? That might explain why they didn't know about the CCTV cameras around the building. Good work, CC."

"Thank you, sir. I've put out an alert on the registration, so if it's sighted anywhere, we'll be notified immediately."

"Have you had chance to go through the film footage looking for our fake nurse?"

"Yes, sir, but it turns out she was a he, or at least might have been a he."

Paolo frowned. "It's not like you to talk in riddles, CC. Care to explain?"

She nodded. "A tall nurse was caught on camera heading towards the lifts, but she didn't get in and doesn't reappear on any of the floors. She was looking down, unfortunately, which makes me think she knew the camera was there. Our people found the nurse's uniform and a dark, short haired wig in the men's toilets on the floor below where she was spotted, so presumably she took the stairs next to the lifts. The clothes and wig were stuffed into a carrier bag and left in one of the stalls. The problem is, we don't know if it was a man dressed as a woman, or a woman who went into the men's toilets to make us think it was a man."

"So no help for us there. Uniform and wig gone for analysis?"

"Yes, sir."

"Let's hope they turn up something useful. Anything else?"

CC shook her head. "Nothing more from me, sir."

Paolo passed a slip of paper across the desk to her. "I want you to get in touch with Gazmend and see if he knows any local thugs going by the name of Bekim or Edar. They are the names of the two men who run the girls to and from the red light district. Apparently they in turn answer to someone called Joey."

CC picked up the paper with the names on it. "Joey? British name? That's unusual, sir. Normally the Albanians are pretty tight and don't let outsiders in."

"I know, so figuring out who this Joey might be is going to be that much harder. Ask Gazmend if he knows of any outsider who has been accepted into his community. We've been concentrating on the Albanian connection, but it might be a British crook who saw an opening and took it."

CC frowned.

"You don't agree?" Paolo asked.

"I suppose that could be the case," CC said, "but then how would he get the contacts to pick up the girls over there?"

Paolo sighed. "If I could answer that I think we'd have the case wrapped up. Let's hope Gazmend can help us on that score."

He turned to George. "The floor's all yours."

George picked up the pad he'd placed on the desk in front of him and rapidly flicked through the pages as if searching for something.

"Got it," he said and folded the pad back to keep it open. "As you know, I've been looking into Albanian businesses with the opportunity to bring in people under cover of legitimate activities. I've narrowed the list down to three likely ones. The first two businesses are Albania/UK/Albania, haulage contractors run by Jetmir Redzepi. Then there is Bogdani Imports, a general import/export company run by Jorgi Bogdani. Also runs regular trips around the country, not just between Albania and the UK."

Paolo nodded. "Well done. They both fit the brief."

George looked up from his pad. "The third on my list is actually the most interesting and the one I think I should dig into first."

"Why's that?" Paolo asked.

"The business is the Albanian Language School. They offer English-language immersion classes to Albanian students, many of whom come over in advance of taking up university places. The students are given a three-week

124

intensive course speaking nothing but English, so that when they get to uni it's easier to understand the lectures. The school handles all the travel and accommodation arrangements and brings in students on a regular basis, so are fully capable of smuggling in people under their legitimate activities."

Paolo sat up straighter. "I like the sound of this one."

George gave one of his rare smiles. "That's not all. You'll like it even more in a minute. When you mentioned the name Joey I wondered if maybe that was the Anglicised version of an Albanian name. The school is owned by Isuf Xhepa. Isuf being the Albanian equivalent of Joseph. You think he could be our Joey?"

"He could be," Paolo said. "Definitely one to look at closely. George, that's excellent work. I want you to find out more about the comings and goings of all three businesses. But I agree with you. Concentrating on the language school makes a lot of sense at this stage. Keep everyone in the loop on what you find. Tomorrow, Dave and I will pay a visit to each of them to see if Bekim and Edar are known to anyone."

"Oh, I thought maybe I could do that, sir," George said.

"No, George, we need your skills on the computer and telephone. Find out as much as you can on each of the businesses' activities over the last year."

Paolo saw the enthusiasm drain from George's face and felt bad, but he was the best of the team when it came to digging into backgrounds. He made a mental note to make sure George knew how much his skills were appreciated.

Dave stood up. "I'm off to see what else uniform have discovered at the hospital. See you all later."

Paolo looked at his watch. "I need to leave in about half an hour. I have an appointment with Katy's psychiatrist this afternoon, so will probably not be back until quite late in the day. I'll be switching my phone to silent while I'm in with her, but if you need to contact me urgently, send a text and I'll call you back as soon as I leave her office."

"Good luck, sir," CC said as she followed Dave and George out. "I hope it's a good meeting."

So do I, Paolo thought, but he had a horrible sinking feeling in his gut that it was going to be the exact opposite. Jessica Carter had sounded far too serious for it to be good news.

Paolo walked into the waiting room to find Lydia already there. She looked up when he entered and the temperature dropped by a thousand degrees. He could almost feel his skin suffering ice burns from the glare Lydia shot at him. He opened his mouth to greet her, but before he could get a word out she deliberately looked back down again, making it quite clear she'd rather be eaten by maggots than speak to him.

He sat down on the other side of the room, praying that Jessica Carter wouldn't keep them waiting. He wasn't sure he could survive too long without getting frostbite. He'd loved Lydia since they'd been teenagers. Theirs had been a young love that blossomed into a deeply passionate marriage. Just a few years ago they'd been an example of the perfect relationship. Sure, they fought, all couples did that, but their disagreements had never lasted beyond a few hours. And look at them now. Mortal enemies, at least from Lydia's side. From his? He just wanted to be able to exist in the same atmosphere without being annihilated by her hatred. Maybe, given time, she'd start liking him again. Right now he'd settle for indifference.

He glanced at the clock on the wall above Lydia's seat. Only two minutes to go, thank God. But those two minutes passed as slowly as twenty. By the time the door opened Paolo was wishing he'd put on thermal underwear.

Jessica Carter smiled at them. "Please come in."

Lydia stood and swept past the psychiatrist. "I hope this isn't some ploy to stop me from getting a second opinion," she said.

Paolo gave Jessica a half smile as he went in. He sat down next to Lydia, who promptly moved her chair as far from his as possible. Maybe he had leprosy and no one had bothered to tell him.

Jessica took her place behind her desk and leaned forward with her arms resting on it. Paolo thought she looked like the most relaxed person he knew.

"I have some good news for you, but it is balanced by a negative aspect," she said. "Firstly, Katy has begun speaking."

Paolo felt like leaping to his feet in celebration. Finally, after months of silence, his baby was able to speak again. His joy was short-lived.

"I don't believe you," Lydia said. "I was with her this morning and she didn't say a word."

Jessica Carter shrugged. "She isn't saying a lot, but what she has discussed with me is the reason I've asked you both to be here this afternoon."

"I'm taking her home," Lydia said, reaching for her handbag and standing up.

"Mrs Sterling, please sit down. Katy has not yet recovered enough to leave the hospital, but I think it won't be long before she is. What we need to discuss here is where she goes when she is well enough to move on."

Paolo had been watching Lydia, but his head shot back to the psychiatrist.

"What do you mean? Surely she'll go home to Lydia's?"

Jessica shrugged again. "Under normal circumstances that would be exactly what I would recommend. However, in light of what happened yesterday and Katy's subsequent revelation, I feel going home with her mother would be the worst possible outcome."

Still standing, Lydia hissed, "Don't be ridiculous. Of course she should be with me."

"Mrs Sterling, please sit down. Katy has asked me to have this discussion with you and her father. She told me what you said to her yesterday morning. She was extremely distressed and says she'll run away if she has to go home with you."

Lydia sat heavily, looking so heartbroken and confused Paolo wanted to reach out and hold her.

"I'm sorry," he said, turning to the psychiatrist. "I don't understand. Why would Katy say such a thing? She loves her mum. I know she does."

Jessica Carter sighed. "I don't know the full details yet. Katy became very agitated when telling me, but it seems Mrs Sterling..."

"I told her I was getting a restraining order to keep you away from her," Lydia interrupted.

All desire to hold Lydia left. "You did what?"

Tears fell down Lydia's face. "Yesterday morning I went to see Katy. She was staring into space, like she always does. I told her I was going to get a second opinion and take her home. And then... and then..." She took a breath. "And then I told her I was going to stop you from visiting until she was well again."

"How could you?" Paolo had never had a violent urge towards a woman in his life, but right now he was glad Lydia had moved her chair so far from his. He wanted to lash out.

Lydia leaped to her feet again. "How could I? It was easy, Paolo. I've told you this before. You're toxic. Everyone you come into contact with gets damaged. Sarah, me and now Katy. We don't want you in our lives."

"Mrs Sterling! That's quite enough. Please, once again, I must ask you to sit down." She waited until Lydia was seated before continuing. "Let me make my position quite clear. Should you go ahead with your plan to put a

129

restraining order in place, I would feel obliged to testify against you."

"What?" Lydia said. "You should be on my side. He upsets Katy."

Paolo wanted to argue his case, but a feeling of incredible weariness stopped him from speaking. He felt detached from the argument raging in front of him. Whatever happened, he wanted what was best for Katy. Jessica Carter's words finally penetrated and brought him back into the room.

"I don't take sides, Mrs Sterling. My only priority is to my patient. Katy became hysterical when she thought you would be able to prevent her father's visits. It is not in her interests to keep them apart, no matter what your feelings may be on the matter."

Lydia laughed. It sounded close to hysteria to Paolo.

"I can't win with you, Paolo. Whatever I do, you always come out on top."

Paolo went to answer, but the psychiatrist got there first.

"It isn't a case of winning or losing, Mrs Sterling. It is a case of doing what is best for your daughter. I want to be able to recommend Katy goes home with you, but I cannot do so if I think there is the slightest chance you will block visits from her father. She needs him in her life if she is to make a complete recovery."

Lydia stood once more. "It's blackmail. You're saying you'll only let Katy come home to me if I go against what I believe is best for her. I loathe my ex-husband, you will never know how much, but that's not why I wanted to stop Katy from seeing him." She scorched Paolo with a glance. "You see, I genuinely believe seeing him reminds Katy of what she went through. If it hadn't been for him she would never have been put in danger. But you two go right ahead and cosy up to each other. Paolo has that effect on the women in his life. Maybe you're the next on his list. If so, be careful."

"That's unnecessary, Lydia," Paolo said.

She ignored him and continued to speak to the psychiatrist. "Clearly I have to go along with whatever you decide. I don't like it and I think you're wrong, but I love my daughter."

"I don't doubt that, Mrs Sterling," Jessica said. "Let's get Katy well enough to go home. By then she will be able to make her feelings clear and we'll both know we're doing what *she* wants."

Lydia nodded and walked to the door. "I'm going to the hospital to tell her I was wrong to try and keep her father away from her. I wasn't, but I'll pretend I was if that's what it takes to get Katy well again."

Paolo watched as the door closed behind Lydia and then turned back to the psychiatrist. He'd thought the day couldn't bring him any more pain, but the look of sympathy on her face almost brought him to his knees.

CHAPTER 17

10th October (morning / afternoon)

"At the roundabout, turn left. First exit. Turn left. First exit."

"That thing will drive me insane, Dave. I could have told you where to find Albania/UK/Albania. Look, there it is at the end of the street," Paolo said, pointing to a dilapidated looking warehouse building.

"You have reached your destination. You have reached your destination."

"And it repeats itself all the time. Turn it off before I throw it out of the window."

"It's the first time I've been on this industrial estate," Dave said, pulling up outside the haulage contractors. "I hadn't realised how big it was. We needed the Satnav."

Paolo got out and closed the car door. "You don't trust my navigation skills?"

Dave laughed. "No comment, but I would like to remind you of a few journeys we've been on where we ended up taking the scenic route."

"Okay, I'll give you that. Right, let's get in and see if anyone recognises the images."

Paolo opened the door and walked into a surprisingly well furnished office. From the outside, the building had looked scruffy and unprepossessing, but the interior was completely the opposite. He approached the young woman manning the reception.

"Good morning, sirs. Can I help you?"

"Yes," Paolo said. "We'd like to speak to Mr Redzepi."

"Is he expecting you?"

"No, but I hope he'll make time to chat to us," Paolo said, pulling out his identification and showing it to the receptionist.

"One moment, please," she said, examining the card before picking up the phone. "Good morning, Mr Rezepi. I have two police officers in reception. They would like to talk to you. Shall I send them?"

She replaced the phone and pointed behind Paolo and Dave to a corridor.

"His office is the one at the end. He said to go through."

Paolo thanked her and nodded to Dave to go ahead. By the time they reached the end, a tall, perma-tanned man was waiting for them in the doorway.

"Come in, come in. Sit, sit. Is it about Connor?"

Paolo swallowed a smile. The man repeated himself just like the Satnav. He and Dave sat down in front of a massive polished walnut desk, which took up nearly the full width of the room.

"No, sorry. Who is Connor?"

"My driver, my driver. You arrested him in the motorway services a few days back."

Paolo looked at Dave to see if he was any the wiser, but Dave looked as confused as Paolo felt.

"We arrested two men that night, but neither of them was called Connor."

Jetmir Redzepi laughed. "Stupid me, stupid me. You most probably booked him as Konstandin Demaci. He was known by everyone here as Connor."

"Ah, that makes sense, except that he didn't mention being employed by you."

"That's because I fired him last month. I'd caught him lifting goods from our customers, so had no choice. Sorry, sorry. I assumed you knew and were here to find out more about his background."

Paolo smiled. "That clarifies matters. No, we're not here for that, but I'll send a uniformed officer out tomorrow to chat to you about Konstandin, if that's okay with you?"

"Fine, fine. What can I do for you if it isn't about that?"

Dave opened his file and slid the two images across the mammoth desk.

"We're looking for information on these two men. Bekim and Edar, we believe they are called."

Jetmir reached forward and picked up the images. "No, no," he said. "I don't know them. No, don't know them."

He flicked the pictures back on the desk. Paolo noticed the man's shaking hands.

"Sorry, Mr Redzepi, but are you sure you don't know either man? Please have another look."

"I don't know them. I don't know them," he said, but made no attempt to pick the photos up again. He stood up. "I'm sorry I haven't been any help to you, but I am very busy. Very busy. Was there anything else? I have much to do today."

Paolo signalled to Dave to pick up the pictures. "There isn't anything at the moment, but would it be okay to come back if we need to ask you a few more questions?"

"What about? I've told you, I know nothing, know nothing about bad men."

"We didn't say they were bad men, Mr Redzepi."

"No need, no need. You are police and asking about them. They must be bad men. I have nothing to do with bad men. Send your uniformed police to me tomorrow. I'll tell them all about Connor. I am very helpful, very helpful to the police."

He came round the desk and opened the door.

Paolo and Dave had no choice but to shake his hand and leave. The door closed before they had moved more than a couple of steps back towards reception. Paolo put his finger to his lips to stop Dave from commenting on the man's behaviour. Stopping at the reception desk, he signalled for Dave to open the folder and took out the images. He put them down in front of the receptionist.

"Before we leave, could you tell me if you've ever seen either of these men?"

She picked them up, one in each hand and studied the faces.

"I can't say for sure, but this one," she said, waving Bekim's image around, "looks a bit like a bloke who came here to speak to Mr Redzepi a few months back. I don't know that it really was the same man, but..." She tilted her head to one side and screwed her eyes up in concentration. "Nah, now that I look at him again, I'm not at all sure it was him. Sorry."

She handed the images back to Dave. "Was there anything else?"

"No, thank you. You've been very helpful," Paolo said. "Please, keep the images. Could you show them to your drivers when they come in? If anyone has any information on either man, perhaps they could call me?" He handed her one of his cards.

"Sure thing," she said, putting the card and images on her desk, and then turned back to her computer.

They walked outside and Paolo waited while Dave went through his usual pantomime of searching for his keys. When the doors were finally unlocked, they got in.

"What do you make of Jetmir Redzepi?" Paolo asked.

"I couldn't work him out at all," Dave said. "He certainly got the wind up when he saw the images, that's for sure."

"Yes," said Paolo, "but was that because they work for him or because he's scared of whoever they do work for?"

"The latter. He looked more scared of them than of us. I don't think they are connected to him, but I would put a month's salary on him knowing who they are and what they do."

Paolo nodded. "My thoughts exactly. Let's move on to the next business. Set up your new toy to find the way."

"Turn right. After two hundred yards you have reached your destination. You have reached your destination."

Paolo grinned. "That sounds just like Mr Redzepi. Did you notice he says some things twice?"

"I did, but my boss says I have to show more compassion and not make fun of afflicted people. Not even when he does it himself."

"Touché," Paolo said. "That'll teach me to keep my thoughts to myself." He looked at the building housing Bogdani Imports. "This looks a bit more upmarket than the haulage place. There must be quite a bit of money in this industry. I wonder what they import."

Paolo pushed open the door and the fragrance of exotic spices wafted over him.

"That answers my question," he said to Dave.

Unlike the haulage company, this was not a case of being smarter on the inside. There was a threadbare two-seater couch pushed against one wall. A plant, half dead and in desperate need of light, stood in one corner. A coat rack, overloaded with coats and jackets, filled one wall and a counter spread across the room with a sign saying 'Reception' hanging above it. The desk behind the barrier was empty, but there was a bell on the counter with a sign asking visitors to press it for assistance, so Paolo did exactly that. A loud ringing sound could be heard from far off in the bowels of the building.

They waited for a few minutes, but no one came, so Paolo pressed and held the button down for a few seconds before releasing it.

"That should bring someone," Dave said. "If only to disconnect the bell."

"Listen," Paolo said as the sound of someone running got closer and closer.

A door behind the empty desk opened and a man Paolo recognised burst through.

"Sorry, I'm here alone at the moment. Can I help you?"

Paolo held out his hand. "Jeton, isn't it?"

Jeton looked surprised. "Sorry, do I know you?"

"No, but I know your cousin. Not only do you look very much like him, but I saw you together at the hospital. I believe you gave him a lift that day because his car was in for service."

Jeton's brow cleared. "Ah, yes, of course. I remember now. You were there with the woman with the green hair."

Paolo laughed. "People do tend to overlook me when I'm with Detective Sergeant Cathy Connor. She works quite closely with your cousin."

Jeton nodded. "Yes, I know. Are you here about... no, I mean... sorry, why are you here?"

"We were hoping to have a word with Mr Bogdani. Is he here?"

"Yes, he's in his office. At the back of the warehouse. I'll take you through to him. We're a bit short-staffed at the moment. Our receptionist is off with the flu."

138

He lifted a section of the counter for Paolo and Dave to pass.

"Before we go to see Mr Bogdani, perhaps you could have a look at a couple of images. You might recognise one of them. It would be really helpful if you could."

"Sure, of course. Is it to do with... sorry, I'm not supposed to know. Forget I said anything. I don't want to get Gazmend in trouble."

Paolo smiled. "In trouble? In what way?"

"I'm staying with him at the moment, so can't help but know about his translating work. When he's been at social services, he comes back really upset. It's hard to be in the same room with him for an hour or so until he's calmed down. He takes it to heart. But I'm not supposed to know where he's been. He says it's to do with data protection, so please don't tell anyone I know about it."

"I won't say a word," Paolo said, passing the two images Dave had handed him over to Jeton. "We have reason to believe these two could help us with our enquiries. Do you know either of them? That one is Bekim and this one is Edar."

The colour left Jeton's face and he trembled. "No! Sorry. I can't help you. I've never seen either of them before." He thrust the images back at Dave. "I'll take you to Mr Bogdani."

Paolo and Dave exchanged a glance as Jeton strode off. Another one upset by sight of the images. These two certainly seemed to have made their mark on the Albanian business community.

The warehouse, in contrast to the deserted reception area, was teeming with activity. Workers moved with precision between rows of shelving, picking boxes to add to trolleys. Paolo assumed they were filling orders for customers. Considering the numbers of workers, the place was almost deathly quiet. None of the men spoke and there was no music blasting out, as there was in many of the businesses on the industrial estate. People moved silently from spot to spot, eyes focused on the job in hand.

Jeton led them across the warehouse to a door in the back wall. He knocked and waited.

"What?"

"Mr Bogdani, there are two police officers here to speak to you," Jeton called through the closed door.

A few seconds later the door opened to reveal a short, wiry man dressed immaculately in a grey three-piece suit. He glared at Paolo and Dave.

"She's lying. I caught her red-handed and if she says otherwise, I've got witnesses to prove what happened."

Jeton held up a hand. "They aren't here about Maris, Mr Bogdani."

"What?" He turned to Paolo. "Well if it isn't about that cow, what do you want?"

"Maybe we could have a chat inside?" Paolo gestured towards the man's office.

"Yes, of course. Sorry. I thought you were here about my ex-secretary. She said she would go to the police when I fired her and I assumed that's what she'd done when Jeton said the police were here. Jeton, what are you standing around for? Get back to work."

The look of relief on Jeton's face as he left made Paolo determined to question him again after they'd finished with his boss. Gazmend's cousin definitely knew something about the two men – and he'd been at the hospital the day the child was murdered. He might have mentioned to someone what ward she was on. If so, Paolo needed to know who he'd spoken to.

Jorgi Bogdani strode to his desk and waved vaguely. "Sit down."

There was only one visitor's chair available. Dave signalled for Paolo to take it and stood next to him.

"We are investigating a case and are looking for information on these two men," Paolo said as Dave passed the images across the desk.

After a cursory glance, Jorgi Bogdani nodded. "Bad news, those two. I'm not sure I can tell you much, but the whisper in the Albanian community is that they are involved in things we wouldn't want our children to know about."

"What sort of things?"

"Drugs, prostitution, all the petty crimes."

Paolo raised his eyebrows. "Would you describe those as petty?"

Jorgi Bogdani scowled. "It isn't murder and it isn't theft. Those are the really bad crimes. If kids want to destroy their lives by taking drugs, they are as much to blame as the pushers. Same with women who sell their bodies. No one is forcing them to do it."

"You're wrong there, Mr Bogdani, at least in the case of prostitution. The case we're investigating involves young girls, children who need to be protected from the likes of these men. Do you know where we can find them?"

"Why would I know? I don't associate with such types? What are you implying?"

"I'm not implying anything," Paolo said, struggling to keep his temper in check. "I'm simply asking if you are able to help us find these two men."

Jorgi Bogdani's scowl deepened. "I don't know them. I only know of them. They are a disgrace to our community. They give us all a bad name. I hope you catch them and put them away, but I don't have a clue where you should start looking."

"Are most of your employees Albanian?" Paolo asked.

"Yes, what of it? Is there a law against giving my own countrymen a helping hand?"

Paolo sighed. God, this man was hard work. "No, there's no law and that wasn't why I was asking. We'd like to show the images to your workers. Maybe one of them can point us in the right direction."

"Oh, I see. Yes, go ahead, but please make it quick. They'll look for any excuse to waste time and the orders have to go out today." He nodded. "Please close the door on your way out. I need to get on with my paperwork. I don't have a secretary and the agency says none of the girls on their books will work here. They say I'm too demanding. Too demanding! No wonder there are so many on the dole. No one wants to work hard."

Paolo and Dave left the office, carefully closing the door.

"Bloody hell," said Dave, "I swear I'll never moan about my boss ever again."

Paolo laughed. "As your boss, I'll make sure you don't. Right, let's show these images around and see if we get any further with his workers than we did with him."

But no one in the warehouse admitted to knowing either man. Many of them assumed the apprehensive look Paolo was beginning to recognise as the reaction to seeing the two faces, which meant those being questioned were lying when they said they didn't know them, but being scared wasn't a crime, so there was little Paolo could do to make them tell the truth.

Handing the images back to Dave to return yet again to the file, Paolo looked around for Jeton, but couldn't see him anywhere. He asked the man working closest to the reception doorway if he had any idea where Jeton might be.

"Gone home, mate. He scooted out of here as soon as you went in to see Mr Bogdani. Looked as sick as a pig, he did. Maybe he's got this flu that's going around. He'll be for it, though, if the boss realises he's skived off."

Paolo thanked the man and turned to Dave.

"I think a visit back here tomorrow is in order, don't you? I'd like to know why our visit spooked Jeton. Right, let's make our next stop. Back to town for the language school. Then, just to show you what a kind and understanding boss you have, I'll treat you to a sandwich at the Nag and Bag."

"I'm overwhelmed, sir. A whole sandwich? All to myself? I don't have to share it with the rest of the office?"

Paolo grinned. "Don't push it, Dave, or you might end up with a bag of crisps instead."

"Even you won't find parking here, Dave," Paolo said as they turned into Conference Road.

There wasn't a space anywhere to be seen.

"You could be right, sir. Oh, hang on, look!"

"That wouldn't have happened if I'd been driving," Paolo said, looking in disbelief as a car pulled out, leaving a spot right in front of the language school.

Dave manoeuvred the car into position and got out.

"I wonder what reaction we'll get here," he said as Paolo joined him on the pavement. "So far the only person who's owned up to recognising the men was Jorgi Bogdani, but he wasn't exactly over helpful, was he."

"No, maybe we'll have better luck in here."

A young man in his early twenties greeted them as they entered the school.

"Good day, may I help you?" he asked in the voice of someone not quite comfortable in English. "I am called Agim Corbajram."

"Hello, Agim," Paolo said. "We would like to see Mr Xhepa. Could you please show us to his office?"

"A pleasure it is for me to do it," Agim replied with a formal bow. "You follow, please."

Paolo found himself responding and half bowed in return. He caught Dave grinning at him.

144

"Any word from you and that packet of crisps is in danger of going the way of the sandwich."

Agim turned back to Paolo. "I am sorry, what is you say?"

"Nothing, just a joke with my Detective Sergeant."

Agim stopped walking. "You are police? Is problem with visa? We all have good visa. School arranges. School arranges all."

"No, no, nothing like that," Paolo said. "We need to talk to the owner of the school on something completely different. I'm sure your visas are all in order. Are you here on a course?"

"Yes. Is good. When I come, I speak little. Now I speak good, yes?"

"Very good," Paolo said. "Certainly much better than I can speak any other language."

Agim looked pleased with the compliment. They followed him down a carpeted corridor to a staircase and then walked up to the first floor. They stopped outside a door marked Principal. Agim tapped on the door and opened it. He said something in Albanian and then stood back to allow Paolo and Dave to pass.

"Goodbye," he said, smiling as he left.

"Welcome. Do come in and make yourselves comfortable," Isuf Xhepa said, pointing to a sofa and two armchairs. "What can I do for you?"

Paolo sat in one of the armchairs and Dave took the other. There was something familiar about the man, but Paolo couldn't quite place what it was.

"Have we met before?" he asked.

Isuf frowned in concentration. "I don't believe so, but it's possible we have seen each other at a civic function. I'm sorry, I didn't catch your names? My student said you were from the police."

Paolo took out a card. "My apologies. I should have introduced myself straightaway. I'm Detective Inspector Sterling. This is Detective Sergeant Johnson. We'd like to ask you if you recognise either of these two men. If yes, could you give us any information regarding their whereabouts?"

Isuf took the images from Dave. His hands shook in what now seemed to be a normal fashion whenever anyone handled the images.

"I've seen them around, but I'm afraid I have no idea who they are or where you could find them. What is it they've done?"

Paolo knew the man was lying about something, but what exactly? He'd certainly recognised the men, but like so many others, he seemed to be scared of them.

"We're looking for them to assist with our enquiries on a case. At this stage we don't know that they have done anything, but we do need to speak to them. You say you've seen them around, could you be more specific?"

Isuf swallowed. "No, I'm afraid not. It could have been anywhere. Maybe in the market or on the street. I'm sorry I can't help you. Was there anything else?"

Paolo and Dave stood up.

"No. Thank you for your time, Mr Xhepa. Sorry to have bothered you."

A smile of pure relief washed over the man's face. "No bother at all. We're always happy to assist the police here."

Paolo waited until they were back in the car before voicing his thoughts.

"Another one who knows something but isn't telling. I got the impression he was very pleased to see the back of us, Dave."

"Yes, I thought that. Where did you think you knew him from?"

Paolo shrugged. "I have no idea. I'm not even sure I know him as such, just that I've seen him somewhere. It might not even be important, but until I remember it's going to bug me."

***

Paolo was glad to get home. He slipped off his shoes and stretched out on the couch. It had been quite a day. He wasn't sure if they were any further forward or not. They hadn't picked up any solid information, but they had established that Bekim and Edar were bad news. Not that they didn't already know that, but it was useful to know they inspired fear over quite a large circle.

He flicked on the television in time to hear the newscaster give the date and time. The tenth of October, just one more week until his birthday. He really should try to work up some enthusiasm about celebrating his move out of the thirties, but knew he wouldn't feel any different at forty than he had at any other age.

He concentrated on the screen, putting thoughts of his own life firmly to the back of his mind. The prime minister was giving a speech in yet another far-flung country, telling its inhabitants how to run their affairs. Paolo wondered how it would be received if leaders of other countries arrived in the UK to tell the government where they were going wrong. He smiled at the thought, but soon lost all desire to smile as the next news item filled the screen.

A spokesperson for Mr and Mrs Bassington, the distraught parents of young Lucy, was speaking, pleading for someone to come forward with information. The words swept over Paolo. He barely heard them. His whole attention was taken up with the parents in the background. In the time since Lucy had disappeared, Mrs Bassington had changed from a woman in distress to a zombie. She stood, silently holding the photograph that still dominated headlines and appeared on posters all over the country. Gone was the well-kept hair, make up and nice clothes. She'd lost weight. It was like looking at someone who'd died and just needed a gentle push to fall down. Paolo shuddered. No parent should have to suffer not knowing who had their child, but that's what was happening to many families in Albania.

He'd track the bastards down, no matter what it took.

CHAPTER 18

17ᵗʰ October (morning)

Pete woke to the sound of buzzing in his ear.

"What the fuck?" He turned over, his head pounding like a jackhammer on speed. He'd had another late night session and had only staggered into bed just after four. What was that noise?

The buzzing kept on, drilling into his brain. The pillow seemed to be vibrating in time with the buzz. Phone, he thought, I put the fucker on mute, but didn't switch off the buzz. He lifted himself up and turned to search for the phone under the pillow. Where was it? He needed to shut off that fucking buzz before he went insane.

He finally found it tucked inside the pillowcase. Joey's name and number flashed on the screen. Pete moved the slider to answer the call.

"Do you know what time it is?" he snarled, catching sight of the bedside clock. "It's fucking eight in the morning, Joey!"

"Yeah, good morning to you, too. Sounds like you're not interested in hearing about a replacement. Funny that,

I thought by now you'd be gagging for it. Oh well, plenty of other customers…"

"Wait," Pete yelled. "Don't play silly bastards with me. What you got on offer and when can I have one?"

"I'm moving a few around. They've each only been with one punter, so are still quite fresh. You want?"

"No virgins? You know I don't like leftovers."

Joey sighed. "No, Pete, my last two virgins are dead. Or have you forgotten our little problems? These are not leftovers. As I said, they've each only had one careful owner."

"How old?"

"What age do you want?"

Pete swallowed. "The younger the better."

"I've got an eight-year-old. She doesn't speak English, so should suit you just fine."

"How much?"

Pete prepared himself for a hefty rise. Joey had threatened as much after he'd sorted out the brat in hospital, but he wasn't going to make it easy for the bastard to rob him.

"A thousand pounds."

"What? Are you fucking mad?" Pete spluttered. "No fucking brat is worth that, especially not one that's already been used."

"Fine," said Joey, sounding too cheerful in Pete's ears. "I'll take my wares to market elsewhere. Ciao."

"Joey! Joey?"

All Pete could hear was the buzz of a disconnected call. The fucker had put the phone down on him. He hit speed dial. Joey answered immediately.

"Yes? Ready to pay?"

"Five hundred, Joey. That's fair. After all, you'll get her back again."

Joey sighed. "I should get her back again, Pete, but you and I both know that sometimes they don't come back from you. By the way, the price is now one thousand two hundred. Fair warning to you here, so pay attention. If you say no again, the next time I mention the price it will be two hundred more."

Pete wanted to tell Joey to get stuffed, but he couldn't. No one else he could trust knew about his preferences. The last thing he needed was for word to get out. Fucking press would have a field day.

"Look, Joey, let's talk about this, okay? How about eight hundred?"

"You're a slow learner, Pete. Listen carefully now. The price has just gone up to one thousand four hundred."

"Joey, I…"

"Pete, do yourself a favour and quit haggling. Say yes, Joey. Thank you, Joey, before the price goes up another two hundred."

Pete swallowed. What the fuck. It was only money and he had enough of it. "Yes, Joey. Thank you, Joey. When can you deliver?"

"Let's see. I'll be picking them up tomorrow morning. What about a lunchtime pizza delivery?"

Pete didn't need to think about it. He could pick up the cash in town this afternoon.

"Sounds good to me. No anchovies."

"Very funny. See you tomorrow."

"Yeah, tomorrow," he said and disconnected the call.

Thoughts of a good fuck made his heart race. He'd barely had any time at all with the last one. He sighed and slipped his hand under the duvet to stroke his cock. It was solid.

"Tomorrow will do me a fucking treat," he whispered as he gave in to the sensation.

CHAPTER 19

17th October (morning / afternoon)

Forty! Paolo shuddered, as he straightened his tie and slipped on his jacket ready to leave for the station. How did so many years pass without him noticing? Funny, it didn't feel any different now that he was no longer in his thirties. Wasn't he supposed to feel something? Wasn't this when the cliché kicked in? Life beginning and all that crap? Maybe he should think about that over the next few days. It might be time for him to make some changes. Get his life sorted out a bit.

His thoughts turned to his girls. Sarah, dead and buried. Would she want him to be grieving still, to the point where he couldn't move on with his life? No, Sarah would be urging him to enjoy himself. She'd been too full of life to want him to give up on his own. And Katy? She was talking now. Not much, but at least she was communicating with them again. Katy, the old Katy, would have been the first to tell him to get back out there and find himself, whatever that meant. As for Lydia... well the less time he spent thinking about his dead

153

marriage the better. Lydia might tolerate him being in the same room as her now, but she still didn't speak to him or even acknowledge his presence.

Okay, he thought, as he opened his front door, that was enough soul searching for this year. He'd worry about finding himself next year when he hit forty-one. Time to get to work.

He managed to forget his birthday for the half hour it took him to drive to the station, but any hopes of it going unnoticed by his team were put to bed as soon as he entered the main office. A massive banner stretched from one side of the room to the other, screaming in vivid red capital letters: Happy Birthday. Helium balloons hovered near the ceiling in a variety of neon colours, all proclaiming the same birthday message.

CC stood up and signalled to the others in the office and everyone began a badly out of tune rendition of *Happy Birthday to You.*

As the final strains warbled into silence, Paolo wondered what the hell he was supposed to do next. This was a first. Normally all he got was a few birthday greetings as the day wore on. Never anything like this.

Before he could speak Dave stepped forward and handed Paolo a parcel.

"We had a whip round," he said. "For your 'life begins at' birthday we got you an arresting present."

Paolo knew something was up because everyone laughed at Dave's words. Cautiously, he undid the wrapping and opened the box. Inside he found a pink

154

whip and a pair of plastic handcuffs lined with pink fake fur. He looked up at the sea of grinning faces and for some peculiar reason he didn't quite understand, felt tears welling. Pushing the emotion to one side, he managed to grin back.

"Just what I've always wanted," he said, "and pink really is my colour."

"It goes with your eyes, sir," called out one of the younger PCs.

Paolo nodded. "Yes, and my eyes are particularly pink when I've spent several hours trying to decipher *your* reports. Ever thought of helping me out by using some punctuation?" He looked down at his gift and then grinned again. "Thank you for these, but I hope you don't mind if I don't fill in a report on how and when I use them."

Dave raised his coffee cup in salute. "That was one of the conditions attached to the gift, sir. Full details in triplicate on each of our desks the morning after."

"I'll see what I can do," Paolo said. He took some notes from his wallet. "Dave, can you organise with the bakery down the road to send in some savouries for lunchtime? Tell them we'd also like a selection of cakes. As it's my birthday I think we can all avoid the canteen for today."

Dave took the money and headed towards the door.

"Come straight to my office when you get back, Dave. You two as well," he said to CC and George.

Half an hour later Paolo nodded to CC. "You look as if you're brimming with news. What have you got?"

"Just got this in, sir. The van used to drop off the girl at the hospital has picked up a parking ticket in Stamford."

"When was this?"

"The ticket was issued two days ago, but it seems that it isn't first one. There was another ticket in a different car park, but still in Stamford, five days ago on the 12th. So it seems likely that the travellers have set up camp not too far from the town."

Paolo felt like punching the air. Something positive at last. "Get on the councils within a five mile radius of Stamford. Find out if any groups of travellers have arrived recently."

CC nodded. "Ahead of you there, sir. I made a list before coming in here. That will be my first job when this meeting's over."

"Has Gazmend had any joy showing the images of Bekim and Edar around the place?"

"Not really, sir. He's getting the same sort of feedback as you did. Those who recognise them won't say anything and the rest genuinely don't know anything about them."

"Has his cousin turned up yet?"

"No, sir. Gazmend says he hasn't seen Jeton for a week. Not since the day you spoke to him at the import place. Gazmend's pretty annoyed with him. Apparently Jeton went straight back to Gazmend's, packed up all his stuff and left. Didn't even leave a note. The first thing

Gazmend knew about it was when you and Dave knocked on his door that evening looking for Jeton."

"I hope Gazmend will let us know if and when Jeton reappears."

"I'm sure he'll do that, sir, but he might thump him first. Reading between the lines, I think maybe Jeton owes him quite a bit of money."

"Fair enough. Right, what have you got for us, George?"

"Not much, unfortunately. I've been keeping tabs on all three businesses, paying particular attention to the language school, as we agreed. So far I haven't been able to unearth anything suspicious. The school has a new batch of students arriving shortly, so I'll keep them under surveillance, just in case more bodies than the expected students come in."

Paolo drummed his fingers on the desk. "Even if they do bring kids in that way, how do they get them past the border controls? Surely everyone would have to be accounted for. How do they arrive, by air or road?"

"By air. Each student's tickets and necessary documentation is organised by the school. In fact, the school seems to do everything, even down to supplying luggage so that they have the right size bags for carry on. They sort out all the books and everything they could possibly need, including places to stay."

"Sounds expensive," Paolo said.

"It is. These students are all from good families with plenty of money. So far I haven't been able to uncover anything even remotely suspicious. The number and documentation of students coming in seems to match with those going home at the end of the intensive course. I can't find any evidence of anyone being brought in who is under eighteen, so definitely not in the age group we're searching for. There also is little to no contact with other towns and cities around the UK. Although it's an international school and you'd expect it to do business with all the university towns, it seems to be limited to contact with Bradchester. I couldn't find even one solitary thing that flagged up anything we could look into."

"Blast," Paolo said. "That one sounded perfect and the owner definitely recognised the men."

George shrugged. "It might still be dodgy, but it seems on the level so far."

"What about the others? Is there anything worth looking into with the import/export, apart from Jeton doing a bunk?"

"Nothing I've been able to find."

"And the haulage contractors?"

"Same result there. All three businesses seem to be completely above board and complying with all the regulations. But I'll carry on digging."

"Thanks, George. There must be something we're missing."

Paolo turned to Dave. "Anything new from uniform?"

"No, sir. They've questioned all the staff and the patients. No one saw the woman after that sighting of her on the CCTV footage. That's a dead-end, I'm afraid."

Paolo looked down at the list he'd made earlier. "And according to the people we've had watching the Zephyr

Road area there's been no sign of any underage kids on the streets. We've had no sightings for a couple of weeks now. I can't help wondering why that might be. Are they keeping them off the streets because they know we're watching out for them? Or are they waiting for new girls to arrive from Albania to take the place of the older kids who will then go on the streets? I wish I knew where they kept the young ones before they get to street working age."

"I would imagine they get passed around," Dave said. "Perverts like to share. As for the girls on the street, as you say, the pimps might have got wind of us nosing around and decided to set up shop somewhere else."

"It's possible," Paolo agreed, "but the last youngster we definitely know was working there was our overdose victim. Maybe the poor kid from the hospital was meant to take the place of an older girl destined for Zephyr Road but something went wrong and they've decided to hold off on putting a new girl out to work for the time being. Perhaps they're waiting until we've lost interest. Maybe we should give them that impression."

Dave sat up and smiled across at Paolo. "Are you thinking of giving them a bit of rope to hang themselves?"

"It's an idea, Dave. Definitely an idea. I'm going to pull surveillance back a bit and see what happens."

What a way to celebrate, Paolo thought three hours later, as he reached for yet another report to read and sign off on. He found himself looking back with nostalgia to the days when he could pass this stuff to his superior and get on with the job of stopping crime instead of adding up numbers about it. A knock on his door saved him from the tedium. He looked up as CC made an appearance.

"Sorry to disturb you, sir, but I thought you'd want to know straightaway. A fairly new travellers' camp has been set up in North Luffenham. Not actually in the village itself, but on a bridle path going through the woods. I've had a look on the map and it seems to be up on the hill a couple of miles outside the village. The council are going through the legal channels to get them moved on."

Paolo stood up. "In that case Dave and I had better get over there right now. They might decide to set up camp elsewhere and then we'd be back at square one. Well done, CC. Good work," he said, taking the map and directions and following her into the main office.

"Dave," Paolo called out. "Stop shoving those sausage rolls in your mouth as if they've offended you and grab your jacket. CC's phone calls might have unearthed our travellers' camp."

He turned back to CC. "Keep searching. If we're lucky this will be the camp, but just in case it isn't, keep looking for others."

She nodded and returned to her desk. Paolo wasn't sure, but thought he detected a slump to her shoulders. She'd been frowning more than usual lately and didn't seem to be as chatty with George. He made a mental note to talk to her later to find out what, if anything, was bothering her.

Following the Satnav's directions, Paolo and Dave pulled up on the side of a country road high above the village of North Luffenham. The entrance to the woods, a wide bridle path, led off from the road. From the way the bridle path was churned up, it was obvious that a number of vehicles had driven along there fairly recently.

Paolo pointed at the ground. "We should have brought wellies with us, Dave."

Dave grimaced. "Bloody hell, sir, my shoes won't be worth wearing once we been down there."

Paolo shrugged. "The joy of police work, Dave. I don't think my local drycleaner is going to be too thrilled to get these trousers in tomorrow. Come on, it might not be so bad further in."

They trudged along the muddy path, slipping and sliding, but managing to remain upright. After ten minutes or so the smell of wood smoke, accompanied by the sound of voices, drifted towards them.

"Nearly there, Dave," Paolo said, trying not to think about the mud clinging to his shoes and the bottoms of his trousers.

"They could have picked a more accessible spot," Dave moaned.

Paolo grinned. "I think the whole point is to choose somewhere as inaccessible as possible so that it's harder to move them on."

They came to a large clearing. A mix of brightly painted traditional wagons was interspersed with a number of white transit vans. Paolo scanned the vans, looking for the registration plate they'd found on the

CCTV footage, and was thrilled to see the van standing at the end of the clearing. He nudged Dave.

"Looks like we're in luck," he said, nodding in the direction of the van.

At his words all conversation stopped. Women gathered children to them and the men stepped forward. One man, much older than the others, hobbled towards them, leaning heavily on a stick.

"This is a private place," the old man said. "What do you want here?"

Paolo showed his card. "I'm Detective Inspector Sterling and this is Detective Sergeant Johnson. We'd like to ask you a few questions about a visit to Bradchester Central Hospital earlier this month."

Those nearest to him gasped.

"I told you!" one of the women hissed to the man next to her.

Paolo smiled at her. "Told him what?"

The woman took a step towards him, but the old man raises his stick and waved her back.

"I'll deal with this, Mari," he said. Turning back, he continued, "My name is Hanzi Recos and these are my people. Any questions you have, you can put to me. Come, we can talk in my home."

Without waiting for an answer, he turned and headed for the largest of the painted wagons. Paolo estimated it to be about 30ft long. Paolo and Dave followed him up the steps. Inside, on the left, a stove was throwing out a lot of heat. Paolo wondered if he should take his jacket off. It was stifling in there.

"Sit," Hanzi Recos commanded, pointing at a small sofa.

Paolo and Dave perched side by side, shoulders rubbing. The old man took a comfy looking armchair opposite them. Paolo looked around at the intricately painted panels filling every available space.

"Lots of work gone into this," he said, pointing at the walls and ceiling.

Hanzi Recos smiled. "It has been in my family for over two hundred years. I cannot take credit for the decoration. But you haven't come here to talk about my people's history or this home, my *vardo*. You are here about that child, I think?"

Paolo nodded. "We know that one of your vans delivered the child to the hospital, but we need to know how she came to be with your people and why whoever dropped her off there didn't take her inside."

The old man nodded. "She was badly injured, but not by us. However, we have not the best reputation with authority, as you must know. We saw she needed help and took her to a place where she would receive that help. Had we taken her inside the chances are high we would have been accused of injuring her."

Paolo opened his mouth to answer, but the old man held up his hand to stop him.

"Before you speak, please do me the courtesy to think about what I have just said."

"You're probably right," Paolo said, "but I believe you. Please will you tell me what happened?"

The old man nodded and yelled something in a language Paolo didn't understand, but he'd clearly called for someone because shortly afterwards a woman came in and sat down. Paolo recognised her as the woman who'd hissed to the man outside.

"Mari," the old man said, "tell the police how you found the child and what we decided to do with her."

"I'd had a fight with Jan, he's my husband, and stormed off into the woods when I heard a noise. I thought it was an animal, maybe injured. I had my knife with me. I thought it was maybe something for the pot."

The woman's face quivered and she fell silent. Paolo became aware of the scratching of Dave's pen as he took notes.

"But it wasn't an animal," Paolo prompted.

"No," she said, "I found a child scrambling under a bush, trying to hide. She was naked and bleeding. I managed to coax her out and took her back to the camp." She shook her head. "I was wrong about the noise coming from an animal. The animal was the one who did that to her. She had blood between her legs and running from behind. I knew she'd been raped front and back."

She fell silent and studied her hands before looking up again. "We couldn't understand her language. The words were all strange to us, but I'm sure she was saying thank you. I wanted to keep her with us, but after the council met it was decided to leave her at the hospital. At least we saved her from whoever had raped her. What will happen to her now?"

Paolo pictured the horror Mari must have felt when she found the child. He didn't want to tell her she'd saved the girl only for someone to murder her in what should have been a place of safety, but he had no choice.

"I'm afraid she's dead. Someone got to her in the hospital."

Mari's hand flew to her mouth. "No! How? That isn't possible, surely?"

"I'm sorry, it's true. Could you tell me where you were camped when you found her?"

The old man answered. "Bradchester Woods. It is one of our regular stops. Almost directly in the centre there is a large clearing with tables and benches. At this time of year few people use the woods for picnics. Before, when it is warmer, we are not able to camp because the council move us on. But in autumn, we rest there for a month or so."

"Is there anything else you can tell us that might help track down the rapist?"

Mari spoke to the old man in their own language. The old man nodded and Mari got up and left the van.

"Please wait. She has gone to fetch one of the children."

After a couple of minutes Mari returned, her hand clasped with that of a boy of about eight or nine. He looked at Paolo, bright-eyed and unafraid.

"Tell the policemen what you saw, Andre."

"I was in the last van and I told my dad someone was following us."

Paolo smiled in encouragement. "What did your dad say?"

"He said I was making it up, but I wasn't. There was one of them posh BMWs hanging back all the way until we stopped outside town. Then, when Mari and her man took the girl to the hospital in their van, the car followed them. I told my dad, but he didn't believe me."

"I do," Paolo said. "Did you get the car's number?"

Andre shook his head. "It was too far back. No one else spotted it, but I did. I love cars like that."

Paolo nodded. "Me too," he said. "What colour was it?"

"Black or really, really dark blue."

"Could you see how many were in the car?"

"It looked like four. Two in front and two in the back."

"That's great," Paolo said. "You're very observant. Were you able to see any of the people closely enough to describe them?"

Andre shook his head again. "No. They were too far away. I think one of them in front had light hair. Lighter than the others."

"And that's all? Nothing else you can think of that stands out?"

Andre stood for a while, eyes up towards the ceiling. Paolo could almost see the wheels turning in the boy's head as he tried to find something to add to what he'd remembered so far. Finally, he gave up and shrugged at Paolo.

Taking one of his cards, he passed it to Andre. "If you remember anything, no matter how small, ask your dad if you can call me."

Andre took the card and slipped it in the pocket of his jeans. "I don't need to ask my dad. I've got my own phone."

"I'm sure you have," Paolo said, "but tell your dad anyway, just so that he knows you've spoken to me. Okay?"

Andre nodded and Mari took him outside.

Paolo stood. At least now they knew how the traffickers had known the child was in the hospital. He held out his hand to the old man. "Thank you for your help. If we need anything more, I'll come back again. Will you stay here long?"

The old man stood and grasped Paolo's hand. "For as long as it takes the council here to get an order moving us on. Wait, I'll give you my mobile number. If we're not here, you can call me."

Paolo waited while Dave added the number to the notes he'd already taken. "You and your family have been a great help," he said.

"I'm pleased someone is bothering about that child," Hanzi said. "The press only care about blue-eyed children from good families. I feel for the plight of Lucy Bassington, but what about all the other children who go missing? The ones who aren't pretty or blue-eyed – who cares about those? No one!"

"I do," Paolo said. "I care."

Hanzi nodded. "I believe you. If any of my people thinks of something to help, I'll call. We get a bad press," the old man continued with a toothless grin. "Sometimes we earn it and sometimes we don't. This time, we're on the side of the angels. Next time..." He shrugged. "Who knows, we might not be."

As they trudged back through the mud to the car Paolo realised he was one of the guilty ones. Before they'd got here, he'd pretty much made up his mind the travellers must have been involved in a bad way. Now it turned out they'd been, as the old man had put it, on the side of the angels this time.

Mari had painted such a vivid word picture of the child's condition when she'd found her, Paolo couldn't get it out of his mind. How many other children were out there suffering in the same way?

CHAPTER 20

17ᵗʰ October (late afternoon / evening)

Paolo stared at the Google Earth images on his computer screen, bringing into focus the layout of the properties around Bradchester Woods. He turned the monitor so that Dave, sitting on the other side of the desk, could see as well.

"Okay, let's see what we have. There's the river to the south and the motorway to the north, so not much help to us there, although I suppose she could have been dumped on the motorway and made her way into the woods. Something for us to bear in mind, but not likely to have happened. There are lots of houses here on the east side," Paolo said, pointing out a large estate on that boundary. He scrolled across to the other side of the woods. "What have we got over on the west?"

He manipulated the image and two large properties came into view. "Ah, yes. I think one of those belongs to Pete Carson," Paolo said. "I don't know who owns the other one, but we can soon find out."

Dave grimaced as if a bad smell had suddenly appeared under his nose. "Pete Carson the over the hill rock star I'm going to have to suffer in a couple of months' time?" he asked. "Maybe if we can get him locked up I won't have to sit through a night of torture. Now there's an idea. He absolutely fits the bill. Our very own Gary Glitter. No problem in getting the public to believe he's involved. You've only got to look at who's been found out in the last year or so. Was he ever on *Top of the Pops*? I bet he was. Well, that proves it. He's our man. Let's go pick him up."

Paolo glanced away from the screen. "You're lucky there's only me in here. Someone else might have thought you were being serious."

Dave grinned. "I am! That'd be perfect. Even Rebecca wouldn't expect me to turn up to a concert where the main act is in jail."

Paolo laughed. "Knowing your Rebecca she'd drag you off to listen outside the prison walls. Anyway, let's get serious for a minute here. There hasn't been a sniff of scandal attached to Pete Carson over the years. Well, drugs, yes, but no accusations of sexual impropriety have ever come to light. Mind you, there are plenty facing charges right now who had always appeared squeaky clean. We need to find out who owns the other house, but you and I are off to pay a visit to Pete Carson just as soon as I've organised uniform to do a door to door on the housing estate on the east side."

Paolo picked up his phone, but before he could dial George tapped on the door.

"Come in," Paolo called. "What have you got for me?"

George glanced at Dave and then back to Paolo. "Nothing, sir. I thought you might be alone."

Dave got up. "I can leave. No problem."

"No!" George said, his voice sounding agitated to Paolo's ears. "It wasn't important. I just wanted to discuss the Christmas rota. That's all. It wasn't important. I'll come back later."

He started backing out of the office.

"Wait! Dave and I are off to have a chat with Pete Carson," Paolo said, explaining what they'd found out so far. "While we're out, could you find out who owns this property?" He signalled for George to come and view the screen.

George nodded. "Yes, I'll get on to it right away."

As he left the office, Dave grimaced again. The bad smell look even more pronounced.

"What's that face for?" Paolo asked when he was sure George was no longer in earshot.

"I'm not sure," Dave said. "There's something funny going on with George these days. He isn't getting on as well with CC as he used to."

Paolo remembered CC's frown from earlier and wondered if there was a connection. Something else he must remember to look into.

"Let me know if you hear anything," Paolo said. "If George has a problem we need to help him through it. Right, let's get uniform organised on the housing estate and then we'll go and see your favourite rock star."

171

Dave drove up to the main gates of Pete Carson's mansion.

"Looks more like a stately home than a rock star's pad," he said as he pressed the intercom buzzer.

"I told you." Paolo said. "He's gone out of his way not to upset the locals. He keeps a very low profile. No wild parties, no quad bike races, nothing like that."

A woman's voice sounded through the intercom. "Yes, can I help you?"

Dave held his warrant card up to the camera on the gate post.

"We'd like a word with Mr Carson."

"I'm his housekeeper. I'm afraid he isn't here at the moment," the woman said. "He's gone to visit his agent."

"What time are you expecting him back?" Dave asked.

"Not until tomorrow. He usually stays overnight when he goes to London."

Dave turned away from the intercom. "What now, sir?"

Paolo thought for a moment. "She might have seen something useful, but I'd rather wait and question her at the same time as Pete Carson. Ask her if she'll be around tomorrow when he's back."

Dave relayed the question.

"Oh, yes, I'm here every day. Mr Carson will be here tomorrow afternoon. Could you come back then?"

"Yes, of course," Dave said.

"Oh, before you go. What shall I tell him you want to talk about?"

"Just routine enquiries about something he might have witnessed," Dave said. "Nothing for him, or you, to worry about."

"Where to now, sir?" Dave asked as he reversed the car out of the driveway.

"Drive on to the next place."

While Dave was negotiating the county roads, Paolo called George. He switched his phone to speaker mode so that Dave could listen in.

"Have you got info on the owners of that property I asked you about, George?"

"As far as I can tell, it's empty, sir. I'm still trying to find out all the details, but up to now I've discovered the owner was something big in the city. When the market crashed he lost everything, couldn't take the strain and topped himself. His wife and kids moved out a couple of years back when the bank repossessed. It's been on the market ever since, but according to the estate agents there's absolutely no interest in it."

"Thanks, George. Good work."

"Yeah, right," George said and then the phone went dead.

Paolo looked at his phone. He definitely needed to set aside some time to find out what was bothering George.

"Did you get all that, Dave?"

"I did, sir. We still going to have a look?"

Paolo nodded. "Definitely. There's nothing to say the house isn't being used by people other than the owners."

But when they pulled up outside the property it was clear no one had been near in a long time. They got out of the car and peered through the locked gates. Weeds had taken root on the drive leading up to the house. Paolo could see the weeds hadn't been disturbed for at least several months as they all stood tall and undamaged.

"There's not much point in trying to get access here," he said. "Let's concentrate on Pete Carson's property and the houses on the other side of the woods."

Dave nodded. "Back to the station?"

"Might as well," Paolo agreed, climbing back into the car. "Nothing more we can do here until tomorrow." He looked at his watch. "I think I'll pick up my car and head off to the hospital. I should get there before visiting time ends."

Dave started the car and reversed out. "How is Katy, sir?"

"She's doing much better. Her psychiatrist says she should be able to go home in another week if she continues to improve."

"That's great news," Dave said.

"It is," Paolo said, but couldn't help wondering if Lydia would make it difficult for him to see Katy once she had her under her wing at home.

Paolo parked and walked up to Katy's ward, saying hello to nurses and doctors as he passed. Visiting twice a day meant he got to know faces, even if he never found out their names. As he approached Katy's room he heard raised voices – Katy's and Lydia's.

He hesitated, not wanting to intrude, but there was little visiting time left and he wanted to see Katy before he went home. He went to push open the door when Katy's voice went up a notch.

"You just won't listen," she said. "It was my own fault. Dad tried to stop me. I disobeyed him."

He couldn't make out Lydia's answer, but whatever she'd said, Katy didn't agree.

"You don't want to believe it. That's cos it's easier for you to blame him than blame yourself. Where were you when I was playing detective? Nowhere! You didn't want me around. You never wanted me. You'd have been happier if I'd died instead of Sarah."

Paolo felt an electric shock run through him. Should he go in? Should he go home and leave them to sort themselves out? He hovered outside the door, hand in the air, feeling unable to go forward or back.

"As long as you can blame Dad, you don't have to look at yourself."

He had to put a stop to this. As he reached out to open the door, Lydia's voice made him wait.

"You're wrong, Katy. I do blame myself. I could have... I should have spent more time with you. It's no excuse, but we all fell apart after Sarah died. All of us. Your dad disappeared into himself. You wouldn't talk to anyone. I wanted to die along with Sarah. But you're wrong about me wishing you'd taken Sarah's place. I love you, Katy. I love you every bit as much as I loved, still love, Sarah."

The sound of Lydia and Katy both sobbing broke Paolo's heart, but now wasn't the right moment to intrude. He waited until the crying stopped and then quietly

175

opened the door, ready to go in, but not wanting to disturb them. As he was about to step into the room, Lydia said something he'd believed he would never hear.

"I'll tell your dad I'm sorry for pushing all the blame his way and I promise I won't try to keep you two apart. Can you forgive me, Katy?"

Paolo quietly closed the door. This wasn't his time. It belonged to mother and daughter. He'd call Katy later and tell her a little white lie, say he'd been caught up in something and hadn't been able to get to the hospital in time. He turned and headed towards the lift. He got in and, just as the doors were closing, a man hit the button. The doors opened again and the man got in. He gestured for Paolo to go ahead and press which floor he wanted, before pressing for his own.

In that instant, it came back to Paolo where he'd seen Isuf Xhepa, the owner of the language school. He was the man in the lift the day he and CC came to the hospital after the child had been admitted. He, too, had waited for CC to press the floor number before pressing his own. Another visit to Mr Xhepa was on the cards for tomorrow. Paolo would be very interested to find exactly what he'd been doing in the hospital that morning.

He walked back down to the car park, intending to go home, but when he saw the pink handcuffs and whip on the backseat he remembered it was his birthday. Did he really want to spend the evening in his flat with no one to talk to? Maybe he should find a restaurant nearby. He'd still have no one to talk to, but at least he wouldn't be alone. Suddenly, he felt a tremendous urge to be surrounded by other people so that he didn't have to think or feel.

He left the car where it was and walked along Chesterfield Road until he came to an Italian restaurant. Perfect! A reminder of his mother's cooking in a place he'd never been before was exactly what he needed right now.

Pushing open the door, he went inside. The smell of garlic and herbs lifted his spirits. The restaurant wasn't that busy, but there were enough full tables to provide a nice buzz of conversation. Paolo was shown to a small table near the back of the room. As he picked up the menu, the door opened again. He looked up and saw Jessica Carter come in. She appeared to be alone. Paolo couldn't make out what was said, but the waitress led Jessica to the small table next to his.

"Small world," he said as she spotted him. He hesitated. Why not? "Would you like to join me, or are you waiting for someone?"

"No," she said. "That is, no, I'm not waiting for anyone. I often eat here as it's so convenient for the hospital. I'm used to eating alone."

Paolo wished now he hadn't said anything. "Sorry, I didn't…"

Jessica smiled. "Actually, I'd love to join you," she said, taking the chair opposite him. "It would make a very pleasant change to have someone to talk to while I eat. But we have to have one house rule. We cannot mention your daughter or ex-wife. Or anything to do with Katy's care and prognosis. It wouldn't be ethical without Mrs Sterling being here."

Paolo smiled. "I'm happy to go along with that."

CHAPTER 21

18th October (morning)

The next morning Paolo arrived at the station feeling happier than he had for a long, long time. His visit to Katy on his way into work had raised his spirits considerably. She hadn't mentioned her mother's visit and seemed to accept his excuse for not coming the night before. Paolo tried to convince himself that was why he felt so cheerful, but in his heart he knew the evening spent in Jessica Carter's company had a lot to do with the fact that he'd woken this morning with a smile on his face.

Not that the evening had been romantic in any way. It hadn't been. But if he couldn't enjoy a few hours chatting and putting the world to rights with an attractive woman, then he might just as well turn his toes up and wait to die.

They'd found they had a lot in common, not least the same sense of humour. Paolo remembered the laughter and automatically smiled.

"Is that our leader I see before me?" CC called out as he passed. "No, can't be. The man is smiling. Help! Our boss has been abducted by aliens."

He turned to her and felt an overwhelming urge to stick his tongue out. Yes, Paolo, very professional, he thought. He settled for grinning instead.

"Very funny, CC."

He looked around and saw George wasn't yet in. Realising now would be a good time to try to find out what was going on, he asked CC to come into his office.

"Shut the door," he said as she followed him in.

"Sounds ominous," she said. "Am I in trouble? I was only pulling your leg. It's just that it was so damn nice to see you come in with a smile on your face."

"What? No, it's nothing to do with that. Take a seat." Paolo waited until she was settled. "Is there a problem between you and George?"

She looked startled. "I don't know. What made you ask?"

"George doesn't seem to be his normal self and neither do you."

CC shifted in her chair as if the conversation made her uncomfortable. Paolo supposed it would. She'd been partnered with George for the best part of a year and they always seemed to get on well.

"As far as I know," she said, "George is fine with me. I certainly don't have a problem with him."

Paolo smiled. "There's a but in your voice. I can hear it."

"But, you're right, he isn't happy. I don't know why and I'm not going to pry. If he wants to tell me…"

"Calm down, CC. I'm not asking you to pry. I'm not asking you to do anything. I just wondered if you knew of anything that might be making George unhappy here at work. You should know me well enough by now to understand I'm only asking to find out if there's any way I can help."

She smiled. "Sorry, sir. Wicked Irish temper. It comes up too quickly. I don't know what's up with George, but you're right, something is. Why not ask him?"

"I'm going to. I just thought you might be able to point me in the right direction before I spoke to him."

She stood up. "I'd help you if I could, but I honestly don't know what's eating him. I tried to find out yesterday and he bit my head off. So good luck with that, sir."

"Thanks, CC. I'll be out shortly to bring you all up to speed."

Paolo waited until everyone was facing him. "Right, let's see where we are at the moment. The feedback so far from uniform is that no one on the housing estate saw or heard anything the night the child took refuge in the woods. That means one of two things. Someone there is lying to cover their own tracks, or she came from this side of the woods," he said, pointing to the map. "As we know, there are only two properties on that side. One is empty and hasn't been lived in for some time. Dave and I were there yesterday evening and couldn't see any signs of disturbance to suggest the house was being used by anyone. The other property belongs to Pete Carson. He wasn't at home when we called there, but his housekeeper assures us he is due back later this afternoon. So that's on our agenda for today. Before I go into detail about the travellers I want to pass on another snippet of information. It may have a bearing on the case, it may not. I remembered last night where I'd seen the owner of the language school before." He turned to CC. "Do you recall the morning we went to the hospital a man rushed into the lift at the last moment?" When she nodded he continued, "I'm fairly certain it was Isuf Xhepa. He might have a perfectly reasonable explanation for why he was there, but he might also have been waiting for us to arrive to find out which ward the child was on. After all, no one could ask at the information centre without drawing attention to themselves."

George raised his arm. "I'd be happy to go and interview him, sir, as you and Dave are busy today."

"Thanks, George," Paolo said, "but I think it's better if I go as I'd like to see his face when I ask him the questions. I mentioned to him when I was there last that I thought I'd seen him before. I'm now wondering why he didn't mention that it was in the lift. Although it's quite likely he didn't see me because he was distracted by CC's hair, which was green at the time."

CC laughed. "How do you like the new colour?"

"It's brown, CC, just brown. I wondered if you weren't feeling well."

She grinned. "Just felt like blending in a bit for a change, sir."

"So I don't get to go out on an interview?" Geoge said, bringing them back on track.

Paolo shook his head. "Not this time. I really think it's better if Dave and I go on our way to visit Pete Carson."

George slung his pad on the desk, but didn't say anything.

"What you're doing here is every bit as important. In fact, in many ways, it's even more vital, George. We need to be fully armed with information when we go to talk to anyone. You are better at digging out that background info than anyone else in this office."

"Yeah, right," George said under his breath, but loud enough to be heard.

Paolo debated picking him up on it, but decided now wasn't the time.

"CC, any news from forensic on the child's clothes? Not that they will be much help as they came from the travellers. And what about the DNA from the semen swabs? Do we know when we're likely to get that result?"

"Nothing of interest on the clothes, sir. No news yet on the DNA, but I'll chase that up and let you know what I find out."

"Okay, everyone. Back to work. Dave, you and I will be off to have a chat with Pete Carson in a few hours. According to his housekeeper she's expecting him home by two. We'll head out after that. Before then, we've got time call in on the language school and find out what took Isuf Xhepa to hospital that day. Okay?"

He'd set his phone to silent, but its buzzing alerted him to a call. Looking down, he didn't recognise the number displayed. Could be the old man from last night. He picked it up and slid the bar across to answer the call.

"Sterling."

"You'd better come quickly," a female voice said. "They've just dropped off one of the kids at the top of Zephyr Road."

The line went dead.

"Dave, change of plan. You come with me. We've got a child to rescue before some pervert picks her up. George, this is your opportunity to get out of the office. CC, you come too. I'll arrange for a couple of uniform to go with you both. CC, when we pick the girl up you and a WPC can take her straight into care. George, I want you and a PC to wait for the car to come back. When it does, don't approach. I need you to follow it and see where it goes. With a bit of luck, Bekim and Edar are going to be chatting to us later today."

CHAPTER 22

18th October (morning / afternoon)

Pete drove in through the gates, tired and glad to be home. He hated London with a passion. He knew it was stupid, after all, he was supposed to be the big rock star, even if it had been many years since he'd been at the top, but he much preferred being home. Here he could indulge his needs without worrying about some fucking snapper catching him unawares.

He parked the Lamborghini Gallardo in front of the ten car garage. He'd put it away later. Right now, he needed something to eat and a sleep. Fucking hotel beds always made his back ache.

And it had been a pointless trip, which made his blood boil even more. Fucking agent hadn't been able to drum up any real interest in his comeback concert. Yeah, he could get him a small mention on the entertainment pages of most rags, but apparently, if a washed up reality star sneezed, that would make a bigger story than his getting back on the road. Reality star? What was that all about? Talentless shits who did nothing but argue in some dead end show were now classed as stars? How the fuck did that happen?

He opened the front door and headed for the stairs. He'd only gone up two when his housekeeper called out.

"Oh, Mr Carson. Welcome home."

"Thanks," he said, barely turning his head.

"I'm sorry, Mr Carson, but…"

Pete spun round.

"But what?" he snarled. "Whatever it is will have to wait, okay?"

Mrs Baxter looked as though he'd slapped her.

He felt bad. It wasn't her fault his agent was a useless piece of shit. "Look, I didn't mean to yell at you, but I'm tired and need to sleep."

"I… I'm sorry, Mr Carson. I wouldn't normally disturb you, but it's the police."

Pete's heart began to beat so fast he thought he was going to puke. As he came back down the stairs his head swam. The police! Now what? Surely the stupid bitch hadn't told anyone about the blood on the gates.

"The police? What happened? Did you call them?"

"No, Mr Carson. They came here yesterday, but didn't say what it was about. They're coming back today."

He forced himself to stand still even though his entire body was screaming at him to run and never look back.

"Did they say what time?" he asked and was pleased to hear his voice sounding normal.

"No, not a definite time. Just that it would be some time this afternoon. They seemed to think you might have witnessed something."

"What sort of something?"

"I don't know," Mrs Baxter said. "They didn't tell me."

It must be to do with that brat who got away, Pete thought. Smile, Pete. Come on, smile and pretend you haven't a clue what it's about.

"In that case, I'd better get up and have a quick shower before they get here. Make me some coffee, would you? I'll be down in about fifteen minutes."

His smile disappeared as he turned and continued up the stairs. His mood, already black, sank even lower. What did the cops know? How had they found him? Thank fuck he'd given instructions for the studio to be cleaned while he was away. Any evidence he'd had girls over there should be gone. Maybe he should ask Mrs Baxter if it had been done? No, not a good idea. That would draw her attention to it. She might put two and two together and actually make four.

As the hot water blasted down on him, Pete tried to get his mind under control. It was no good panicking. He had to find out what made the cops pick on him. *If* they were picking on him. Hadn't she said something about being a witness? But to what? He hadn't seen anything the police would be interested in apart from his own actions. No, it must be to do with the brat escaping. Maybe he should call Joey. He might know what the fuck was going on. On the other hand, did he want Joey to know the police were sniffing around? What if it turned out it was nothing to do with that brat after all? What if it was something completely different? If he told Joey before he even knew what was going on, maybe Joey wouldn't let him have one of the girls he was moving around to different homes.

He decided to wait and see what the police had to say. He could always call Joey for help later. Maybe he was overreacting.

He climbed out of the shower and grabbed a towel. Catching sight of himself in the mirror he shuddered. No way could he go to prison and become some fucker's bitch. He'd kill himself first.

As he dressed, he ran over events in his mind once more. Joey was sure he'd got to the girl before she'd had chance to talk, so she couldn't have pointed fingers at him. Relax, Pete. You've got nothing to worry about.

But, as he dressed, his hands were shaking so much he couldn't do up the buttons on his shirt. Fuck it, he thought, I'll wear something else. Ripping the shirt off, he threw it on the bed. He grabbed a tee shirt, pulled it over his head and went downstairs. A few mugs of coffee and he'd feel better.

A couple of hours later the intercom sounded and Pete's heart started up that sickening heavy beat that made him want to puke. He'd drunk so much coffee by then he was almost high. For the whole afternoon his mind had been running overtime on all that could have happened. He'd picked up his phone at least a hundred times, but stopped himself from calling Joey.

He let Mrs Baxter answer the intercom and open the gates. Waiting for them in the drawing room, he tried to relax, but his hands shook. Head swimming, he fought off wave after wave of nausea. It felt as if an hour had passed before the door opened and Mrs Baxter came in with two men.

Pete recognised the older of the two. He'd been on television some time back doing some sort of press conference asking for help to track someone down. Pete couldn't remember the details, but he knew the police had found the man they'd been hunting. Shit, that wasn't good. That meant these two were heavy duty cops. Not here about an unpaid parking ticket.

"Good afternoon. I'm Detective Inspector Sterling and this is Detective Sergeant Johnson. Sorry to trouble you, but we need your help."

Pete forced himself to stand and smile. "Hello, take a seat. Mrs Baxter said you'd be coming over. How can I help you?" That was good, he thought, voice sounded okay. "Mrs Baxter, could you bring us some coffee, please?"

The two coppers sat down, but Sterling shook his head.

"No coffee for us, thank you. We'd like Mrs Baxter to stay, if that's okay with you. She might have witnessed something and not realised it was important."

The bastard actually smiled at him! He knew something, Pete was sure of it now.

"Yeah, fine, no problem," Pete said. "Sit yourself down, Mrs Baxter. Let's see if we can help out, shall we?"

"We're looking into a rape and murder," Sterling said. "The victim was picked up by some travellers in the woods a couple of miles from here."

"Dear God, no! What is the world coming to?"

Pete tuned out the waffle from Mrs Baxter. So he was right, they were on to him. He had to keep calm.

"Sorry," he said, "I'm not sure what that's got to do with me? If she was murdered a few miles from here, well…" He couldn't think how to finish his sentence, so left it there.

Mrs Baxter chimed in. "I agree with Mr Carson. Why would you think we saw anything if it all happened in the woods? I expect it was the travellers. Dirty nasty people, they are."

"No," Sterling said and looked at him in such a way that Pete wished the man would have a heart attack and die. "We have reason to believe she was attacked in one of the houses near the woods."

"Well, it certainly wasn't this one," Mrs Baxter said. "In fact, let me tell you this is a respectable house. Just because Mr Carson used to be in that band you needn't think he's a bad person, because he isn't. Treats us well, he does. And, what's more…"

"Do you know, I think would like some coffee, after all," Sterling said, smiling at Mrs Baxter. Pete wanted to punch him.

Mrs Baxter glanced at him for permission to go, but what could he do apart from smile. She got up and left the room. Left him to face the two coppers on his own.

Sterling stared at him. The other one hadn't said a word since they'd arrived. He just sat there scribbling in his notebook. Pete wondered what he'd written down. They'd hardly said anything so far, so what the fuck had he been writing?

190

"Sorry about interrupting your housekeeper, Mr Carson. It was clear she doesn't know anything. So maybe it's best if we have a chat with you on your own."

Pete leaned back and stretched his legs out. "Sure thing," he said, "but I don't know how I can help you. I haven't seen any young girls around here."

Sterling looked over at the other cop, then smiled and nodded. What the fuck? What had he said to make the bastards so fucking happy?

"Who said anything about a young girl?"

"What?" Pete said. "You did!"

"No," Sterling said with that fucking sickening smile that made Pete's hands itch to smack it away. "I didn't mention the victim's age. I didn't mention the gender either, but you can be forgiven for jumping to conclusions on that point. How did you know the victim was young?"

Pete tried to remember exactly what the bastard had said, but couldn't. The fucker was trying to trap him. He shrugged.

"I just assumed it. Not sure why. I suppose most rape victims are young. What was she, about eighteen or so?"

Sterling looked at him as if he was a piece of dog shit.

"No, Mr Carson, she was quite a lot younger than that. We think she was between ten and twelve."

"I'm bloody sure I've have noticed if she'd been hanging around here," Pete said. "Sorry, I can't help you."

Sterling smiled at him again and Pete wondered what was coming next. The bastard looked far too happy.

"What happened to your face?" Sterling asked.

"Nothing. What do you mean? What's my face got to do with a rape and murder?"

"I didn't say there was a connection. I was just wondering how your face came to be scratched like that."

Pete felt his heart go into overdrive. Fucking hell, the man must have bloody sharp eyesight. The scratches he'd got in the woods were barely visible. Even Mrs Baxter hadn't noticed them, or if she had, hadn't commented. His mind went blank. What could he say that would sound plausible?

"Cat," he blurted out. "My agent has a new kitten. I was playing with it and it suddenly went commando on my face."

"Really?" Sterling asked with that fucking irritating grin.

At that moment the door opened and Mrs Baxter came in carrying a tray with coffee and cakes.

"Would you like a slice of Dundee cake? I made it myself," she said.

The two cops stood up as if someone had choreographed their movements. Pete wondered if they had some signal between them.

"Thank you, Mrs Baxter," Sterling said, "but unfortunately we find we can't stay for coffee after all."

Thank fuck for that, Pete thought. They've swallowed it. But the cop's next words made him sweat all over again.

"Thank you for your time, Mr Carson. We'll be back if we need to ask you a few more questions."

192

"Oh, do you mean about the intruder?" Mrs Baxter said.

As the two policemen sat down again, Pete wanted to strangle his housekeeper.

"Someone broke in?" Sterling said.

Pete knew he had to put a stop to this before Mrs Baxter could mention the blood on the gates. Fuck it, what could he say?

"No, we weren't burgled," he answered before she could drop him in it. "Sometimes people climb over the gates to try to get an autograph or pinch a trophy. You know, just something to prove they've been into the house of a famous person? Anyway, that's what happened. We didn't report it because you people have far more important things to do – like chasing rapists and murderers. Isn't that right?"

He realised he was babbling and stopped. The coppers were looking at him funny. Had he overdone it? No, they stood up again.

"You should always report crimes, Mr Carson. We certainly look into any suspected wrong doing very carefully. In fact, we'll keep a close eye on this property from now on. Just in case anyone tries anything."

Was the bastard trying to frighten him? Well, if he was, he'd fucking succeeded. Pete managed a smile, although it almost choked him.

"Good to know," he said. "I'll show you out."

But Mrs Baxter wasn't having that. "No, Mr Carson, that's my job. You sit yourself down and enjoy the coffee and cake."

She left, almost sweeping the police in front of her. Pete waited until they'd gone and then jumped up to listen at the door. Please don't mention the blood, he begged silently.

"Poor Mr Carson," he heard his housekeeper say. "He works so hard. Such a nice man he is underneath all that rock and roll strutting. I hope you will keep a watch on the house. He's right, you know. We often get people wandering the grounds who shouldn't be here."

Pete couldn't make out what they answered, but heard the door close a few seconds later. Thank fuck for that. But then his mind began racing. They knew. Somehow they knew he was involved. He waited until he heard the sound of car wheels on gravel, then pulled out his phone.

Walking to the door, he put his eye to the crack and saw Mrs Baxter heading off to the kitchen. With shaking hands, he hit speed dial.

Joey answered on the first ring. "Can't talk now, Pete. I've got a problem on my hands."

"So have I," Pete hissed. "The cops have been here."

"Fuck! What did they want?"

"They asked me about a rape and murder. They didn't say so, but I know it was the brat we lost in the woods."

"*We* lost? You fucking lost her. Anyway, what did you tell them?"

"Nothing! I told them I'd seen nothing and knew nothing."

"Okay, good. Keep it that way. I've got to go. Two of my men are being followed by the cops and I need to know what's happening with them."

194

The line went dead and Pete stared at the phone as it if might bite him. Police onto Joey's men? What more could go wrong?

CHAPTER 23

18th October (late afternoon / evening)

Paolo's mind was running over everything Pete Carson had said. Even more to the point, the things he hadn't said. Pete certainly hadn't asked the right questions. Surely he should have wanted to know more so that he could help find a killer?

"That was sharp of you, sir, spotting those scratches. I only saw them after you'd mentioned them," Dave said as they waited for the gates to open.

"Luck, pure luck," Paolo answered. "The marks are really faint, but the light caught his face at the right angle, just for a moment, when he moved and they showed up. Without that, I don't think I'd have spotted them either."

"What did you make of his answer about the cat?" Dave said as he manoeuvred the car through gateway and pulled into the road.

"Bullshit, pure and simple. The scratches weren't deep enough to come from a cat, not even a kitten. He looked as if he'd plucked that excuse out of thin air," Paolo said. "I wonder if we can come up with a valid reason to ask his agent if he has a cat. Not that it matters at this stage. The scratches were too random for an animal. They would fit being scratched by bushes or branches running through the woods, though."

"So you reckon he's involved?" Dave asked.

Paolo nodded. "I'm almost sure of it. Gut feeling says he's in it somehow. Unfortunately, we can't do anything without firm evidence. I can just imagine trying to get a warrant to search his place on the strength of a gut feeling. The way he was sweating, he knows something, that's for sure."

"You think he's the one bringing the girls in?"

Paolo shook his head. "No, I don't think so. I think he might be a customer, but I don't think he's the trafficker. Whoever is doing that has to have some strong connections in Albania. As far as I can remember, our Mr Carson doesn't have any links outside of the UK, but we'll look into that, just in case."

"Just a customer?" Dave asked. "Or do you think he's our murderer?"

"I'm pretty sure he'd have been recognised if he'd gone to the hospital, even dressed as a woman," Paolo said, "but he might be the bastard who raped the poor kid. As it stands at the moment, even if we get some usable DNA from that child, we can't even ask Pete Carson for a sample to check against it. We need to dig into his past. Find out if there were any rumours about him being interested in young girls back when he was on the road with The Vision Inside. I don't remember any talk, but then not every paedophile is obvious about it. It would be better if they were. Easier to find and put away."

Dave hit the steering wheel with both hands. "I hate them. The bastards ruin lives. Worse than murderers they are. I'd like to cut their hands and pricks off and…"

"Hey, keep your mind on driving, Dave! We nearly went off the road there."

"Sorry, sir."

Paolo glanced across. Dave was chewing his bottom lip as if he wanted to destroy it. Not for the first time, Paolo wondered about his detective sergeant. Dave had demons nibbling at his mind, that was for sure, but Paolo had no idea why. He wanted to say something to comfort him, but before he could frame a sentence, Dave spoke again.

"If he had the girl in there, how did she get out?"

"Good question," Paolo said. "The gates are only opened from the inside or by someone with a gadget in their vehicle. It's hardly likely he would have let her run off into the woods stark naked."

"What was the housekeeper was saying about intruders?"

Paolo smiled. "Mrs Baxter is top of my list to question again when Pete Carson isn't there to interrupt her. She seemed to think he should have told us about an intruder. I found it very interesting how quickly he moved in to shut her up. I think she might know more than she realises. I wonder how George is getting on following that car."

Right on cue, his phone rang, but it was CC's name up on the screen, not George's.

"Yes, CC, what's the situation with the girl?"

"She's been placed in detox, sir. Poor thing is in a terrible state. According to the doctor she's covered in genital warts, showing she's sexually active. Not that we need that kind of evidence to know she's been put out to work. She's in no fit state to talk. Won't be able to give us any information for quite some time, depending on how she handles detox."

Paolo sighed. "Poor kid. Have you heard from George?"

"Not in the last hour, sir," CC answered. "Last I knew he was still following the car that came back for the girl. George said it pulled up and waited for a bit, realised something was up and drove off. That was hours ago and they've been driving around town and the countryside ever since."

"Okay, thanks. We'll see you back at the station."

Paolo filled Dave in on what CC had told him and then dialled out. George answered, but it was clear from his tone that he wasn't happy.

"This is pointless, sir. They know I'm onto them and have taken me on a bloody tour of Bradchester."

"Where are you now?" Paolo asked.

"At the motorway services north of town. They pulled in here about fifteen minutes ago. Uniform and me, we're sitting in the car park like a couple of Charlies."

"Okay, stay there. Dave and I will come over to back you up. If they move off again, keep on them and let us know where you're headed. I think it's time we had a chat with that pair."

Paolo ended the call and turned to Dave. "Change of plan. Head to the motorway services. We're going to bring in the two men who ferried the girl to Zephyr Road."

Dave smiled. "Good. I can't wait."

Dave's smile made Paolo feel he might not be the best person to take into the interview room when they questioned the two men. He decided to give George a shot at them.

Dave pulled up next to George's car. Paolo jumped out and stood next to the driver's window.

"Hi, George. Where are they now?"

"Dark BMW over there in the far corner, sir. They parked up and haven't left the car since we got here. I'm bloody sure they know I've been following them."

"Okay, I'm going to go and have a chat with them. You stand by in case I need back up."

Paolo turned and signalled to Dave to come with him. As he walked away he heard George mutter.

"Always bloody back up."

"Just hold on a second, Dave," Paolo said and stepped back to the car.

"Do you have a problem, George?"

Paolo was surprised by a look of venom on George's face, but it passed so quickly, he couldn't be certain it had ever been there.

"No, sir, no problem. Why do you ask?"

"I thought I heard you say something," Paolo said.

200

George cast a quick look at the uniformed officer sitting next to him. Paolo couldn't quite work out what the look was intended to imply, but George's next words were definitely a lie.

"I said, 'Let's hope you don't need back up.' Sir."

"Okay, fine. I hope you're right," Paolo said and returned to Dave's side. As they walked across the car park, Paolo changed his mind about inviting George in on the interviews. He'd bring in CC instead.

Putting thoughts of George and his problems to one side, Paolo tapped on the driver's side of the BMW. The window slid down and Paolo felt like punching the air. The man looking up at him was a perfect match for one of the identikit images Michelle had helped the artist to compile.

"Why has your man been following us?" the man said before Paolo could speak.

"He just wanted to ask you a few questions. We're investigating a child prostitution ring and think you might have witnessed something that could help us."

"How would we know anything?" The man looked at his companion, a dead ringer for the second identikit image. Michelle was spot on with her observations. "Do you know about child prostitution, Bekim?"

"No, not me," the man answered. "I only like grown up prostitutes. What about you, Edar? You like humping children? "

Both men laughed and Paolo felt as if he'd wandered into a bad comedy routine.

"The thing is, when you were in Zephyr Road, you might have seen or heard something that could help our investigation. Would you like to come to the station and have a chat?"

Once again, both men laughed. "Sure, why not?" the driver said. "We'll follow you there."

"That's not necessary," Paolo said. "You can come with us in our cars. Someone will bring you back here afterwards. Your car will be safe enough in the meantime."

As if they had rehearsed it, both men nodded and got out of the car. This is too easy, Paolo thought. Far too easy.

After more than two hours' questioning each man separately, Paolo's blood pressure was close to explosion point. The men couldn't have been more helpful, except that they knew nothing and could tell the police nothing. They even voluntarily handed over their mobile phones for Paolo to check past calls, which meant, Paolo was sure, there would be sod all that was incriminating to find on them. He left the interview room in search of George and found him in the canteen.

"Mind if I join you?"

George looked up from the newspaper he was reading and pointed to the seat opposite.

"Not at all, sir. Bit unusual for you to take an evening tea break, isn't it?"

As he sat down, Paolo nodded. "I haven't come for tea. CC and I have been interviewing the two men you

202

followed and getting nowhere. Did they stop anywhere while you were on their tail?"

"From time to time, yes, but it felt like they were doing it to jerk my chain, not for any other reason. Neither of them left the car at any point, if that's what you're asking."

Paolo smiled. "It's one of the things, yes."

"I'd have told you if they had. You didn't need to come looking for me to ask that," George said, pushing his cup away so forcefully the tea slopped over the rim and trickled across the table, soaking into the newspaper.

"Whoa, steady on, George. I wasn't implying you'd left anything out of your report. The thing is, these two are being far too helpful. They've even handed over their phones, which tells me they're not going to be of any use to us. Did you see them discard anything while they were driving? I'm wondering if the phones are back-ups, kept just for this purpose. If that's the case, their real phones were discarded somewhere along the way."

George glared at Paolo. "Sir, everything I saw and everything I heard is in my report. *I'm* not in on the interview, so I don't know what's being said up there, but I did everything right."

Paolo sighed. "I have to get back upstairs, but I think we should have a chat, don't you? Something is eating away at you and we need to resolve it."

"There's nothing wrong with me, sir. It must be your imagination. Unless, of course, someone has been complaining about me?"

Paolo shook his head. "No, nothing like that. Just my own observations. Come up to my office in about an hour. Even if, as you say, there's nothing wrong, we need to clear the air."

George shrugged. "If you have a problem with me, fine, I'll be there."

Paolo sighed and thought about explaining that responses like that indicated there definitely was something wrong, but he had to get back to the interviews upstairs.

"See you in an hour," he said and left George to his sopping wet newspaper.

Paolo sat down opposite Bekim and started recording the interview once more. Time to give the man a bit of a jolt. He passed the identikit image across the small table.

"Recognise yourself?"

Bekim laughed. "Is very good. Looks very like me, but is not me."

"I think it is. We have a witness who provided the information some time ago. How would we have this image unless someone had seen you dropping off and picking up the girls?"

"I don't know. Maybe is fixed? I tell you. Edar and me, we do, how you say it? A good deed. For this we get harassed. Human rights not given."

"I'll repeat my earlier offer. Would you like a solicitor to sit in on this interview?"

"Is no need. We pick up hitchy hiker girl. We take her where she say. We leave her there. Your men follow. We

204

do nothing wrong. Your man, he see this. He follow, follow, follow until you come." Bekim shrugged. "Why I need solicitor like bad man? I do good deed for hitchy hiker girl. You ask girl."

Paolo smiled. "We intend to do exactly that."

Bekim grinned back. "So you go ask. I wait here and then you say, sorry, Bekim, we get it wrong. You good man. We make the compensation for you."

Bekim laughed so hard Paolo hoped he'd choke. There was nothing more he could do. They hadn't caught the men doing anything they could prove was illegal. The hitchhiker story wasn't one they could disprove until the girl was out of detox, and possibly not even then if she followed the same path as the others they'd taken off the streets. None of them were prepared to say who they'd been held by or even where they came from. Each and every one was terrified of the consequences if they spoke out. The bastard sitting opposite knew full well he was safe. But only for the time being. Paolo swore silently. He'd shut this organisation down no matter what it took.

Paolo stood. "Interview terminated 7:23 pm. You are free to go. I'll arrange transport back to your car."

As he left the interview room, Paolo heard the man whistling. He recognised the song even though it was totally out of tune. Queen's *I want to break free*. Not if I can help it, Paolo thought. He looked back into the room, hoping to intimidate Bekim, but the man continued murdering the song. If Paolo had his way, the only people breaking free were going to be the kids being trafficked by scum like Bekim and his friends.

Paolo put his head round the door of the interview room where CC was questioning Edar.

"A moment of your time, please, Detective Sergeant Connor."

He watched CC terminate the interview for the benefit of the recording tape and then stepped back into the corridor. She came out and closed the door behind her.

"What's up, sir?"

"Has this one said anything new since I was last in the room?"

CC shook her head. "Just repeating the same old good Samaritan junk as before."

Paolo sighed. "We're going to have to let them go. I'll arrange a car to take them back to the motorway services. I'll also organise a round the clock watch on them. I want to know where they go, who they meet and why. With a bit of luck they might just lead us to the mysterious Joey, but even if they don't, we might be able to pick them up in the act of ferrying the girls to and from the streets. I'd like to see them use the hitchhiker excuse then."

***

Paolo sat at his desk going over the events of the day in his mind and making notes to remind himself of all the things he still had to do, like re-interviewing the owner of the language school and setting up meetings with the former members of The Vision Inside. If Pete was a paedophile, surely at least one of band would have noticed something odd about his behaviour.

God, he was tired. He'd promised himself an early night, but it was already gone eight and he still had to chat to George. He wasn't looking forward to that, but something was eating away at the man and Paolo needed to find out what it was before George's attitude rubbed off on the rest of his team.

Ten minutes later George tapped on the office door and came in.

"You wanted to see me? I hope it's not going to take too long, sir. We were supposed to go off duty a couple of hours ago."

"Take a seat, George. This won't take long." He waited until George had settled himself opposite. "Okay, let's not pretend we don't know why you're here. What's up? You're not a happy man at the moment."

"I *don't* know why I'm here. I work hard; do whatever is asked of me; put in the hours. What more do you want? What do you mean, not happy? Am I supposed to tell jokes? Be the office clown?"

"No, that's not what I meant at all. I'm concerned about you. Your general attitude these days is aggressive, like now. I'm just trying to find out why. What's happened recently to change you from someone happy in their work to…"

"To what? Who says I'm not happy in my work? Is it one of our team? If so, that's crap."

"George, calm down. No one has said anything about you. This is my own observation."

"Amazing, sir, I didn't think we spent enough time together for you to have observed me. I'll make sure to smile more from now on when you're in the room."

"Is that it? Do you feel overlooked by me?"

"Sir, you choose who goes out with you on jobs. Usually it's Dave, sometimes it's CC. I don't really care either way. All I'm saying is that I spend most of my day in the office and you spend most of yours outside or in here. You see me for maybe a couple of hours at most. I think you're reading too much into whatever it is you think you've seen. I'm perfectly happy." George stood up. "Can I go now? It's been a very long day and I'm dying for a pint."

Paolo nodded and watched him leave. George was right, he didn't spend much of each day in his company, but he was also not being truthful. Something had turned him sour, but Paolo was no nearer to knowing what it was than he had been earlier in the day.

He looked at his watch. Eight-thirty. It was a bit late to call in to see Katy, but he was sure the staff would turn a blind eye if he didn't stay too long. Maybe, afterwards, he'd treat himself to another meal at the Italian restaurant near the hospital. He wondered if Jessica might be there. He could do with a pleasant end to a very unproductive day.

CHAPTER 24

Paolo tapped on the door and went into Katy's room. She was standing at the window, but turned round as he came in.

"Dad," she called out and ran into his arms. "Are you here for a proper visit this time? You only stayed five minutes last night."

Paolo hugged her, feeling life didn't get much better than this. Katy was on the mend at last. He let her go and she climbed onto her bed, sitting with her back against the headrest. Paolo sat facing her in one of the visitor's armchairs, fighting an urge to yell with joy at the look on his daughter's face. Katy looked more like her old self than ever.

"Sorry about last night. We worked late and I've got an office steadily filling up with files and papers screaming at me to deal with them."

She ignored the part about the paperwork. "What are you working on? What's the case, Dad?"

Paolo wanted to chat naturally, as they had in the past, but he couldn't. He wouldn't. The last time he'd let Katy know anything about one of his cases was the reason she was in the hospital. He shook his head.

"Nothing exciting. You'd be bored to tears if I told you."

"I'm bored to tears anyway. Go on, Dad, tell me."

Paolo was saved from answering by the entrance of Lydia.

"Tell Katy what?" she asked, walking over to the bed and dropping a kiss on Katy's head before sitting in the other armchair.

"I've been trying to get Dad to tell me what he's working on, but he won't."

Lydia flashed a look at him and Paolo raised his hands in surrender.

"Don't get mad at me. I've not said a word."

Amazingly, Lydia smiled. "I believe you. You're here early. Did you get a call from Jessica as well?"

Paolo could feel a blush rising up from his chest and flooding his face. He prayed Lydia wouldn't spot it. Jessica hadn't needed to call him this morning because they'd shared a table again the night before in the restaurant. Although she hadn't mentioned Katy or said why she wanted to see him and Lydia, she'd asked him to be at the hospital at nine this morning. He looked at his watch. It was ten to nine.

He avoided answering Lydia's question directly. "She should be here soon. I wonder what she wants to talk to us about."

Lydia gave him a strange look, almost as if she knew he'd twisted out of telling her there'd been no need for Jessica to call him. He felt absurdly guilty, which was ridiculous. They'd sat at the same table and chatted about life in general. Nothing more than that.

He was relieved when the door opened again and the psychiatrist came in.

"Good morning, everyone. Thank you, both, for coming in on a Saturday morning, but I'm afraid this was the only time I had available and I didn't think either of you would want to wait to hear this. Katy can go home on Monday."

"Yes!" Katy yelled, punching the air.

Jessica smiled. "You don't get rid of me that easily. I'd like to see you as an outpatient for a few months. Just to make sure you're doing okay." She turned to Paolo and Lydia. "When Katy leaves she'll be given an appointment to come to my office for visits, as I'd like to get her away from the hospital environment. I'd like to see her weekly for the first month and then we'll see how she is after that. Maybe we'll cut it down to once a fortnight, or even monthly."

Paolo stood and shook Jessica's hand. "Thank you; you've done an amazing job."

"Not me," she said. "Katy's the one who's worked hard to get to where she is now." She turned to Katy. "See you on Monday."

As Jessica left the room, Paolo turned to Lydia, annoyed that she hadn't said a word while the psychiatrist was in the room, but his feelings of irritation disappeared when he saw the tears streaming down Lydia's face. She was clearly trying hard to bring her emotions under control, but failing.

Katy climbed off her bed and knelt in front of Lydia. "Don't cry, Mum. Please don't cry."

Lydia reached out and pulled Katy to her. "I thought I'd lost you forever."

"Never," Katy said. "You don't lose me that easily."

Paolo didn't know what to do. Should he go and leave them to it, or should he stay? He'd never loved Katy more than when she looked up at him and winked.

"Go and do your paperwork, Dad. See you this evening?"

He nodded and moved to the door. The last sound he heard was of Katy soothing her mother. Amazing how things changed. It wasn't that long ago it had been the other way round.

He walked into the station feeling better about life than he had for a very long time. He tried not to work Saturdays, but today was a good time to finally clear some of those files still littering his desk.

As he sat at his desk, he allowed his mind to wander back to the night before. Sharing a table once again with Jessica had sent him home smiling. She was a good companion. Intelligent, articulate and funny. Although she'd told him about the meeting she'd arranged with Lydia and had left a message on his answering machine, she didn't let slip any idea what the meeting might be about. He was pleased she hadn't mentioned Katy's prospective return to normal life. It proved she stuck to the rules about patient confidentiality.

He shook his head and focused on the files in front of him. Thinking about Jessica Carter wasn't a good idea. She was Katy's doctor. Nothing more than that. But he still spent the next few minutes dwelling on their time together the night before.

He dragged his mind back into work mode. He needed to get in contact with the former band mates of Pete Carson. That was going to be tricky. He couldn't mention his suspicions without proof, but he needed to find out if Pete had shown any inclinations towards very young girls back when they were all together. He'd have to leave off interviewing them until he had a bit more to go on.

That left the owner of the language school. He was definitely one to investigate. Was it coincidence he was at the hospital the day the girl was murdered? Maybe, maybe not, but he'd better have a bloody good reason for being there.

Paolo sighed. He'd put it off as long as he could. It was time to get on with his least favourite chore. He picked up the first file and began reading.

CHAPTER 25

21st October (morning)

Paolo smiled and put his phone on the desk. Katy was back at Lydia's and the move had gone smoothly. Incredible as it seemed to him, Lydia was the one bringing him up to date on where they were. It was like talking to the person he'd known before tragedy had torn them apart. Funny how life turned around when you least expected it.

He got up and went in search of Dave. He found him by the coffee machine looking like he'd found fifty pence after losing ten pounds.

"What's up, Dave? Coffee even worse than usual?"

Dave smiled, but it was a poor effort. "Is that even possible?"

"Probably not," Paolo said. "If it's not the coffee, what's put the frown on your face?"

"It's this case. It's getting to me. I hate the thought of those poor kids being forced to … well, just being forced. I want to rip the bastards to shreds."

Paolo felt the same way, but knew now wasn't the time to say so. "Come on, get your jacket. We're going to visit the language school again. Let's find out what Isuf Xhepa was doing at the hospital that morning. More to the point, why did he wait until the last minute to get in the lift with me and CC? Maybe it was a clever way of finding out what floor the girl was on. Throw that rubbish away. I'll treat you to a decent cup on the way."

Dave dropped his half full cup in the bin. "You're on, but I want one of those fancy coffees with half a dozen names to it."

Paolo laughed. "You'll get a straightforward coffee and like it."

"Yes, sir. Anything you say, sir."

As they turned towards the entrance, George appeared. Paolo was about to offer to bring back coffee for him and CC when they returned, but before he could speak, George turned and went back into the main office.

"Blimey," Dave said, "what's eating him?"

Paolo shook his head. "Come on, let's get out of here."

Dave pulled the car into the curb, almost directly outside the school. Paolo grinned. Having Dave as driver was like ordering ahead and having the perfect parking spot reserved. He was about to get out of the car when his phone rang. He looked at the display. CC. He signalled to Dave to wait and answered the call.

"Yes, CC, what have you got for me?"

"Bad news, I'm afraid, sir. Surveillance have lost Bekim and Edar."

215

"What? How? I thought they were keeping a tight watch on both of them?"

"They are, or rather, they were. The pair drove to a warehouse on the industrial estate and parked outside. A couple of hours later the car was still there, so one of the surveillance team decided to take a closer look. Turns out the warehouse was empty, completely gutted. Seems they went in through the door at the front and disappeared out the back."

"Shit! That was our only real lead. Who owns the warehouse?"

"George is looking into that at the moment, but it looks like it's been empty for the best part of a year. There was nothing inside at all."

"Okay, thanks, CC. Keep me informed if anything new comes up."

"Will do, sir."

Paolo ended the call and put the phone back in his pocket.

"That didn't sound like good news, sir," Dave said.

"It wasn't," Paolo said and explained what had happened. "Seems like our surveillance aren't as invisible as they think they are."

Dave shrugged. "Either that, or they guessed we'd put someone on them and took avoiding action just in case."

"You could be right. Come on; let's hope we have more joy with Isuf Xhepa."

They climbed out and entered the school. As they walked in, a group of students were congregating in the entrance hall. In the melee, Paolo recognised the helpful student from their last visit, but couldn't recall the young man's name when he came over to greet them.

"You come second time. Is problem? We go on trip to field for castle in Lest... Lest... is hard to say."

"A field trip to Leicester to see the castle?" Paolo asked.

He and Dave moved to one side as the students filed out.

"Yes. Bus is wait for me. I need take you to Mr Xhepa?"

Paolo smiled. "No, that's not necessary. We can find our own way up to his office. You go with the others and enjoy your day out."

The young man bowed and again Paolo felt an urge to copy him. Seeing Dave's grin out of the corner of his eye, he knew his detective sergeant had seen his slight movement. They waited until the students had left and then walked along the corridor to the staircase. Walking up to the first floor, they found their way to the principal's office, but made no attempt to go in. The man was clearly on the phone and not at all happy with the person on the other end.

"Judging by the yelling going on in there, we'd have found this room even if we hadn't known where to come," Dave said.

Paolo nodded. Isuf Xhepa was giving someone hell. Given that they couldn't hear the other side of the argument, Paolo guessed the school principal wasn't getting his own way. It was a pity he couldn't understand Albanian. He'd have loved to know what had angered the man so much, but they could only wait until the flow of incomprehensible words came to an end. One thing was for sure, regardless of language, it was obvious Isuf Xhepa was far from pleased by what he was hearing.

"Not a happy bunny by the sound of things," he said to Dave.

"Nope. Glad I'm not on the end of that tongue lashing."

They waited another couple of minutes and then heard the unmistakeable sound of a receiver being slammed back onto the phone.

"I think that's our cue," Paolo said and tapped on the door. Without waiting for an answer, he went in with Dave right behind him.

"Good morning, Mr Xhepa. Sorry to trouble you, but I wonder if you could help us. Would you mind if we asked you a couple of questions?"

"What about? I'm very busy. How did you get in? The door is supposed to be locked when the students aren't here."

Paolo moved towards the desk. "Do you mind if we sit down?" he asked, settling himself on one chair as Dave took the other.

"Yes, I do mind. I told you. I'm very busy. And you didn't tell me how you got in here. I think I should speak to my solicitor about this harassment."

Interesting, thought Paolo. This is a completely different reaction to when we were here last. Again he wished he'd been able to understand whatever had been said on the phone.

"The students were on their way out when we arrived, so the door was open. I'm sorry if you feel we're harassing you, but I can assure you that isn't our intention, but please feel free to call your solicitor."

He watched as the school owner made a concerted effort to bring his temper under control.

"No, I see. I'm sorry if I was a little agitated. Business doesn't always go according to plan and I'm afraid I took my irritation out on you. What can I help you with? I've already told you I have seen those two men around town, but don't know them. What more can I say about that?"

Paolo smiled. "No, that's not why we're here. I don't know if you recall, but a few weeks back, we shared the lift in Bradchester Central."

"If I did, I don't remember it. Why are you asking about that?"

"Are you sure you don't remember? I was in the lift with a woman. She had vivid green hair. I would have thought that might stand out in your mind."

Isuf closed his eyes in thought. "Yes, now you come to mention it, I do recall the woman, but I'm afraid I don't remember seeing you. Is it important? Is that why you're here?"

Paolo nodded. "In a way, yes, it is. Would you mind telling us why you were at the hospital that day?"

The colour drained from Isuf's face. "What business is it of yours? Why should I tell you about my private affairs?"

"You don't have to tell us anything, of course, but it would be very helpful to our enquiries if we knew why you were there."

"How? In what way? This is ridiculous. Get out."

"Do you read the papers?" Paolo asked.

Isuf looked bewildered at the change of direction. "Of course I do."

"Then you might recall that later that same day a child was murdered in the hospital. We are interviewing everyone who was there. In order to remove you from our list of potential suspects – not that I'm saying you are on it – but to take away any possibility of you being involved, we'd simply like to know why you were in the hospital that day."

Isuf looked down at his hands and moved them under the desk, but not before Paolo had seen how much they were shaking.

"I would like you to leave now. I don't have to tell you anything unless you are going to charge me with something. Are you?"

Paolo could feel his temper rising. If the man had nothing to hide, why not say why he was at the hospital that day?

"If I find you're in any way involved in what happened to the child, I swear..." He took a deep breath. There was no point in losing his temper. "If you aren't involved, I give my word whatever information you give today will remain between us."

Isuf kept his eyes down, almost as if he couldn't bear to look at Paolo as he spoke. "I have nothing to say."

"You do realise I cannot leave it at that? We are investigating a murder."

Isuf looked up. "Do whatever you want, but if my reason for being at the hospital gets out, I will know it came from you. If that happens, I'll sue you and destroy your career. Now leave and don't bother coming back. I had nothing to do with any murder."

Paolo stood up. Dave followed him from the office and closed the door behind them.

"Phew!" he said. "How are we going to find out? There's no point in asking at the hospital and we don't have enough to request a warrant."

"No, but that doesn't stop us from keeping a very close eye on him."

They went downstairs with Paolo thinking about Isuf's reaction when they first arrived. Why had he been so defensive before he even knew why they were there?

Paolo opened the front door for Dave to go through and made sure it closed behind him to activate the locking mechanism.

"Did you get the feeling Mr Xhepa has something to hide?" Paolo asked as they reached the car.

"Yes. You think it's to do with our case?"

"I'm not sure, but I definitely think he's up to something. He really didn't like us being there today. Even if his reason for being at the hospital that day is innocent, I think we should still keep an eye on his activities. His reaction was completely over the top and there must have been a reason for it."

They got in the car. Dave fastened his seat belt and turned to Paolo.

"Where to next, sir?"

"Let's go out to the import business on the industrial estate and see if there's any news of Jeton. He seems to have disappeared off the face of the earth. If they're telling the truth, not even his family have seen him since the day we spoke to him about Bekim and Edar. As you know, I've had people watching his wife, just in case she leads us to him, but so far the most exciting thing she's done is go shopping twice in one day in Tesco's. The officer on duty says it's like watching paint dry."

Dave laughed. "Yeah, I've done some of those stints. The boredom is deadly. Staying awake is the hardest part."

"You can say that again. Hang on; you've reminded me of something."

He pulled out his phone and called George. "Any news on that warehouse where surveillance lost Bekim and Edar? Dave and I are on our way to the industrial estate. We could take a look round while we're over there."

"It's a bank repossession and they haven't been able to offload it. It was previously owned by a small construction company that went out of business. It's one of those complicated set ups where the parent company is registered offshore, but the insolvent part had its roots in Leicester. I'm still digging to try to find out who really owned it."

"What's the address?"

As George gave it to him, he keyed it in to the Satnav.

"Thanks for that, George. See you later," Paolo said, but the line had already gone dead.

"What made you think of that?" Dave asked.

"You talking about surveillance reminded me how we'd lost Bekim and Edar. That wasn't a spur of the moment thing. They deliberately went to that warehouse because they knew it was empty, but more importantly, they had to have had transport of some sort waiting for them out the back. Someone knew about that warehouse and set it up. Either that was someone who was connected with the failed business, or it was someone who worked nearby and had seen it go under. Let's go there first. We can check in on the import business afterwards. A few minutes won't make any difference to see whether Jeton is there or he isn't."

But as it turned out, they didn't have to make a detour. Dave pulled up outside the empty warehouse, which was only two buildings along from the import company.

Climbing out of the car, Paolo pointed at the warehouse and back to the place where Jeton worked.

"Nice and convenient, isn't it? I'm beginning to think Jeton knows more than he told us. Let's hope he's back in work."

But they were out of luck. No one had seen Jeton since the day of their first visit.

"You know, Dave," Paolo said when they were on their way back to the station, "it's looking more and more likely Jeton is involved somehow. Whether or not he's the one bringing the kids in, I don't know, but there must be a connection between Jeton's disappearance and us asking about Bekim and Edar. I wonder where he went."

CHAPTER 26

28th October (morning)

Dave pulled the car into the drive outside Pete Carson's mansion.

Paolo nodded in the direction of the intercom. It seemed incredible to him that three weeks, all but a day, had passed since the child had been murdered. Ten days had fled since they'd last been to this house. He was getting nowhere fast, but maybe he'd get a bit closer to the truth this time. He glanced at his watch. Nice and early, less chance of the singer being up and about.

"Let's hope we can speak to the housekeeper without Pete Carson interfering."

Dave nodded, then reached out and pressed the button on the intercom.

"Hello, can I help you?" Mrs Baxter answered.

Pete flashed his badge at the camera.

"Oh dear, Mr Carson is upstairs sound asleep. Should I go and wake him?"

"That's not necessary, Mrs Baxter," Paolo called across Dave. "We've just come to get some more information on the intruder. We can ask you all the questions we have and don't need to disturb Mr Carson."

"Oh, that is kind of you," she said. "I'll put some coffee on for you."

The gates opened and Dave drove through. Paolo gave a sigh of relief. This was working out exactly as he'd hoped. The car came to a stop in front of the garages and they got out.

"I wonder how many cars he has," Dave said. "I bet every garage is full."

"Unless one of them is a black car used to ferry the girls to and from Zephyr Road, I don't really care. Let's keep our minds on the job."

They walked up to the front door where Mrs Baxter greeted them with a massive smile.

"I knew you'd be back. Mr Carson said not to bother you, but it isn't right, is it? People just take advantage all the time. Come in. I hope you don't mind if we go through to the kitchen. We're less likely to disturb Mr Carson if we talk in there. Would you like some cake with your coffee?" she asked as they reached the kitchen at the back of the house.

Paolo sat down at the polished oak table. "No cake for me, thank you. Just the coffee will be great."

"And you, young man? Have you got room for a piece of homemade cake?"

Dave's eyes lit up and he nodded. Judging by Dave's reaction, Paolo guessed whatever Rebecca's charms were, they didn't include home baking.

He waited for Mrs Baxter to sit down.

"When we were here before you were very concerned about an incident. You said someone had broken into the grounds, but not into the house, is that right?"

"Yes. I wouldn't have known anything about it if it hadn't been for the gardener's assistant. Tony spotted the blood."

"Blood?"

"Yes," Mrs Baxter said, nodding vigorously. "That's how we knew someone had been in the grounds. If I'd known you were coming I'd have asked him to come in today, but Tony only works three days a week here."

"Never mind, Mrs Baxter," Paolo said. "We can always have a chat to Tony at another time. Why don't you tell us what happened and when."

She screwed up her face. "It's the when that's a problem to work out. I can't quite remember when it was, you see."

"Okay, don't worry, we can come back to that. Let's concentrate on what Tony found."

Paolo was pleased to see the frown disappear. "Oh, that's easy. Tony came to me and said there was blood on the drive near the side gates. The ones closest to the studio where Mr Carson does all his recording. So I went with him to see and there wasn't much, but it was enough, you know? Anyway, so I told Tony to power hose… oh, no, sorry, I've got that wrong. First, Tony said to me, 'where do you think the blood's come from?' and, of course, I had no idea, so we had a good look round and found there was blood on the gates as well." She smiled. "And *that's* when I told him to power hose everywhere."

Paolo and Dave exchanged a glance. That sounded like the death knell to any evidence they might have been able to find. But maybe not. There might still be traces.

"Did you discuss this with Mr Carson?"

She nodded. "Yes, but we decided not to bother you as whoever had broken in had gone and not really caused any damage, apart from the blood, of course. He or she, we get all sorts hanging around, must have cut themselves climbing over. Blood's a nasty thing these days. Aids and such like. That's why I told Tony to clean it up straightaway."

The kitchen door opened and Pete Carson came in. He looked as if he hadn't slept in at least a week.

"What's going on? Why are you here again?"

Mrs Baxter jumped up. "Oh, Mr Carson, if I'd known you were awake, I'd have brought you up some coffee."

"Never mind that now," he said. "Why did you call the police back without telling me?"

"She didn't," Paolo said. "We're simply following up on our last visit when we heard about your intruder."

"I told you, we didn't want to make a fuss about it."

Paolo smiled. "Yes, sir, I know, but now we've been told about the blood on the gates, well, that puts a different light on things."

Pete sat down heavily. "Does it. Why? I haven't asked you to come back here."

"No, but it's our civic duty to investigate when we know a crime has been committed."

Pete glared at him. "You don't know any crime has been committed here. It could have been –"

"We are fairly certain a crime has been committed here, Mr Carson, and we intend to investigate it fully, starting with getting forensics out to take samples from the gates and the drive. Don't worry," Paolo said, leaning towards Pete, "whatever happened to cause that blood to appear on your gates, we'll find out about it."

"Well now," said Mrs Baxter, smiling broadly, "isn't it great to know the police can find time to look into all crimes, not just the ones that make the headlines!"

Pete looked down, avoiding Paolo's eyes. "Yes, it's just great."

Leaving Pete Carson in the kitchen, Mrs Baxter led them back to the front door.

"You must excuse Mr Carson, he's never at his best early in the morning. We must have woken him when you arrived. You will look into the blood on the gates, won't you?"

Paolo nodded. "Mrs Baxter, I give you my word, the blood on your gates will get my full attention."

They walked back to the car, Paolo's mind running on speed. As soon as the car doors were closed, he pulled out his phone to arrange for forensics to come over to do the tests.

"You think there's anything to find, sir?"

"I don't know, Dave. The power hose wouldn't have cleaned away everything, but we don't know how much blood there was to start with. By the look on Pete Carson's face, he seemed to think there might be something to find. I was pretty sure before today that he was involved. Now I'm convinced of it. I think we've now got enough reasons to justify a chat with his former band mates. There must be something in his past that will trip him up if he was interested in kids."

"If he is, I hope to God we can put him away. You know what the other prisoners will do to him – give him the justice we can't. I hope they rip the bastard into shreds."

Dave accelerated away from the garages, wheels spinning.

"You sound as if it's personal."

Dave nodded, tight-lipped. "It is."

CHAPTER 27

28th October (morning)

Pete looked at Mrs Baxter as she bustled around the kitchen clearing away the coffee cups and wanted to smash her face in. Stupid, stupid, stupid fucking bitch had no idea what she'd done to him. How the fuck was he going to get out of this one?

She turned and smiled at him. "Aren't they kind? I never dreamed they would go to so much trouble for us. We should have called them in sooner. I feel so safe now, don't you, knowing they are going to be watching out for us all the time. I don't suppose anyone will get in or out now without them knowing about it."

She turned back to ferry cups to the sink and Pete felt as if he'd been hit in the gut with a wrecking ball. What if they came back and searched the studio? He had to get rid of the brat Joey had delivered a few days earlier.

"I'm off to the studio, Mrs Baxter. I don't want to be disturbed, no matter what it is. Not even if the police come back to talk to us. Tell them I'm out. Tell them whatever you want, but do *not* bring them to the studio.

I'm in the middle of a very tricky section on my latest track and can't break off for anyone. You got that?"

She looked worried. "You sound angry, Mr Carson. Have I done something wrong?"

Pete forced a smile onto his face. "No, of course you haven't. I'm just not used to being up at this time in the morning. You know what I'm like. Up all night and then sleep most of the day. But as I'm awake, I'll go over and work."

"Would you like some breakfast before you go?"

Pete shuddered. "No thanks. It's too early for me to eat."

"Shall I bring you something later?"

He shook his head. "No need. I'll call out for pizza."

She smiled at him. "I've never known anyone to love pizza as much as you do. I swear not a week goes by without that pizza van coming to deliver. I can't stand the stuff myself, but each to his own tastes, that's what I say."

Couldn't agree more, thought Pete, as he left the kitchen. But right now I need to get rid of the brat. He was bored with her anyway, so she'd be no loss, but he'd better lay off for a while until the cops found someone else to get their claws into.

Pete walked across to the studio and keyed in the security code. The brat was curled up in the corner, covered with a blanket. She looked up at him, fear and longing on her face. She wanted a fix and knew what she'd have to do to get it, but he couldn't take the chance on keeping her. He'd have to call Joey. Although, it would make more sense for the pizza van to come at lunchtime, which gave him a couple of hours. Turning to double lock the door, he smiled. Yeah, why not have a farewell fuck?

He unbuckled his belt and pulled the blanket off the girl. That would have to go with her when she went. All his stash would have to go as well. He couldn't leave anything behind, traces of the girl or any drugs, just in case that fucker Sterling sent in people to search this place. He wouldn't put it past the piece of shit to pretend he was doing it as a public fucking service.

Looking down at the girl, he decided to have one last go with her before he sent her back.

"Get up," he said, signalling with his hands what he wanted her to do.

She knelt in front of him in the way he'd trained her and set to work. He was already feeling better. The phone call to Joey could wait for an hour or two.

CHAPTER 28

31ˢᵗ October (morning)

Paolo stood in front of his team, noting the looks of frustration on their faces. It reflected the way he felt. So far they'd interviewed all of the band members except one and none of them remembered anything bad about Pete Carson, which was pretty incredible considering Pete's drug taking and outrageous behaviour had brought about The Vision Inside's downfall. The fact that they all spoke of him like he was some kind of saint told Paolo there was some serious covering up going on, but there was little he could do about it at the moment.

"Right, as you know, the only member of The Vision Inside we haven't yet spoken to is the drummer, Don Carmichael, and he arrives back from the Caribbean this afternoon. He's agreed to have a chat with Dave and me at the airport hotel before travelling on to his next destination. Let's hope he can give us something useful. God knows, we've had little enough to go on." He sighed. "The forensic team went over every inch of Pete Carsons gates and drive. They found miniscule traces of blood, but say they don't yet know if there is enough to test. We'll find out the answer to that in a few days, but it's not looking good."

George threw a file on the desk. "You're concentrating your efforts on this Carson pervert. What about the Albanian side of things? What was the point of digging into those businesses if you're not following up on them?"

Paolo caught the murmur of discontent whispering around the room. If he didn't put a stop to this, George's attitude would spread.

"You're right, George. The Albanian side of things is where we'll find the traffickers, so let's recap where we are so far with the three main suspect businesses. First, the language school. Isuf Xhepa wouldn't give us his reason for being at the hospital on the day the child died. He may have been finding out which ward the girl was on, but we have no way of proving that. All we know for sure is that he was there. Full stop. However, the last time Dave and I went to interview him, Isuf Xhepa's behaviour was odd to say the least. We will be watching him very carefully when the next batch of students arrive, but that's a month off yet."

Turning to the board behind him he pointed to the next business on it. "The import business itself looks clean enough, but there are two things that don't smell right. Firstly, Jeton, Gazmend's cousin, was at the hospital when we went to see the child before she was murdered, so he knew exactly where to find her."

A voice from the back called out. "Which is more than we know about him and his ex-wife, sir."

Paolo smiled. "Exactly. They have both fallen off the face of the planet. There isn't a sign of either of them anywhere. Surveillance has let us down badly on this case. The ex-wife went into Tesco's and didn't come out again. Did she meet up with Jeton in there? Did he or someone else give her clothes and a wig to disguise herself? Did she go into the toilets looking one way and come out as someone completely different? It's beginning to look like it. Let's not forget that our other disappearing act, Bekim and Edar, used an empty warehouse almost next door to where Jeton worked, which is another possible connection to add to the tally."

He picked up a piece of paper from the table in front of the board. "This stays within these four walls, but I am bringing in a new Albanian interpreter from London."

CC called out. "You have doubts about Gazmend, sir?"

Paolo turned to her. "Not really, CC. My main reason is saving Gazmend's feelings. It looks more and more as if his cousin might be involved in some way. I don't want to put Gazmend in an awkward position. I'd like you to tell him that we've given up on questioning the girls we have in care. Say we realise now they are too far gone on drugs, or simply too traumatised to talk."

She nodded. "Will do, sir. I'm sure he'll buy that because we haven't been to talk to the girls for a while now for exactly those reasons."

"When the new interpreter arrives, a woman, she'll be working closely with Jessica Carter, the clinical psychologist who has helped my daughter so much. I've spoken to her about the girls in care and she's offered to give her time free of charge, working through the interpreter, to try to help the girls. In the process, she might find out a few facts we can use to flush out the traffickers."

When he mentioned Jessica's name, Paolo felt a blush rising up through his body and prayed no one in the room picked up on it. Sharing a table with her most evenings had become a very pleasant habit and it was over one of their chats that she'd made the offer. No need to mention that now, though, Paolo decided. Let them think it had happened during one of his consultations with her about Katy.

He turned back to the board. "This final business, the haulage contractors, is also very interesting. When Dave and I went to ask about Bekim and Edar, I left my card with the receptionist. She hasn't been there very long, but thinks there's something not quite right about the set up. If she has any information, she'll pass it on. So you see, George," Paolo said, smiling in his direction, "we are still keeping a very close watch on all three concerns. The reason we are concentrating on Pete Carson is that we believe, strongly believe, that he is a customer of the traffickers. Even more than that, we are convinced he was in some way responsible for what happened to the child before she was found by the travellers." He sighed again. "Unfortunately, so far we don't have a single shred of provable evidence."

"So he gets away with it!" George said.

Paolo took a deep breath before replying. The last thing the team needed was an argument breaking out in front of everyone.

"No, George, he's not going to get away with anything. That's why we're watching his place day and night and will pounce if there's so much as a hint of DNA linking the blood of that child to the blood on his gates. We just have to be patient for the time being." He nodded to the group. "That's it for now. Dave and I will be out for most of the day. We're off to Gatwick to chat to Don Carmichael, but you can reach either of us on our mobiles."

The Gatwick Elevation wasn't the kind of airport hotel Paolo sometimes used for overnight stops if he had an early departure. This was luxury with a capital L, he thought, as he took in the marble floors and gilt fittings glinting in the soft lighting hidden behind elaborate structures pretending to be artworks instead of light fixtures. It was the kind of place that made you want to whisper when you asked for directions.

"How the other half live, sir," Dave said as they waited for someone to show them to Don Carmichael's suite.

"I don't know about waiting for a plane, I'd be happy to have my holiday right here," Paolo said. "It's ten times better than the hotel I stayed in last year in France and that was supposed to be five star. If that was five, this place must be ten at least."

A young man in the purple and gold hotel livery left the reception area and walked over to where Paolo and Dave were seated.

"Mr Carmichael asked me to show you to his suite. Would you come with me, please?"

Paolo reluctantly heaved himself out of the low armchair. He'd have been happy to be kept waiting another hour or so while he relaxed in that chair. Something so comfortable most probably cost more than he earned in a month. They followed the young man to the lifts. He inserted a card into the operating mechanism, but didn't press a floor number. The doors closed and the lift moved upwards.

"That's neat," Paolo said. "Is that to stop other guests going up to certain floors?"

"Yes, sir. Only those actually staying on the top floor get one of these cards and we never give them out to their visitors."

Paolo wondered what it must be like to be so rich you could afford to stay in a place like this. Not just rich enough for the lower floors, but rich enough to buy the privacy of a top floor suite. The members of The Vision Inside must be rolling in it if this hotel and Pete Carson's mansion were examples of the wealth they had.

The lift doors opened and they followed the porter to the end of the corridor. He tapped on the door and they waited a few moments. The door opened and the least famous member of The Vision Inside appeared. Instead of the aging rocker Paolo had been expecting, Don

Carmichael could have posed as a business tycoon ready to attend a board meeting.

"Come in," he said, gesturing to Paolo and Dave to move past him. "Thank you, Simon."

Turning to the porter, he grasped the young man's hand and Paolo thought money was exchanged, but it was so neatly done, he couldn't be sure. He found himself liking the man, without quite knowing why.

"Take a seat. Please, make yourselves comfortable. What can I get you? Tea? Coffee? Something cold?"

"Nothing for me, thank you, Mr Carmichael," Paolo said.

Dave shook his head. "Not at the moment, thank you."

"Call me Don, please. Mr Carmichael makes me sound like I'm in trouble." He frowned. "You said it was to do with Pete. What do you want to know? I haven't seen him in years. In fact, when he got in touch about reforming the band, it was the first time I'd spoken to him since we split up."

Paolo sank into another comfortable armchair and seriously considered robbing a bank to be able to afford this lifestyle.

"Without going into details, we need to ask you some questions about Pete Carson's activities off stage."

Don sat down opposite them. "Okay, I have a feeling I can guess what you want to know."

Paolo raised an eyebrow. "Really? Your fellow band mates didn't give us the impression there *was* anything to know."

Don laughed. "Well, they wouldn't, would they? Their income is mainly from royalties on our old stuff. It still gets a fair amount of air time. You might not realise it, but a lot of our music is used to sell products on television and a couple of the latest shows use our tunes as their signature theme."

"Are you saying they kept quiet to protect their earnings?"

Don nodded. "Of course."

"Which implies," Paolo said, "that there is something in Pete's past that would threaten those royalty payments. So why are you prepared to tell us if they weren't?"

Don smiled. "Because I am not reliant on the royalties for my lifestyle. Before I joined The Vision Inside I'd gained a first at university in business studies. From the moment we made our first serious money, I started investing in various businesses. The royalties are nice, but I don't need them."

"Why did you guys break up? The story in the press was drugs and drink. Was that all there was to it?"

Don poured himself some water. "Are you sure I can't get you anything to drink? No? Okay, here's what happened. It wasn't the drugs; we were all doing those at the time. I don't think there was band back then who didn't have a constant supply of stuff on tap almost. We gave out that Pete's use had rocketed, but that wasn't really true. Sure, he was using, but he had it under control."

"Go on," Paolo said, when Don stopped.

"We were on tour and we'd all gone out to eat after a gig. All except Pete, who'd said he was tired and wanted an early night." Don laughed. "An early night! It was two in the morning, but that's the way life was on tour. Getting to bed when the sun came up and sleeping most of the day. Anyway, Pete said he was too tired to come out to eat with us and he went back to the house we'd hired for the week. We'd only been in the restaurant for half an hour when Jimmy, the bass guitarist, who was allergic to shellfish, said something he'd eaten must have been contaminated. He blew up like the Michelin man and we got into a right panic, but he said it was no hassle. We just had to get him back to the house where he kept an emergency supply of injections his doctor had given him."

Don went quiet and Paolo guessed what was coming next, but stayed silent to give him time to find the words.

"The bastard couldn't have been expecting us back for another couple of hours at least." He looked at Paolo. "You know, don't you?"

Paolo nodded. "I can guess, but we need you to tell us. I can't prompt you."

Don shrugged. "No, I suppose not. I don't even want to put it into words, but I'll have to. We opened the front door and Pete must have heard us because he appeared at the top of the stairs wanting to know why we were back so soon. Jimmy went off to get his injection from his room at the back of the house and then we heard someone crying. Really sobbing her heart out."

"Go on," Paolo said.

"I ran upstairs, pushed past Pete who tried to stop me from going in his room. There was a young girl on the bed. Turns out she was from a local children's home. I have no idea how Pete found her or how she came to be in the house. She certainly hadn't been there earlier when we left for the gig. At least, I don't think so. While I was calming the poor kid, there was a massive noise going on behind me. The other guys beat the shit out of Pete – put him in hospital for a week."

Paolo thought back to the time the press had been full of Pete's injuries. "Is that when the papers reported he'd fallen from an upper floor window while high?"

Don nodded. "That was the story we gave them. We took the child back to the home and made a hefty donation to their charity funds. Then we dumped Pete at the hospital." He shrugged. "And that was the end of The Vision Inside."

Dave stopped writing and looked up from his notes. "Why didn't you carry on without him?"

"Because he was the gifted one. It was his music, his voice that people paid to listen to. The man is an absolute genius when it comes to music, but a sick bastard outside of that."

"Why didn't you report him to the police?" Paolo asked.

Don sighed. "There is no good answer to that question. I could say things were different then, which they were, but that doesn't excuse the fact that we didn't do the right thing. We covered it up and went our separate ways."

"So why are you breaking your silence now after all these years?" Paolo asked. "Why not keep quiet? We wouldn't have known if you hadn't told us today."

"If I'm honest, I don't think I would have come forward looking for anyone to tell, but you contacted me asking about Pete's past and I knew I had to tell you the truth. It was time."

Paolo stood up. Dave put away his pad.

"You realize you aided and abetted a paedophile, don't you?" Dave asked, his voice close to a snarl.

Paolo looked at him and was astounded to see Dave was trembling and looking at Don as if he wanted to punch him.

Don nodded. "I know that now, but back then it wasn't... we didn't see it. Look, I'm sorry, we should have reported it to the police, but we didn't. I'm doing my best to make up for it. I know it's too late for –"

"It's too late for the kids your friend has abused over the years," Dave said. "I'll wait for you downstairs, sir."

He left without looking again in Don's direction.

"He's right, you know," Paolo said. "That young girl probably wasn't the first and definitely wasn't the last. I'm sure once we have enough to arrest Pete Carson many of his other victims will come forward. It's possible there will be a charge to answer, for you and your former band mates."

Don nodded. "I knew that was a possibility, but it's a chance I'm willing to take. I should have done the right thing years ago. You have no idea how bad I feel that I've left it until now."

Paolo held out his hand. "Thank you for telling us. I know it couldn't have been easy."

They shook hands and Paolo left. As he went down in the lift he wondered what had caused Dave's reaction. He'd never seen him so aggressive with a witness.

He found him in the car.

"What was that all about?" Paolo asked, getting in and adjusting his seatbelt.

"All what?"

"The way you spoke to Don."

"He covered up for a bloody kiddie fiddler, Paolo. I don't know how you could stand there and be polite to him. It's because of shits like him that abusers get away with it. No one says a bloody word when they should."

"Dave, is there something you want to talk about? Something I can help with?"

Paolo waited, but Dave shook his head.

"Nope. Not a thing. Let's head for home."

Paolo realized he'd have to let it go, but vowed to be there if ever Dave decided to open up.

"Well, that's another piece of the puzzle in place," he said as Dave pulled out of the hotel car park.

Dave nodded. "Pete won't have stopped. There'll be many other victims. It's a pity we can't put an ad in the paper asking them to come forward."

"We do at least have another lead to follow. We can find out from the children's home how the hell that young girl ended up in Pete Carson's bed in the early hours of the morning. Thanks to Don we know which home it was.

I have a feeling there's a very sordid story waiting to be uncovered in that place."

His phone rang and he pulled it up to look at the screen. He didn't recognise the number, but it was a Bradchester one.

"Sterling."

"Hi, this is me," a voice whispered so softly Paolo had to press the phone firmly to his ear to make out the words. "Angela, from Albania/UK/Albania Haulage. I have to see you. I can't speak now, but I really need to talk to you."

"I'm on my way back from London. Can we meet this evening?"

"Um, no, I can't. What about tomorrow? I can pretend I'm going to the supermarket. Can you meet me at the Zero coffee shop in the shopping centre? It's right next to the elevator when you come in from the car park on the ground floor? Say ten past one? If you get there first, can you try for a table right at the back so that no one can see us?"

"Sure thing, I'll do that. But can you tell me what it's about?"

"I think our trucks are being used for smuggling people into the country."

CHAPTER 29

1st November (morning / afternoon)

On his way into work Paolo noticed the headlines were once again concentrating on Lucy Bassington. It seemed someone claimed to have seen her in London. He couldn't help but remember the old traveller's words. Would the newspapers be so interested in her case if she hadn't been pretty, blue-eyed and from a middle class family? His heart said of course they would, but his head knew that wasn't true. Putting such thoughts to one side, he entered the station. He needed to bring his team up to speed.

Half an hour later, he was leaning against a desk at the front of the main office. He'd finished his talk, covering his visit to London with Dave.

"So, all in all, it was a very positive trip and it's given us a bit more to substantiate our suspicions about Pete Carson's predilections. Before I move on to the next bit of news, does anyone have any questions?"

His heart sank. He should have guessed George would be the first to wave a file in his direction. Please let it be something positive this time, he thought. George's negativity was having a serious effect on some of the younger officers. No matter how many times he raised the issue, George was adamant there was nothing wrong.

"Yes, George?"

"Surely we have enough now to bring Pete Carson in for questioning?"

Paolo shook his head. "Afraid not. You know what will happen if we move too soon. He'll arrive here with an expensive solicitor in tow and we won't get a word out of him. If we wait until we have some solid evidence…"

"But we have!" George interrupted. "We've got the blood on the gates and drive, we've got Don Carmichael's testimony and we know Pete Carson is a kiddie fiddler. What more do you need?"

"George, you know better than that. You've been in the force long enough. Don Carmichael's statement has already been sent down to London. That rape, if it happened, bear in mind we only have one person's word for it at the moment, but let's say it did take place, that rape was out of our jurisdiction. We can't do anything apart from notify the specialist child protection section in London. They have said they'll treat it as a priority and will be looking into the care home where the girl was living at the time."

"That's shit! You've given away our strongest hand."

"No, George, what I've done is enlist the help of a crack division trained to deal with cases from years back where the abuse has only just come to light. They've promised to share with us anything that would impact on our current case."

George flipped the file he'd been holding onto his desk. "As long as they do. You know what they're like down in London. Real glory boys. All about the spotlight and polishing their halos in public."

Paolo was about to issue a reprimand when he remembered what had caused the break-up of George's marriage. His wife had left him for a London-based CID officer.

"I think we have to let them get on with it, George. It's now their business, but what's happening here in Bradchester is ours and we need to concentrate on that."

"Exactly!" George said. "We've got the blood evidence. Even a high-priced solicitor won't be able to ignore that. We've got evidence."

"Not yet, we don't. We're still waiting to hear back from the lab people. They weren't at all hopeful there was enough blood collected to run the tests to prove anything conclusively. Until they give us something solid to act on, that blood evidence might just as well not exist."

"So he might get off the hook even though we know that kid was probably in his place?"

At George's words, a babble of conversation broke out. Paolo waited for the murmurs to die down before continuing. Looking around the room, he made eye contact with each officer in turn.

"Don't worry, we won't let Pete Carson get away with anything. I give you my word, if he's involved, we'll get him, but our main priority is catching the traffickers. I'm pleased to say we've finally caught a break on that."

Another murmur broke out, but this time it sounded positive. Several officers sat up a bit straighter, leaning forward to hear what Paolo had to say.

"We have a contact in Albania/UK/Albania haulage who Dave and I are meeting up with today. She says she has information pointing to them being involved in people smuggling. This could well be the tipping point for us. Solid information at last."

Paolo and Dave arrived half an hour early at the shopping centre, just so that they could make sure of a table at the back, but they needn't have worried. It seemed that everyone wanted to sit out on the concourse, watching the world go by.

The tables inside were empty, but they walked to the rear anyway and took a table behind a supporting column. They were completely hidden from passers-by.

"I hope she doesn't look in and think we're not here," Dave said.

Paolo smiled. "More to the point, I hope the waitress realises we're here. The coffee smells good."

Dave laughed. "What world do you live in, sir? Waitresses in a coffee shop? Not a chance. I'll go and order for us. What would you like?"

"Coffee," Paolo answered. "What else?"

Dave picked up a menu from the table next to them and handed it to Paolo.

"Most of these sound like meals. Any chance of a straightforward white coffee?"

"I'll see what I can do, but I'm not making any promises," Dave said.

He came back a few minutes later and handed Paolo a cardboard cup. Paolo took a sip and was amazed. Coffee heaven. He might need to come here on a regular basis.

They'd almost drained their cups before Angela arrived, cardboard cup in hand. She sat next to them, with her back to the room. Paolo noted how scared she looked.

"Don't worry; no one can see you from outside. This table is nicely tucked away."

"Yes, I know, but still…". She shrugged. "I'm not really cut out for this cloak and dagger stuff. I can't stop long. I only get half an hour for lunch and had to tell my boss I needed some extra time so that I could go to the supermarket."

Dave pulled out his pad and waited.

"Just relax," said Paolo. "Drink your coffee while you compose yourself. Then tell us what makes you believe the trucks are being used for people trafficking."

Angela nodded and took a sip.

"It all started after you'd come to show those images around. I overheard my boss say something to one of the drivers that sounded a bit odd at the time, but I didn't really think anything of it, you know? Odd, but not suspicious."

"What did you hear?" Paolo asked.

"The boss was talking to Sam; he's like the head of all the drivers. I think he's been part of the company since Mr Redzepi started it."

"Sam?" Paolo asked. "Not Albanian?"

Angela shook her head. "No, I think he's from Leicester, or somewhere near there. I get the impression he's got some sort of stake in the business. I believe he's related to Mr Redzepi's wife, but I'm not certain. I've not been there that long, so don't know all the ins and outs. Anyway, I had to take some papers for signing and heard voices, so I waited outside the office. Mr Redzepi can get a bit funny about being interrupted when he's got someone with him. I heard him say, 'We'll have to leave the next shipment for a while. I don't think it's safe at the moment.' Then they went on to talk about something else, so I went back to my desk to wait for Sam to come out."

Dave stopped writing. "How did you know it was Sam?"

"I recognised his voice, but also he had to walk past my desk to go out to his truck, so I knew it was definitely him."

"But it wasn't that incident that made you suspicious?"

She took another sip of coffee, the cup quivering in her hand.

"No, it was a number of things. Just small stuff, nothing on its own looking out of place, but when you add it all together, it didn't feel right. I did a bit of digging and found there was more money coming in than we'd actually done trips for."

"What makes you think the extra money is coming from people smuggling?" Paolo asked.

"Nothing! I didn't. I mean, I didn't think the money was coming from anything in particular. I just thought maybe Mr Redzepi was holding back on the tax return, that was all. But then yesterday morning I overheard another conversation." She blushed. "I deliberately eavesdropped this time."

"Go on," Paolo urged when she fell silent.

"I won't have to go to court or anything like that, will I?"

"I don't know," Paolo said, "and that's the honest truth. It all depends on what you tell us and what happens as a result."

She looked uncomfortable, as if she wished she hadn't called in the first place.

"Look, I don't think I want to say anything else. I shouldn't have… it's nothing to do with me. I'm sorry. I'd rather go, if you don't mind."

Paolo knew he had to say something to get her to stay. They could watch the business, but there was more chance of catching them in the act if they had some solid information to work with.

"Please don't go," he said. "Children as young as six and seven are being smuggled in to be passed along to paedophile rings. Please help us put a stop to it."

Angela looked up. "No, oh no, that can't be right. What I heard was about men. I'm sure it was. Not children." Tears filled her eyes. "My daughter is six. Please don't tell me they use kids the same age as Natalie."

Paolo shrugged. "I wish I could lie to you, but I can't. Please, Angela, tell us what you overheard."

Her lip trembled and Paolo wondered which way she would go, but then she nodded.

"I saw Sam go down to Mr Redzepi's office. I'd figured out by now that whatever was going on, he was right in the middle of it. So I waited until he'd been in there a few minutes and then picked up some papers I needed Mr Redzepi to sign and went and stood outside the door."

Paolo noted Dave scribbling furiously to keep up. They worked well together. He nodded for Angela to continue.

She looked at her watch. "I have to go, so I'll just give you the bare bones of what I heard. Sam is going to Albania and bringing back some men to work over here, they said men, not children. The men are sold on to some other people. I don't know who, but Sam and Mr Redzepi keep the passports so that the workers have no way of getting home again."

"When does this happen? Did you manage to find out?"

Angela was already getting to her feet. "Yes, the truck arrives at Hull, coming via Rotterdam, on November 15th. I have to go. Please don't get me involved if you don't have to. Surely if you catch them with the people hidden in the truck, you won't need me?"

Paolo stood up. "I promise you, if I can keep your name out of this, I will. You've given us some really valuable information. Thank you."

She turned and almost ran from the coffee bar.

"Come on, Dave, back to the station for us. We need to get in touch with our colleagues in Hull. Finally, we've got something tangible to work with."

They arrived back at the station. To give Dave time to type up his notes, Paolo called for his team to assemble in half an hour. He went into his office and picked up the phone to find out who dealt with people trafficking in Hull, but before he could dial out, CC came in.

"Sorry to disturb you, sir, but we've had a call from the homeless shelter. Someone called John wants to speak to you. He left his number and says it's urgent that you call him back as soon as you come in. It's about Michelle." She put the paper on his desk.

"Right, thank you, CC. I'll do that right now. While I'm busy with John, could you find out for me who we need to liaise with in Hull to have a lorry stopped and searched as it leaves the ferry? I'll fill you in on the exact details in the meeting."

"Sounds good, sir. I'll get the names and numbers for you."

He waited until she'd closed the door and then dialled the number she'd left. A man's voice answered almost immediately.

"John, here."

"Hello, John. This is Detective Inspector Sterling. You left a message for me to call you. Something to do with Michelle?"

A long sigh greeted his words.

"Oh thank God you've called. You have to do something. Ten minutes ago a black car pulled up outside. Two men jumped out and grabbed Michelle while she was having a smoke."

CHAPTER 30

1st November (afternoon / evening)

Paolo ended the call and raced into the main office.

"Our witness, Michelle, has been picked up. It sounds like she's been grabbed by Bekim and Edar. They must have found out she was the one who gave us the identikit details. Dave, you need to take my place here and outline what we learned from Angela. CC, have you found the names and numbers for the people we need in Hull?"

"Yes, sir, I have them here."

"Good. Pass the info to Dave and grab your jacket. I want you to come with me to see what we can find out from John at the shelter. The rest of you, gather round Dave. He'll allocate tasks to each of you after he's brought you all up to date on the latest developments."

He headed towards the door, but was stopped by George. "What do you want me to do?"

"Sorry, George, I have to go. Dave will fill you in."

"He's not my superior, *sir*," George said, with too heavy an emphasis on the sir for Paolo's liking.

He leaned in towards George and lowered his voice so that the officers nearby wouldn't be able to overhear.

"I know he isn't, but he was there with me when we spoke to an informant. He was the one who took the notes and probably noticed even more than I did *because* he took those notes. All of which means, if I can't be here, then he is the best person to pass on the information and decide who should follow up on what and when."

George shook his head. "Smacks of favouritism to me."

Paolo sighed. He really didn't need this. "I don't have time right now, but when I get back I need to talk to you. This constant griping has to stop."

He turned back to the room. "CC, you ready?"

She handed over a sheet of paper to Dave. "Yes, sir. I was just explaining my scribbling so that Dave could follow it."

"Good, let's go. The more time we mess about here, the less chance there is of finding Michelle before something happens to her. I have a really bad feeling about this."

Paolo parked his car behind the church and jumped out as soon as he switched off the engine. He barely gave CC time to get out before pressing the button for the central locking.

"Sir, if you don't mind my saying so, you seem to be taking this a bit personally."

Paolo stopped midstride and turned back to face her.

"I know I am. She trusted me, CC. She put her faith in me and now she's God knows where with people who didn't hesitate to kill a child in the hospital. The same bastards who shoot kids full of drugs and farm them out to perverts. What do you think they're going to do to someone they think grassed them up?"

"Sir, she knew what she was doing when she gave the info. It's not your fault if –"

"It may not be my fault, CC, but I am responsible."

"We don't know yet that it was definitely Bekim and Edar."

"I'd put my pension on it, but I've brought the identikit images with me, just to make certain that's who it was. Come on; let's see what we can find out."

They entered the shelter and the overpowering smell of unwashed bodies, stale urine and boiled vegetables hit them like a solid wall. Paolo, at least, had been expecting it, but he heard CC gag and realised she'd been taken by surprise.

"Try not to breathe too deeply," he said. "You'll soon adjust."

They'd only taken a few steps when a tall man came rushing towards them. He was so thin Paolo was amazed he could remain upright. The clothes hanging from his frame looked as if they'd been bought for someone three times as bulky.

"I'm John," the man said. "I know it's cold, but can we talk outside?"

Paolo caught the look of relief on CC's face and nodded. "Yes, of course."

They went out and stood next to the wall where Paolo had chatted with Michelle a few weeks earlier. On that day it had been warm enough to pretend summer hadn't left. This afternoon, a raw November wind whipped round corners and bit through clothing, regardless of how many layers a body was wrapped up in. Even so, CC looked much happier out here in the cold than back in the warmth of the shelter.

"I've been calling her mobile," John said, "but no one is answering. It goes straight to voicemail. I know she had it with her when the men came."

"Can you tell us what happened?" Paolo asked.

"Michelle had come out on a smoke break. I realised we would need more bread rolls for this evening and came out to ask her to chat up her contact in the local bakery. They give more generously to her than to anyone else. If I go I'll end up with half of what she manages." He stopped. "Sorry, none of that's important."

His voice quivered and Paolo realised John wasn't just upset at losing a valuable team member.

"You care for her, don't you?" he asked.

John nodded. "She was, *is*, such a brilliant person. Funny and very, very intelligent. We were, you know, sort of getting to know each other."

Paolo nodded. "I liked her. She'd found a way out of the life on the streets. Tell me what you saw."

"I'd just opened the door to come out when a black car pulled up. I think it was a BMW, but I'm not good with cars, so it might not have been. Two men jumped out and grabbed Michelle. One got in the back with her and the other drove off. I ran after the car, but it went screaming down the road like it was jet fuelled."

"Did you get the registration number?"

"That's what really frightened me. It didn't have any plates. It was almost as if they knew they might be seen. Michelle had told me, if anything happened to her to call you. That you'd know what to do."

Paolo felt as if a fist of stone had punched him in the gut. More proof that Michelle had trusted him to make sure she stayed safe.

"Did you get a good look at the men?" he asked.

John nodded. "Enough to know I'd recognise them again if I saw them."

Paolo pulled out the images of Bekim and Edar. "Are these the men?"

John's face lit up. "Yes! That's great. If you know who's taken her you can get her back, right?"

The stone fist punched harder. "I'm afraid it's not that easy, John. We know who they are, but not where to find them." He put his hand on John's arm. "I promise I'll do everything possible to make sure no harm comes to her."

But even as he said the words, he knew they meant nothing. If Bekim and Edar had taken Michelle there wasn't much hope of seeing her again. Not alive, anyway.

They arrived back at the station to find Dave and George in the middle of a yelling competition. Paolo took one look and exploded.

"What the fuck do you think you're doing?" he yelled.

The room went quiet. Dave turned to Paolo, his face ashen.

"Sorry, sir, things got a bit out of hand."

Paolo forced himself to calm down, but it was hard. Already upset over Michelle's disappearance, his anger was close to erupting. Taking a deep breath, he hissed a command.

"I can see that. I want both of you in my office."

George opened his mouth to speak, but Paolo cut him off.

"Now!"

He strode to his office, not looking to see if Dave and George were behind him. He'd have them hung by their toes if they weren't. Only when he'd moved round to sit behind his desk did he look up. Dave shut the door and turned round. He kept his eyes down, almost as if he couldn't bear to face Paolo. George, though, glared as if the debacle in the main office was nothing to do with him and he couldn't understand why he'd been called in like a naughty schoolboy.

"Sit down," Paolo said.

"I'd rather stand, if it's all the same to you, sir," George said.

"No, it bloody well isn't. Sit down!"

George sat, pointedly taking his time. Paolo had to clench his hands together under the desk to stop himself from throwing something at him.

"I couldn't believe what I was hearing when I came in. You two yelling at each other like kids in a playground. What the hell was that all about?"

Dave finally looked up. "Sorry, sir."

"I didn't ask for apologies. I asked what was going on. George, would you like to start?"

George shrugged. "Why not ask your golden boy what he told me to do."

Dave turned in his chair. "I didn't *tell* you to do anything. I asked you."

"Same thing," George said. "You didn't waste time before throwing your weight around."

Paolo banged his desk. "That's enough. Dave, I'll hear your version of what happened and then, George, I'd like to hear yours, minus the stupid remarks. Just what actually was said and done. Go on, Dave, I'm listening."

"I filled everyone in on what we'd discovered about the possible delivery of people in the truck arriving in Hull on the 15th. Then I looked at the information CC gave me just before she went out with you. I handed out tasks as I thought you would have allocated them."

George snorted. "Suck up. But you're right. I'd have got the crap jobs whoever handed them out."

"Bloody hell, George, what is your problem?" Dave asked. "You've been as miserable as sin for months."

"What's wrong with me has fuck all to do with you."

Paolo again banged his hand on the desk. "That's enough. What did Dave ask you to do that you feel was beneath your capabilities?"

George scowled. "I offered to go to Hull to liaise with the officers there, but apparently that's out of my league. You and the Chief's special nephew here will be going on that trip."

Realisation hit Paolo with the force of a lightning strike. "When did you discover Dave was the Chief Constable's nephew?"

George shrugged. "I can't remember when exactly, but when I saw the preferential treatment you were giving him, I did a bit of digging. That's like being a detective, *sir*."

Paolo looked across at Dave. "Go back to the other office. George and I have things to sort out."

Dave stood up. "I really am sorry, sir."

Paolo nodded. "We'll discuss it later."

As Dave closed the door behind him, Paolo sighed. "You're wrong if you think I'm giving him preferential treatment, George. I came down harder on him than on any of you when he first arrived, purely and simply because I didn't want someone foisted on my team who wouldn't pull his weight. I, too, thought his being the chief's nephew would mean he'd expect the easy path to promotion, but he isn't like that and you know it."

George laughed. "I don't know anything of the sort. Between him and CC they get all the cushy jobs and I get the shit that's left over."

"That isn't the case at all."

"Isn't it? I never go out with you on interviews. I'm usually stuck here in the office doing the donkey work so that you and your pets can go off and be the glory boys. Even when I spent the best part of a bloody day following those two pimps, I wasn't allowed to take them in. Oh no, that had to be down to you and wonderboy."

"Firstly, Dave didn't sit in on those interviews."

263

"No, your other pet did that!"

"And secondly," Paolo continued, "I have used your talents to the full. Like it or not, you are the absolute best in this station at ferreting out information. I don't know how you do it, but you come up with the goods every time I ask you to. That's why you tend to get used more here than out on the streets. It certainly isn't because I don't value you."

Paolo waited, but George looked down at his hands and kept quiet.

"Would you like me to put in a transfer request on your behalf? I could have you moved to another region. I don't want to lose you, but I also can't have the undercurrents you've added to the team recently."

He waited for a response. Finally, after what felt like an hour, George looked up.

"I'm sorry, sir. I don't know what's got into me recently. I've never minded being the backroom boy. I know I'm good at that, but seeing CC and Dave always out and about... I dunno, it made me feel as if you didn't even see me at times."

Paolo smiled. "Now it's my turn to apologise, if that's how I've made you feel. I can assure I'm very well aware of your contribution into every investigation. I'll try to make sure you aren't stuck in the office all the time, but honestly, George, you are the best information gatherer we have, so you'll have to bear with me until I can find someone who is in your league."

Paolo stood up and walked around to stand next to George.

"I really do value your contribution to the team. We wouldn't function anywhere near as well without your talents. Don't ever think differently."

He held out his hand. George stood and shook it.

Paolo smiled. "Let's get back to work. But, before you go, have you told anyone else about Dave's relationship to the Chief?"

George shook his head. "I almost blurted it out when we were having our slanging match, but you arrived back in time to stop me."

"Good. Keep it to yourself. You won't be the only one who imagines Dave's getting preferential treatment if the word gets out."

He looked surprised. "So even CC doesn't know?"

"There are only three people on my team who do and that's me, you and Dave. I'd like to keep it that way, okay?"

"Yes, sir."

Paolo waited until he'd gone and then let out an enormous sigh. Sometimes he thought looking after a bunch of three-year-olds after an all-day sugar feast might be easier.

CHAPTER 31

15th November (night – Hull)

From the moment they'd crossed the Humber Bridge, Paolo began to worry about Dave. It was almost as if he'd retreated into a world Paolo couldn't enter. He'd barely spoken for the past hour. That alone was unusual for him, but when Paolo had asked him about his plans for the weekend with Rebecca, he'd clammed up completely. All wasn't well in that relationship, but Paolo couldn't figure out what. Dave and Rebecca were crazy about each other, so there probably wasn't anyone else involved.

His thoughts were interrupted by the Satnav telling them to turn left, following the signs for King George Dock & Ferries.

"It'll be strange, sir, you not being in charge."

Paolo shrugged. "I knew that would be the case as soon as we passed the information along. It's decent of them to invite us up here to join them."

"What will happen, though, after tonight? Do we get the bastards or does Hull hang on to them?"

Again, there was something in Dave's voice that made Paolo wonder why he was taking it so personally. In a way, he was almost relieved Dave wouldn't be interviewing anyone up here.

"Let's wait and see what we find on the lorry. We'll work with Hull on this one. I just want to find out who is bringing in the kids to Bradchester and shut the bastard down. Let Hull have the mules, I want the mule driver."

And find whoever ordered Bekim and Edar to pick up Michelle, Paolo thought. Two weeks and not a sign of her. Part of Paolo's brain knew she was probably dead, but the rest of him refused to give up looking until someone found her body. Maybe he was wrong and they were just keeping her prisoner. Yeah, right. Fat chance of that. The best case scenario was that they'd forced her back onto the streets, in which case, she'd turn up somewhere. Paolo never thought he'd be praying a woman had been forced back into prostitution, but that was preferable to her being killed, or even tortured, to find out what she'd told him.

They reached the ferry terminal and Paolo was relieved when Dave's voice broke in on his uncomfortable thoughts.

"Well, that was a doddle to find, sir. Let's hope our hotel is just as easy," he said as he pulled the car over to the side of the road.

Paolo stretched his legs out as far as they could go within the confines of the car. "Yes, a good night's sleep and we'll be ready to meet up with our Hull colleagues bright and early tomorrow. We need to be at the station by six. Apparently the ferries here are always on time, so at eight tomorrow we'll be waiting for the doors to open and the lorry to roll off."

"I'm Detective Chief Inspector Collins."

Paolo held back a yawn as he shook hands and introduced himself and Dave. Maybe Dave's snoring was the reason he and Rebecca weren't quite as close as they seemed. Paolo felt as if he'd only just dropped off when the alarm sounded at five.

Collins let go of Paolo's hand and smiled. "Good to meet you. Thank you for the tip off. We've been convinced for a while now that some of the trucks are bringing in illegals from all over Eastern Europe. We've had an influx of them over the past couple of years, but haven't had much joy catching anyone with bodies on board. Yours is the first solid lead we've had."

Paolo nodded. "You're looking for adults; we think the truck is bringing in kids for the sex trade. Let's hope one of us gets lucky. Our source said men, but we're hoping that wasn't correct. Other than that, the person was pretty sure of the facts, but we've no idea if anything was changed without the informant knowing."

Collins smiled. "Let's go and find out which one of us is going to hit the jackpot, shall we?"

"I'm glad we're not outside in this, sir," Dave said as snow flurries drifted past the windscreen.

"From the point of view of not freezing to death, I agree with you, but I'd really like to be in on the action when the truck arrives. Speaking of which, look!"

Paolo pointed to the ferry where a lorry was being forced out of the queue by unmarked police cars that had been parked nearby.

"Come on, Dave, time to play *follow the leader*."

They drove behind the convoy to a hangar. Once they were inside, officers moved to close and bar the doors. Anyone inside would be staying there until the doors opened again. Dave parked over to the side of the hangar.

As they got out of the car, Paolo nodded towards the truck's Albania/UK/Albania sign emblazoned on the side.

"They made it nice and easy to pick them out of the queue. Let's go and watch the thing being taken apart. God, I hope this proves Jetmir Redzepi is involved. We need a break on this case."

Two hours later the truck had been unloaded of its cargo and only the shell remained. Paolo and Dave watched as a team of men demolished the interior panel by panel. They'd covered about three-quarters of the panels when a shout went up.

The adrenaline shot through Paolo, making his head throb. At last. If there were kids in there, they'd be terrified. Paolo knew Collins had an interpreter on hand, but he wished he'd brought along Gazmend's replacement. Ejona was really making progress with the girls in care. They were finally opening up to her.

Another panel came free.

"We've got people in here," one of the officers inside the truck called out. "Some of them look in a bad way. Bring the medics."

Dear God, those poor children, Paolo thought, but the first person helped off the truck wasn't a child. Neither was the next, nor the next. A steady stream of grown men appeared. Paolo moved over to where Collins was directing operations.

"Seems my informant was right, in more ways than one," Paolo said.

"How do you mean?"

"Men and not kids. I'm pleased you've got what you wanted, but unless Redzepi is also shipping kids in, it doesn't take me any further forward. Time for me to go and find out if he's the villain I'm looking for. You'll keep me informed of whatever you uncover up here?"

"Yes, of course. You'll do the same with regards the owner of this outfit?"

Paolo nodded.

Collins held out his hand. "Good luck and thanks once again for the tip-off."

CHAPTER 32

18th November (morning / afternoon)

Paolo felt like smashing his head against the wall in frustration. Every time it seemed as if they'd come close to a breakthrough, the door shut faster than he could force a foot across the threshold. Redzepi was in custody, but they wouldn't be able to hold him for much longer unless something concrete came up proving he knew about his brother-in-law's illegal activities. So far both men were sticking to the same story. Sam Bristol was taking full responsibility for bringing in the illegals and saying his wife's brother knew nothing about it. Redzepi was claiming shock and outrage to think his brother-in-law would do such a thing. Paolo knew they were lying and so did Collins in Hull, but unless Angela was prepared to stand up and say so, they couldn't prove Redzepi's involvement. Paolo just had to hope the books they'd confiscated would unearth something he could use.

But even if they found definite evidence he'd known about Sam's activities, that didn't bring Paolo any closer to finding out who was shipping in the kids. Sam Bristol's denial on that score had seemed genuine enough, but who knew how good a liar the man might be. He was prepared to lie to keep his wife's brother in the clear, so what else was he lying about?

Nearly three weeks had passed since Bekim and Edar had snatched Michelle and there hadn't been sight nor sound of any of them since. She was probably dead, but until Paolo found her body, he wouldn't let up on the search. As for the two thugs who'd taken her, Paolo vowed to track them down if it took him a decade to do it.

He glanced through the window separating his office from the main room and saw Dave slumped over his desk. That was something else Paolo needed to sort out. Dave had come into the station this morning with a face that suited a Monday, which was unusual for him after a weekend with his beloved Rebecca.

Paolo sighed. After their shaky start, he'd become close to his young detective sergeant and didn't like to see him falling apart like this.

He walked to the door and called out for Dave to come through. By the time Dave arrived, Paolo was seated back behind his desk.

"You wanted me, sir?"

"Yes, come in and close the door."

Paolo waited until Dave sat down, studying the young officer's face. His eyes looked raw. He'd either been crying or on drugs. Paolo's money was on the tears, but how to raise it?

"Everything okay, Dave?"

"Yes, fine. What did you want me for? Redzepi's book uncovered any gems for us?"

Paolo shook his head. "Not yet. The financial forensic guys are busy taking them apart number by number, but they've not come up with anything we can use so far. No, I called you in because I'm concerned about you."

Dave smiled, but Paolo could see it was an effort. "No need to worry about me, sir. As I said, I'm fine. In fact, I'm planning a night out tonight now that I'm free and single again."

"You and Rebecca split up?"

Dave nodded and stood. "It's been on the cards for ages now. We just weren't meant for each other. It's all for the best. I don't know when I've been happier. If there's nothing else, sir, I've got quite a lot on my desk that needs sorting out."

Paolo shook his head. "Nothing more at the moment."

Dave turned to go, but Paolo called him before he reached the door.

"If you want to talk, Dave, I'm maybe not the best person to help with relationships, but…"

"You're all right, sir. There's nothing to talk about."

He went out, closing the door behind him. Dave was clearly hurting, but maybe it was no more than a lover's tiff and he would get back with Rebecca. Not meant to be together? Paolo smiled. If ever people were made for each other, it was those two.

His thoughts were interrupted by the phone on his desk. Glad of the distraction, he picked up the receiver.

"Sterling."

"Good morning, Detective Inspector, this is Ejona Bejko. I wondered if you had a couple of minutes to chat to me about the girls in the social services hostal."

"Yes, by all means. Would you like me to meet you somewhere?"

"No, that won't be necessary. I simply wanted to bring you up to date. I don't know if you are aware, but I've been translating for Jessica Carter, the psychologist. She has been amazing with the girls and we think we've made a minor breakthrough."

Paolo wasn't surprised Jessica had got through to the girls in care. He knew from experience how good she was. Social services had done the right thing, letting her in on this case. He smiled. He was getting to know her quite well. They had dinner together, well, sat at the same table in the restaurant, three or four times a week. It was amazing they never struggled to find something to talk about, considering they didn't talk about Katy, or his work.

"Are you still there, Detective Inspector?"

Paolo pushed thoughts of Jessica to one side. "Yes, sorry. You were telling me you'd made a breakthrough."

"A few of the older girls are now prepared to look at photographs to see if they can identify any of the men who held them captive, or who abused them when they were first brought to the UK."

"That isn't a minor breakthrough in my eyes," Paolo said. "That is the best news I've heard in a long time. I've got a few suspects in mind, so will gather together some photos for you. I'll call you as soon as I've got them."

"That would be very good. Thank you. I'll wait for your call before arranging for Ms Carter to come with me to show the images."

"Would it be possible for me to see their reactions when you show them?"

Ejona hesitated. "No, I don't think that would be a good idea. They might feel intimidated by your presence. I would prefer it if only Ms Carter and I were present."

"Of course," Paolo said, not happy he couldn't witness their reactions first-hand, but short of bringing them to the station and putting them in an interview room with a two way mirror, which would be even more intimidating, there was no way to watch them without being in the room.

He said goodbye to the interpreter and replaced the receiver. At last, some good news. He moved the mouse, bringing this screen to life. One image would be easy to source. Pete Carson's face had been all over the local news recently, promoting his New Year's Eve concert. If Paolo could prove he'd been abusing any of the girls they had in care, then Pete could kiss his concert goodbye. He printed off several head shots of the singer.

Redzepi's image was also easy to get, as the man was still in custody. Paolo needed to move quickly, before they were forced to let him go due to lack of evidence. If the girls identified him, that would change everything.

The only image he needed now was Jeton's. He might be involved, he might not, but the way he'd disappeared, taking his ex-wife with him, made him look very suspect. Definitely another one for the photo gallery.

He got up and went into the main office and stopped at CC's desk.

"Can you get in touch with Gazmend and see if he's got a photo of his cousin we could use?"

"Yes, of course, sir. Who are we going to show it to?"

He told her about the interpreter's call.

"Should I mention you've brought in another interpreter, sir? Remember I told Gazmend we'd dropped that line of enquiry. He might feel slighted if he knows he and Diellza have been replaced."

Paolo nodded. "Good point, CC. No, don't tell him. Just say we want to use the picture as we're treating Jeton's disappearance as a missing person's case."

"Right you are, sir. I'll call him now."

Paolo was deep in thought, wondering if what he felt for Jessica might one day be reciprocated, when a light tap on his office door disturbed him. He looked up as CC, closely followed by Gazmend, came into the room.

"Gazmend wanted to see you, sir. He's concerned about his cousin."

Paolo indicated the chairs opposite his desk. "Yes, of course, please take a seat."

Gazmend sighed and passed a photograph across the desk. "This is the only image I have of Jeton, but I don't think it will be very useful as we were only about twelve when it was taken." He shrugged. "We were never very close as children. He grew up in Leicester and I moved here with my family shortly after this photo was taken.

We've only recently got to know each other again since Jeton moved here a couple of years ago."

Paolo picked up the photo. Gazmend was right; it wasn't going to be any use to him. The boys were some distance from the camera and, besides, were far too young for the girls in social to recognise Jeton.

"You've no idea where Jeton and his ex-wife might be?" Paolo asked.

"No, if I knew, I would tell you." He shrugged again. "Please don't think I'm being rude when I say this, but I'm not stupid. You think my cousin has something to do with the child trafficking, don't you?"

Paolo considered his options. He could lie, but it would be far better to have Gazmend on his side. He nodded.

"It is beginning to look that way, yes. He disappeared shortly after we visited his place of work and his wife went missing a little later. You can't think of anywhere he could have gone? Perhaps back to Albania?"

Gazmend shook his head. "Not as far as I know. The two men you've been asking about, Bekim and Edar, I have recently discovered from one of my contacts that Jeton was seen frequently in their company. I had no idea, but as I said, Jeton and I weren't exactly close."

"And yet he came to stay with you when he had marital issues?"

Gazmend smiled. "Close or not, when family come knocking on the door asking for help, Albanians will never turn anyone away. I did my best for him, but now I'm wondering if he took me for a fool."

"How do you mean?" Paolo asked.

"He was always interested in my translating work with social services. I thought he was just being polite, but looking back, maybe he was digging for information to find out if the girls were talking." He shrugged again. "I don't know if that is what he was doing, but it could have been."

"Tell me something," Paolo said, "the morning we called you to the hospital to translate whose idea was it for Jeton to drive you?"

Gazmend looked horrified. "It was Jeton's. My car wouldn't start and I was about to call for a taxi when he offered to drive me in his car on his way to work. But what are you saying? You think he killed that child? No! I'm sorry, but I cannot believe that."

Paolo shook his head. "I wasn't implying he killed her, but maybe he wanted to find out which ward she was on and driving you was an ideal opportunity."

Gazmend stood up. "I don't believe my cousin is a killer, and I don't believe he came with me for any reason other than to be helpful. But if I'm wrong, I promise you I will do everything I can to find him and hand him over to the police." He glanced down at the photograph. "I'll leave that with you. Maybe your technical people can do some sort of age advancement with it. Jeton and I are almost the same age. Our fathers were brothers. His blood is my blood. He would no more disgrace it than I would. I'm sure you'll find he had nothing to do with these terrible crimes."

Paolo waited until Gazmend and CC had closed the door before picking up the phone. If Gazmend couldn't supply a photo, it was time to arrange a warrant to search Jeton's house. Surely there would be a more recent image there they could use.

Paolo stopped by Dave's desk. "There's no point hanging around here. We won't get the warrant until tomorrow. A trip out to the warehouse where Jeton worked might yield us a bit more information. Grab your jacket and let's go."

As they walked towards the entrance George came in, looking very pleased with himself.

"Nice to see you looking so happy," Paolo said and immediately wished he'd kept his mouth shut as the look of joy faded from George's face.

He nodded at Paolo, scowled at Dave and carried on into the main office.

"Blimey," Dave said, "I'm really not flavour of the month with him."

Paolo shrugged. "I thought I'd sorted out his issues, but it seems I was wrong. I'll chat to him again tomorrow, but let's get going now. The warehouse will be closed by the time we get there if we don't get a move on."

They pulled up just as the daytime workers were leaving. Paolo and Dave walked towards the group milling around outside waiting for lifts home.

"Have any of you heard from Jeton?" Paolo asked.

"Nah, mate," one of the women replied. "You've already asked most of us that question when he first went missing."

"You should chat to his mate from the café down the road," another woman called out.

Paolo headed over to her. "Who's his mate?"

"The cook," she said. "He and Jeton have known each other for yonks. Went to school together, I think."

"Many thanks," Paolo said. "Come on, Dave, it's time for a cuppa."

As they walked down to the café Paolo repeated what the woman had said.

"Sounds promising," Dave said. "Let's hope the mate hasn't already left for the day."

The café was typical of many found on industrial estates. It catered for workers in need of a filling meal, not for those looking for fine dining, but the smells coming through from the kitchen were enough to make Paolo hungry. A large board spelled out the daily menu where nearly everything came with chips. Not good for the heart, Paolo thought, but comfort food just the same. Few of the tables were in use, but at five thirty in the evening that wasn't surprising.

Paolo walked forward and showed his identification to a girl busy wiping down the counter with a cloth that looked as if it carried more germs than the surface it was supposed to be cleaning.

"Could we have a word with your chef?"

She laughed. "Chef? That's a bit posh for this place." Turning her head, she yelled towards a beaded curtain, which Paolo presumed hid the kitchen. "Tony, you'd better come through. Looks like your past has caught up with you."

A tall, massively overweight man in a what could once have been described as whites, but were now covered in a multitude of stains in various shades, barged through the beads.

"What are you on about, Sally? I'm cleaning up back there and don't have time for your shit."

She smiled and pointed to Paolo who still had his badge on show.

"Oh," Tony said. "Have you come about Jeton?"

"Have you got somewhere private we can talk?" Paolo suggested. He turned to Sally. "Perhaps you could bring us some coffee?"

"Sure, why not? It's not as if I've anything else to do in this dump."

Tony raised his eyes, but didn't say anything. He led Paolo and Dave to a table set apart from the others.

"This is our staff table. No one can overhear us if we keep our voices down," he said. "Have you got news of my mate? I've been worried sick about him."

Paolo sat down and studied the chef. He was younger than he'd thought at first, but his size made him look older. He seemed genuinely concerned, but that was an easy emotion to fake.

"I was hoping you'd have news for me," Paolo said. He waited while Sally put cups of surprisingly good smelling coffee in front of each of them. When she'd gone back to the counter, he continued. "Jeton has been missing for some time now. Did you know his wife was also missing?"

"Sonia? No, can't say as I did. But what's she got to do with anything? They split up. Jeton had moved in with his cousin."

Paolo nodded. "Yes, we knew that, but she also seems to have disappeared, so it looks likely they are together."

Tony scowled. "Look, what are you getting at? I thought you were here because something's happened to Jeton, but now it sounds like you think he was up to no good and did a runner. That's shit. No way. He's a good bloke."

"Calm down. No one has said anything about Jeton being up to no good. We're just trying to find out more about him to help us in our search."

Paolo waited and saw the mulish look leave Tony's face.

"Sorry. It just sounded like you were making out he was bad news. I've known Jeton since we sat next to each other in primary school. He's my best mate, so I'm not going to let the likes of you stitch him up."

"No one is trying to stitch him up, but we really do need to find him. He might be able to help us with our investigation."

"Isn't that cop talk for we think he's guilty of a crime?" Tony asked. "When I hear that on those crime programmes I think to myself, I bet he's wanted for whatever it is they're looking into and then the next week most times we hear the bloke has been arrested. So don't tell me you don't think Jeton's done something. I won't believe you."

Paolo took a sip of coffee and put the cup back on the table. "Okay, here's the truth. We do think Jeton might be involved in something very serious. If he is, we need to find him. If he isn't, we need to be able to rule him out so that we can concentrate on others. So, do you have any idea where we should start looking?"

"You've been round his cousin's, I suppose?"

Paolo nodded.

"Oh, pity. I'd been hoping Gazmend had got him to go over to Albania for the charity."

"What charity?" Paolo asked.

"Didn't Gazmend mention it? No, I suppose he wouldn't. They're very modest, that family."

Paolo smiled. "I'm sure they are, but I'm still waiting to hear what the charity is all about."

"He works with an orphanage in Albania. His charity brings young girls over here for short holidays. Two, maybe three times a year."

CHAPTER 33

19th November (whole day)

Paolo stopped by the court on his way to the station and collected the warrant, but his mind was running on what they'd discovered about Gazmend the night before. Was it possible that the person they'd been hunting for had been in front of them all the time? Paolo's heart beat faster as the thoughts chased each other round his head. Gazmend had been at the heart of the investigation, right from the outset. Only he understood Albanian. He and Diellza could have been saying anything to the girls in care and no one would have been any the wiser.

Before jumping to conclusions, though, he needed George to find out all he could about the charity Gazmend had set up in Leicester. Why there? Why not here in Bradchester?

He arrived at the station ahead of everyone else and used the time to reduce his mounting pile of reports before his team trickled in one by one. Standing up and moving from behind his desk, Paolo felt his blood pumping. They were getting closer to cracking this. He was sure of it.

He stood in front of the board and called them all to attention.

"I've got the warrant to search the house where Jeton lived with his wife before he moved in with Gazmend," he began. "Dave, that's our job for this morning. George, I want you to find out all you can about a charity Gazmend runs in Leicester. The charity brings young girls over a few times a year from an Albanian orphanage."

At his words a mass of noise rose from his officers.

"That sounds right dodgy, sir," called a voice from the back of the room.

"I agree, which is why I've given the job of ferreting out the information to George. He's the best we have for that. If there's anything untoward, he'll find it."

He smiled at George and was surprised to see an answering grin. Was it what he'd just said? No, now Paolo came to think of it, George had arrived looking particularly pleased with himself this morning. Whatever the reason, a happy George was much easier to work with than a sullen one.

"CC, I want you to contact Ejona Bejko and ask her to try to find out if any of the girls knew Gazmend other than as an interpreter. They may not tell her, of course, if he is part of the trafficking gang for fear of what might happen to their families, but it's worth a try."

"Right, Dave and I will be out for a few hours on the search. Any news, call me."

Paolo and Dave stood in the kitchen of Jeton's house. They, together with the uniformed officers, had searched every corner of the place and hadn't found a single thing that incriminated Jeton.

"In fact," Paolo said, "the only good thing to come from this morning's work is that we've got this." He pointed to the picture of Jeton and his wife on their wedding day. "At least I can pass that over to the interpreter with the images of Pete Carson and Jetmir Redzepi."

"Weird, isn't it, sir, that there's no computer in the house?"

"I suppose so, but so many people now only use laptops or tablets, so that might not be suspicious, but I'll tell you what is," he said. "This place was immaculate when we arrived. Not a thing out of place. You'd think, if they'd both done a runner, there would be clothes scattered where they'd packed in a hurry. Or at least something to show they'd left on the hop. But no, this place was as neat as my late granny's house after she'd been spring cleaning."

"You think someone came in and cleaned up?"

Paolo nodded. "We're not doing any good here. Let's drop the images off at the interpreter's and head back to the station."

As they entered, CC called out, "The lab dropped off the test results, sir. I've put the envelope on your desk."

"Great, thanks," Paolo said, rushing through to his office.

He snatched the envelope and opened it, scanning the results as he moved round to his chair. The word inconclusive jumped out. He slumped down, feeling as if he'd run into yet another brick wall. His earlier positive feelings disappeared to such an extent, he found it hard to summon up the energy to concentrate on reading the full DNA report. The tests on blood samples gathered from the gates and drive at Pete Carson's home were inconclusive due to there being insufficient material to conduct a thorough examination. Sighing, he stood up. Whether he wanted to or not, he had to share this crap news.

He walked into the main office, forcing himself to act in complete contrast to the way he felt. If he showed any negativity, it would rub off on his team and they didn't deserve that. Summoning a smile from the depths of his being, he stood at the front of the room.

"Okay, listen up, everyone. Dave and I found nothing of any use at Jeton's house, unfortunately, but we were able to pick up a photo to hand over to the interpreter. As you know, unless Redzepi decides to talk, we will have to let him go in another couple of hours. So Dave and I will be chatting to him again…"

He was interrupted by his phone. The display showed DCI Collins' name.

"Sorry, I have to take this," he said. Turning his back to the room, he swiped the phone to answer it. "Sterling."

"Hi, DCI Collins here, from Hull."

"Please tell me you have some good news. We could do with it here."

Collins laughed. "Well, it's your lucky day, then, because that's exactly why I'm calling you."

Paolo listened and the more he learned, the more his spirits rose. He ended the call and turned back to a room full of eager faces. They'd clearly picked up on the tone, if not the content, of the call.

"Good news at last," he said. "As I'm sure you've all gathered, that was DCI Collins from Hull. Sam Bristol, driver of the lorry smuggling in the illegals, and also the brother-in-law of the man we currently have in custody, has finally offered up something we can work with." He grinned. "I'm not sure how Collins achieved it, and I don't want to know, but he somehow convinced Sam that he would go down not only for smuggling the men, but also for trafficking children into prostitution. He didn't need to be told what the other prisoners would do to him if they thought he aided child sex offenders. Apparently he worked it out for himself."

Paolo settled himself on the edge of a desk. "Here's the story so far. He and Redzepi work for our mysterious Joey, but they only bring in men, who are then sold for slave labour around the country. Apparently Sam didn't seem to think that was much of a crime, but there you go. Anyway, it gives us something to use against Redzepi."

CC punched the air. "Did Sam name his brother-in-law as being involved, sir? Did he give us enough to hold Redzepi for a bit longer?"

"He sure did. Names, dates and numbers. Once Sam started talking it seems he couldn't stop. But there's more. Joey is not only into people smuggling. According to Sam, Joey is the king of crime in Bradchester. The two bullies we had in here, Bekim and Edar, are his main enforcers of the protection and loan rackets he runs. Businesses pay to be protected, presumably from Bekim and Edar, and ordinary people are given loans at ridiculous rates of interest, meaning they end up so deep in debt they'll never get out again. No wonder most people came close to passing out when we showed their pictures around."

Dave laughed. "Seems if we can only work out who Joey is, the crime rate will drop and we can all have a nice relaxing Christmas break."

Paolo grinned. "Considering we still have over a month to go before Christmas, we might get lucky. You never know. The main thing, though, is that Redzepi must know who he's been working for. We just need to find a way to make him tell us. Time for us to have another chat with him."

He stood up and noticed the DNA report on the desk where he'd been sitting. It was a pity to bring everyone down when he'd finally given them some hope, but it had to be done.

"Sorry, I've also got some bad news to temper the good. The DNA results on the blood taken from Pete Carson's place are inconclusive. Not enough material to work with."

At the chorus of groans, he instinctively looked over at George, expecting an outburst. But George didn't look upset at all. In fact, he looked positively cheerful. Maybe the talk he had with him had done some good after all.

"I thought you'd have been more annoyed than anyone, George. I know you were worried Pete Carson would get away with it."

George shrugged. "He'll get his just deserts one day. Life has a habit of paying back when you least expect it."

"I'm pleased to hear that. But don't worry, we will get Carson. I'm sure of that. By the way, I know you haven't had much time, but have you discovered much on Gazmend's charity?"

George smiled. "Quite a bit actually, sir, and it looks as though it's all on the level. As you say, a few times a year the charity brings in between six and ten girls, mainly under the age of ten. They come from an orphanage by coach and get a whistle-stop tour of Europe on the way. They stay here in the UK in a hotel at the expense of the charity for up to a week, but usually four or five days, and then they return home stopping in different places to those they visited on the way out."

"The girls definitely leave again?" Paolo asked. "It isn't a front to get the girls over here and not send them back?"

"From what I've found out so far," George said, "the same number goes home as arrives. I'll dig some more, but lots of the Albanian businesses in Leicester contribute to the charity. I think it's on the level."

Paolo nodded. "Good work. In the meantime, give me the details on the orphanage in Albania. I'll be seeing our new interpreter tomorrow to find out if the girls recognised anyone from the photographs. It might be worth asking her to call. See what the people running the orphanage have to say."

Paolo and Dave entered the interview room and went through the formalities. Switching on the tape and recording the date, time and people in the room.

"Mr Redzepi, are you sure you wouldn't like legal representation?" Paolo began.

"As I've told you over and over, why should I need it when I have done nothing wrong? Today you will have to let me go. I will then go to see my solicitor to find out how to sue you and this force for damages."

"You may not be going home today, I'm afraid. You see, your brother-in-law has been very helpful."

Redzepi laughed. "Oh, please, not that old trick. Sam hasn't told you anything about me because there is nothing to tell."

"Really?" Paolo said, putting a sheet of paper on the table and turning it so that Redzepi could read the dates, names and numbers. "Sam has been most helpful, don't you think?"

Redzepi gave the paper a quick glance. "It's nothing to do with me. Sam has obviously been running this scam for a long time. I was duped into believing he was an honest man."

"I wonder if your books will prove that when we pass this information over to the financial forensic squad."

For the first time, Redzepi looked ill at ease, but he remained silent.

Paolo spun the paper back towards him. "That's not all Sam told us. We now know all about Joey and his various business activities. It seems you've been working hand in glove with him for a number of years to smuggle in men who believe they have a job and a better life to come to, but end up as slave labour. Sam says neither of you are involved in the child sex racket, but maybe you are and Sam doesn't know about it."

Still Redzepi stayed dumb, but Paolo was pleased to see the man was starting to sweat.

"On the other hand, if you're not part of that particular set up, surely you would want to help us shut it down. The traffickers are bringing in kids as young as six. I'm sure the courts would be much more inclined to be lenient if you were to help us put Joey out of business, particularly that one. All you need to do is tell us his name."

Redzepi opened his mouth and closed it several times. At last, thought Paolo, we'll know who we're after.

"Joey?" Redzepi said. "I don't know anyone called Joey and now I find I have changed my mind. I would like to call my solicitor and I have nothing more to say until he gets here."

CHAPTER 34

19th November (evening)

Paolo closed the door on his apartment and sighed with relief. It had been one hell of a day. He'd been seriously tempted to go to the Italian restaurant again, but didn't want Jessica to feel he was stalking her. Besides, he wasn't sure he'd be the best of company tonight. Fair enough, they'd had a bit of a breakthrough with Sam spilling his guts, but Redzepi had clammed up and refused to say another word.

He flopped onto the couch and picked up the remote, flicked the button and slung it next to him. Maybe a spot of television was what he needed to make him forget work for a while. The DNA result had been a real blow. Without that, they had no way of tying Pete Carson down.

As the screen came into focus, Paolo couldn't believe his eyes. There he was – Pete Carson giving a press conference to promote his concert, grinning at the cameras as if he hadn't a care in the world. And he probably hasn't, Paolo fumed.

He reached for the remote, but paused as he saw the smile leave Pete's face. Paolo hadn't heard the question, but whatever it was, it had clearly knocked Pete sideways. Paolo turned the volume up in time to hear the question being repeated.

"Would you like to comment on information I've been given about your involvement in a child abuse ring?"

The reporter was from the local paper. Paolo often saw him hanging around the courts. He didn't normally cover celebrity events, so must have gone there deliberately to ask the question. But who the hell was his informant? Paolo felt sick. Dear God, please don't let it be anyone on the team, he prayed, but he already knew in his heart it couldn't be anyone else.

"I have no idea what you're talking about," Pete Carson said over the riot that had erupted when the question was repeated.

The reporter smiled as if he alone held the key to Fort Knox and no one else even knew there was gold inside.

"I think you do, Mr Carson. Would you like to comment on a current investigation which I believe led senior detectives to take blood samples from your gates and drive?"

Paolo wanted to throw the remote through the screen, but needed to find out how much the reporter had been told. All the reporters were now yelling questions and Pete Carson looked as if he was going to throw up all over them.

"I repeat. I have no idea what you're talking about," he shouted over the din.

"Apparently, the Chief Constable's nephew is part of the team, which my informant tells me is why the investigation is a bit of a shambles. But that's neither here nor there. Would you like to comment on the allegation that you're part of a paedophile ring operating here in Bradchester?"

Pete Carson jumped up. "That's a lie! I'm not going to stay here to listen to you spouting a pack of lies."

Pushing his chair to one side, he stormed from sight, closely followed by reporters and cameramen jockeying for the best position.

Paolo hit the mute button. No wonder George had been looking so bloody smug. He must have leaked to the bloody press. Standing up, he paced up and down the lounge. He had to get rid of some of this pent up energy. Grabbing his jacket, he headed for the door. A long walk should clear his head and calm him down.

He walked, as he thought, aimlessly, until the enticing smell of garlic and herbs wafted on the air. His subconscious had brought him to the restaurant. He owed it to his inner whatever to go in, surely? Not because he wanted to see Jessica, but because he was hungry and this was a restaurant, right? Yeah, right. And if he believed that he'd swallow anything. From outside he couldn't tell if their usual table was occupied. Only one way to find out.

Opening the door, the fabulous aromas doubled in intensity and his mouth began to water. He glanced towards the back of the room, but no one was sitting at the table they often shared. Oh well, he'd just have to eat alone. As he took a step towards the table, Jessica appeared from the cloakroom area near the tiny bar. She saw him and smiled.

"Hello," she said, coming over to stand next to him. "I didn't think you were coming in tonight."

"I nearly didn't," he said. "Mind if I join you?"

For answer, she smiled again and led the way. As they sat, he felt her scrutiny and looked up.

"Tough day?"

He nodded. "A bit up and down."

"Want to talk about it?"

He shook his head. "No, I think we should stick to our rule. No work chat and that way we can't cross any lines we shouldn't. Fair?"

"Fair," she said, "but only if you can shake off whatever cloud you're sitting under."

Paolo grimaced. "Is it that obvious?"

Jessica laughed. "Without resorting to shop talk, I *am* a psychiatrist. If I can't spot when someone's troubled, I'd better find myself another profession."

Forcing himself to forget the cares of the day, Paolo picked up the menu. At least the day would end on a high.

Two hours later, and he was well fed and at peace with the world. Whatever tomorrow would bring would happen whether he worried about it or not. Glancing across at Jessica, he realised how much he enjoyed her company. Maybe she enjoyed his. Deciding to stop being such a wimp, he sat up straighter.

"I need to ask you something," he said.

"Oh, oh. That sounds ominous. You haven't forgotten your wallet, have you? Planning to leave me to pay the full bill?"

He smiled. "Not quite as bad as that. I was wondering if you'd like to go out somewhere one evening. See a show, or something."

Jessica didn't even appear to think about it. "I'm afraid not," she said, shaking her head.

"Sorry, I shouldn't have asked," Paolo said, feeling like a fifteen-year-old who'd just been turned down for the first time. "I won't ask again."

Jessica smiled again. "I hope you do," she said. "I'm saying no because I'm still seeing Katy as an outpatient. Ask me again when her treatment is finished. As long as you haven't morphed into an axe murderer by then, I might just say yes."

CHAPTER 35

20th November (morning)

Paolo picked up the newspapers on his way into the station, dreading what the headlines might be on the more lurid tabloids. He wasn't surprised to see 'Paedo Pete?' as the main theme, the question mark keeping the newspapers just about on the right side of libel. Thankfully, there was little about the police informer, but he knew that would soon change. In fact, if he had anything to do with it, the person responsible would face more than a press enquiry.

He'd watched the news the night before, when the reporters had followed Pete home to his mansion and taken up residence outside both gates. Within half an hour, a private security firm had arrived to ensure no one had access. In fact, the only vehicle they'd let in had been a pizza van. Paolo found himself hoping Pete choked on his meal.

As he entered the station, the duty sergeant called him over.

"The chief wants you to go up as soon as possible." He gave Paolo a sympathetic smile. "I expect it's to do with that bloody reporter last night."

Paolo could see the man was dying to ask who the chief's nephew might be. Damn! They'd managed to keep that relationship under wraps, and now it was all over town.

"Thanks," he said. "I'll go up now."

He climbed the stairs to the third floor and made his way to the Chief Constable's office. Tapping on the door, he took a deep breath and went in when he heard Chief Constable Willow's bark. "Enter!"

One look at his boss's face was enough to tell Paolo he was in for a rough ride.

"Come in. Shut the door and tell me who the bloody hell you've been blabbing to. Who knows in this station that Dave is my nephew?"

Paolo wasn't prepared to give George up without speaking to him first, so he shrugged.

"I can't answer that yet, sir. But I will find out."

"You'd bloody better. That reporter implied not only that Dave was incompetent, but that he's here because he's my nephew. You know full well I haven't put any pressure on you to favour him in any way. If he's crap at his job, tell me and I'll turf him out."

Paolo hadn't been asked, but decided to sit anyway. He wasn't an errant schoolboy, so there was no reason to act like one. He waited until the chief wore out his rage. It didn't take long. Willows was generally a fair man.

"I have an idea who the leak might be, but until I've looked into it, I don't want to do any finger pointing, sir," Paolo said. "Funnily enough, the leak might turn out not to be such a bad thing. I don't mean about Dave," he said as Willows showed every sign of getting worked up again. "If Pete Carson is a paedophile, this might prompt some of his earlier victims to come forward."

"Yes, and it might also bring forward a few who weren't victims, but want to get their names in the paper."

Paolo shrugged. "We always get a few of those, regardless of the case we're working on."

Willows scowled. "You're right. Not sure what they get from it, but some people seem to like their fifteen minutes of fame, even if it's for repulsive reasons."

Paolo went back downstairs feeling as if he'd got of lightly. Willows was angry, but not with him. As he walked through the main office he stopped by George's desk.

"I'd like to see you in my office, please, George."

"I've just…"

"Now!" Paolo said, barely keeping his temper in check.

George sighed as if he were the most put upon person in the universe. Paolo had to count to ten just to keep himself from yelling.

"Close the door, George," Paolo said as he walked behind his desk and sat down. "Take a seat. I need to ask you some serious questions and I'd like truthful answers."

"Of course. What do you want to know?"

300

Paolo wondered how to phrase the question, but there was no gentle way to put it. He'd have to confront the issue full on.

"Did you watch Pete Carson's press conference last night?"

A massive smile crept over George's face. "I did and I'd like to shake the hand of whoever gave out that information. We know he's guilty and can't do a damn thing about it. Now everyone else knows what he is."

"Was it you?"

The smile dropped from George's face. "Was what me?"

"The person who leaked to the press. Was it you?"

"Why are you picking on me? It could be anyone out there," he said, pointing to the outer office. "It could even be your blue-eyed boy."

Paolo shook his head. "Not according to the way the reporter spoke of him. That sounded like a quote from someone who'd found out Dave's relationship to Willows and was angry about it."

"So because I know and don't like Dave, you get to accuse me? That seems a bit unfair, if you ask me."

Paolo leaned forward. "I'll find out who leaked. Whoever it was will be out of the force. I'll make sure of that. If it wasn't you, it has to be someone who knows about Dave and Willows. Have you told anyone?"

George stood up. "No, I bloody well haven't. If you've got a leak then you need to find it and plug it, but you're not going to use me as an easy scapegoat. Is there anything else, *sir*?"

Paolo winced. "Yes, have you found out anything more on Gazmend's charity?"

"Only confirmation of what we already knew. It's on the level. The kids arrive via Europe where they get to see the sights, stay a few days and then go home again. None of them get left behind."

"Okay, thanks."

"Happy to be of assistance," George said, voice dripping with sarcasm.

Paolo decided there and then, whatever happened, whether George was the leak or not, he would arrange for him to be transferred.

He glanced down at his desk as George left and discovered a post it note in CC's handwriting asking him to call the interpreter. She had news on the girls' reactions to the photographs. Praying it was something that might take them closer to establishing the identity of Joey, Paolo dialled the number on the note.

"Hello, is that Ejona? Paolo Sterling here."

"Thank you for calling me back. We've had a small breakthrough with the girls. None of them recognised Mr Redzepi, but they all reacted strongly to the photograph of Jeton. Unfortunately, they are all too terrified to speak out against him."

"Did any of them identify him by name?" Paolo asked.

"No, only as Joey, but there was no doubt they knew him as a person to fear."

"Thank you. And the picture of Pete Carson? Did any of them react to that?"

Paolo heard a sharp intake of breath. "Seven of them broke down in tears when they saw his photograph, but none of them would say why. I believe Jessica Carter may be able to help them with whatever trauma they are going through. She is very good with them, as you know."

Paolo smiled. He didn't need outside validation to know how good Jessica was at her job. This could be the breakthrough he needed. If any of the girls could be persuaded it was safe to speak out against Pete, he could move on him. Knowing the type of person Pete was, there was a fair chance he'd spew up information in an effort to save his own skin.

He thanked the interpreter again and was about to put the phone down when it occurred to him how alike Gazmend and Jeton were. There was still something nagging at the back of his mind about the charity Gazmend had set up. It seemed strange he'd never mentioned it.

"Ejona, if I give you a number to call in Albania, would you ask the people who run an orphanage about their experience with a charity set up over here?"

"Yes, of course. What do you want me to find out?"

Paolo laughed. "That's the problem. I'm not really sure. The charity gives free European trips to young girls. They leave the orphanage by coach, travel through various countries to here, where they enjoy a couple of days sightseeing, then go back to Albania stopping at different places to those they viewed on the way out."

"Sounds like a good charity. I'm more confused than before. What questions should I ask the orphanage?"

"Could you find out if the girls are distressed in any way when they come back? Do they seem to have been traumatised by the trip? I don't really know, to be honest. I'd just like to be sure that the charity is doing what it says and isn't a cover to bring kids over here and use them until they end up in the same state as the girls you're working with."

"I'll get on to them right now and call you back. Will you be in your office for the next hour or so?"

"I should be, but let me give you my mobile number, just in case I'm called out."

He thanked her and replaced the receiver. Maybe he could bluff his way with Pete Carson. Give the impression the girls had spoken out against him, without actually saying they had. It was worth a shot. He was still deep in thought when Dave rapped on his door and came in, clearly distressed.

"Paolo, they all know I'm the chief's nephew and I feel like I've turned into a bloody leper. None of them, apart from CC, will even talk to me this morning."

Sighing, Paolo stood up. Pete Carson could wait for half an hour. First, he needed to sort out the children in the sandpit.

By the time he'd given his team a good talking to and convinced them that Dave wasn't there as a result of nepotism, his head was aching. He left them looking a bit sheepish and trying to make it up to Dave for jumping to conclusions. All except George who'd said all the right words, but without any sense that he'd meant them.

Paolo sat down and scribbled a reminder of things he needed to deal with – George's transfer topped the list. Willows had made it clear there would be an enquiry into the leak over Carson; if George was the culprit, as Paolo firmly believed, could he really transfer him right now? No, he couldn't. It wouldn't be fair to his new boss if George was guilty and it wouldn't be fair to George to make it look as if he was being sent away in disgrace if he was innocent. It seemed like Paolo was stuck with him until he knew for sure, one way or the other.

Second on his list was a visit to Pete Carson. He was about to get up and call for Dave to go with him when the phone rang.

"Sterling."

"Hello, it's Ejona. I made the call for you and it seems you can relax. I spoke to several people at the orphanage and they all look on Gazmend Dushku as some sort of saint. Apparently, the girls come back full of stories of the wonderful time they had. Mr Dushku's charity tries to offer this treat to as many of the orphanage's children as possible. In fact, it seems that they are able to place the children who have been abroad with new families much easier than those who have never left the orphanage."

"And none of the children are accidently left behind, or have an accident that means they have to stay?" Paolo asked, knowing even as he spoke that he was looking for evidence that didn't exist.

Ejona confirmed this. "They all arrive back. Not one child has been left behind on any of the trips the charity organised. As I say, they regard Mr Dushku as someone very special."

"Thank you, Ejona. Don't forget to add the cost of the call to your bill."

She laughed. "I won't. Let me know if there's anything else I can do."

Paolo had no sooner replaced the receiver than the phone rang again. At this rate he'd never get out to question Pete Carson. He snatched up the phone.

"Sterling."

"Oh, thank goodness. I kept dialling and your number was engaged. I didn't know what to do."

"I'm sorry, who is this speaking?" Paolo asked. He'd recognised the voice, but couldn't place it."

"It's Mrs Baxter. Mr Carson's housekeeper. When you were here about the blood on the gates you gave me your card and said to call you if I had any problems."

Paolo could hear the hysteria rising in the woman's voice. "I remember," he said. "How can I help you?"

"It's Mr Carson," she sobbed. "He's dead!"

CHAPTER 36

20th November (afternoon)

Paolo stood next to Dave, keeping to one side of Pete Carson's studio while Barbara and her team worked on the singer's body. Evidence of drug use littered the table, leaving them in little doubt of how he'd died. The question now though, was to decide whether the overdose has been deliberate or accidental. Not that Paolo cared one way or the other. At least there was one less pervert to prey on vulnerable children.

"This place, it stinks," Dave said.

Paolo nodded. The stench was incredible. Pete had clearly been dead for several hours and his body had emptied its fluids where he lay.

"You should be used to smells like this now, Dave."

"That's not what I meant, sir. I meant stink in the other sense. Kiddie porn on the computer, handcuffs, blood on the floor. I dread to think what that bastard did in here. I wish he was still alive. I'd like to cut his fucking balls off and –"

Paolo grabbed Dave's arm and pulled him outside. "What's going on, Dave? You can't lose it like that in front of everyone."

Dave was shaking from head to toe. "There's fuck all wrong with me, sir. It's the bastards that fuck up children and ruin their lives."

"And you're swearing. I've never heard you swear like this. You want to tell me why you're taking this case so personally?"

Paolo waited. At one point it looked as though Dave was going to tell him, but in the end he shook his head.

"No reason. I just don't like the idea of people like Pete Carson abusing kids. That's all."

"You going to be okay to go back in there? I need you to keep it together."

Dave nodded. "I'm fine now. Honestly."

As they went back inside, Barbara was straightening up. She walked over to them.

"Definitely an overdose. Maybe he couldn't face the public after he'd been outed," she said.

Paolo looked around. "Something isn't right here. No evidence of a pizza delivery."

Dave looked at him as if he'd lost his mind. "Sorry? You've lost me, sir."

"I was watching the news last night. The only vehicle that made it through the security guards was a pizza delivery van. Two things strike me as odd about that. Firstly, if you're about to OD, would you send out for pizza? Secondly, we know the van came, but where's the evidence? No pizza box, or anything else to show a delivery."

Barbara signalled to her team to take the body outside. "When I get the stomach contents analysed we'll know for certain, but I think you're right. I'll let you know as soon as I can," she said. "Or will you be coming to the autopsy?"

Paolo nodded. "Let me know and I'll be there."

He watched her follow her team out and then turned back to Dave.

"Okay, so why would a pizza van come here if it wasn't to deliver pizza? Maybe it wasn't dropping anything off, but doing a pick up instead. I'm wondering if there might have been a child here with Pete and he panicked when the news broke and called for someone to take the child away." He picked up the phone. "I'm going to get CC to watch the news from last night. We need all the information we can get on that pizza van."

When he'd finished the call, he slipped the phone back in his pocket.

"Let's go over to the main house and see what Mrs Baxter has to tell us about Pete's last few days."

They settled into the kitchen chairs where they'd sat on the day Pete had tried to stop Mrs Baxter's from telling them about the blood on the gates and drive. The only difference was that the housekeeper was sobbing and couldn't stop.

"I don't believe what that horrible man said last night," she said, when she was finally able to speak. "Mr Carson was always good to me and to the other staff. I'd have known if he'd had young girls in here. But he didn't! He didn't ever bring anyone back. He was a good man."

She dissolved into tears again and Paolo handed her a tissue from the box on the table. After another good blow, she was able to halt the flow.

"Can I ask, what made you go over to the studio this morning? Is that part of your regular duties?"

She shook her head. "No. We only clean the studio when Mr Carson says… said we should do it. He hated for his place of work to be disturbed. The door has a special lock and he changes the code, so we could only go in when he told us the new code. I was so worried about him. He came back from the press conference in such a state. Said he was going to the studio and didn't want to be disturbed. And that was the last time I saw him alive."

Paolo passed her another tissue.

"Thank you. It's so sad. The world will think he was like that Gary Glitter, but he wasn't."

"I'm sorry, Mrs Baxter, I'm confused. If you didn't know the code, how were you able to open the studio this morning?"

"I went over and knocked and knocked and knocked. When he wouldn't open the door for me I came back here and looked out the list. He didn't realise, bless him, but he used the same codes over and over. I just tried them all until I got to the one that worked. And I found him like that."

"Were you here when the pizza delivery came?"

310

Mrs Baxter lips moved into a smile briefly as she shook her head. "Did he order pizza? I'm not surprised. I've never known anyone eat as much pizza as Mr Carson. I swear that pizza van was here every week." She sniffed. "I don't blame you, personally, but I do blame the police. That reporter got his information from the police. He said so. It's not true and you need to find out who's been spreading such ugly lies."

As the tears began to flow once more Paolo stood up and nodded to Dave to join him. He patted Mrs Baxter on the shoulder.

"We're going now. I promise you I'll get to the bottom of the leak, but I'm afraid you're going to have to get used to the idea that Pete Carson was not as nice as you'd believed."

While Dave negotiated the country roads, Paolo called CC.

"Were you able to get the film footage?"

"Yes, sir, and I've put out an alert on the van. Good news is we were able to get a clear shot of the number plate. Bad news is the plate is a mock up. The number doesn't exist."

Paolo sighed. "Why am I not surprised? Good work, CC."

"Are you coming back to the station?"

"Yes, we're on our way now. Why?"

"Gazmend called and wants to see you. It seems someone has told him you've brought in an outside interpreter and he wants to know what he's done wrong."

Paolo entered the main office to find Gazmend waiting for him. Sitting next to CC's desk, he was laughing at something CC had said, but the laughter died when he looked up and saw Paolo approaching. The interpreter stood up.

"Next time you're in my part of town, CC, I'll buy you that lunch I've been promising you."

CC smiled. "I won't hold my breath. I've heard that offer so many times and I'm still hungry."

Gazmend turned to Paolo. "I'm sorry to interrupt your day, but could I have a word with you?"

"Sure. Come through to my office. Would you like some coffee?"

"No, thank you. CC has force fed me so many cups my veins are running on pure caffeine."

Paolo gestured for Gazmend to go ahead and followed him into his office.

"Take a seat," Paolo said, closing the door to give them some privacy. "What can I do for you?"

Gazmend waited until Paolo had sat down before answering. "I'm not really sure how to put my question, to be honest."

Paolo kept quiet. He didn't want to put words into Gazmend's mouth. The silence stretched out between them.

"Am I no longer involved with the child trafficking case?" Gazmend asked eventually.

"You are, but I've also brought in an additional interpreter."

"May I ask why? Are you not happy with the way I handled things? I thought you trusted me."

Paolo hesitated. "What makes you ask that? I was expecting you to ask me if I thought your skills were lacking, or some other aspect of your service."

Gazmend shrugged. "I know my language skills are good. Better than good. I've lived here most of my life, so I'm not likely to make mistakes when interpreting. I've been helping out the police for years now, but suddenly you bring in someone new. To my mind, it can only be a matter of trust." He looked down at his hands, then looked up and smiled ruefully. "I assumed it was because you suspect my cousin of involvement and wondered if I would pass on evidence against him if any of the girls named him."

"We do think Jeton might be involved, but I didn't side-line you because I didn't trust you. There were two reasons for bringing in another person. Firstly, I felt it was important that the girls were able to communicate with a woman."

"But my wife is the one who talks to the girls! I only go with her because I am accredited and she is not."

"Yes, I know, but as I said, there were two reasons. The second, and more important, reason was to avoid putting you in the position where you, or your wife, would have to give information that might lead to your cousin's arrest. We were trying to save your feelings, rather than not trusting you to do the right thing."

"Ah, I hadn't thought of it from that angle," Gazmend said. "And have any of the girls spoken out against Jeton?"

Paolo smiled. "Now, you know I can't answer that."

Gazmend laughed. "And yet, if I'd been the one doing the interpreting, I would have known the answer." He suddenly looked serious. "I don't know where he is. Just in case you think I'm covering up for him. I want you to know. I have no idea where he's hiding or if he's even still in the country."

"I believe you," Paolo said, "but if he should get in touch…"

Gazmend nodded. "Yes, of course, I'll let you know." He stood up and moved towards the door. "Oh, one last thing. I received a phone call from the orphanage in Albania whose children my charity gives cultural trips to. May I ask why you're investigating my charity if you have no reason to distrust me?"

"We have to follow up all leads. It was possible that someone in your charity was using it as a means of bringing the girls into the country."

"I thought it might be something like that," Gazmend said. "The orphanage people were horrified to think you might put a stop to the culture trips."

Paolo shook his head. "Even if it were in my power to do so, which it isn't, why would I want to prevent children in care getting some enjoyment from life?"

"That's what I told them," Gazmend said. "Will you be using my services on other crimes? Or am I now of no further use to you?"

Paolo smiled. "I'm hoping the Albanian crime situation will resolve itself when we get to the bottom of the trafficking ring, but I'd like to be able to call on you, if needed."

Gazmend opened the door. "For the sake of my community, I hope I'm not needed," he said. He waved farewell and left, closing the door behind him.

Paolo sat, mulling over the turn of events. Once again, there was something that nagged at the back of his mind, but what was it? He went through each snippet of conversation. What had today's chat achieved for Gazmend? Was he just trying to find out what Paolo knew? Or was he genuinely concerned that he'd been pushed out?

The niggles were growing. Paolo picked up the phone. He'd put a watch on Gazmend. Even though there was nothing concrete to suggest he was involved, there was something not quite right. At the very least, he might know where Jeton was hiding. That denial, distancing himself from his cousin, was a little too pat.

CHAPTER 37

29ᵗʰ November

Paolo drummed his fingers on his desk in frustration. He couldn't believe it had taken nine days to find the pizza van, but it had finally turned up. Not that it was any use to them. It had been discovered, burnt out, on waste ground near a fly tipping site. If the council hadn't decided to clean up the site and put a fence round it, the van might have remained there forever.

And that wasn't the only reason for his irritation. The surveillance on Gazmend had revealed precisely nothing. He hadn't met with anyone he shouldn't, hadn't made any suspicious moves. In short, he was so squeaky clean Paolo wondered if Gazmend had realised he was being watched. He shook his head. There was no reason to suspect the interpreter, apart from a feeling that he was not as clean cut and honest as he'd always appeared.

The internal enquiry on the press leak had also, apparently, led nowhere. The reporter refused to reveal his source and swore no money had changed hands. Paolo was still inclined to believe George was behind the leak, but unless evidence came to light, there wasn't anything he could do about it. He'd virtually frozen George out of the investigation, not wanting to take a chance on more evidence being shared with the press.

He frowned as he glanced at today's headline. Mrs Baxter was dominating the front page yet again claiming Pete had killed himself as a direct result of police harassment. And even his death wasn't as clear cut as Paolo would have liked. Barbara's report gave cause of death as an overdose, but she was unable to say one way or the other whether it had been self-inflicted, or assisted. Paolo would have put money on the latter, but without proof, there was nothing he could do about it. Who would want Pete Carson dead? Apart from the girls he'd abused, of course. The answer had to be the unknown Joey. When the news broke at the press conference, Pete must have become a liability which had to be dealt with. Why else would a bogus pizza van come to call just before Pete died?

Feeling as if he'd reached dead-ends on every avenue, he was about to go in search of Dave to go yet again to question the various Albanian business owners, when George tapped on his door.

"Can I come in? Or are you busy?"

Paolo gestured towards a chair. "What can I do for you?"

George carefully closed the door before coming over to the desk and sitting down. He looked haggard and ill at ease.

"I... er... I need your help, sir."

"In what way? If I can help you, I will," Paolo said.

"The… er… the inquiry about… you know… um…"

"The inquiry into the press leak?" Paolo asked.

"Yes," George said. "You won't have been told yet, but… er… I think… that is… someone is going to… the money's been traced."

"George, are you telling me you took money to leak to the press? Is that it?"

Paolo looked in disbelief as George nodded.

"And you want me to help you? How?"

"You could say you gave me the go-ahead to give the leak."

"What? Are you mad? Why would I do such a thing?"

"Look, sir. I'm going to lose my job, my pension. I might even end up inside. Please, you've got to help me."

Paolo shook his head. "I won't lie for you. If it comes to it, I'll speak up for you, but I won't lie."

"You would if it was for one of your favourites."

Paolo banged his fist on the desk. "Oh, for God's sake, George, give it a rest! I don't have favourites, but even if I did, anyone who sold out our investigation in the way you did would deserve whatever came their way."

George shuddered. "I'm sorry. I didn't mean to say that. I came in here to ask for your help, not to get into a fight with you. You do have favourites, though. You've always overlooked me when it comes to the best jobs."

"Are you implying it was my fault you went to the press?"

George's shrug said more than any words could have done and Paolo felt his temper rising.

"Dave and CC get to go out with you…"

"That's enough! You spout the same words over and over, George. Even if you have been overlooked, and that is most definitely *not* the case, do you really feel that jeopardising our investigation was the way to get even?"

"I didn't do it to get even."

"No, sorry, I forgot. You did it for the money. The only reason you've come in here today is to try to cover yourself because you know you're about to get found out. Well, I'm sorry, but don't expect me to help you on this. I can't trust you anymore."

George stood up and leaned forward, giving Paolo the impression he'd like to climb on the desk to get even closer.

"You never did trust me. If you had, I wouldn't have gone to the press. And I didn't do it just for the money. I did it because you were too bloody timid to do what needed to be done to put a stop to bloody Pete Carson's perversions."

"You've left me with no choice. I have to report this conversation. You realise that, don't you?"

"What do I care? I'm screwed anyway and you're to blame."

"Gather your stuff and go home, George. I'll do my best for you when the hearing takes place, but…"

"*I'll do my best for you,*" George repeated, mimicking Paolo's voice.

He moved away from the desk and turned towards the door. Paolo watched him. Did he have a genuine grievance? George wasn't good with people, which was

319

the main reason Paolo hadn't taken him out on interviews
– and he was incredibly good at fact finding. On the other
hand, Paolo had known George felt undervalued. Clearly
he hadn't done enough to change that conviction.

"George," he called.

Turning back, George sneered. "Don't bother.
Whatever you've got to say, it's too late and I couldn't
give a shit."

As the door slammed, Paolo wondered if any others on
his team felt overlooked. Sighing, he put George and the
inevitable consequences to one side. He had work to get
on with.

By the time evening came, Paolo was glad to get home
and shut his front door on the events of the day. His team
had watched in silence as George emptied his desk. No
one had asked why, but it seemed they had all come to the
same conclusion, because none of them spoke up as
George left. Paolo had gone out afterwards and brought
them up to speed on the basic facts. He'd been surprised
by the lack of response, expecting people to exclaim as if
they couldn't believe it, but not one word of shock had
been expressed.

Paolo shrugged off his jacket, pulled a can of cool
drink from the fridge and settled down to watch the news.
Sometimes he wished he didn't have to put himself
through the daily diet of death and destruction, but
keeping up to date with events was part and parcel of his
job. He took in the world events with only half his mind.

The other replayed over and over every aspect of what he knew about Joey.

Part of him was convinced Gazmend's charity was involved, but every inquiry down that road led to another dead-end. The girls arrived, the girls went home. What was he missing? Maybe he was looking for clues that didn't exist.

World events over, the programme switched to UK news and Paolo was saddened to see yet another appeal on behalf of young Lucy. Even though the coverage of her disappearance never left the headlines, no lead had yet produced a concrete piece of evidence.

Paolo couldn't help wondering how different Lucy's life would be from now on, even if she were found. It was the same for the Albanian girls who were shipped to the UK. They would lead such different lives to the ones they should have had; they'd become different adults to the ones they should have grown into.

He stood up to get another cool drink. As he walked into his kitchen, the refrain, different lives, different girls, beat like a tattoo in his head. He opened the fridge and an idea came to him with the blast of cold air.

What if? He shut the fridge door, all thoughts of another drink forgotten, and rushed to pick up his phone. Dave had said he was going to work late, bringing his reports up to date. He answered on the first ring.

"Are you still at the station, Dave?"

"Yes, sir. I'm leaving in about ten minutes. You need me to do something?"

"I want to run an idea past you."

"Fire away."

"Gazmend's charity brings Albanian kids over on a culture trip and then they go home again, but what if the girls who leave are not the same ones who arrived? What if he's sending home different girls?"

"But why, sir? What would he gain from that? Besides, we know Joey keeps the kids and puts them out on the streets when they are too old for the paedos."

"Bear with me for a moment. What if little Lucy and who knows how many other girls who have gone missing this year have been taken for a specific purpose?"

"Well, obviously they have been," Dave said. "Lucy's probably been taken by some pervert who got his kicks and then killed her. That's why there's been no sign of her since she disappeared."

Paolo sighed. "I know. That could well be the case and that's what the press are saying, but what if she hasn't been found because she is no longer in the country? What if she was sent to Albania in place of one the kids the charity brought over here?"

"Bloody hell, I hope you're wrong, sir."

"So do I, Dave, but I have a really strong feeling that I'm right. When is the next culture trip due to arrive? George had the notes on his desk. Can you go and have a look?"

Paolo waited, more and more convinced he was right as he listened to the sounds of paper being rustled.

"Found it!" Dave said. "They are due to arrive in Leicester on December the eight and leave again on December the twelfth."

"Excellent," Paolo said. "I'm going to arrange one of our photographers to take some surveillance images. I want photos of each girl as she arrives. I bet the same girls aren't on the coach when it's time to go home again."

CHAPTER 38

12th December

Paolo listened intently, thanked the caller and then slipped the phone back into his pocket. Turning to Dave, he nodded.

"That was CC. The coach should be here in about twenty minutes. She's still on its tail and it doesn't appear as if the driver has any suspicion he's being followed."

Paolo looked at the line of police cars waiting to move out on to the motorway to form a road block. He wanted to make sure the coach had gone beyond all possible escape exits before setting it up. He had another group of cars waiting for the coach to pass the exit before this one. As soon as they saw CC's car, they'd follow behind her, effectively blocking any chance of the coach reversing back to an exit when the driver realised he was heading into a roadblock. His phone rang again.

"Sterling."

"CC here, sir. I've just passed the turn off and the unmarked cars have come on behind me."

"Great," he said, ending the call and signalling to the drivers to take up their positions.

"Do you still think they've switched the kids, sir?" Dave asked.

A hollow pit opened in Paolo's stomach at the thought that he might be wrong. If he was right, he was saving kidnapped kids from being shipped abroad and possibly saving the girls brought into the country from entering the sex trade here. If he was wrong, his job was on the line. He'd had to force the idea through against some strenuous opposition from upstairs. With no evidence and only a hunch to go on, it was made really clear that any fall out would be down to him and him alone. He'd considered the two possible outcomes and decided the chance of saving children from a life as sex slaves far outweighed any risk to his career.

Traffic had crawled to a trickle as the police on the roadblock allowed vehicles through. In the distance, Paolo could see the bus stuck firmly within the line of cars and lorries. Even without the police cars behind, the exit was blocked, but Paolo was glad he hadn't left anything to chance.

Eventually, the bus came level with the roadblock and Paolo walked over to the driver's side. He indicated with sign language that the driver should follow the police car in front. The driver nodded and moved his bus off the motorway. Paolo jumped into Dave's car and they trailed behind, leaving the roadblock to be removed and traffic returned to normal. The bus was led into the car park of the motorway services and immediately surrounded by cars.

Paolo's heart was beating fast as he approached the stationary coach. This was where he found out if his hunch had been a good one. The driver opened the doors and Paolo climbed the steps, signalling to a uniformed officer to take the driver outside.

The bus was completely silent. None of the young passengers were awake, which was surprising considering the flashing lights and noise levels outside.

"I think they're drugged," Paolo said.

He pulled a page of images from a file and compared the passengers to the photographs the surveillance team had taken when the coach first arrived. Five of the sleeping girls were very similar in colouring and build, but not exact matches. His heart jumped when he realised one of them was Lucy Bassington. Maybe it was her colouring that had kept her from being shipped out sooner. She was the only fair haired child on the bus. The Bassingtons were going to be very relieved parents tonight, but what of the other four who clearly didn't belong? Where were their parents and why hadn't there been news of their disappearance? They were questions to be answered later. For now, the children's welfare had to take priority.

"Call for medical, will you, please, Dave. We don't know what they've been given. We also need social to be around when they wake up. God knows where they've been held or what's been done to them."

He got off the bus and walked over to the driver.

"Do you speak English?"

The driver looked confused. "What is problem?"

"Please give me your phone."

"Why? What is problem? I take girls home to Albania. You have no right to stop me."

Paolo smiled. "I have every right. Five of those girls are British citizens and you are an accomplice to kidnapping and possibly worse charges, depending on what's been done to them. Now, I would like your phone, please."

The driver trembled. "I do nothing. I drive, is all. I know nothing. I bring girls. I take girls. I do no wrong."

Paolo shook his head. "Your phone. Now!"

The driver rummaged in his pockets and produced an iPhone. Paolo quickly scanned through the recent call log.

"He hasn't made or received any calls for over an hour. Take him to the station," he said to the uniformed officers holding the driver. Turning to Dave, he continued, "We need to move fast in case there's someone waiting for him at the ferry port. We don't want Gazmend and his friends to realise anything's up. First stop, Gazmend's house."

"Open up, police!"

The door opened a little. Paolo could see one half of a woman's face. She looked terrified. He stepped forward.

"Diellza, we have to speak to Gazmend. Is he home?"

She shook her head.

"Could you stand back and let us in, please?"

327

Soundlessly, she opened the door and stood to one side. She said nothing as police officers streamed into the house and began a systematic search. After a few minutes, Paolo was told the house was empty of all but Diellza, who still had not moved from her place against the wall.

Paolo took in her bruised arms.

"CC, could you come with me? I want to chat to Mrs Dushku in the sitting room. She's looking a bit fragile and might be glad for some female support."

He wanted to go gently with Gazmend's wife. She looked as if she'd been through enough trauma, but he couldn't spare the time. If Gazmend got wind of the fact that Paolo was closing in on him, he'd have time to hide his tracks.

"Diellza, I need you to help me. Please. Children's lives are at stake."

The woman nodded as tears ran down her face.

"Did Gazmend force you to threaten the children in care?"

She nodded again.

"Do you know where he keeps the girls not yet old enough to go on the streets?"

"Can you protect me from him? And from the people who work for him?"

"If we can put him away, you'll be safe. Please, Diellza, help us. Help us find the children he's selling."

She shook her head. "I can't. He'll kill me."

CC took Diellza's hand. "I'll get you into a refuge. You'll be safe there until after the trial and once Gazmend's in prison, he won't be able to do anything to you. Please, we have to find the children before he has chance to move them. Do you know where he keeps them?"

"No, but I can give you some addresses to try. Gazmend has many, many businesses." She turned to CC. "If I give you the information, you will take me to the refuge? Tonight? Promise me."

"I promise."

Paolo passed Diellza a pad and pen. She wrote down several business names and addresses, many of them on the industrial estate. As she handed the pad back to Paolo, her hands shook so badly the pen fell from her grip.

Paolo leaned down and picked up the pen. "Are any of these more likely to have hideaways than others?"

"That one," she said, pointing to a construction equipment supply company. "He had cellars dug out and built. He never told me why, but I guessed." She touched her blackened eye. "Promise me one thing," she whispered. "Promise me he won't come home tonight. If he finds out I told you where to go…"

Her voice trailed off, but Paolo didn't need to hear the rest.

"If we can find him tonight, I give you my word he won't be released to hurt you ever again."

She nodded, as if reassured and Paolo felt the weight of yet another person's safety settle on his shoulders. He prayed he'd do a better job for Gazmend's wife than he was able to do for Alice, who'd so nearly found a new life as Michelle.

Paolo sent squads to each of the businesses on the list. He was leading the search in the supply company and, like the others, was waiting for the time to tick over to nine exactly. They had to enter all the businesses at the same time to avoid any chance of someone giving a warning.

Lights were on in office across the street from where they waited. Paolo hoped it was Gazmend in there. He wanted to be the one to take him in.

He looked at Dave, crouched next to him behind the car, and nodded.

"Now!"

They rushed across the street and a uniformed officer kicked the door open. Paolo, right behind him, saw Gazmend rise from behind a desk.

"What the fuck is going on?" Gazmend shouted. "All you had to do was knock."

Paolo ignored the question and signalled to the officers.

"Handcuff him and take him outside."

He waited until they'd removed Gazmend from the premises. "Right, I want this place torn apart. His wife seems to think there are rooms underground. Let's find them. Dave, you and I will take this office, the rest of you, spread out into the warehousing area."

The officers split into pairs and moved off. Dave and Paolo began the painstaking task of tapping on walls, moving furniture and feeling for loose floorboards looking for hidden doorways. In the end, they discovered the door almost by accident. They'd worked their way systematically from the entrance towards the rear of the long office and found nothing. They had only the rear wall to check out when Dave rested against a massive filing cabinet. As he put his weight on it he felt a slight movement.

"Paolo, I think I might have found it."

Paolo put down the rug he'd picked up and hurried over. Together they shoved, but although it gave a little, it didn't shift as much as they'd hoped. Getting down on his knees, Paolo looked underneath. There was a lever which he pulled and wheels dropped down into place. He clamboured back up.

"I think it will go now, Dave."

They had barely touched it when it slid easily to one side, revealing a door.

"The lever works from the back as well as the front, so we need to be careful. Some of Gazmend's men could be down there," Paolo said, stopping Dave from opening the door and rushing through. He waved his phone at Dave. "I'll get some backup."

When the uniformed officers arrived, Paolo opened the door and stepped onto a well-lit landing with steps leading down to a corridor with a series of doors on each side and a single door at the end.

"There's about a dozen rooms here," Paolo whispered. "Dave and I are going to open the door at the far end. I want two of you to come with us and the rest wait up here in case anyone tries to run from the other rooms."

He nodded at Dave and they crept down the steps and along the corridor, closely followed by the two uniformed men. There wasn't a sound from any of the rooms as they passed and Paolo wondered if they had been soundproofed so that no noise would carry to the office above. When they reached the end of the corridor, Paolo held up his hand and then pointed to his chest. He was going in first. The others nodded to show they understood. Hand on the handle, Paolo took a breath and then turned it quietly, leaning against the door as he did so.

The door flew open to reveal a single bed against one wall. The bed was occupied, but a man's shocked face was all Paolo had time to register before Dave shoved him to one side and wrenched the man from the bed by his neck.

"Get Dave off him," Paolo ordered the officers as he moved to the naked child cowering on the bed. She was one of those who'd arrived from Albania just a few days earlier.

He reached out to cover her with the blanket, but she scrambled away, screaming words he couldn't understand. Pulling out his phone to call for CC and a WPC, he glanced back to see Dave being restrained. The man, Edar, had been handcuffed by two other officers who'd come down to join the fray.

"CC, we need you and as many WPCs as we have available. We've got at least one child in serious need of female support."

He looked back to see that the child had grabbed the blanket and was hiding underneath it. A classic case of if I can't see you, you can't see me, Paolo thought, wondering how old she was. Maybe six or seven, certainly no older.

He was tempted to let Dave have his way with Edar, but that would play into the bastard's hands.

Moving out into the corridor, he saw the officers had opened all the doors. The rooms on either side were much larger than the end room and were laid out as dormitories. There were six beds in each room and all the beds were occupied.

An officer came out of one of the rooms, dragging Bekim.

"I found him hiding under one of the beds, sir."

"I did nothing," Bekim said. "I just feed, but not touch. I not touch. I tell you all, yes? Then you be kind. Like me. I kind to girls. I feed, but I not touch."

Paolo didn't trust himself to go near the man until he'd had chance to bring his emotions under control. Not only did he understand Dave's rage, his own made him feel as if his head was about to explode.

"Get him out of my sight."

CHAPTER 39

17th December

Paolo stood in front of his team. They were still traumatised by what they'd found five days earlier. Most of the girls were now with social services, but a few were still in hospital. Paolo would be going over later that day to have another talk with the child they'd found under Edar. Mentally, she had made a remarkable recovery, but physically, she'd sustained much internal damage and wouldn't be leaving the hospital for some time yet. He hated the thought of putting her through any more suffering, but she was the only one prepared to talk to them. The others all had families who they were protecting, but Adelina was a genuine orphan. She had no one.

"As you know," Paolo began, "Bekim hasn't stopped talking since we arrested him. Thanks to his information, the bodies of Michelle, Jeton and his wife were uncovered yesterday on a construction site operated by one of Gazmend's companies. Bekim says Jeton recognised their photos as being men he'd seen many times in his cousin's company. He'd rushed off to warn Gazmend to have nothing to do with them. When Gazmend saw that Jeton guessed the truth, he had to die."

"But why kill his ex-wife, sir? She didn't know anything, did she?"

Paolo sighed. "No, she was completely innocent. Her disappearance was to make us think she'd run off to be with her ex. It piled the suspicion on Jeton."

Paolo spared a thought for Alice. She'd so nearly made a new life for herself and Gazmend had destroyed her.

"Several other bodies have also been found," he continued, "but we have not yet been able to identify them. It seems that many unsolved crimes over the last few years might have had one of Gazmend's companies involved in some way. He is still denying all knowledge and putting the blame firmly on Bekim and Edar, but we'll leave that to the courts to sort out."

He sighed. "News from Albania is not so positive. The orphanage claims ignorance of any girls being switched in the past and, unfortunately, we have no way of proving otherwise."

At the roar of disapproval, Paolo held up his hand. "Yes, I know. I feel the same way. They claim they have always received back the same girls who left and would have reported it had the girls in the bus arrived at the orphanage. The Albanian authorities have promised to look carefully at what's been going on in the orphanage. We have to rely on them doing so because we obviously have no authority. Fortunately, Interpol has now taken over that aspect because it looks as though the ring was

Europe wide. I've spoken to the officer in charge and he says he is sure there will be evidence to prove the orphanage was complicit. Don't worry, the people there will go down."

He waited for the cheers to fade out before going on. "Interpol say girls were being exchanged all along the route on the return journey. UK kids handed over in France, for example, were swapped for French children, who were then taken to Germany and so on. Which means, of course, that the driver's claim of innocence in all this is a crock of shit." Paolo paused, remembering the driver's look of outrage when it was made plain he was under arrest along with all the others. He wondered how many lives he'd been responsible for transporting into hell. "Gazmend's organization has been trafficking children for years. It's going to be a major job to track down all those he's sold on, if it can be done at all. But the Interpol officer sounds determined to do so. For the sake of all the kids who've been snatched from the street and put to work God knows where, we can only pray they are successful."

A chorus of cheer greeted that comment. When it died down Paolo glanced at his notes and picked up where he'd left off.

"As you know, Lucy Bassington has been reunited with her parents. She has been through hell in the time she was kidnapped, as have the other four British girls on the bus. They were snatched from care homes around the country. We are keeping them here in our social services while the courts decide where they should go.

336

"Fortunately for us, Gazmend kept good records of where he'd farmed out the girls here in the UK. We've passed the paperwork to the special crimes unit and they have broken up a massive paedophile ring, arresting close on two hundred men. That's being kept out of the press until the operation is complete, but the news will break in a few days. It's thanks to your work, team, that this was possible." He raised his coffee cup. "Here's to you."

"Thank you, sir. What about the street girls? Have we managed to track them all down?" one of the WPCs called out.

"We believe we've taken into care all the girls who Gazmend was running on the streets. Bekim was very helpful there, telling us where they were held and who by. Some may have taken the opportunity to disappear, but without money or passports, I doubt they will get very far. As always, we have people out looking out for underage runaways."

He gathered up his papers and headed back to his office, but was stopped by CC as he walked past her desk.

"Sir," she whispered so that only Paolo could hear, "what's happened to Dave? We haven't seen him since the night of the arrests."

"Dave was in need of a break, so he took a few days' leave. He'll be back tomorrow."

"Good," she said. "The place isn't the same without him."

Paolo was careful to keep his smile to himself. Only a year before Dave and CC couldn't be in the same room without war breaking out.

"I'm going to the hospital in about half an hour to meet the interpreter who is talking to Adelina, the poor kid Edar raped. She is our only link to the orphanage. I'd like you to come, just in case she reacts badly to a man being in the room. I wouldn't blame her if she did."

"No, sir," CC agreed. "I can't begin to imagine what effect this will have on her."

"Or on any of them," Paolo said. "It's hard to picture anyone recovering from this level of abuse, but many do. We'll just have to give them as much help as possible."

Paolo parked, as he frequently did, in the area reserved for the hospital administrators. It always amused him that the admin offices were sited right next to the clinic for sexually transmitted diseases. He would never say so out loud, but considering the fact that those at the top earned more than the doctors and nurses they controlled and didn't seem to give the staff the respect they deserved, it was a fitting place.

He shivered as he waited for CC to climb out. The temperature had dropped several degrees overnight and he was glad he'd picked up his gloves and scarf before leaving home this morning. They walked briskly to the main entrance and arrived just as the first snowflakes fell.

"Hey, sir, you think we're getting a white Christmas?"

Paolo looked up at the grey sky. "Could be. I'm kind of hoping the snow holds off until the day and then clears up again immediately afterwards."

"That sounds very bah humbug of you, sir."

"It wasn't meant to be. I was just thinking of the idiots who will go out on Christmas Eve or to office parties this week and get plastered and then still try to drive home. It's bad enough when they do that in good conditions. In the snow and ice, it's a recipe for disaster. Still," he said, looking at the trees turning white, "I agree, the world does look prettier in the snow."

They made their way to the ward where Adelina was being treated and found the interpreter chatting to the two WPCs outside her door.

"Ejona, thank you for coming. You've met CC, I believe?"

Paolo was amazed to see a blush spreading over the interpreter's face as she nodded.

"Yes, we know each other," she said.

He turned to CC and saw that her neck had gone very red and a small smile played on her lips. Putting two and two together, Paolo was glad for her. She'd taken the breakup of her last relationship badly. Ignoring the crackling atmosphere between the two women, he signalled for Ejona and CC to enter the room ahead of him. He didn't want Adelina's first sight of her visitors to be male.

The child smiled at Ejona, but looked nervously at Paolo.

"I'm going to sit over here in the corner as far from her bed as possible," he said.

He waited until CC had settled on one side of the bed, ready to take notes, and Ejona sat on the other before framing his first question.

"Could you ask her how long she'd been in the orphanage?"

Ejona translated and turned to relay the answer. "All her life. She has no idea who her parents were."

"And the other girls who were on the coach with her. How long had they been in the orphanage?"

Ejona chatted a while and then translated again. "Between two weeks and just two days. They came in one by one at different times, but were all put into the same dormitory. Adelina says they were all taken on the way to school or from a park near their homes."

"Why didn't they call for help on the journey? The bus must have made several stops."

Paolo wished he hadn't asked the question when he saw how distressed Adelina became.

"She says they were too scared. One of the girls did try to run away, but the driver caught her and beat her. After that they slept all the time."

"I expect they were drugged," CC said. "Like the girls who were being shipped out of the country."

"It shows the driver was definitely involved," Paolo said. "Not that there was ever any doubt about that. Would you please show her the photograph of Gazmend? He is claiming ignorance of the trafficking, putting all the blame onto Edar and Bekim."

Ejona took the photograph from Paolo and turned it so that Adelina could see it. Immediately, she began to sob and cried out.

"No, no, no, no!"

When Ejona and CC were able to calm her down, she told them what had happened when they arrived in Leicester.

Ejona's voice shook as she translated. "Gazmend looked her over, lifted her dress and pulled her pants down to see what she was worth. He told her he had a buyer for her and wanted to make sure she was clean and hadn't been used at the orphanage. They spent one night in a cellar in Leicester and then they were moved to the place where you found her. She was farmed out to a man for two nights and had only been brought back earlier that day. Edar raped her twice. The second time was when you arrived."

Paolo felt sick listening to Adelina's experiences, but he had to ask the questions if they were going to be able to put Gazmend and his sick accomplices away for a good long stretch.

By the end of the interview he would have given anything to spend a few hours alone with Gazmend in a soundproof room. He stood and thanked Adelina, asking Ejona to tell her that he would make sure she was well cared for. If he had anything to do with it, she wouldn't be going back to the orphanage. He intended to do everything in his power to ensure she stayed in the UK. At least he could pass on her testimony to Interpol as proof the orphanage was involved.

Ejona came out of the room with them, leaving the child to rest.

"I've been meaning to call you, Paolo," she said. "I've listened to the music tape you found in Pete Carson's studio and translated the Albanian. You were right, it was a child's voice. She was crying 'help me, mama' and that man recorded it to use on his record." She took a deep breath. "I've never hated anyone, but I am glad that man is dead. I hope he rots in hell for all eternity."

"So do I, Ejona," Paolo said. "So do I."

He and CC walked back to the car park in silence. Paolo was glad he felt so comfortable with her that he didn't need to make small talk. The last thing he wanted right now was to discuss inanities. His mind had been bludgeoned by what that poor child had gone through – and she was just one. God alone knew how many had been subjected to Gazmend's brutality.

They reached the car and Paolo pressed the key fob to open the doors. As he got in, he glanced over at the STD clinic. He wouldn't have noticed the man if he hadn't acted so furtively, looking around as if scared of being spotted. Paolo smiled to himself, that was another mystery solved. No wonder Isuf Xhepa, the owner of the language school, hadn't wanted to say why he'd been at the hospital that day. Paolo cast his mind back to the floor button Isuf had pressed. The lab was on that floor. Isuf must have been sent to get a blood test. Owning up to having a sexually transmitted disease wasn't something anyone would find easy, and it would have put him high up the suspect's list if Paolo had known about it.

"Where to now, sir?"

"The station, CC. I want to tell Gazmend face to face that his empire has collapsed. I also want to let him know that everyone he shares a cell with will know exactly why

342

he's inside. Pete Carson may or may not be burning in hell, but once the other prisoners know what he's in for, Gazmend will experience hell on earth and, you know what, I don't have a single shred of sympathy."

CHAPTER 40

18ᵗʰ December

Only a week to go before Christmas, Paolo mused as he looked at the pile of files that had once again grown to ridiculous proportions. He wondered if he'd be able to clear his desk before he took a few days off. Probably not, he decided, but couldn't work up too much regret at the thought.

Gazmend's little empire falling apart had cleaned up a great deal of crime in Bradchester: prostitution, loan sharking and protection rackets, just to think about a few, but as a direct result, Paolo's paperwork mountain had escalated. It seemed a fair price to pay.

His thoughts were interrupted by a tap on the door. He looked up to see Dave peering round it.

"Come in," Paolo said, pleased to see his young detective sergeant back again. "Take a seat."

"Thanks, sir," Dave said. "I'm sorry about the way I reacted when we found the children. I, er, I wondered if you had a moment. I need some advice."

"If it's to do with Rebecca, you know my advice there. Get in touch with her and make it up."

As Dave looked across at Paolo he was shocked at the look on the younger man's face.

"That's just it, sir. I want to, but this case, it's done my head in. I can't sleep, I can't think straight."

Paolo thought about the best way to handle the situation. Dave was clearly in need of a sympathetic ear, but if what Paolo suspected was true, Dave needed professional help, not simply a chat with his boss.

"Dave, right from the outset you've taken this case personally. Is there a reason for that?"

Dave nodded, but didn't answer.

"Something in your childhood?" Paolo asked.

Dave nodded again, but this time opened his mouth to speak. No words came out, so Paolo waited. Eventually, Dave grimaced.

"No details, sir, but when I was a kid, really young, our next door neighbour used to babysit." He shrugged. "I suppose you can guess the rest. I should have excused myself from this case, but I couldn't. I needed to see people being brought down. Made to suffer for what they did. Unlike Uncle Greg. He died last year, and I had to go to his funeral and pretend he was as great as all my family thought he was."

"You want my advice?"

Dave nodded again. "That's why I'm here."

"Get in touch with Jessica Carter. I don't know if she'll be able to take you on as a patient because of her role in helping the girls we've rescued from Gazmend.

345

There might be a perceived conflict of interest, but she'll certainly recommend you to someone she trusts."

"That's what I want to do. Finally deal with all this crap in my head. Maybe then I can get back together with Rebecca."

As he heard the pain in Dave's voice, Paolo's heart went out to him.

"Why not talk to her?"

"I don't want her to know," Dave said.

"You don't have to tell her what happened to you as a child, but you could allow her to be there for you now."

Dave stood up. "I'll give it some thought, sir." He smiled. "Thanks for listening. If Ms Carter is as good a listener as you, I'll be in safe hands."

Paolo watched him go. As good a listener as Jessica? No one could be. Paolo smiled at the thought of getting to know her better. Katy was making such excellent progress that she would soon be out of counselling. Then there would be nothing to stop him from asking her out properly. He wondered if she would go to the Italian restaurant over the Christmas period. As Paolo had no plans, other than spending some time on Christmas Day with Katy, he intended to visit the restaurant every evening, just in case Jessica made an appearance.

Was he falling in love with her? He wasn't sure, but one thing he did know, he loved spending time in her company.

Forcing himself to stop daydreaming, he took the top file and opened it. Work was the best way of getting

Jessica out of his head. Not that he wanted to, but he had to be sensible.

A couple of hours later another knock on the door gave him the opportunity to take a welcome break from the reports. He looked up, surprised to see Lydia standing in the doorway.

"I hope you don't mind me turning up like this," she said, closing the door behind her and coming into the office.

Paolo's heart began to race. "Katy? Has something happened to Katy?"

Lydia shook her head. "No, she's fine. May I sit down?"

Relief made Paolo feel weak. "Yes, of course. I'm sorry, I should have offered."

Lydia smiled. "I took you by surprise. I didn't think, though I should have known you'd assume I was here about Katy."

"I'm not saying you're not welcome," Paolo said, "but, why are you here?"

"Firstly to congratulate you. I should have guessed it would be you who'd find that young girl."

"I can't take credit for that. I had no idea she would be on the bus. It was pure luck – for her and for me."

She smiled. "That's as may be, but it doesn't change the fact that Katy thinks you're even more of a hero." She crossed her legs and leaned back, looking nervous. "Secondly, I suppose in a way, I am here about Katy, but not because there is anything wrong with her."

Paolo must have looked as confused as he felt because Lydia sat forward.

"I don't know how to put this, Paolo, so I'm going to come straight out with it. Katy loves you and she loves me. She would really like us to get back together again and, believe it or not, so would I." She smiled again, not realising she was taking Paolo visions of the future and crushing them. "I'd like you to come home. Not just for Christmas. For good."

END

ABOUT THE AUTHOR

When not working on her crime novels, Lorraine Mace is engaged in many writing-related activities. She is a columnist for both Writing Magazine and Writers' Forum and is head judge for Writers' Forum monthly fiction competitions. A tutor for Writers Bureau, she also runs her own private critique and author mentoring service. She is co-author, with Maureen Vincent-Northam, of *The Writer's ABC Checklist* (Accent Press). Other books include children's novel *Vlad The Inhaler – Hero in the Making*, and *Notes From The Margin*, a compilation of her Writing Magazine humour column.

Find her at:

Website: www.lorrainemace.com

Blog: http://thewritersabcchecklist.blogspot.com

Twitter: https://twitter.com/lomace

Facebook: https://www.facebook.com/lorraine.mace.52

Á

Proudly published by Accent Press

www.accentpress.co.uk

Praise for Other Books by Anna Carey

The Making of Mollie

'I loved Mollie – she is rebellious … thoughtful and funny.'
thetbrpile.com

'A girl's eye view of early feminism … exciting, vivid … with the
impulsive and daring Mollie.' *Lovereading4kids.co.uk*

'For junior feminists … a must-read.' *The Irish Times*

'Mollie's struggles are strikingly relevant to the teenagers of today.'
Sunday Business Post

Mollie on the March

'I cannot tell you how much I adore these books. They're funny and
clever and Mollie is a BRILLIANT character … I found myself moved
by the plight some of these women endured in their struggle to win
rights that we take for granted today.' *Louise O'Neill*

'It's wonderful but also brought home how hard the struggle was, how
scary, and that's giving me courage to keep on pushing for our
rights today.' *Marian Keyes*

'Just as charming as the first … a deeply relatable story and a welcome
reminder that Irish history has more to it than nationalist rebellions.'
The Irish Times

The Real Rebecca

'Definite Princess of Teen.' *Books for Keeps*

'The sparkling and spookily accurate diary of a Dublin teenager. I
haven't laughed so much since reading Louise Rennison. Teenage girls
will love Rebecca to bits!'
Sarah Webb, author of the *Ask Amy Green* books

'This book is fantastic! Rebecca is sweet, funny and down-to-earth, and
I adored her friends, her quirky parents, her changeable but ultimately
loving older sister and the swoonworthy Paperboy.' *Chicklish Blog*

'What is it like inside the mind of a teenage girl? It's a strange, confused
and frustrated place. A laugh-out-loud story of a fourteen-year-old girl,
Rebecca Rafferty.' *Hot Press*

Rebecca's Rules

'A gorgeous book! ... So funny, sweet, bright. I loved it.' Marian Keyes

'Amusing from the first page ... better than Adrian Mole!
Highly recommended.' *lovereading4kids.co.uk*

'Sure to be a favourite with fans of authors such as
Sarah Webb and Judi Curtin.' *Children's Books Ireland's
Recommended Reads 2012*

Rebecca Rocks

'The pages in Carey's novel in which her young lesbian character announces her coming out to her friends and in which they give their reactions are superbly written: tone is everything, and it could not be better handled than it is here.' *The Irish Times*

'A hilarious new book. Cleverly written, witty and smart.' *writing.ie*

'Rebecca Rafferty ... is something of a Books for Keeps favourite ... Honest, real, touching, a terrific piece of writing.' *Books for Keeps*

Rebecca is Always Right

Fun ... feisty, off-the-wall individuals and a brisk plot.'
Sunday Independent

'Be warned: don't read this in public because from the first sentence this story is laugh out loud funny ... This book is the funniest yet.'
Inis Magazine

'Portrays a world of adolescent ups and downs ... Rebecca is at once participant in and observer of, what goes on in her circle, recording it all in a tone of voice in which humour, wryness and irony are shrewdly balanced.'
The Irish Times

ANNA CAREY is a journalist and author from Dublin who
has written for the *Irish Times*, *Irish Independent* and many other
publications. Anna's first book, *The Real Rebecca*, was published in
2011, and went on to win the Senior Children's Book prize at the
Irish Book Awards. Rebecca returned in the critically acclaimed
Rebecca's Rules, *Rebecca Rocks* and *Rebecca is Always Right*. *The Making
of Mollie* (2016) was her first historical novel and was shortlisted for
the Senior Children's Book prize at the 2016 Irish Book Awards, and
was followed by more of Mollie's feisty feminist activities in *Mollie on
the March*.